Bryan Davis tells a terrific tale teeming with perilous predicaments, fascinating fantasy features, and likeable, charismatic characters who grow in their faith. The engaging writing style captivates the mind and the Christian themes captivate the heart. This epic novel is a superb start to a sensational series.

SHANNON, AGE 24

When I first picked up this book, I didn't know what to expect. By the time I finished the first chapter, I couldn't put it down! I love the way Bryan Davis mixes dragons and faith. It is a very touching experience.

ANNABETH, AGE 13

Bryan has a natural flow in his writing that make his characters come to life through his in-depth description of each character and the way the narrative evolves. I would heartily recommend this book to any fan of the genre regardless of age as the book has a broad appeal to all ages and all walks of life.

JOHN B., AGE 59

I recently reread the Dragons in Our Midst series and fell in love all over again, probably even more so than the first time. Bryan Davis's writing really makes the story and characters come alive. The Dragons in Our Midst series is a fresh take on the fantasy adventure genre, mixing dragons, knights, and the Arthurian legend with modern day. Even a reread makes you want to keep coming back for more.

MADI T., AGE 20

Mr. Davis's work *Raising Dragons* and the series that follows are some of the best Christian fantasy I have ever read. They are the perfect example of an author's work that challenges his readers to learn and grow. He also has a great way of leading his readers to Christ and to become more mature Christians. The series is great fun to read, no matter your age.

JEREMY D.

Books by Bryan Davis

The Astral Alliance Series

Across Astral Realms
The First Starborn
At the Speed of Mind

Dragons in our Midst

Raising Dragons
The Candlestone
Circles of Seven
Tears of a Dragon

Oracles of Fire

Eye of the Oracle
Enoch's Ghost
Last of the Nephilim
The Bones of Makaidos

Children of the Bard

Song of the Ovulum
From the Mouth of Elijah
The Seventh Door
Omega Dragon

Dragons of Starlight

Starlighter
Warrior
Diviner
Liberator

READERS ALSO LOVE BRYAN'S DRAGONS IN OUR MIDST SERIES

As parents of boys who are avid readers, my wife and I struggled to find reading material that fed their appetite while reinforcing the virtues we value. Bryan Davis is a good man and a great storyteller. And this series is an all-time favorite my sons still speak of, even now into their college years!

MARK T. HANCOCK, HUSBAND AND FATHER, CEO OF TRAIL LIFE USA

One of the best blends of contemporary fantasy and allegory that I have read, Dragons in Our Midst will have you hurting and rooting for Billy and Bonnie. If you love fantasy, King Arthur, and hopeful adventures, this is the story for you.

SCOTT APPLETON, AUTHOR OF THE SWORD OF THE DRAGON SERIES AND THE NEVERQUEEN SAGA

It all started with a boy who could breathe fire and a girl who had wings. Dragons in Our Midst invites readers to lift up their swords and join Billy Bannister and Bonnie Silver as they battle dragon slayers, uncover ancient legends, and—of course—come face to face with dragons. Bryan Davis delivers a clean, complex series that challenges and uplifts its readers. When I was a teenager, Billy and Bonnie's story captured my own heart and imagination. And today, its poignant messages of faith, sacrifice, and courage endure and stand ready to inspire the next generation of young readers.

JESSICA SLY, AUTHOR OF *THE PROMISE OF DECEPTION*

WHAT READERS ARE SAYING

Raising Dragons is an excellent start to a thrilling, inspiring, and faith-building series. Bryan Davis's unique meshing of legends, myths, and truth is incredibly creative. Together with his strong storytelling and thought-provoking themes it makes for an unforgettable ride. Bryan Davis's books exceed any others in the genre for thematic depth and yet are just as gripping and exciting story-wise as other books of the genre (or even more so). Bryan Davis is my favorite author, and I hope he will become yours too when you dive into the fascinating world of dragons and slayers, of light and darkness, and of truth and deception in *Raising Dragons*.
JOSEPH B., AGE 17

If you love fantasy, you NEED this book! You won't be able to put it down! If you love dragons, you'll love this book! Dragons aren't just portrayed as big bad beasties, as in other books—they're actually heroes! Are you a Christian who wants a deeper relationship with God? This book models that too! Are you seeking God, but always afraid of committing? This book models what true faith looks like and shows that you can love and trust God through everything!
NICK B.

Absolutely brilliant. This is not your typical dungeons and dragons book. Even at 28 I find this book/series addicting. Mr. Davis combines faith and fantasy flawlessly. There are books about King Arthur, Merlin, and dragons aplenty, but to find one whose story line spans centuries and also teaches modern Christian values, that is rare. Mr. Davis includes many unexpected twists and turns and a story line so unique it simply cannot be rivaled. *Raising Dragons* is guaranteed to pique the interest of readers of all ages.
LORI W., AGE 28

Tales of Starlight

Masters & Slayers
Third Starlighter
Exodus Rising

The Reapers Trilogy

Reapers
Beyond the Gateway
Reaper Reborn

Time Echoes Trilogy

Time Echoes
Interfinity
Fatal Convergence

The Oculus Gate

Heaven Came Down
Invading Hell
My Soul to Take
On Earth as it is in Hell

Wanted: Superheroes

Wanted: A Superhero to Save the World
Hertz to Be a Hero
Antigravity Heroes

Standalone Novel

Let the Ghosts Speak

To learn more about Bryan's books, go to
www.daviscrossing.com

BRYAN DAVIS

ASTRAL ALLIANCE

– BOOK TWO –

THE FIRST STARBORN

The First Starborn
Volume 2 in the Astral Alliance series

Print Edition ISBN 13: 978-1-946253-14-9
Ebook Edition ISBN 13: 978-1-946253-15-6

First Printing - September 2023

Printed in the United States of America

Part 01

Beta Four

I clutched a stone protruding from the steep cliff face, my fingers aching. Two other stones loomed a meter or so higher. If I couldn't reach up to grab them, my sweaty fingers would soon slip, and I would fall for sure.

Closing my eyes, I mentally focused on my real goal, not to climb my way out of a volcano, but to conquer this endurance test, make myself stronger for the next step—to find my father, likely banished to Beta Four, the frozen prison planet. To do that, I would need every gram of strength my body could provide. I had to be strong, for him.

I lifted my foot and pushed the toes of my sneaker into a tiny crag, then vaulted and grabbed the higher stones. But now my dangling feet had nothing to stand on, either stones or crags. A hundred meters below, a pool of lava waited for any misstep. Even from here I could feel the heat rising from the bubbling cauldron. One false move meant certain death. Or did it?

I whispered, "This isn't real. This isn't real." But my sweaty T-shirt and workout pants said otherwise, as did the pain roaring up and down my spine and into my trembling arms.

A clicking sound rose from below. Still dangling, I searched for the source. A hairy spider five times my size skittered up toward me, seconds away, its fangs dripping green venom.

I muscled up with both hands and scrabbled with my feet until one dug into another crag, then I leaped to the next handhold, then the next, clawing my way toward the top of the cliff. When I reached it and rolled onto the rocky ledge, I rose to all fours and looked down, gasping for breath as sweat dripped from my chin.

A loud thud reverberated. The spider dissolved into black sparkles and blew away like sooty dust. The lava cauldron disappeared, and the entire scene faded to white, revealing the four walls, ceiling, and floor of the ship's hologram training room, including the two circular heating coils that created the simulated lava's heat, still glowing orange but cooling quickly.

Leaning against a wall near the exit door, Crystal and Zoë looked on, both wearing workout tank tops. "Blazes, Megan," Crystal said. "Almost literally. But you were super quick."

Zoë rubbed the brand on her upper arm, probably inflamed by sweat from her climb a few minutes earlier. "Yeah, quicker than both of us. By far the fastest climb of the sisters trio."

I smiled. Zoë liked mentioning that we were sisters, all three infused with the same DNA. Not long ago, they chose to be marked on the upper arm with a dragon-shaped brand covered with my mother's ashes, a design that resembled my pirate brand. We didn't look alike at all—Crystal with lily-white skin and blonde hair, Zoë with ebony skin and black hair, and me with khaki skin and brown hair. No one would guess we considered ourselves sisters.

"I wonder how fast you could do it with your bracelets on," Crystal said. "Where'd you put them?"

I pointed at the floor a few meters below. "Down there." Directly under me, my power bracelets lay where I had left them alongside my two necklaces, one holding my original dragon's eye locket and the other the locket I took from my mother's corpse. "Maybe a little faster with them. They charge my leg muscles but not my arms. And everything seemed so dangerous. I might've been too amped up by adrenaline to remember to use them. Any idea why it was so hard?"

Sonya's half-human, half-mechanical female voice responded. "Because I set the motivation factors to nine out of ten." Her tone seemed more civil than usual, but it probably wouldn't last.

"That explains the giant spider and stalagmites," I said, "but what about the difficulty?" I sat upright and let my legs dangle over the edge of my perch, the ceiling about half a meter above my head. Several centimeters below my feet, two sets of moveable handholds and footholds slowly hummed downward on their tracks. Although the holographic images somehow made them look and feel like rocks, now they seemed ordinary, nothing more than simple white wall protrusions. "I could barely budge the handholds, even with all my strength."

"Because I increased the gear ratio to seven out of ten," Sonya said.

I narrowed my eyes. "So you set both the motivation and difficulty factors higher than usual?"

"Correct."

"But why? It's not like I'm training for the Galaxy Games."

"To allow you to collect more stress points in a short amount of time. You haven't made your goal for the week." Her tone shifted to snarky. "You were in the *slacker* category. Your success today raised you to merely *lazy*. Now you can work toward *wet-noodle* status."

Crystal flapped her lips. "Don't listen to that slave driver, Megan. You broke your mother's speed record, even at the tougher settings. You're the Astral Dragon's all-time female champ."

Sonya copied Crystal's lip noise. "So says the blonde bookworm. If she would pay as much attention to her own exercise instead of reading her badly written novels, she could rise above slimy-slug status."

"Hey!" Crystal pushed away from the wall. "I'm way stronger than a slug! And I'm not nearly as slimy."

Zoë rolled her eyes. "Sonya, what is your snark level set at?"

"One hundred percent. To answer in the common language for less-capable minds, my snark is at full throttle."

Zoë set her hands on her hips. "Who gave that order and why?"

"Perdantus. He wanted to test his negotiation skills against a snarky opponent. Although he is literally a birdbrain, his conversational skills are better than I expected. His vocabulary is recherché."

Crystal blinked. "What in blazes does *that* mean?"

"Exquisite," I said. "Unusually high quality."

Crystal huffed. "I call that a Willis word. You've been studying with Perdantus too much."

"Yeah," Zoë said. "I thought it meant highfalutin, pompous jibber-jabber. Come back to Planet Normal where you belong." She looked at Sonya's remote console, embedded in a wall alcove. "And set your snark level to zero. We've had enough of your digital lip."

"Snark level will be set to zero in ten seconds," Sonya said. "Only Captain Willis has immediate obedience authority, not so much for Lieutenant Bristle-brush hairdo. Have you ever heard of a comb? Or better, a garden rake?"

Zoë pinched the ends of her curls. "Is it that bad?"

Wincing, I replied in concert with Crystal. "Yeah. Pretty bad."

"Don't let Sonya get you down," I said. "We're all looking pretty rough. Three weeks in a wormhole without a shower will ripen anyone."

"Ripen?" Crystal repeated. "You mean rot. Why does it take so long to travel, anyway? In a novel I read, ships could zap from one part of the galaxy to another in an instant."

"Yeah. Fun stories but not real, at least not yet. The Alliance was working on instantaneous-travel technology, but for some reason, it was too dangerous. My father liked to talk about it. He told me people died in the tests."

Crystal shuddered. "Okay. I'll take slow, simmering stink over rotted-corpse stink any day."

I smiled. "Glad you're adapting. But no worries. I'll fix the water pressure valve when we get to Beta Three. Someone there should have the part we need. Then we'll go to Beta Four to find my father. Until then, we'll have to endure bird baths from a basin."

Perdantus flew in, landed on Crystal's shoulder, and spoke in chirps, a language we all had learned. "A bird bath is quite suitable for a silver jay, but I …" He grimaced. "What is that foul odor?"

Crystal smirked. "Me, Mr. Nimble-nose. I did my wall climb a little while ago." She lifted her arms. "I just need to air out a bit."

"You do that." Perdantus flew to Zoë's shoulder and inhaled, then grimaced again. "Unfortunately, the odor isn't much better over here."

"Get used to it." I scooted off the ledge and landed on the floor, bending my knees on impact. I picked up my locket necklaces and bracelets and snapped the bracelets on my wrists. "You're stuck with three smelly girls for a while."

Perdantus fluffed his feathers. "Very well. I realize that I was warned about this possibility. I will adapt."

"Good thing." I wrapped my old locket's chain around my neck and fastened it in back, then my mother's. "You don't have a choice."

"Captain Willis," Sonya said, "while you were exercising, I completed my analysis of the data drive you retrieved from the dead girl."

"What did you learn?"

"The data was encrypted using Alliance methods with which I am not familiar. You should keep the drive with you in case you have an opportunity to have it analyzed by an Alliance computer."

I frowned. "So you have no intel for me at all?"

"Not from the drive. Zoë scanned the documents from Thorne's lockbox and entered them into my system. I matched the names and addresses to people and places in a relatively new database. All but one of the people have been reported missing or dead. The one person who remains is named Omen. Thorne's scribblings revealed no last name."

"Omen?" I repeated. "Where does he live?"

"According to an invoice Thorne kept, Omen lives on Delta Ninety-One, though Thorne's poor handwriting makes me uncertain."

"Delta Ninety-one? I've never heard of it."

"It is an Alliance outpost planet," Sonya said. "Its harsh environment makes it unsuitable for colonization. Only a few people live there, likely no more than a hundred."

I nodded. "Understood. Maybe we can dig into it later."

"According to Thorne's paperwork," Zoë said, "he was selling bee eggs and DNA to his customers. I guess that's more valuable than glowsap because they could copy his mines on other planets. Plenty of people would pay a lot for that knowledge."

"There is more," Sonya said. "Based on Captain Willis's estimate of how much bramble bee glowsap was in the Nebula One's cargo hold, I conclude that Thorne and his contacts could not have harvested that much."

"Well, maybe they've been storing it for years," I said, "or even decades."

"Negative. Glowsap is not flammable after one year. It is still valuable, but it would not create the massive explosion you experienced."

I furrowed my brow. "Where else could Admiral Fairbanks have gotten so much glowsap?"

"According to my calculations, it is virtually impossible. Your estimate is twenty-three times more than all of Thorne's contacts could have harvested in one year, assuming they had a mine as prolific as Thorne's, which is unlikely for new operations."

I nodded. "Right. Thorne had well-trained kids that—"

The lights in the room flashed off, then on, and continued like a strobe. "Warning," Sonya said. "Anomalous readings from the wormhole indicate a potential collapse."

I sucked in a breath. "Collapse? Is the warp engine malfunctioning?"

"That possibility exists. Not all readings are coming through. In any case, catastrophic damage is likely in less than five minutes at which time everyone on this ship will perish."

"Can we just shut down the warp drive? Terminate the wormhole passage on our own?"

"Affirmative, but since the warp drive could be malfunctioning, that option might also be risky. We could end up in a deep space gap, and with the warp drive possibly broken, we would be marooned there."

"I'll take risky over certain death." I waved a hand. "Crystal. Zoë. On my six."

"On your six?" Crystal said. "What in blazes does that mean?"

"Follow me. I'll explain later." I dashed out the door to the lower-level hallway, scurried up the ladder to bridge level, and sprinted to the captain's chair. The front viewing window displayed the scene in front of the ship. The surrounding tunnel of dazzling light appeared to be narrowing as an exit hole in the distance grew smaller and smaller.

Crystal and Zoë rushed onto the bridge and took their seats, Crystal in the first-mate's chair, Zoë at the navigator's station. Zoë read the data on her screens, her eyes darting. "Claw of the dragon! Everything's scrambled. I can't get a sensible reading."

Crystal's eyes widened as she looked out the window. "We're about to get popped like a pimple!"

"Sonya," I said, "the wormhole exit is closer than we calculated. That means the warp engines folded space fabric more than expected, but we'll still come out in the Beta system, right?"

"Your explanation is not precise, but it is close. In short, if we can make it to the hole before the collapse is complete, we will exit relatively near our planned destination. If not, the Astral Dragon will disintegrate into millions of molecules dispersing across the galaxy."

Crystal gulped. "I don't like the sound of that."

I toggled the switch that retracted the ship's wings and grasped the steering yoke. "Sonya, I need data—current size of the hole relative to our ship, how many minutes till we reach it, the size it will be when we get there, and time till catastrophic wormhole collapse."

"The exit hole is currently one point nine times the size of our ship, and arrival will be in three minutes and seven seconds. At that moment, the hole will be point eight six times the ship's size, which, of course, is too small for passage. Collapse will occur in two minutes and twenty-four seconds."

"If we push the warp drive to maximum, can we make it out before the hole is too small?"

"Impossible to calculate in the time remaining. The Astral Dragon has never attempted a higher warp-drive setting than the current one, and since the drive could be malfunctioning, increasing the warp factor could—"

"Never mind. Everyone strap in. Perdantus, find a safe place. Too late to put on pressurized suits. They wouldn't do us any good anyway." While Perdantus flew out of the bridge area, I slung the seat straps over my body, buckled in, and unlocked the warp drive throttle on my console. The moment I heard two more clicks from Crystal's and Zoë's seats, I pushed the warp-drive throttle three notches higher to maximum.

The surrounding tunnel boundary blurred, and the exit hole shot toward us, shrinking like the jaws of a hungry beast. Colorful lights sparkled around the perimeter and radiated toward the center. Since our warp engine folded the space fabric, pushing the throttle merely crinkled the fabric further while leaving the exit point intact, a super dangerous shift since we didn't have time for Sonya to calculate the results.

I pushed a button that set the targeting grid on the viewing window. "Be ready to fire at hostiles."

"Why?" Zoë asked. "We're not coming out at a common trade point. Pirates shouldn't be around."

"Not pirates. Prison guards." I eyed the oncoming exit hole, now about thirty seconds away. "The warp shift could've altered our exit point enough to put us in range of Beta Four's security scanners. The moment we punch through, I'll need you to get a fix on our location."

"Will do, Sister."

"I'm locked and ready," Crystal said as she grasped a targeting joystick with a trembling hand. "But blazes, Megan! How are you staying so calm? We're an albatross trying to squeeze through a pigeonhole."

"I know. It'll be tight." I checked the wing status—fully retracted. But, like Crystal said, the hole still looked too small. More sweat trickled down my already-damp back. In seconds, we could all be dead. "And trust me. I feel the danger. I'm just not showing it."

"Yeah. Easy for the experienced pirate to say." Crystal firmed her lips and stared straight at the viewing window. "Okay. I'll be a Megan Willis clone. Bring it on. The more danger, the better." She looked down, a skeptical frown growing. "It's not working."

Ahead, the hole shrank further, now looking much flatter, more like a coin slot than a wormhole exit. We could fit widthwise, but our height? I shook my head. Not good. Not good at all.

Sonya piped in. "Five seconds to exit. The hole is too volatile to determine its safety."

"Everyone brace yourselves." As we zoomed into the slot, I gritted my teeth and whispered to the Astral Dragon, the deity, not the ship, "Please help us."

Something popped. Sizzles crackled all around. The ship's lights flashed chaotically. Then everything fell dark and silent.

"Megan?" Crystal said, her voice puny and shaking. "Are you alive? Zoë?"

I exhaled. "I'm alive."

"Same here," Zoë said. "Sonya? How about you?"

"I am functioning at full capacity, but the ship has automatically shifted to stealth mode—full silence and complete darkness."

I blinked at the darkness. Since my parents and I used the ship to sneak up on various Alliance bases, we needed that mode in order to approach undetected. "What triggered the shift?"

In the quiet blackness, Sonya's voice sounded more mechanical than usual. "I am conducting a full sweep of all processes to be sure, but it seems that the top of the ship grazed the exit hole boundary. The exiting protocol assumed that we were under attack, thereby triggering stealth mode."

"Makes sense. Can you override?"

"I can, but I advise waiting until I complete a damage check. It is safer to stay in stealth until we know the capabilities of the ship. I estimate two minutes to complete the sweep."

"Give me a damage report when it's done." I breathed a sigh. "We can relax now, at least for a couple of minutes."

"All right," Crystal said. "Now you can tell me what *on my six* means. It's been biting my brain ever since you said it."

"It's something my father taught me. He and I used to prattle back and forth with barbs and jabs, mostly fun stuff, but when things turned serious and we had to get somewhere quick, he would say, 'On my six.' It means follow me. Or I would say to my father, 'on your six,' if I wanted to let him know I was following him."

"I don't get it," Crystal said. "How does it mean 'to follow'?"

"Picture an analog clock on the floor. The person leading is at the center, facing the number twelve, and the person following is on the six. The follower is on the leader's six. Got it?"

"Yeah. Perfectly clear. Except I have one question."

"Okay. Ask it."

"What's an analog clock?"

I rolled my eyes. "Remind me to show you a picture later." I looked out the viewing window—a fairly dark scene. Only a few stars dotted the blackness, though one light near the center outshone the others. "Zoë, is that a star or a planet directly ahead of us?"

Zoë's voice drifted through the dimness, her face barely visible in the glow of her console screen. "I was just getting our bearings, but I think it's Beta Four."

"Not Beta Three? I guess the shift really put us off course, like I thought it might."

"A little, I think. The two planets are pretty close to each other right now. We could make it to Three in about an hour, and if we stay on our current course, we'll be at Four in just a few minutes."

"Then we definitely need to stay in stealth mode. We're already in scanning range."

"Maybe …" Zoë's eyes darted as she studied her screen. "I don't see any patrol crafts. No cruisers. No drones. No pods. Nothing."

I unbuckled and rose from my chair. A tiny light on my console caught my attention, the power LED on the data drive I took from Penelope's coffin. I pulled the drive out of its slot, pushed it into my pocket, and walked closer to the viewing window. "How is that possible? Maybe prisoners can't get off that icy rock on their own, but guards are needed to watch for stooges who could drop by and pick them up."

"Like us," Crystal said. "I mean, not the stooges part, but we *are* planning to snatch your father from the planet."

"Exactly." I scratched my itching scalp. "I don't like this. I don't like it at all. It has *trap* written all over it." As the light drew closer and brighter, its identity as a planet became clear. I spun toward my crew. "Zoë, plot a course to put us in a safe orbit, out of range of planet-based missiles. Sonya will show you the protocol on your console."

"Got it." Zoë began tapping on her screen.

I tried to focus on Crystal, but only her silhouette sat in view. "Scan the surface for a base of operations. We're looking for lights, warmth, movement, any sign of life."

"You got it, Captain." Crystal's console light turned on, revealing her face as she studied the screen.

"Captain Willis," Sonya said, "the only damage is to one shield panel on top of the ship. We will be vulnerable to attack at that location."

"Is it beyond repair?"

"Affirmative. It will have to be replaced. To answer your next question, we have no spare shield panels in inventory."

I smiled. "That was pretty close to snark. Are you sure the level is set to zero?"

"Affirmative. I was merely anticipating your question. Zero snark does not reduce my efficiency."

I looked out the window again. With Beta Four now closer, its icy surface clarified, much of it visible between cloudbanks here and there. Exploring the planet in search of one person could take a long time, especially if other prisoners or dangerous creatures lurked, but nothing could stop me from trying. "We'll continue our approach and worry about the shield later."

"Understood. The captain, of course, is well aware of the ambush potential."

"I'm aware, but we can't be running from shadows." I looked at the ceiling. "Set bridge to twilight and your snark level to forty. I need my old Sonya back."

"Yes, you do." The lights flickered on to a dim setting, making the bridge viewable. "And old Sonya thinks that the spider on Beta Four is telling the fly named Megan that all is well. Come to my web and visit me. But I know you will pay no heed to this warning, so now I am anticipating your next move. Your father's parka is at the bottom of the clothing compartment."

I grinned. "You're quite the mind reader, Sonya."

"Reading your mind is usually entertaining, Megan, but the plot is often predictable."

"Well, you've known me since I was only—"

"Wait," Crystal said, scrunching her brow at me like I might be crazy. "A parka? Are you thinking of landing the Dragon on Beta Four now? Shouldn't we scan for hostiles first?"

"We're not landing the dragon. I'm taking the glider to the surface. Less chance of being seen."

"How many passengers does it hold?"

"Just a pilot. It's super small. Undetectable on radar." I winked. "Perfect for pirates sneaking into places they're not supposed to go."

She narrowed an eye at me. "This is serious! You can't go alone. You need someone on your six to watch your back."

"I'll have someone." I blew a shrill whistle. "Perdantus!"

He flew in and landed on my shoulder. "You called?"

"Yep." I rubbed his chest with a finger. "You once told me you prefer cold weather, like you had on Delta Ninety-eight."

He glanced at my finger as if suspicious. "Yes, we silver jays are a hearty lot when it comes to low temperatures. Why?"

I drew my hand back. "I need you to come with me. I'm going to Beta Four. It's an ice planet. Like Delta Ninety-eight after a big battle storm."

"Oh. I see. Well, if I can help you in your quest to find your father, then …" Perdantus fluffed his feathers. "I am up for the challenge."

Zoë flashed an annoyed frown. "I'm glad our brave bird gets his chance, but what are Crystal and I supposed to do while you're gone? Play checkers?"

"Nope." I withdrew a communications bud from my pocket and inserted it in my ear. "You and Crystal will monitor my progress and watch for danger. The glider's scanner doesn't have nearly the range the dragon's does, and it doesn't have any weapons like some of the Nebula series pods do. I might need you to come to my rescue."

Crystal rolled her eyes. "What would we do? Scoop you out of a nest of giant ice spiders or blast an army of snow zombies?"

I shrugged. "Maybe. I haven't seen a snow zombie in at least three years, five years for an ice spider, but you never know."

Crystal huffed. "And people think novel reading zapped *my* brain."

"My brain's been zapped more times than I can count." With Perdantus still on my shoulder, I walked to our sleeping room as I spoke through the earbud's microphone. "Listen," I said, my voice now audible in the ceiling speakers, "I'm not going to land the Dragon out in the open and expose it to a possible trap." I flipped up the clothing trunk lid and fished out my father's parka along with a spare work uniform—long-sleeved with insulated pants. I also grabbed a weapons belt, complete with a flashlight and a holstered laser pistol, good for about twenty blasts. "When you expect guards and don't find any, it smells like an ambush."

Zoë's voice piped into my ear. "Admiral Fairbanks didn't seem surprised when he heard your father's voice coming from the ship. Maybe he knew the security here was gone."

"Good point, but I think he was at least a little surprised. Guards or no guards, it's still hard to get off the planet." I gave my shoulder a shrug. When Perdantus flew off and alit on the trunk's open lid, I put the uniform on over my exercise clothes. "That's how I know my father's alive. Fairbanks thought he should still be on Beta Four."

"Can't argue with that," Zoë said. "Speaking of Fairbanks, should we ask Sonya to check for any buzz about where his wife might be? Don't remember her name, but she's bound to be hot on the trail of whoever killed him."

"Camille Fairbanks." I tied the drawstring on the uniform's waistband. "Sure. Ask Sonya. And also ask her to check for any messages from Oliver. He knew to send an update to my mailbox on Beta Three."

"Will do, Sister."

I put the belt on, then the parka, and zipped it in front—quite a bit too big for me, but it would do. "Any update on your scans, Crystal?"

"I spotted something just now," Crystal said. "Come take a look."

"On my way." I pulled a pair of thick gloves from the parka's pocket. "Let's go, Perdantus."

He fluttered to my shoulder and rode along as I hustled back to the bridge, slowed by the winter gear. After a few seconds, he slipped off, then flew the rest of the way and landed on the back of my chair. "Your parka is slick," he said as I arrived, "but at least it hides most of your odor."

"Good thing. The glider doesn't have windows to let the stink out." I stood behind Crystal and looked at her screen. It showed a magnified view of a two-story gray building with a big door on one side. "Supply warehouse, maybe? Or a hangar?"

"Can't tell. No movement anywhere. But there is a heat signature in the center of the building. Really faint." She pointed at the spot. "It's like a blur. If I hadn't been looking for something, I never would've noticed it."

I leaned closer. "But you're right. It's there. Could be someone sick or dying, so that's where I'm going first." When I stepped back, I looked at Zoë and Crystal as both cast disappointed frowns at me. "Listen, I know you feel like you're being put on the useless shelf, but I'm the only one with experience in this kind of stealth mission. I guess you could say I'm the sneakiest. I've broken into some pretty secure places."

Crystal touched her chest. "*I'm* plenty sneaky. My magic powers can get me pretty much anywhere. One look into my eyes and even snow zombies will do whatever I tell them, at least for a little while."

My parka's zipper started sliding down by itself. I scowled at Zoë. "Stop that!"

She grinned. "Just a reminder that I can unzip, unfasten, or unlock just about anything with my mind. Hard to be sneakier than that."

"Okay, point taken." I rezipped the zipper and set my fists on my hips. "Which one of you wants to take my place in the glider and cross an unpredictable number of mind-numbingly frigid kilometers, tiptoe across deep chasms covered by thin ice sheets, avoid convicted murderers who would slit your throat just for the warmth of your blood, and face beasts that could gulp you down like a screaming, kicking kernel of popcorn?"

"My talents are needed here." Zoë refocused on her screen. "I'm the navigator."

Crystal lifted an arm and sniffed. "And I'm the smelliest. The beasts would track me down too quick."

I crossed my arms and nodded. "I thought so."

Zoë pointed toward the docking station. "Then stop procrastinating. Get your butt in that glider and go find your father."

"Wait. There's a way you can come with me." I opened a cabinet under Sonya's console and withdrew a receiver deck—a circular platform the size of my palm. I showed it to my crew. "With this."

Crystal narrowed her eyes. "What is it?"

"As long as I'm in range, it'll project your holographic images from the ship to me and send views from its camera to you. My father invented all sorts of cool tech like this. Sonya will teach you how to communicate with it."

"Yes," Sonya said, "I will teach them, but you need a lesson in planet exploration yourself. You have not asked for an environment report."

I heaved an impatient sigh. "Humans live there. I assumed it was habitable."

"It is a punishment planet that eventually kills those who are exiled there. You need to be ready to face the negative elements. The air temperature ranges from twenty-two degrees below zero Celsius at night to six degrees below zero during the day. Gravity is seventy-nine percent of the level we create with our onboard gravity engine. You will feel lighter on your feet and be able to move larger objects than usual. The oxygen level is twelve point three percent, similar to what you will find on a moderately high mountain peak on Alpha One. You will feel out of breath until you adjust. The atmosphere also contains a high level of methane, a combustible gas, so be aware in case you need to start a fire. Another problem is a higher-than-safe percentage of radon. It is a carcinogen that eventually kills those who are exiled for a long period of time, which is why being a prisoner there is a death sentence in the long term and why a guard's duty at the station is limited to one year."

"Okay. Good to know." I spun toward the ship's dock. "Let's go, Perdantus." Still encumbered by the extra clothing, I jogged to the hatch, spun open its locking wheel, and walked across the ramp toward the airlock door. On the way, I stopped and grabbed an adult-sized pressure suit and helmet from a hook and began putting the suit on over my clothes, making me bulkier than ever.

Perdantus landed on the empty hook. "In the event of an air leak in the glider, I assume that you will stuff me into your suit so that I can breathe your air."

I fastened the front of the suit, tight over the parka, especially with the air tank pulling the material toward the back. "That's right."

"Your fetid air."

"Great word. Stinky. Foul. Noxious. I have more synonyms if you need one."

"No. Any of those will do." He flew to my shoulder again, now able to perch there more easily. "I will take the risk."

"I knew I could count on you." I tucked the helmet under my arm and opened the airlock door. As it slid to the side with a long hiss, I walked in, put my helmet on, and fastened it in place. "Sonya," I said into the helmet microphone, "Crystal and Zoë are co-captains while I'm gone. If I can't give commands, they're in charge."

Sonya's voice buzzed in my helmet. "Co-captains? Those two? They don't know their port from their stern."

"Maybe not." I pushed a button on the wall that opened the top hatch to our craft, a single-seat glider with sleek, swept-back wings, and climbed inside, Perdantus still on my shoulder. "But you're smart enough to figure out what they're saying."

"This is true, but it will put pressure on my artificial patience."

When I scrunched into the tiny seat, my elbow knocked an empty paper cup that sat in a holder next to the armrest. A coffee stain at the bottom of the cup raised a reminder about my father's love for coffee. He had left the cup here long ago. I didn't have the heart to toss it out.

I reached a finger toward the front console's airlock control. A thud reverberated and shook the Astral Dragon. I drew my hand back. "Sonya, what was that?"

"We are being attacked." The glider's top hatch closed over us. "Emergency protocol engaging. Shields going up."

"Emergency protocol? That means the airlock will—" A hidden valve hissed. "Sonya! I'm losing air in the glider!"

No answer came through.

I pressed the button to open the hatch, but nothing happened. The emergency protocol had taken over. In a few more seconds, the glider would be out of air.

"Not to be a complainer," Perdantus said, "but the air seems to be getting a bit thin in this glider."

"I know." I unfastened my helmet, grabbed Perdantus, and pushed him underneath, then refastened it and sent air from the tank into the suit.

He fluttered his wings, tickling my cheek. "I was afraid of this exact scenario, and your parka is no longer masing your odor."

"Hush and settle down." I withdrew the communications disk from my vest pocket, turned it on, and set it atop the glider's control console. "I have to see what's happening out there."

A white ghostly image appeared above the disk. Crystal and Zoë stood side by side as if looking at something, maybe the viewing window. With so little air in the glider now, the sound waves barely reached my ears. "Megan's gone," Crystal said. "We dropped her off at Beta Three to look for repair parts while we scanned Beta Four for life."

A new voice entered, female and unfamiliar. "Nonsense. Megan Willis would never leave the Astral Dragon under the command of two inexperienced girls."

I sucked in a breath. A woman was communicating from another ship. Could she be Camille Fairbanks?

"Megan must be in the ship somewhere, and if you don't turn her over to me, I will destroy the Astral Dragon. I know your shields are up, but we have enhanced torpedoes on board that will not be deterred by your shields. My understanding is that you are already familiar with this weapon, seeing that Megan detonated one in my husband's ship and killed him."

I gulped. Yes, she was Camille Fairbanks. We had heard that she was more brutal than her husband ever was. She probably wouldn't hesitate to blow the Dragon to pieces. She was hungry for revenge, and it seemed that I had only one choice to save the ship and my crew.

I pointed the disk's camera at my face and spoke into the helmet's microphone. "Sonya, patch me to the bridge and show the communication's disk camera view to our caller. And don't answer. Just patch me through."

When the comm shift clicked, I spoke with a commanding voice. "Camille Fairbanks, this is Megan Willis, captain of the Astral Dragon. I saw your husband die, and he died bravely, but he was a monster, a child predator, and he deserved to burn in his own ship's inferno. You have no right or reason to exact revenge against those who tried to stop his rampage."

Camille's voice piped into my helmet speaker. "I am not interested in your opinions about my good husband, Megan Willis. You will either meet my demands and surrender, or I will destroy your ship. You have five seconds to signal your compliance and provide your location on the ship."

"I am in the Astral Dragon's escape glider. If you want me, come and get me." I pushed the comm disk into my vest pocket, buckled my seatbelt, and pressed the launch button. The mechanism catapulted the glider with Perdantus and me out of the belly of the Astral Dragon and into space.

With one hand on the glider's yoke and the other on the console, I engaged the rear thrusters and blasted farther away from the Dragon. The surge shoved my body against the back of the seat and Perdantus into my hair, but I couldn't take the helmet off. We probably had zero air left in the glider.

Perdantus squirmed forward, now pressed between my cheek and the helmet, but he stayed quiet, smart enough to know better than to complain.

Without a viewing camera at the aft, I turned and looked back through the glass dome covering the glider. A huge ship flew over the Astral Dragon and gave chase, exactly what I had hoped for. Camille didn't want to waste any time. Even in the few seconds it would take her to fire torpedoes at the Dragon, I would be long gone, not even a tiny blip on her ship's scanners.

Now, with her on my tail, I had to take cover or her much faster ship would catch me. I pulled the comm disk out again and set it on the console, its camera pointed at me. A holographic image of the Dragon's bridge reappeared above the disk, showing my two crew members, Zoë, now in the captain's chair, and Crystal sitting next to her. "Crystal. Zoë. Switch back to stealth mode while I make a run for it. Don't let her find you, or our ship's a dead dragon."

"Sure thing," Zoë said, "but how're you going to hide from her?"

"By heading to the planet. My glider's a lot more maneuverable than her ship. I can go places she can't. Just send the coordinates of the building Crystal saw to the glider's navigation computer."

"Will do. Keep in touch."

"Nope. I have to shut off all transmissions for a while. Everything's going dark. I'll contact you when I'm safe." I turned the disk off, slid it back into the vest pocket, and shifted the glider directly toward Beta Four with the thruster still on maximum. "All right, Perdantus, the ride's probably going to get really bumpy. Hold your breath and find something to hang on to. Maybe my hair."

Perdantus let out grunt-like chirps. "I *have* been holding my breath and not only because of the odor. I am being squeezed from both sides."

"Can't help you with that. We'll be in breathable air in about—"

A laser blast zipped past us on the left, then another on the right, both barely missing. "Blazes! Those were close! She must have some kind of advanced aiming mechanism to lock in on a glider this size."

Perdantus squeezed out a few more chirps. "Can you do something to counter it?"

"Yep. Watch this." I shifted the yoke up and down and side to side, making the glider dance. My body bounced with it, held in place by the seat's straps.

Several more laser blasts streaked by, missing us by a wider margin. "She's guessing now, but she's not giving up. Let's see if she follows us into the planet's atmosphere." I pulled up the coordinates of the building where Crystal saw the heat signature and set a course for that spot, a path that would first dive to the planet and then skim the surface the rest of the way.

Below, a cloudbank covered the ground, veiling the terrain. Without a more sophisticated scanner, I couldn't tell if the clouds might be hiding a deadly obstacle, like a mountain or a canyon, but I couldn't risk slowing my dive.

With only seconds remaining before penetrating the mist, I looked back. Camille's ship now followed from only a few kilometers behind, its silvery metallic shell glimmering in the planet's rising sun. Soon, she would have to extend her ship's wings to catch the air and turn into a glide. Otherwise, she would crash into the surface. The shift would force her to decelerate, but with my tiny craft, I could wait until the last second to pull up, allowing me time to scoot out of sight.

The moment the tips of her wings appeared, sliding out of their sockets, I faced the front again. When our glider plunged into the cloud, I turned parallel to the planet's surface. The sudden shift pushed me down in my seat, making it feel like a whale decided to sit on my lap, but after a few seconds, the pressure eased.

Now flying blind with billows of fog splashing against the window and with the glider bucking hard, I opened a vent and allowed a stream of misty air inside, then took off my helmet and set it on my knee. Perdantus fluttered out of my hair and perched on the yoke, his claws tight as he gasped for breath. "This has been ... quite a ride."

"Nothing compared to the crash we'll suffer if we fly into a mountain. I have to rise to see where we're going and then burrow under again. It's going to stay bumpy."

He bobbed his head. "Understood."

I angled the wings and ascended a few meters, enough for the top of our glass dome to peek over the bank. About a hundred meters ahead, a ridge protruded above the clouds, icy and desolate. I had only a few seconds to decide whether to go over it and risk being seen by Camille or dive down, turn sharply, and skirt the ridge, using the terrain to conceal the glider, though that option would make the journey longer.

The image of the blurred heat signature flashed to mind. Although it was a million-to-one shot that my father's body lay in that building, I couldn't risk losing another second. I pulled the yoke back, making the glider shoot upward into the clear. Like an airborne kangaroo, we leaped over the ridge and dove again, but the cloudbank was no longer there, only a long, snow-covered slope toward a glacial valley—U-shaped and, like everything else, covered by ice, though the curved ice made it appear as though water had flowed at one time, maybe a river centuries ago.

After glancing back and seeing no pursuing ship, I flew a meter or so above the frozen river's meandering path, more or less following the computer's charted course. Now out in the open, I felt like a sitting duck, ready to be zapped by an angry hunter.

As I flew, Perdantus studied the landscape. "This world looks like Delta Ninety-eight during the peak of an especially cold winter. I have seen this much snow and ice before, but only once in my lifetime."

"Oh? How old are you, Perdantus?"

"In Alpha-one years, I am twenty-three. We silver jays usually live to about thirty years of age, forty at the most, though I have heard a tale about one particularly ornery fellow who lived to be forty-five." He let out a chirping laugh. "They say he was too mean for the grim reaper to drag away. He fought the reaper off and tied him up with a discarded shoelace."

I laughed with Perdantus in spite of my worry. "What finally killed this ornery old bird?"

"They say he accidentally flew into a—"

A laser blasted a hole in the river in front of us. A blizzard of crystals erupted into the sky. Icy fragments pelted the windshield as more shimmering streaks knifed past us. Ahead, the frozen river disappeared into a hole in a mountain face, only seconds away. "We're trapped!"

"Can we turn?" Perdantus asked as more near-miss laser bullets sent ice shards flying. "Go straight up?"

"Not without decelerating. If we do that, we're cooked." I pointed forward. "We gotta get through that hole."

Perdantus looked toward it. "It's so small. Can we fit?"

"Not with the wings extended. I'll have to retract them, hit the river's surface, and slide in." I lowered the glider to mere centimeters from the surface, pressed the console button to draw the wings in, and shut off the thrusters. We landed smoothly on the river and began sliding toward the hole, now two seconds away, but a laser blew a divot directly in front of us. I grabbed Perdantus with one hand and my seat's armrest with the other. The glider struck the divot and flipped us into an out-of-control tumble through the opening.

Holding my breath as the straps kept me in place, I rode with the bounces and somersaulting lurches. My chest heaved. My stomach churned. Finally, the glider slowed to a stop with me sitting upside down in the pilot's chair.

I opened my hand, releasing Perdantus. He fluttered down to the glass-domed top a few centimeters below my dangling hair and looked up at me. "Are you all right, Megan?"

"Yeah. I think so." I unbuckled and let gravity lower me to a scrunched sitting position next to him. "You?"

He fluffed his feathers and shook them out. "I believe that I have survived unscathed, but if that ship is so determined to destroy us, hiding here won't keep us safe for long."

"You're right about that." I reached up and pressed the button that opened the glider, but nothing happened. "Mechanism probably isn't powerful enough to open while I'm sitting on the hatch. It would have to lift the whole glider to get it open."

"You could push up with your enhanced legs."

"Good idea." After turning my body to press my feet against the pilot's seat above and flexing to charge my muscles, I grasped the latch handle, turned it, and shoved with my legs. The glider lifted, and the hatch creaked open, barely enough to allow me to push myself out before the glider fell back into place with a heavy thud. The glass cracked, leaving a head-sized hole in the dome, big enough for Perdantus to exit.

I rolled over a rough sheet of ice, climbed to my feet, and looked back at our entry. The opening of this tubular cave cast light from about a hundred meters away. It wouldn't take long for Camille to land somewhere close and send her goons in. I had to figure out a way to prevent an attack.

Perdantus flew up to my shoulder. "What now?"

"I'm thinking." A breeze blew in, cold on my bare cheeks. The air channeled farther into the cave, over a head-high ridge of ice that had halted the glider's skid. The airflow meant that the cave had another exit, but could we get to it? "Perdantus, while I check for Camille, can you fly deeper into the cave and see where it leads?"

"Of course." He leaped off my shoulder and flew over the ridge.

I shed the spacesuit and tank but left the parka on. Feeling lighter than usual, I padded to the cave's entrance, pressed myself against the adjacent wall, and peeked out. Camille's ship sat on the frozen river fifty-or-so meters away. The Nebula series craft, about the same size as the Nebula Nine, had aimed its prow toward my vantage point. Meter-tall letters on each angled side announced its identity—Nebula Seven.

From where it sat, it could send a barrage of laser blasts or even a photon torpedo into the cave, but Camille likely realized that a barrage might miss me and collapse the ceiling just inside the opening, preventing anyone from finding me.

The front hatch opened, revealing the ship's exit ramp as it lowered. At least fifteen soldiers hustled out, all armed with laser rifles. Wearing what appeared to be cleats of some sort, they had no trouble keeping traction on the ice. They lined up and stood at attention as if waiting for a command to attack.

I stepped well back from the entrance. There was no way I could fend off that many soldiers, and without cleats of my own, I couldn't run as fast as they could. I had to either sneak away or block their access, but if I did that, would I be trapped?

I hissed into the cave, "Perdantus!"

"Coming." He flew out of the dimness and landed on my shoulder. "There is another way. It is a rather narrow tube, but you can fit if you crawl. It leads to a chamber with a spacious exit to the outside."

I imagined crawling through a narrow, rocky tube. "Can an adult male fit?"

"I believe so."

"Then they could come after me. Maybe I should blast the ceiling near the opening here and make it collapse." I shook my head. "No, then Camille would know I have another exit."

"True. She knows you're not a fool."

I raised a finger. "Or I could set some bait."

"Goad her into collapsing the cave for you?"

"Exactly. She's thirsty for a steaming cup of revenge. Maybe I can make the water boil." After unzipping my parka to expose my weapons belt, I stepped out of the cave into the open. Dark clouds obscured a rising sun to my left, and a cold breeze from the same direction made me blink to keep my eyes from drying out. Maybe a snowstorm was coming. That might force her hand more quickly than otherwise.

I pulled my laser blaster from its holster, and shouted, "You'd better not send anyone in here, or you'll be sorry."

To prove my prowess, I fired at the closest soldier, hitting his foot. He dropped to a knee and groaned while the others looked at the ship as if begging for a command to charge. A woman wearing a parka walked down the ramp, halted at the bottom, and looked at me, gloved fists on hips pressing her parka against her narrow waist. Her lanky form made her look younger than I expected, though her short gray hair, barely visible under her hood, said otherwise, and her commanding posture told me even more. She had to be Camille Fairbanks. "Megan Willis," she said, "your foolishness seems to have no bounds."

Perdantus whispered into my ear, "She has taken a negotiation stance and led off with a verbal barb in order to measure your temper. You know what to do."

I whispered in return, "You've taught me well. Let's give *her* temper a bit of a test." Hoping to show Camille that I had no fear of her, I squared my shoulders. "Camille Fairbanks, your bloodlust for revenge in support of your parasitic husband is pathetic. While he's rightfully being eaten by worms, you think in the rancid sewage you call a brain that killing me, the little girl who bested a decorated admiral at every turn, will somehow restore honor to that vomitous buzzard, a so-called man who fed on the corpses of innocent children."

While Camille lowered her hands but kept them balled as fists, Perdantus whispered, "That was brilliant, but perhaps a bit overdone."

"Nope. I've got her pegged as an ego freak. She needed the coldest slap in the face possible to make this work."

Camille shouted, "From the stories I heard, my husband could have killed you several times. Since you were a condemned criminal, he should have summarily executed you."

I retorted in a sassy tone. "Too bad for him. He's a rotting carcass, and I'm still kicking."

Camille stood quietly for a moment, heavy breaths puffing streams of white vapor, a clear sign of rage, though she kept her voice in check. "If my husband had any faults, showing mercy to a child was one of them. I won't make the same mistake. But I know what you're doing. You're hoping to bait me into sending my troops into that cave, only to be picked off by you as they enter. Well, I won't risk their lives over the likes of a petulant rodent like you, and since a storm seems to be on its way ..."

I whispered to Perdantus without moving my lips. "Here it comes."

"I agree. Be ready to run."

Camille shouted toward the bridge. "Fire the enhanced torpedoes. I want her atomized."

I hissed, "Let's go!"

Perdantus took wing and zipped into the cave. I dashed after him, but my feet slipped out from under me. I fell flat on my back and slid a meter or two before slowing enough to scramble up again. Perdantus flew quick orbits around my head while frantically calling, "Hurry! Hurry!"

"I'm trying!" I set my feet on a rougher portion of ice, flexed to activate the electrical impulse to my legs, and leaped. While I sailed forward, an explosion erupted behind me. A concussive wave shoved me through the air even faster. The boom jolted my senses. I fell on my stomach and slid until I rammed my shoulder and head into the glider.

I rolled up to a seated position and looked back. Only a narrow shaft of light pierced a gap in a pile of rocks and ice that blocked the entrance. I looked at my hand, no longer holding the laser gun. I probably dropped it during the explosion and it now lay somewhere under the debris.

Blood dripped in front of my eye. I dabbed at a cut on my forehead. Not too bad, but with sweat seeping into the cut, it stung.

Another blast rocked the cave. More debris cascaded from above, sending a wave of dust across my face and shutting out all light. Now in darkness except for the blinking console lights in the glider, I rubbed dust out of my eyes and looked around, unable to see anything but vague shapes. "Perdantus, are you all right?"

"I believe so." His voice came from the ground near my leg, barely audible over the ringing in my ears. "It seems that my auditory senses have been injured."

"Same here. Like trying to hear through cotton." I touched the bud lodged in my ear. Whether or not it still worked, I couldn't tell, but I needed to make sure all electronics were shut down. I toggled the bud's power switch to its off position, reached into the glider, and powered the console down, dousing the last remaining light.

The sound of a spaceship engine hovered overhead, probably Camille's, searching for any sign of me. "She'll scan for heat signatures. We have to make it look like we died in the blast."

"How can we hide our own heat?"

"Not easily." I pulled the flashlight from my belt, flicked it on, and searched the icy rubble between us and the tunnel entrance. When I found a narrow space under a fallen boulder, I crawled toward it. "Quick. Follow me."

I took my parka off, tossed it to the side, and slid into the space in a fetal curl. When Perdantus hopped into the space with me, I turned the light off and refastened it to my belt. "The heat signature from the glider will be easy to detect. Since the shape is distinct, Camille will be able to recognize it. She'll also probably be able to see my signature since I'm far enough away from the glider, but the more rocks and ice between me and her, the weaker my signature will be. And as I get colder, my image will fade even more. I hope she'll think I died, and my corpse is cooling."

Perdantus chirped in my ear. "A brilliant plan."

"Not really. Mostly guessing." As I lay quietly, cold air seeped through my shirt and pants, chilling my skin, not bad so far, but I had to let my body chill a lot more if I hoped to convince that bloodthirsty witch that her torpedoes had done me in. With ice surrounding me, it wouldn't take long to resemble a cooling corpse, but even a short time in this freezer would be torture.

Above, the droning hum of the ship's hovering air blasts continued. The cold darkness felt like death itself. My skin tingled, and a hard shiver rattled my body. My teeth chattered, but, try as I might, I couldn't stop them. How long would she continue her search? I had no way of knowing.

To take my mind off the chill, I whispered to Perdantus, shivers fracturing my words, "You were ... about to tell me ... how that old ... silver jay died."

"Oh, yes." His own words seemed slower than usual, but they remained steady. "They say he flew into a—"

A loud grinding noise interrupted, coming from above. A light appeared from a small hole in the ceiling, expanding to a meter-wide circle on the ground. A tube poked through the hole. With a miniature camera embedded on the forward end, it snaked lower and began turning, as if searching.

I steeled my body against the shivers and stayed perfectly quiet, though the bitter cold air continued knifing into me from head to toe.

A man's voice emanated from the probe. "Megan Willis, Camille Fairbanks is offering you an opportunity to surrender. You will be executed quickly instead of suffering in this tomb until you freeze to death. If you are in here, respond. This probe has a sensitive microphone. We will be able to hear you."

A new shiver crawled across my back, but I couldn't let it take over and throttle the rest of my body. Staying quiet and motionless might be my only chance to survive.

The voice continued. "Cavern scan indicates total blockage by debris. She appears to have no way to escape. Conducting closer infrared scan." A red light beam emanated from the probe. It swept around the chamber and stopped at the glider. "Heat signature for an escape glider identified. No one appears to be inside."

The beam rotated and halted on me. The light ran along my body from my feet toward my head. I closed my eyes and held my breath, begging the shivers to cease. "Human heat signature identified. Body temperature is well below normal limits. It is likely Megan's corpse."

I opened my eyes. The red light flicked off, and the probe receded toward the hole in the ceiling. When it disappeared, I squirmed out from the crevice and tried to straighten, but my joints wouldn't move. They seemed locked in place.

A new shiver broke through. I rolled to my back and shook hard, hugging myself. My teeth chattered. My bones ached. Light from the hole in the ceiling allowed a view of my parka, but it lay well out of reach. I couldn't possibly crawl that far to get it.

I coughed as I spoke between chatters. "Perdantus ... my coat ... I can't ... get to it."

"I will see what I can do." He flew to the parka, grabbed the hood's drawstring, and pulled. His claws slipped on the ice, prompting him to beat his wings and try to fly, but the parka appeared to be frozen to the floor.

He dropped the string. "I will try something else." With another flutter, he flew low to the ground toward the glider.

My joints still rigid, I tried to relax my muscles, but the shivers continued assaulting my limbs and torso, thwarting my efforts to stay calm. Finally, a sense of darkness washed into my mind, and the tension eased. Was I dying? Freezing to death?

Something popped. A sizzling noise followed, blending with louder crackles. Warmth filtered into my skin and crawled along my body—soothing, luxurious warmth. The darkness faded, and my joints loosened.

A flickering light caught my attention. Flames danced in and around the glider, a backdrop for Perdantus as he hopped toward me. "It seems that you are getting relief from the fire."

"Yeah. A lot." I sat up and blinked. "How did you do it?"

"I followed the scent of fuel that leaked from the reservoir, cracked by the crash impact, I suppose. I dipped a discarded cup in the fuel and carried it to a bank of wires that had broken loose. After reading the instruction labels, I found the glider's ignition wires and clipped them with my beak, set the ends in the fuel, and pushed the start button. The fuel ignited and began burning the cup. I flew more combustible items to the flames, set them ablaze, and carried the fiery pieces here and there in the glider until the inferno seemed to be of adequate size."

"Wow, Perdantus. That's amazing." I rubbed my arms, now no longer stiff. "You saved my life. Thank you."

He bowed his head. "An incident like this is exactly why I accompanied you. I am less vulnerable to cold, and I have built-in tools at your disposal. I am gratified that I was able to help."

"Same here. More than gratified. Thanks again."

Smoke rolled into me like a gray wave, making me blink and cough. Above, some of the smoke curled toward the hole Camille's goon drilled. Soon the smoke would seep out, providing a signal, but she was probably long gone by now, satisfied that I was dead. I could continue warming myself for a while, at least until the smoke got too thick.

Something crackled. Sparks spewed from the glider. One of the sparks ignited a loud pop in the air only a meter in front of us, a fist-sized explosion that sizzled and died away. Then another explosion to the left, twice the size of the first, sent a flash of light from floor to ceiling.

"Methane pockets. We'd better bolt out of here." I shot to my feet. Trying not to breathe too much, I pulled my parka from the floor, ripping a bit of the fabric to set it free. After sliding my arms into the sleeves, I pulled the flashlight from my belt, flicked it on, and pointed the beam at Perdantus. He stood on the ground and looked up at me, appearing smaller than usual somehow. "Can you fly up to my shoulder? We can't stay here."

"I am trying to overcome an episode of dizziness." His body teetered. "My strength is flagging."

I scooped him into my hand. "You worked hard, and oxygen was already low. The fire's slurping the rest." I swept the flashlight beam around. The debris blockade stood only a few meters away, impassable, as the goon had said. If I hadn't been able to scurry out of the danger zone in time, I would have been buried under that crushing pile of rubble. Death had stalked close multiple times—much too close.

A third pop, the loudest yet, burst close enough to sting my ear. I spun and aimed the flashlight at the ridge beyond the glider. "Let's scoot."

After climbing over icy ridges and hiking along narrow tunnels, all with Perdantus clinging to my shoulder, I crawled through a low-ceilinged passage, the flashlight in hand as I scrabbled forward. With oxygen at a relatively low level, I had to stop at times to catch my breath. Fortunately, my lighter-than-usual weight helped.

Soon, a faint glimmer appeared in the distance. When I reached it, a square stone about twice the size of my head blocked the way. I pushed on the stone, but it wouldn't budge.

I craned my neck to look at Perdantus. "I thought you said we could get out this way."

He glanced around. "This area is unfamiliar to me. Perhaps we took a wrong turn."

"A wrong turn?"

"Yes. I fear that my perceptions have been addled by the various crises, especially the lack of oxygen."

Sighing, I again set my hand on the stone. Since light passed through gaps at its edges, it might be movable. Gathering my strength, I pushed once more. The stone slid a few centimeters with a grinding complaint. "That's a good sign, but it's hard to push in this position."

Perdantus hopped to the ground. "Perhaps use your legs. You can energize them."

"Let's see if I can turn around." I curled myself into a ball, rocked to my back, and set my feet against the stone, my knees bent. Using both legs, I pushed, but it wouldn't budge. I flexed my biceps to activate the bracelets. The charge sent an electrical impulse through my skin's conductive ink down to my calf muscles. I rammed my feet against the stone. It slid forward and dropped out of the way.

After turning again, I wormed through the newly opened passage. I looked out into a manmade building with four walls and a high roof, my head about twenty centimeters from the floor. This channel appeared to have been an air vent before being blocked for some reason.

Pushing my hands against the edges of the opening, I squirmed out and rolled onto the floor on the other side. Muted light poured in through a huge open door to the right. This place appeared to be an abandoned hangar for transport ships.

Perdantus flew out of the shaft and flitted to my shoulder, still unsteady. I looked at him out of the corner of my eye and spoke softly. "This is where Crystal saw the heat signature, but I have no idea which part of the building it came from."

"Allow me to fly out to check for Camille's ship. I need to test my abilities."

I glanced through the open hangar door. Outside, snowflakes swirled in a light breeze. Not bad, but it could get worse. "Careful. Looks like a storm might be brewing."

"I won't be long." He flew awkwardly toward the door, apparently still battling ill effects from our harrowing escape.

Hoping to search the building in a methodical way by starting at the door, I followed Perdantus, my knees and ankles stiff from crawling through the cold passages, though the parka had kept my upper body warm. When I arrived at the enormous doorway, I looked out. Snow and ice covered an expanse of flatlands that extended to a semicircle of ridges, maybe a couple of hundred meters high.

I visually traced the frozen river that sliced through a ridge about a kilometer straight ahead and swept at an angle to my right where it had punched through the hole in another ridge, the one we used to escape, now blocked by debris.

I narrowed my eyes at the river. Its course through the ridges meant that it likely flowed freely at some time, maybe seasonally, but it seemed impossible to know how long seasons lasted here. And with no vegetation in sight, how did the ecosystems work? What kind of creatures could live in this cruel environment? Did animals hibernate during a winter that lasted many Alpha-One years? Could plants go dormant under the ice for that long?

Movement at the river caught my eye. Water roiled where Camille's ship had blasted a hole in the ice, exposing the water. An appendage appeared, then another, then a third. A creature with six hairy limbs crawled out of the hole. Agile and flexible, it looked like a furry octopus, its dark gray coat flecked with yellow spots, and its head resembled a bear's. White vapor rose from its wet fur and spewed from its mouth as it bellowed a low, mournful note, maybe annoyed at being awakened from its slumber.

Not wanting to be seen, I stepped to the side and peered around the door frame. The creature set its nose to the ground and crept slowly along the river, as if tracking a scent. At least it wasn't heading in my direction.

I turned toward the inside and spotted a metal grating near the center of the chamber. It covered a square opening at the floor's lowest level, probably a drain, but with everything so cold, it seemed that water would freeze before it could travel all the way to the hole. Maybe heating coils under the floor prevented that, and those coils provided the heat signature we saw from space. I strode to the hole as fast as my stiff joints would allow.

A pole with an attached sign lay on the floor nearby. I lifted the pole to its upright position and read the head-high sign's Humaniversal words—*Wishing Well.*

I furrowed my brow. Strange. How could a drainage hole be a wishing well? Probably some kind of joke.

I pushed my fingers through the gaps in the grating and lifted it off the hole. After sliding the grating to the side, I peered down into the darkness. The heat signature could also be nothing more than a Beta-Four rodent that found a warm spot to sleep.

Not wanting to shout into the hole and possibly alert Camille, I waited for Perdantus to return. Less than a minute later, he flew to the sign and perched on it. "I found where the ship was when it fired the torpedoes at us. It is now gone and nowhere in sight. I also flew high enough to gain a wider perspective and found no signs of machinery or human life anywhere."

"Then Camille thinks I'm dead."

"Most likely."

"Perfect. She'll probably leave the Astral Dragon alone." I knelt next to the wishing well and called, "Hello? Is anyone down there?"

No one answered.

Perdantus fluttered down to the floor next to me. "That sign is written in Humaniversal. Perhaps you should use that language."

I rolled my eyes. "Stupid me." I leaned closer to the hole and called again, this time in Humaniversal. "Is anyone down there?"

A frail voice rose from the depths. "I must be dreaming again." It sounded like a man's voice, old and gravelly. He coughed, then continued, stronger now. "Of course I am dreaming. No one is left. They all abandoned me. Forsaken forever."

My heart raced as I spoke rapid-fire. "You're not dreaming. And you're not forsaken. I can try to help you out of there. My name is ..." I pressed my lips together—probably not a good idea to give away my identity to a stranger. "I'll definitely try to help you."

"Do you have a key to the manacles on my wrists? If you do not, then your willing kindness is no more than a phantom, for desire without ability is like a ghost who seeks a redemption that flees its grasp."

I squinted. "What are you, some kind of philosopher?"

"In a manner of speaking. I assert truths that few have the foresight to grasp for themselves."

"Is that why they call this hole a wishing well?"

"That is a label of ridicule, I assure you. They regularly tossed coins in here and asked me foolish questions, like who will I marry or when will I die. If I chose not to answer, then they wouldn't feed me. So I had to respond in order to survive. Unfortunately, my answers always seemed to come true, and I have been the wishing-well prophet ever since. One guard actually began charging money for others to ask me questions, so I became a valuable curiosity to him."

"Before you go on with your story, let me look for a key to your manacles."

"Yes. Of course."

I rose and scanned the chamber. The walls and floor appeared to be completely bare, as if someone had swept the entire place clean. Searching for a key could take hours, and I still might not find it. I looked at Perdantus, again perched on the sign. "I can go down there and see if there are any weak links in his chains. Maybe an electric shock from my hands would break him free."

Perdantus tilted his head. "How would you return?"

"Based on the sound of his voice, he's not real far down. I could charge my legs and jump out, but I don't have a way to get him up. I would have to call for the Astral Dragon to come in and send a line down. This hangar is plenty big enough for her to dock here."

"That seems to be the only option, but you'll have to hope Camille isn't monitoring communications from the planet."

"If she's sure I'm dead, I doubt she'd do that." I stripped the parka off, pulled the communications disk from its pocket, and turned it on. Hoping to get a better signal, I walked closer to the entrance. When I halted, Perdantus flew at my side and landed on my shoulder.

After a few seconds of inactivity, the ghostly image of the Astral Dragon's bridge took shape with Zoë and Crystal again in the officers' chairs as they looked at the viewing window. Static sizzled through the image. They had to be farther away than I expected. "Hey, you two. Glad to see you got away from Freaky Fairbanks."

"Yeah," Crystal said. "She shot after you faster than a buttered bullet. We felt like neglected orphans. Forgotten. Abandoned."

"Don't be so dramatic. Where are you now?"

"Almost to Beta Three. We checked your mailbox for messages, and guess what? Oliver's there. On Beta Three. Right now."

"Oliver?" I smiled. Learning that he was okay felt so good. "What did he say?"

"He said he could fix the water-pressure valve, so we decided to hightail it there, hoping maybe Calamity Camille would follow us instead of you. We even sent her a video of you that Sonya had in storage, pretending it was live, but we haven't been able to tell if she took the bait or not."

"She didn't take it. She attacked me here on Beta Four, but I escaped. She thinks I'm dead, so that's good." An image came to mind—Camille's Nebula ship turning about to chase the Astral Dragon once she was satisfied that I was dead. "But she might be coming after you now. Watch your six."

"Is that like 'I'm following you' again?"

"Not exactly. It means watch your back for someone following you."

"Got it, and good call. Our six just became a bullseye target. Sonya just picked up a blip. We've got a Nebula ship tailing us. Pretty far away, but not far enough. We'll go to stealth mode to see if we can shake her."

"Okay. I'll sign off. But come back for me when you can. The glider is a burnt trash heap, and I'm in the building you saw when you were looking for—" The hologram crackled and disappeared.

Prickly heat surged across my skin. Not only were my crew members in danger, but if Camille intercepted the communication, she might come back to Beta Four with a vengeance. And even if not, and she managed to cripple or destroy the Astral Dragon, Perdantus and I would be marooned. And my hopes to rescue this stranger might be dashed no matter what.

"That is a worrisome development," Perdantus said from my shoulder.

"No kidding." I slid the disk back into my pocket. "While we're waiting for word, we'll see what we can do to help our friend in the wishing well. If I had a rope, I could climb down there and use it to haul him up. Otherwise, I'll just have to drop and hope for the best."

"I will search for a rope." Perdantus flew off my shoulder and across the huge chamber.

"Don't get lost," I called, but he was probably already out of earshot, especially after the torpedo's deafening blast.

I put the parka on, walked back to the wishing well and aimed my flashlight beam into the depths, but the darkness seemed to swallow the light. I called, "Is there room for me to jump if I can't find a rope? I mean, would I crash into you?"

"I can easily move out of the way. In fact, I have three pillows I could place in the drop zone, so to speak. The pillows are dirty, but they would soften your impact."

"Pillows?" I turned the flashlight off and reattached it to my belt. "Then I guess they had at least some heart."

"You could say that. You see, whenever I prophesied in a manner that pleased them, they rewarded me in some fashion, as if they were tossing treats to an obedient dog. If that's heart, then I was their beloved mongrel puppy."

"A diseased heart, then." I sat cross-legged next to the hole. "What happened if you told them something they didn't like?"

"No food for days. Once when I told them they would all perish from a plague, they poured oil down here then dropped a lighter."

"That's awful! How did you survive?"

"I was able to snuff the lighter before the oil could ignite." He chuckled. "Since I used one of their pillows to do so, you might say that I snuffed the puff with their own fluffy stuff."

I added a chuckle of my own. "That's pretty clever."

"I have a lot of time to come up with witticisms. It keeps me from going insane."

"What about food and water? When was the last time you ate or drank?"

"If I am counting correctly, I have not eaten anything in nineteen days. As for water, I am able to use my body heat, such that it is, to melt ice."

"Oh! How stupid of me!" I stripped my parka off and pushed it into the hole until it dropped. "Maybe that'll help."

The sound of arms sliding through sleeves rose from the hole. "Well, this is nice. Quite warm for my old bones. But considering the size, you must be bigger than I imagined."

"It was my father's. Too big for me. But it was all I had. My mother's parka burned when we …" A lump swelled in my throat, slicing off my words. I took a deep breath and waited a moment for the lump to shrink. "Never mind about that. You mentioned that whatever you said always came true. What about everyone dying from a plague?"

"I suspect that's exactly what happened. The day before everyone left, I heard angry voices. Someone mentioned a pox. Another wailed about wanting to die here so his family wouldn't catch whatever he had. Obviously it was a deadly, contagious plague of some kind. In any case, I think they planned to execute all the prisoners. They even shot bullets into the well. Although they missed, I groaned as if I had been hit. They were none the wiser."

The lump returned, making me squeak. "*All* the prisoners? Do you know if any escaped?"

Perdantus landed on the floor next to me and dropped a key into my hand. "I was not able to find rope, but I found that key on a hook in a wall alcove not far from here."

I slid the key into my pocket. "Let's hope it's the key to the manacles." I grabbed the flashlight again, turned it on, and pointed the beam downward as I scooted until my legs dangled into the hole. "I have to jump, so get the pillows ready."

"I have already done so, but I am concerned that you will not be able to leave after you arrive."

"No worries. I have that covered."

"Very well. I am out of the way, but I will stay close enough to catch you if need be."

"All right. Here goes." With one hand on the floor, I pushed myself into the hole and dropped. A split second later, the flashlight beam illuminated the three pillows, allowing me to time my impact so I could bend my knees to compensate. When my feet struck one of the pillows, it slid forward, and I toppled back, but something supported my shoulders, keeping me from falling as chains rattled nearby as well as coins clinking on the floor.

"I've got you, Miss." An old man with kind eyes, barely visible at the edge of the beam, let me down slowly until my head pressed against one of the pillows. The moment my cheek touched the fabric, it emitted a familiar odor—like dirt, but not just any dirt, soil in a place far back in the recesses of my memory.

"Thank you," I said as the man helped me sit upright. With every move, the chains dangling from his manacles jingled, sometimes brushing my ear with warmer-than-expected metal links. The odor of fuel oil tinged the air, barely noticeable. "It's not as cold down here as I thought it would be."

"Cold enough." He breathed a stream of white vapor. "But temperate compared to the surface. I am usually quite cold but not dangerously so. I have several layers on under your wonderful parka."

"Well, it's good that you can tolerate it, and I'm glad the parka helps." I folded my hands in my lap. "I never asked you your name."

He picked up one of the pillows, pushed a pair of chains to the side, and sat on it in front of me. "No one has asked me my name in years. They just call me Prophet, but my real name is Barnabas. Use whichever you wish."

I let the name Barnabas tumble in my mind. Like the pillow aroma, it seemed familiar, but, again, I couldn't place it. "Barnabas will do." I withdrew the key from my pocket. "Let's see if this will work on your manacles."

He extended a wrist. "Please do."

I found the keyhole and tried to insert the key, but it wouldn't fit no matter which way I turned it. "Blazes!" I grabbed a chain with both hands and felt the links for any sign of weakness but found none. Using an electric jolt probably wouldn't work. "I'll have to think of another way to break you out of here."

"Then I hope you are cleverer than I am. I have failed with every attempt." He leaned closer and half closed an eye, widening the other— bloodshot and weepy in the flashlight's glow. With only a few wisps of white hair on his mottled scalp and loose skin on his nearly skeletal face, partially hidden by a scraggly beard, he had to be more than eighty Alpha-one years old. "You look familiar. What is *your* name?"

I bent back, wondering if I should reveal my identity to a condemned prisoner. He seemed too eager. "I'm not sure yet if I should tell you—"

"Megan?" Perdantus flew down and alit on my knee. "Are you all right?"

I concealed a swallow. He had revealed my name, but Barnabas probably didn't understand a silver jay's language. "I'm fine, Perdantus. Just talking to Barnabas."

After glancing at Barnabas, he focused on me. "I saw no rope, but I did see a strange, potentially dangerous creature that emerged from the river. It stayed far away from this building, so we should be safe, at least for now."

"Good. I saw it earlier. Thank you for the report and your vigilance."

Barnabas narrowed both eyes, accentuating the deep creases in his forehead. "I take it that you understand this bird's frantic chirps. Perdantus, you called him?"

"Yes. He's my friend. We're travelling together. He's highly intelligent and resourceful."

Barnabas nodded. "I once knew a bird like that. Long ago, it was. A parrot by the name of Sophia. But that is neither here nor there. A more urgent issue is the fact that you did not bring a rope, though you said you had an escape in mind. Are we both stuck down here?"

"I called a spaceship that's close by. I'm hoping it can get here in the next few hours with a way to rescue us. Even if it doesn't come, I'm not stuck. I can jump out."

"Nonsense. The best human athletes in the galaxy could never leap that high." His genial chuckle returned. "Unless aided by a trampoline, but, as you can see, I don't have a …" He squinted and leaned closer again. "What is that around your neck?"

I looked down. My mother's dragon's eye locket had fallen out from behind my shirt and dangled in full view. I enclosed it in my hand and dropped it into hiding with the other one. "A keepsake. It's personal."

"May I have a closer look?"

I shook my head, my body suddenly trembling. "It's … it's a locket. An heirloom. I don't want anything to happen to it."

"My guess is that you can't open it. Maybe you don't even know that it contains a priceless treasure within."

My mouth dropped open, but I couldn't help it. "How do you know so much about my locket?"

Barnabas pointed at himself. "Because I fashioned it with my own two hands, and I put the dragon's eye ruby inside." He gazed at me with an intensity that seemed to bare my soul. "Megan, I am your great-grandfather, and I made that locket for your mother."

I gasped, and my words tumbled out like spilled BBs. "My great-grandfather? But my mother always called you Pops, not Barnabas, but of course she wouldn't call you by your first name. I probably heard someone else call you that, and that's why it seemed familiar, and that's why the pillow smelled familiar. I remember that I thought you smelled like dirt, or maybe moss, like musty moss, I guess, and she told me you made her locket and mine, that you tied my dragon's eye to her life force and her dragon's eye to mine, so I could look at it to know if she was still alive."

I took a breath and stared at him. His gaze now averted, he seemed to be staring at something far away. A tear trickled down his withered cheek. I didn't have to ask why. Since I had my mother's locket, he figured out the reason.

Leaning forward, I grasped his hand and held it with both of mine as I ran a finger along the manacle. "Pops, she died saving my life. She never stopped fighting. She was a hero."

His murmured words sounded like a sad song. "That's no surprise, Pumpkin."

The nickname made me smile, like a long-lost memory of something sweet and warm.

He sniffed and brushed the tear away as he made eye contact again. "Did she die in battle?"

"Sort of. She was commanding the Astral Dragon, and a Willow Wind named Thorne possessing a human body tried to steal her life to become immortal. I know that sounds crazy but—"

"No, no." He waved his free hand as the attached chain rattled. "I assume this Willow Wind used a special incantation. Did it succeed? Is he immortal?"

I shook my head but kept my mouth closed. How could I tell him that *I* killed my mother? That I stopped her heart to keep her life essence from flowing to Thorne? "His plan failed, but my mother died anyway. I'd rather leave it at that. But I will tell you that the dragon's eye does work. Somehow it gives me power, though my ruby stopped glowing because she's dead. I suppose her ruby is still glowing because I'm alive. I know it used to glow after she died. I saw it. But I closed the clasp since then, so I can't check to be sure."

He pointed at my shirt. "Have you experienced extra-power episodes after your mother died?"

"Once, back when I saw her ruby glow. I guess I haven't needed extra power since then. I've been relying on my bracelets." I touched one of the bands around my wrist. "They electrify my hands and supercharge my legs. But the ruby also gave other kids power, kids who were born on Gamma Five. It's like I became a dynamo and made their powers … um … more powerful, I guess. And I got stronger, too. But it didn't always work. Sometimes I gave them power, and sometimes I didn't. It seemed unpredictable."

"Gamma Five kids." He stroked his beard. "I am familiar with these wonders. In my circles we called them Starborn children, or just Starborn. They are a recent phenomenon, rising from the mysteries of the universe during the past fifteen years or so."

"That recent? But how? If a planet has the ability to give power to kids born there, how could it suddenly start?"

"It didn't start because of an inherent ability in the soils or atmosphere of a planet. This power to empower, if you will, was sown there or perhaps released there by a human."

I lifted my brow. "A human? Who?"

"I'll let you deduce the person's identity." He pointed at me. "You, Megan, are a catalyst, a dynamo for the Starborn. How is it possible that you can empower the already powerful? Charge what is already charged? Maximize what is already beyond normal maxima?"

The questions seemed so simple, yet so hard, and my answer felt boastful, but I said it anyway. "Because I'm more powerful than they are?"

"Correct. And now for a more difficult question. How can you be more powerful than the Starborn and yet be similar in kind, demonstrated by your ability to infuse them, though you were not born on the planet where they gained their gifts?"

It seemed that Barnabas's thought process streamed into me, like the answers came to mind from outside my head. "I got the power from a greater source, the source that put the power into the planet."

"Exactly right. You received your power directly from the original source while the other Starborn received theirs indirectly, as if it were from a battery charged by the original source in the past. You are a conduit of the power. A channel. Power flows through you to others. Therefore, my guess is that all of the Starborn children are younger than you are."

I nodded. "Oliver, Crystal, and Zoë are all younger than me, and the dead kids I found in the Nebula One were younger."

"Then you are the first Starborn. The original receiver from the original source."

New warmth coursed along my skin. That label, the first Starborn, echoed in my mind. It sounded good, though loaded with responsibility. "Were my parents the original source?"

He lifted a finger. "One of your parents must have had access to the source. And the reason you will be able to guess which one is because of a fact you already mentioned. Your dynamo abilities didn't always work."

I blurted my guess without thinking. "My father."

He lowered his finger and smiled. "And how did you arrive at that conclusion?"

"Well, I'm not sure. Maybe because I had a dragon's eye that connected to my mother, not my father. If she were the source, the power probably would have worked every time." I shrugged. "Just a guess."

He pointed at me, again rattling the chains. "You guessed correctly. Your keen mind serves you well."

"But how could her dragon's eye work at all?"

Barnabas folded his hands, intertwining his fingers. "Marriage … real marriage ordained by God … makes a man and a woman into one flesh. She receives power, comfort, and support from him, and he receives the same from her. Since they were unavoidably separated, her source of power became intermittent, and since she channeled his power to you through her dragon's eye, that power also proved to be intermittent."

I caressed my locket, the one that used to connect to my mother. "I think I understand. But …" I focused on him again. "How did my father get that power? And how did Gamma Five get it from him?"

"That I do not know. Some mysteries remain to be solved. So let's move on to matters we can work with now." He nodded toward my chest. "I assume the dragon's eye in your mother's locket still glows because you're alive, though you can't see it."

"Right. Like I mentioned before, I saw it glowing after she died." I pulled the chain, drawing the locket out again. "I need her thumbprint on the back to open it."

"May I hold it?"

"Sure." I pulled the necklace over my head and laid it on his palm.

He set his thumb on the locket's back panel. It popped open, re-vealing the glowing ruby. "I encoded this locket to open either for your mother or for me. Yours is also encoded to allow me to open it."

"That makes sense. You're the creator. You should have access."

"And so should you. It's yours now." He closed the locket and pressed his thumb on the back for several seconds. This time it didn't open. "Now set your thumb on it and hold it there."

I complied.

"Now lift your thumb and press it again like you're trying to open it."

I did as he instructed, and the little door popped open.

"It is now encoded with your print." He extended the hand with my mother's locket still on his palm. "Place yours here, please."

I drew the necklace over my head and set it next to the other. "Okay. But I know this one doesn't glow."

"I can restore it."

"How? Whose life essence can you tie it to? And how do you do it? My mother said you used some kind of ancient ceremony."

"She exaggerated. Or maybe I exaggerated to impress her. But that's not important. All I need is the blood of the person your mother's dead dragon's eye will be tied to. Since we already have an eye tied to yours, it would be redundant for you to have another one."

I shrugged. "Then yours, I suppose. No one else is around." I nod-ded toward Perdantus, adding a wink. "Except him."

Perdantus hopped back. "Since I am a different species, I am sure I would be an exceedingly poor candidate."

When I translated for Barnabas, he chuckled. "He's right. Since he is not human, it wouldn't work with him, but I have a different person in mind."

"Seeing that I cannot be of help here," Perdantus said, "I will fly back to the surface and watch for trouble. It's possible that some condemned prisoners still lurk on the planet, and they might be dangerous. Besides that, the river creature might come to the hangar. I will watch for it."

I gave him a nod. "Good idea."

He flew straight up and quickly disappeared from sight.

"And now …" Barnabas struggled to his feet, the chains again rattling. "Now that I understand your abilities, I will reveal a secret that you likely never knew. Your father was imprisoned on this planet for a while—"

"Yes. I knew that. He was supposed to be executed, but somehow he—"

"You didn't let me finish." Barnabas shuffled to a leather pouch on the floor, his feet pushing a few coins out of the way. He bent slowly and picked up the pouch. "He was actually down here with me for a short time."

I sucked in a breath. "Down here? Why?"

"He was trying to rescue me. When he heard that the prisoners would be executed, he dropped into the well to try to get me out."

My heart thudded. I could barely keep from shouting. "Okay. Okay. Then what happened?"

"That's when the guard fired shots down here. They didn't know your father was with me. They were trying to kill me, not him. As I told you before, I groaned, pretending to be hit, though I wasn't struck. Yet, your father was. A bullet grazed his calf. Not a life-threatening wound, but it bled a good deal." He opened the pouch and withdrew what appeared to be a white bandage, stained red. "He tore his undershirt and wrapped a strip of it around the wound. Once the blood flow eased, he took it off. Then, when he couldn't free me from my chains, I begged him to leave. After several minutes of arguing, he finally did, but only after promising that he would come back for me when he could."

"How did he leave?"

"He brought a rope with a grappling hook. He was able to throw it topside and catch something, then he climbed out. He took the rope with him, I assume to conceal the evidence."

I looked up, imagining the process. "How long ago was that?"

"Fifteen days."

"Fifteen? Then he escaped after my mother died. Did he say where he planned to go?"

Barnabas shook his head. "I'm concerned that he might have caught the plague. He had a fever while he was here, though he didn't realize it until I felt his forehead."

"But you didn't catch it," I said, "so maybe he's all right."

"I have never been sick a day in my life. But when I discovered the fever, I checked his back for another symptom. Red spots were already breaking out on his skin."

I clapped a hand over my mouth and spoke between my fingers. "Oh, no! How often is it fatal?"

"I wouldn't know, but it was dangerous enough to shut down this prison planet and kill everyone they could find. The most efficient way to stop an epidemic is to kill those who are infected, though it is also the cruelest method."

I winced. "So my father might be dead after all. If the plague didn't kill him, maybe the guards did."

"That's what I intend to find out." Barnabas sat again and spread the blood-stained material on the ground between us. "Your father's blood is within these fibers. If we combine it with your blood, I can tie your dragon's eye to your father's life essence. You see, the ancient lore says that life is in the blood, and it is undoubtably true. This ceremony worked with your mother's ruby and with yours. It should work again. But I will need your help."

"What do I do?"

He pointed at the cloth. "Add your blood to his."

"That won't be hard." I touched the bleeding spot on my forehead. "Quite a bit still oozing here."

He eyed my forehead closely. "I assume you received that wound unwillingly."

I laughed under my breath. "It's not like I go around trying to get injured."

"Understandable, but to bring life to that which is dead requires a blood sacrifice that is willing."

I rolled his words through my mind. How odd they sounded. But he seemed perfectly convinced of their truth. "If willingness is needed, then the power in the blood isn't physical. It's metaphysical."

He drew his head back. "Well, you certainly have an extensive vocabulary for someone your age."

"I suppose so, but it annoys people sometimes."

"I have experienced the same. But you're right. The blood requires a connection that is not merely physical. It has a spiritual aspect." Barnabas glanced around for a moment before pointing at the hole above us. An icicle hung from the side of the wall leading toward the top, ending at a point about a meter above my head. "Would you please retrieve that icicle for me?"

I rose and snapped off the lower several centimeters of the dirty ice, then sat again. "So I just jab myself and drip blood on the cloth?"

He nodded. "That is the first step."

I set the icicle's point at the center of my open palm, pricked the skin, and pushed until blood oozed around the wound. After setting the icicle to the side, I closed my fist and made it hover over the cloth.

A drop of blood fell, then another. The fibers of my father's undershirt, already stained dark red, absorbed the new blood and spread it into the old.

Barnabas set a finger close to the edge of the combined blood. "The water in your blood is infusing his, thereby reconstituting it, and that allows the two to intermix."

A third drop fell, then a fourth. Barnabas waved a hand. "That should be enough." He plucked the tiny ruby from my locket, set it on the cloth's bloody spot, and put the lockets down nearby. "Since this life-force connection is spiritual, it requires a prayer to catalyze it."

"Catalyze. That means to bring it about. To make it work."

"Correct. I called you a catalyst earlier. You make things work."

"But are you sure we should do it? Won't it make my father vulnerable?"

Barnabas cocked his head. "What do you mean?"

"Suppose someone else knows how to do what Thorne did to my mother?"

He blinked. "But you said the incantation didn't work."

Tears welled in my eyes. I had to tell him more. "The incantation was working, and it would have killed her, but I stopped him before it could."

Barnabas stared at me, his eyes riveted on mine. "You killed her, didn't you?"

As I nodded, a tear spilled to my cheek, and my voice spiked. "She asked me to. Begged me to. We couldn't let Thorne become immortal."

He brushed my tear with a thumb. "I understand. You took the life of someone you love. You did it to stop a catastrophe that would surely kill others. That is a sacrifice more painful than any other."

My throat narrowed, forcing me to swallow. "It was gut-wrenching. I want to make sure it doesn't ever happen again."

"Where there is a life connection, there is always a channel that can be compromised by an invading force. When I first created the links, I was unaware of the potential for danger. I learned about the incantation later and devised a safeguard against it. It's not easy to accomplish, but I am sure I can do it."

I nodded. "Perfect. Let's do that."

"Very well." Barnabas grasped my wrist, set my palm on the dragon's eye, and pressed down. He spoke with a deep, resonant voice, no longer weak and gravelly. "Our Creator God, we come before you now with a great request."

His odd words again tumbled through my mind. Creator God? I had never heard a prayer like this before.

His eyes twinkled. "Megan, do you have questions? The Creator won't mind a pause in our prayer."

"Um … yeah. I guess so. My parents always prayed to the Astral Dragon. I know he's real. He visited me a couple of times, like in visions. He helped me more than I could ever explain."

"The Creator God appeared to you in a way you could understand. In our realm, he sometimes appears to his followers as a great white dragon. In other realms, he appears as a lion, a bear, a dove, among others, but, still, there is only one Creator God. In one realm I have heard about, he came to the people as a man, and I predict that he will do the same in ours someday. I can only hope, for that is *our* only hope."

I shook my head. "I don't understand."

"Nor do you need to. But be assured that I will apply the necessary safeguard for your father."

"Good. Let's go on."

Barnabas cleared his throat. "Great Creator, by your power and goodness, I ask you to connect this dragon's eye ruby to the life essence of Julian Willis, Megan's father. As long as he lives, let this ruby shine. Let it glow. And if he has already passed on to your care, grant us comfort over our loss and give Megan guidance as she seeks to carry his light and yours to bring about your purposes in every world she visits." He took in a deep breath and exhaled with a low, "Amen."

"Amen," I echoed.

He lifted my hand. Smeared with blood, the dragon's eye glowed. I stared at it, barely able to believe what I saw. New tears spilled as I squeaked out, "He's …" I swallowed again. "He's alive?"

"He is alive, my dear. And now I can add a tidbit that I haven't yet mentioned. As something of a prophet, I am able to tell you that your father is no longer on this planet. Now that I know he is alive, that means he has departed somehow."

My voice rattled. "That's … that's good to know." I touched the ruby with a fingertip and looked at the intermingled blood—my blood and my father's. In a very real way, we had become one, not just in the blood, but also in purpose. I was his conduit, though I didn't really understand how he could have so much power or why. Still, wherever he was, I needed to find him so we could carry on his mission together, now my mission as well, to topple the oppressors in our galaxy and set everyone free.

I smeared the blood on each cheek. I had no idea why. It just felt right. At least for a while, I would wear the symbol of our combined purpose for all to see.

"Now the safeguard," Barnabas said. "To make sure your father can never be attacked by a sorcerer like Thorne."

My tears still trickling, I nodded, too choked up to say anything.

"Put your mother's ruby on the cloth. Since it's connected to your life essence, we need to protect that one as well."

When I did so, he picked up the icicle, stabbed his own hand with it, and set it aside. He copied my actions to drip blood on both rubies. He laid his own hand over the pair and spoke in his praying voice again. "Creator God, I ask you to use my life's essence to guard the lives of the two people connected to these rubies. If someone tries to steal life from one of them, let my life be taken instead."

I lifted my brow. He was protecting us with his own life? He didn't mention that. And how could I interrupt a sacred rite? But it probably didn't matter. The chances of someone doing what Thorne did had to be practically zero.

"And," Barnabas continued, "let my essence become a curse so that the thief is poisoned by my presence and caused to perish instead of living on perpetually." When he lifted his hand, his blood sizzled on the two dragon's eyes. He stared at them without saying another word, his expression sad.

"Um …" I cleared my throat. "I have a question."

He continued staring. "Ask it."

"How can you safeguard both lives? Let's say you die protecting my father. How could you protect me after that? You'll be dead."

"In a way, I already am. You see, as a prophet, I know that I am near death, perhaps with only days to live. I have some sort of lung condition that is making it difficult to breathe."

"Like cancer? I heard that radon in Beta Four's atmosphere can cause it."

"Perhaps so. In any case, now that we have completed this ceremony, my death will come even sooner."

I blinked hard. "So what you did for me will make you die quicker?"

"That is exactly what I mean, but you shouldn't fret. All you need do now is set the dragon's eyes into their lockets and put them on."

I pinched my dragon's eye, easy to identify since it was a bit smaller than the one that now connected to my father's life. I dropped it into its locket and did the same with the other ruby and locket. During the process, I glanced at him. The wrinkles in his face seemed to deepen, and his skin turned ashen, as if the ceremonies had drained him somehow.

After draping both lockets over my head and fastening them at the back of my neck, I nodded. "Done."

He dipped a finger in his own blood and smeared it on each of my cheeks with the other smears. "Now the bond is complete and since there is no need for you to have two dragon's eyes, I advise that you give yours, the one that is connected to your life, to someone who needs to know you're alive, someone who would be helped by the power it can infuse. When you give it to someone, go through the same procedure I did to transfer his or her thumbprint to allow access."

"I understand."

"Good. It is now time for the final step." He took in a deep, rasping breath, then exhaled with a gurgle. His body toppled over, leaving a semitransparent copy of himself sitting upright, unshackled by manacles. The copy shook his head and blinked. "Well, dying wasn't as difficult as I thought it would be."

I gasped, glancing between his fallen body and the speaking copy. "You … you died? You're a ghost?"

"After a fashion. I am a disembodied spirit, but I will not yet ascend to the Creator because I have bound myself to the task of ensuring safety for you and your father. Since I am disembodied, I am able to protect you both. And I am glad to do so. I am extremely old, long past my time for usefulness, and now I can rise from this pit and actually be of benefit in my chosen protector role."

I stared at him, my heart pounding. A shiver raced along my skin, part from cold and part from fear. I was actually in the presence of a ghost. My great-grandfather had just sacrificed himself for my father and me. He died, and he seemed happy about it. Who was I to question his decision? Yet, a different question came to mind.

"Does ..." My voice trembled, and I couldn't steady it. "Does that mean you'll be travelling with me?"

"That is my intent. I will enter the dragon's eye that is connected to your father and reside there. I don't know if I will be able to see or hear what is happening beyond the boundaries of the gem, but I am confident that I will be able to help you if you call upon me."

I smiled. "Like a genie in a lamp?"

He chuckled. "An apt parallel. But I won't be able to grant wishes, only a request for advice. My first bit of advice is to call on me only in your darkest hour. Once I leave the ruby in order to give you help, I will not be able to enter again to continue protecting you and your father."

A final shiver raised goose bumps on my arms, this time from awe and reverence. An amazing man, a prophet, had given his all. And he did it because he loved me. More than that, he loved his creator and wanted to serve him.

"Then should we go now?" I asked.

"After I enter the dragon's eye that connects to your father." Barnabas's ghostly form thinned and flowed toward my chest. He streamed into the locket through tiny gaps around the perimeter, and disappeared.

I trembled once more, harder than ever. The entire episode felt surreal, like an eerie dream. Somehow the ghost of my great-grandfather dwelt in my locket, and now I could take him with me.

I rocked forward to my knees and kissed him on the head, his corpse's skin cold and clammy. "Farewell, Pops. I love you so much."

After taking the parka from his body, putting it on, and fastening the other locket in place, I rose to my feet and looked up at the opening to the wishing well. Something hummed above, and engine noise rumbled, then a thud shook the ground—the telltale sounds of a ship landing.

I stood quietly and listened for more than a minute. Why hadn't Perdantus flown down to warn me of a newcomer? It seemed odd that he hadn't provided an update. I needed to get up there and find out what was going on.

I activated my bracelets with a muscle flex, leaped, and sailed toward the light, but it quickly became clear that I might not make it all the way. My momentum nearly gone, I reached for the lip of the hole, slapped at it, but fell short. Something grabbed my wrist and hauled me upward. The furry octopus? I sucked in a breath and flexed again, charging my hands with electricity. It was time to fight.

06

Just as my head rose above the top of the hole, the grip on my wrist released. Someone shouted in pain. I dropped but threw my arms out just in time to catch the hole's lip with both hands. As I hung with my legs dangling, I looked around. A Nebula series spaceship had landed in the hangar, its wings extended, its passenger ramp open, and the bottom of its hull only a few meters over my head. Could it be Camille's ship?

A step away from the hole, a humanlike figure wearing a thick, hooded coat shook his hand, his face hidden from view. "Why did you go and shock me, Megan?"

I gasped. "Oliver?"

"Yeah." He pulled his hood down, revealing his shaggy dark hair and narrow face. "I was trying to help you."

Grunting, I extended a hand. "Well, help me now."

He grabbed my wrist and hauled me the rest of the way up. Once I set my feet safely on the floor, he smiled. "Looks like I got my wish from the well."

I brushed dirt from the front of my parka. "Really? You were wishing for me?"

"Definitely. You're the best friend I have."

I wrapped him in a tight hug. "Same here, Oliver."

He returned the embrace, then pulled back, worry lines in his brow as he touched my cheek. "You have blood there. Both sides. Are you hurt?"

I shook my head. "Long story, but I'm fine."

"Good. Anyway, I was also wishing for you for another reason. I need your help. Camille Fairbanks captured the Astral Dragon and her crew."

I gasped. "That's terrible! Do you know if Crystal and Zoë were all right? I mean, did you hear if they were hurt?"

"As far as I know, they're okay, just taken by Camille. I had to tell her a hundred lies to keep from getting taken myself. I convinced her that I am now the captain of the Nebula Nine, and I was taking the ship to Beta Three for repairs and restocking before going to Alpha One for decommissioning after the death of my father and his crew. Standard practice is to decommission an older ship after a disastrous journey that caused the deaths of three or more officers. I think that's because people will believe the ship's cursed. Anyway, since Emerson confirmed my story, she believed it."

I widened my eyes. "Emerson lied? That's hard to believe."

Oliver shook his head. "Every word he said was true. He's really good at telling the truth while still making you believe something else is true."

"Yeah. He is good at that." I looked up. "So any idea where Camille is taking Crystal and Zoë?"

"To Gamma Five. She set up some kind of training camp for gifted kids. That's all I know."

"Gamma Five?" I nodded. "Okay. That makes sense. But in a cruel, sadistic way."

"What do you mean?"

I wagged a finger toward him. "You remember what Thorne was doing. He bought Gamma Five kids who hadn't displayed any powers and watched them to see if they developed. Then he could sell them to the highest bidder. Apparently Camille wasn't content to wait or pay that much money, so she's grabbing the kids while they're young, maybe even taking them from the cradle, and she's quarantining them in the camp until she discovers if they're gifted. That way, she'll already have them for her crusade to make her SS Squad, whatever that is."

Oliver nodded. "I'm thinking someone on the Nebula One survived and ratted out Crystal and Zoë to Camille. After what they did to the admiral, it was pretty obvious they're both gifted."

"Then we'd better get going to Gamma Five. Not because I'm worried about them, though. With their powers, they could probably take over Camille's ship by the end of the day, but they might pretend to be compliant so they can find where the Gamma Five kids are being held."

"True, but don't underestimate Camille. She's been dealing with gifted kids for quite a while. She probably knows how dangerous they can be."

"Good point. We need to get there on the double." I glanced around the hangar for Perdantus. "Have you seen our favorite silver jay?"

Oliver pointed over his shoulder with a thumb. "On patrol outside. Something about a river monster. I said I'd watch for you to come out of the wishing well. He told me about Barnabas." Oliver peered into the hole. "So what happened to him? Is he still down there?"

"His corpse is." I grasped Oliver's arm and guided him toward the Nebula Nine's ramp. "Part of the long story. I'll tell you on the way to Gamma Five."

As we walked up the ramp, Perdantus flew in and landed on my shoulder. "The monster from the river has gained several fellow monsters, and they are all creeping toward us. Although their approach is slow, we should not delay our departure."

I nodded. "Understood."

Once we had boarded, Oliver gestured toward the captain's chair. "It's all yours."

I shook my head. "No way. You're the captain of the Nebula Nine. But I'll be glad to be your first mate."

"Greetings, Captain Willis," Emerson said. "It is good to have you on board again."

I looked at the flashing console lights on the wall opposite the ramp. "It's great to be here, Emerson, but I'm not the captain of this ship anymore."

"Captain is still your Alliance rank, and by virtue of your previous standing, you have the right to the chair and the command of this ship."

"There, see," Oliver said, waving a hand toward the console. "Emerson knows you're the true captain."

"All right. All right." I shed the parka, draped it over the back of the chair, and sat. "But I'm counting on my co-captain to set me straight if I do something stupid."

Oliver seated himself in the first mate's chair. "As if you'd ever do anything stupid."

From my shoulder, Perdantus chirped, "I have seen Megan do some things that I would consider inadvisable, but never something stupid. In any case, I think it would be stupid to tarry here another moment longer. We have friends in danger, and at least four river monsters will be close enough to accost us in a matter of minutes."

"Then let's go." I inhaled deeply and pointed at the ramp. "Emerson, close the hatch and prepare for takeoff."

"With pleasure, Captain Willis."

As the ramp rose, Oliver and I buckled in, while Perdantus flew to a secure spot, probably in the laundry area where he had often gone during previous takeoffs and landings. The Nine's engines hummed their familiar takeoff song, sounding like the purr of a big cat as the ship rose from the floor and its landing feet retracted. "I assume Dirk's not here," I said. "Where is he?"

Oliver shook his head. "We'll trade stories once we're in space. But no worries. He's doing great. We just have to fly without anyone in the engine room. Shouldn't be a problem. I just had the engines tuned up on Beta Three."

"Perfect." I pushed the button to raise the control yoke from the console and set a hand on the throttle. "Emerson, plot a course for Gamma Five while I shoot us out of here."

"Navigation plan commencing."

Oliver grinned as he tightened his belt. "Punch it, Megan."

I pushed the throttle forward. The Nebula Nine shot out of the hangar, pressing our bodies against our seats. As we zoomed over the river and across the icy expanse, I angled the wings' flaps to send us into a steep climb. The familiar queasy sensation of leaving my stomach behind actually felt good for a change. My father was alive and no longer a prisoner on this frozen planet. And where was he now? I had no way of knowing. But at least I could breathe a sigh of relief and concentrate on finding Crystal and Zoë.

When we pulled away from Beta Four's gravitational influence, I looked at Emerson's suggested route to the Gamma system. Using warp drive would get us there in three Alpha-one days, which meant that Camille's route would take just as long. Since she probably left already, she would get there before we could, unless, of course, she planned to stop somewhere else along the way.

"Emerson, can you detect any recent warp-engine use nearby, you know, like opening a wormhole? That usually leaves evidence behind, right?"

"Correct, and the particles are detectable for about an Alpha-one day. At this time, there are no telltale signs of warp-engine activation anywhere in the Beta system."

I scrunched my brow. "Interesting. That means Camille hasn't left yet or she's taking a longer route."

"I am detecting radio transmissions from a Nebula series ship in the direction of Beta Three. They are encrypted, but the signals indicate that she is likely close by."

"Right. Alliance ships probably don't patrol the Beta system much anymore. So that's likely to be Camille's ship."

"Should I plot a course to intercept?"

I shook my head. "With those enhanced torpedoes, she could obliterate us. We're better off in stealth mode."

"Meaning sneaky-pirate mode," Oliver said. "Megan's an expert."

"I suppose I am." I imagined Camille orbiting Beta Three, probably only an hour or so away. Why was she hanging around? To get repairs done on the Astral Dragon so she could safely take it to the Gamma system with her? Or maybe she lurked for other reasons. "Any sign of the Astral Dragon?"

"None," Emerson said. "But she could be running dark."

"If we engage warp speed, Camille can detect our departure, right? And she'll probably be able to read that the tell-tale signs came from a Nebula-class ship."

"Your assumptions are correct."

Oliver leaned toward me. "Are you thinking she's waiting to make sure that I was really heading for the Alpha system?"

"That's one possibility. It was easy for you to go to Beta Four undetected because you didn't use warp speed, but you would've used it to go to Alpha."

Oliver nodded. "So she's scanning the area waiting to see the signs."

"Maybe we should give some to her. She won't know that we really went to Gamma instead of Alpha."

"But couldn't she send a message to the Alliance to find out if we reported the Nebula Nine for decommissioning?"

"Good point." I spoke toward the ceiling. "Emerson, how much time would we lose if we go to Alpha One first and then to Gamma Five?"

"Approximately one Alpha-one day. It will take two days to travel to the Alpha system, then two days to travel to the Gamma system from Alpha. The total of four days is one day longer than the original course would take."

"Set the new course. We'll go to Alpha One, dock the Nebula Nine for decommissioning, and then steal her and head to Gamma Five, making it look like someone else stole her, of course."

"Steal her?" Oliver blinked hard. "Are you serious?"

I winked. "What's the matter, Oliver, haven't you ever stolen a spaceship before?"

"Well, um, no. But I guess you have."

I grinned. "More than once."

"It would not be stealing," Emerson said. "According to section twelve of the Alliance regulations, when a ship is decommissioned, it may be brought back into service in an emergency by order of the officer in charge of the ship at the time, and that officer has sole discretion regarding what constitutes an emergency. Since Megan is the officer in charge, she has the authority to take the Nebula Nine for any reason that she considers to be an emergency."

I muttered, "Digital fuddy-duddy."

"I heard that."

"Good." I set the course to follow Emerson's new guidance. "All right, Oliver, we have one hour and seven minutes till we get to the best warp-drive position. In the meantime, I'll tell you my story, and you tell me yours." I whistled. "Perdantus, come join us, please."

When he flew in and landed on my console, I told Oliver about my escape from Camille and my meeting with Barnabas, and Perdantus filled in some details that I forgot to mention. I showed Oliver the dragon's eye in my locket, the one that proved my father was still alive. I didn't mention Barnabas's ghost being in the gem, though I did mention that he died while I was with him, probably a victim of lung cancer.

Oliver described how he and Dirk flew to Delta Ninety-five with the kids we had freed from slavery on Delta Ninety-eight. There they joined the other children we had left on the planet after rescuing them from bondage. The new colony was thriving, with plenty of food and water for everyone.

After that, he delivered the ashes of the Nebula Nine crew, including those of his father, to an Alliance office in the Alpha system, leaving them there with an anonymous note. He also included Renalda's remains along with enough data for them to locate someone in her family. Then he dropped Dirk off on Alpha Three where his father had been released from prison, and the two were happily reunited.

Oliver breathed a delighted sigh. "That was a great moment. Dirk and his dad actually danced together. I wish you could've seen it."

Goose bumps spread along my arms. "I can imagine it. Dirk deserved a happy ending."

"Anyway," Oliver continued, "after that, I hightailed it to the Beta system, knowing that's where you'd be going. I got there about the same time you did even after all my stops, because the Nebula Nine is faster than the Astral Dragon."

I blew through my flapping lips. "In your dreams. We took our time because we had water-pressure problems and waited for Beta Three to orbit closer to Beta Four. That way we could get repairs done on Three and then hop over to Four."

"Yeah, Crystal told me about that. No showers. I guess that's why you smell the way you do.."

I gave him a pretend scowl. "What do I smell like?"

"Um … you smell natural. You know, like you've been out doing important things. The way every hard-working captain should smell."

I let a grin break through. "A tactful answer. But I'll be glad to use the shower on the Nine."

"And we will be glad as well," Perdantus said. "Oliver was kind. I will be more blunt. You stink."

Smiling, I waved a hand. "Oh, go be a blunt nuisance somewhere else."

Once we had made our warp-speed launch into an Alpha-system-bound wormhole, I found a spare Alliance uniform in storage as a new commlink earbud. Glad to shed the smelly garb I was wearing, I took a shower and changed into the fresh clothes, transferring the data drive I had found in Penelope's coffin to the new pants. The change of clothes felt so good, but my newfound comfort made me wonder how Crystal and Zoë were faring. As prisoners, they likely didn't enjoy the same benefits.

When I returned to the bridge, Perdantus was perched on the first mate's console, and Oliver leaned close, apparently having a discussion with him.

"What's up?" I asked as I slid into the captain's chair and inserted the earbud.

Oliver looked at me. "Emerson thinks someone might be following us."

"Through the same wormhole?"

"Right. Another force is affecting the passageway."

I scrunched my brow. "That's really weird. When we were going through a wormhole in the Astral Dragon, something affected that passage. We wondered if it could be warp drive problems, but maybe it wasn't."

"So is some force out there monkeying with warp travel?" Oliver asked. "That's pretty farfetched."

"Or someone was following me then. Sonya probably didn't know to look for that, but Emerson did because he was programmed by the military. And that reminds me." I fished the data drive from my pocket and plugged it into a port on my console. "Emerson, can you look at the data on this drive? Sonya said it's encrypted, and an Alliance computer might be able to crack it."

"I will try," Emerson said. "With Alliance protocol, there are many possible encryption keys and multiple levels, which means that I will probably have to go through millions of time-consuming iterations in order to fulfill your request."

I concealed a smile. "Emerson, are you saying the job is too difficult for you?"

"No. I am merely warning you that you will not get an answer in a short amount of time. It could take weeks."

I let the smile break through as I nodded. "Oh, okay. I understand. You're not as fast as you used to be. I've heard that computers can slow down with age, though I didn't think it would happen to you."

"After reviewing your request and conducting a quick scan of the data, I am confident I can decrypt it in days instead of weeks."

"That'll be fine, Emerson. Thank you."

Oliver leaned close and whispered, "Mistress of manipulation?"

I whispered in return. "Nope. Motivation." I raised my voice above a whisper. "Back to the subject. My father programmed Sonya, and he probably relied on our stealth modes to keep us from being followed. Besides, he always captained the Astral Dragon and would've watched for that himself. I don't have as much experience."

"Fair enough," Oliver said. "But what do we do about it?"

I straightened in my seat and looked out the front viewing window. "Shields up and stay the course. If a ship's following, it'll have to wait for us to come out of the hole before it can attack. And if it does, we'll be ready."

During the two-day trek through the wormhole to the Alpha system, I checked the status of every device on the Nebula Nine. Although Emerson had been with Oliver to make sure he commanded the ship correctly during his treks with Dirk, Oliver had much more to learn. To make the right decisions quickly, he needed to know what the Nine could and couldn't do. Since Captain Tillman took a much longer than normal route to get to the Delta system, hoping to avoid detection, I had worked as the main mechanic here for months. I knew every centimeter of the ship, and we now had plenty of time to scrutinize every nut and bolt.

We also laid out plans to dock the ship for decommissioning, a brainstorming session that raised reminders of plotting to help the slave kids escape from Thorne. Based on past experience, though, we knew that complex plans never worked out perfectly. We had to be ready to improvise.

Since Oliver had his stuff in the captain's quarters, he slept there, while I slept in the first mate's quarters where Gavin Foster once resided. Perdantus roosted the first night with Oliver and the next two nights with me, deciding that I smelled, in his words, "the less noxious of the two."

Although Emerson reported no new signs of the Nine being followed, we kept our shields up the entire journey, which meant consuming more fuel than usual, but since we had a short journey ahead, that didn't present a problem. We could get water and refresh the isotopes for our fusion engines on Alpha One.

When the day came to leave the wormhole, Oliver and I strapped into our seats while Perdantus stowed himself away once more in case the exit caused a shake. With the viewing window showing the sparkling wormhole exit in the distance, we read the data on our consoles. "Emerson," I said, "it looks like the wormhole exit is contracting."

"Affirmative. It is an unusual occurrence, but the potential for danger is minuscule. We will exit without incident."

"I wonder if the ship following us figured out how to minimize the effect."

"That is likely. A skilled pilot would not make the same mistake twice."

I tapped a finger on my chin. "And now I'm wondering how that ship escaped the collapsing hole, assuming that's what happened. We barely slipped through the opening, and the Astral Dragon isn't a huge ship."

"Perhaps it was shadowing you more closely than you realized. As you mentioned earlier, you were not scanning for a wake rider."

"A wake rider?" I said. "What's a wake rider?

Oliver snickered. "Cool. Something Megan doesn't know."

"Hush. I'll bet I can figure it out." I focused on the wormhole exit, magnified on our viewing window, now about ten minutes away. "A wake rider is probably a ship that doesn't have warp-drive engines. It stays close enough to a warp-drive ship to travel through the wormhole using the tunnel the leading ship makes, like a surfer riding the water wake that a boat makes. If the ship doesn't stay close enough, the wormhole collapses around it."

"That is correct," Emerson said, "and in anticipation of your next question, I scanned for evidence of a wake rider while you were talking and found no signs of a trailing engine."

"What if the captain shut off the engine?"

"The wake does not provide enough of a pull. The trailing ship would have to use at least impulse power to stay in the wake."

I drew a mental picture of a small ship tailing the Nine. "Even if it's really tiny? Like a one-person glider?"

"That is possible, though extremely dangerous. The slightest wrong move would destroy the glider."

I turned toward Oliver. "One time my father wanted to track an Alliance vessel. He flew our spy glider to the rear of this huge ship and attached to the docking hook. They didn't go to warp speed, so it wasn't as dangerous, but they never knew he was there."

Oliver glanced toward the rear of the ship. "Are you saying a spy glider might be attached to our backside right now?"

"That's exactly what I'm saying." I spun my chair toward Emerson's console. "Is there a way to check for attachment?"

"I can rotate the rear camera," Emerson said. "We should be able to see any ship that might be back there."

"Do it, and put it on screen."

The front window shifted to a view of the retreating flashes of the wormhole, the angle changing as the camera moved. Soon, a glider appeared, firmly attached to our rear towing ring, nearly identical to the one I flew from the Astral Dragon.

Oliver's mouth dropped open. "You nailed it, Megan."

"Yeah. But what do we do about it?"

"We can use a console switch to detach the ring." Oliver used his fist to simulate the glider's movement. "The glider will fly off into oblivion."

I shook my head. "We can't kill the pilot. Even if he's an enemy, he hasn't made a threatening move." I mentally scanned everything near the docking ring. What could we use to capture that glider? I had to come up with something in a hurry. The moment we exited the wormhole, the glider would probably detach, and we would lose our chance to see who was following us. "Emerson, let's magnify that glider's aft."

The glider's rear half filled the viewing screen, showing a metal ring on the back. "Looks like it has its own a towing ring, not detachable."

"You are correct. It is a standard Nebula series glider. They all have that ring in case they need to be towed."

"And we're equipped with a hook and line to tow it, pretty close to where the glider's attached."

"Affirmative."

I rose from my chair. "I can work with that."

"You will need to work quickly," Emerson said. "We have approximately seven minutes until wormhole exit."

"Oliver, I'll turn my earbud on. Watch the glider and keep me up to date." I jogged toward the bridge ladder.

A faint, "will do" sounded from behind me as I reached into my ear and toggled the bud on. I grabbed both sides of the ladder and slid down three levels to the lowest deck where I found a pressurized suit, helmet, gloves, utility belt, and magnetic boots. After putting them on in a flash, filling the suit with air from the tank, and toggling the magnets on with my toes, I hurried through the airlock procedure to the trapdoor. The recovery ladder hung just above it.

I pulled the trapdoor open, activating the ladder, and stepped onto its lowest rung while holding the sides with both hands. As the ladder lowered, I mumbled, "C'mon. You're too slow."

"What's too slow?" Oliver asked through my earbud.

"This blasted ladder. How much time left?"

"Three minutes, seven seconds."

"Not good." I pulled line from the belt spool, attached the carabiner to the ladder to secure myself, and pushed my body downward, feet first. I glided to the recovery platform below where my boots attached to the metal floor.

Wanting to keep the ladder out of the way, I pressed a button on the floor that halted its descent, the lowest rung still well above my head. I held to my safety line and eased over to the towing chain and wench mechanism embedded in the ship's frame. After freeing the chain's hook from its mooring, I walked with it out to the edge of the platform, reeling out the thick metal cable.

I knelt in front of the glider and peered inside. The person sitting in the pilot seat wore a full flight suit, complete with a helmet that included a reflective visor that prevented the pilot's face from being seen. He appeared to be looking straight at me, but he couldn't do anything to stop my plans. If he detached his glider before the wormhole exit, he and the glider would disintegrate.

Oliver's voice entered my ear again. "Thirty seconds to go. Emerson said the tighter hole will make the exit rougher than usual. You'd better finish and strap in somewhere."

"Easier said than done." Still holding the cable, I stepped onto the glider, walked to its aft, and attached the hook to the towing ring.

"Ten seconds. Megan, what in blazes are you doing?"

"Almost done." I ran to the platform, locked the spool to keep more cable from spinning out, demagnetized my boots, and leaped for the ladder.

The moment my gloved hands touched the lowest rung, the ship bounced. The ladder rung shot upward, slipping from my grasp. My feet slammed against the platform and the rebound sent me flying toward the glider, but my safety line tightened, and the belt squeezed my gut.

The recoil pulled me back to the ladder. I grabbed the sides and hung on while the ship continued bouncing. The glider detached from its own mooring and spun a 180 turn, but the tow line kept it from escaping, As it flew up and down, then side to side, it looked like a frantic dog trying to break free from a leash.

When the ship stopped bouncing, Oliver called through my earbud. "Megan, you're not in the camera view. Are you all right?"

"A little shook up, but fine. I'm hanging on to the ladder. I guess you can see the glider's in tow."

"Yep. Nice job."

"Now to reel it in." After magnetizing my boots, I pushed down from the ladder, floated to the platform again, and walked toward the spool mechanism. Before I could get there, the glider turned around and landed on the platform next to me, as if surrendering.

From the inside, the pilot opened the door and stepped out. The pilot's shape and stride told me right away that I had assumed wrong. She was a woman, not much taller than me. Her voice came through my earbud. "Greetings, Megan. We have a lot to talk about."

"How do you know my name?" I touched my helmet. "And how can you talk through my earbud? It's a secure frequency that only my father knows."

She patted me on the back. "Let's fasten my glider, then we'll board your ship and I'll explain."

After we reeled the tow line, pulling the glider tight, we rode the ladder up to its top. Once there, I closed the trapdoor and we went to the next higher deck, going through the airlock procedures along the way.

When we were safely on the air-filled deck, I took my helmet off and held it under my arm. The woman did the same and shook out shoulder length auburn locks. Her face—high cheekbones and narrow chin—seemed familiar, but I couldn't place it. She took off her gloves and extended her hand. "I'm glad to finally greet you, Megan Willis. I am very familiar with your father. I am here at his request."

"My father?" I took off my own gloves and shook her hand. "What's your name, and how do you know him?"

"My name is Jillian, and he is my brother. My twin brother."

I gasped. "So you're my aunt?"

Jillian nodded. "Ever since you were born."

"But my father never mentioned a twin sister. He told me about an older sister who died when he was young. I found a photo of her once. That's when he told me about her." I squinted. "And now I see the resemblance. That photo was of *you*."

She smiled, much in the same way my father always did. "Yes, that was me. And your father wouldn't have mentioned me at all if you hadn't found the photo. You see, after going to flight school together, we parted on bad terms. I became an Alliance officer, and he turned to piracy, or freedom fighting, as he called it. It wasn't until much later that I realized that his course was the right one, but I chose to stay put and see what I could do to help his cause from within the Alliance ranks."

"Wow!" My smile grew so wide, my cheeks hurt. "So Julian and Jillian. Twins. That's so cool."

"Yeah," Oliver said in my earbud. "Super cool. Emerson and I heard everything. Come on up to the bridge. I'll get some snacks and drinks, and we'll welcome Jillian to our humble space abode."

Oliver, Jillian, Perdantus, and I sat around the mess table in the dining area while Emerson guided the Nebula Nine toward Alpha One, a three-hour journey after our recent wormhole exit. Jillian and I had taken off our pressurized suits and laid them on the floor, but I kept my magnetic shoes on since I forgot to bring my normal shoes up from where I left them.

While we munched on broccoli tacos, reheated from the last meal Dirk had prepared, I told Jillian our story, though she knew much of it and said we would learn why she knew when she told her story. I included our idea to decommission the Nebula Nine and "steal" her for our next mission, an idea that she found exciting.

I finished our tale and waved for Jillian to speak as I took a bite of my taco—crunchy and better tasting than I expected.

Jillian pulled her hair back and tied a band around it to make a ponytail. "Your story sounds like a nightmare, but it explains a lot." She nodded toward my hands. "Like those bracelets and the line-art tattoos. I thought they were a fashion statement, you know, like a fad, kids channeling an ancient warrior princess or something, but I didn't want to say anything and sound like an out-of-touch fossil. Glad you cleared that up."

I swallowed a bite and smiled. "You're no fossil. Not a day older than ninety, right?"

"You're so funny." She kicked my foot and winced, not remembering that I was wearing metal shoes. "Now, as I mentioned earlier, your father and I attended pilot school together. We finished at the top of our class, tied for first place. Lots of jokes about that, like twin peaks in pods, space cadets since the womb, stuff like that, though I won't mention the more, shall we say, salty comments.

"Anyway, to break the tie, we engaged in a dogfight, flying battle pods." She glanced at the three of us in turn. "They're like my glider, only twice as big and armed with lasers. To make the battle safe, we used red laser light instead of destructive laser bullets, and we covered our pods with a grid that counted the hits. The first to score three hits would win. Every hit was transmitted to the scorekeepers at the base planet while we flew through an asteroid field."

Oliver swallowed his final bite. "Let me guess. You won."

She nodded. "I did, but I cheated."

I nearly choked on my bite, but I managed to swallow it. "You cheated? How? Why?"

"We were tied at two hits each, and he outmaneuvered me around an asteroid and had me dead to rights—a fish stuck in a boot. The moment I knew he would fire, I shut off all power. That deactivated my detection grid. He hit me, but it didn't register. When he flew past, I powered up and nailed him from behind. My third hit counted, and that ended the contest. Bingo. I win, you lose.

"As we flew back to base side by side, he glared at me but didn't contact me on the radio, and I didn't dare contact him. I know he expected me to do the honorable thing and confess, but I kept my mouth shut, and he didn't say a word to the officials." Jillian shrugged. "And that's why we had a falling out. I was recognized as the top pilot in our class, and, after refusing to shake my hand, he stormed out of the awards ceremony to calls like 'Sore loser' and 'Can't stand getting beat by a woman.'

And every barb was like a whip on his back, but he didn't say a word to anyone."

My heart sank. I wanted to like Jillian, my newfound aunt, but this story made her sound like a vain witch. She had to be leading us to a better outcome. I decided to withhold judgment.

Jillian let out a long sigh as she shook her head sadly. "I was such a toad. My lust to get that award tarnished his reputation and destroyed our relationship. And even worse for him, when his commanding officer demanded that Julian apologize to me, he refused. He was denied his commission and drummed out of the service. And I still didn't breathe a word about my cheating. And neither did he."

"Then what happened?" The question rolled off my tongue before I could stop it.

She smiled in a sheepish manner. "I became an officer in the Alliance fleet, and I moved quickly up the ranks. After twelve years, I became the captain of a cargo ship, which was a fast climb for someone my age, especially for a woman. Soon after that, I was told I would be promoted to a Nebula ship if I could safely transport some vital cargo to our battle cruisers on the front lines of our ongoing war against the rebel fighters in the Zeta system.

"By then, Julian had become a pirate, not siding with the Alliance or the rebels, though I didn't know it at the time. Anyway, during my trek to Zeta, Julian and his band of pirates isolated my ship from my escorts and disabled it. When he and his raiders boarded and subdued my crew, he and I came face to face on the bridge. He told me he knew beforehand that I was the captain of the cargo ship, and he targeted it so he could open my eyes to the corruption in the Alliance. Well, *I* thought I was carrying relief supplies to our fighters. The crates were marked as containing food, water, and clothing. Julian said I was actually transporting dangerous weapons to the rebels, that I had a traitor on board who was planning to kill me and deliver the weapons to my enemies.

"You see, one of the Alliance rulers was actually a plant by the rebels, and …" She waved a hand. "Too much detail. Suffice it to say, that both factions were rotten to the core, and Julian's quest was to empty the corrupt pockets of both sides and return as much as he could to the people who had been looted by the tax collectors. Anyway, back to the juicy part of the story. He marched me down to the cargo hold and pried one of the crates open with a crowbar. It held parts for an advanced class of weapons that could have shifted the balance of power to the rebels."

Jillian displayed her thumb and index finger with a tiny gap between them. "I felt about two centimeters tall. Humiliated. I said nothing as he bound the wrists of my crew, and three of his men marched them to the Astral Dragon as prisoners. When we were alone on my ship, he looked me in the eye and said, 'You have an escape glider. I invite you to use it. If you stay here, you will die when we destroy this ship in fifteen minutes. If you take your glider and escape, I suspect that you will choose one of the corrupt factions to join. Then, we will eventually meet again in battle, and I will show no mercy. But if you want to become a freedom fighter instead, I'm sure you're competent enough to find me and we can discuss it further.' Then he left me alone on the bridge.

"Obviously, since I'm not a ghost, I escaped in the glider. I rejoined the Alliance, but only because I was already an officer there and I could investigate more about Julian's claims. I found that the corruption was far worse than I imagined. With few exceptions, I discovered utter sewage all the way from the uppity admirals down to the deck swabbers. But I stayed put and kept my head low, hoping to figure out who was at the top of the food chain.

"A couple of years later, the Alliance captured you and your parents. After they were sentenced to death, I wrote a letter to the judge begging for clemency. I confessed my cheating ways and said that I drove him to become a pirate, that he was the most talented pilot in the history of the school, and it would be a terrible waste to kill him. Just send him to exile and allow me to try to bring him to sanity." Jillian shrugged. "The judge said okay. Which surprised the bean dip out of me. I did exactly what I said I would do, but the only way they allowed me to visit him on Beta Four was in a one-person glider. No risk of him escaping that way. And that's the vehicle I've used ever since. Anyway, during our conversations, I apologized to him profusely, and he forgave me, but that's as schmaltzy as I'm going to get. We were brother and sister again."

Jillian settled back in her chair and folded her hands. "And now that the background is out of the way, I'll tell you why I was following you. The last time I visited Julian on Beta Four, I found him wounded, shot in the leg and sick with a pox—feverish and delusional, babbling something about a prophet in a wishing well that we had to rescue, but it sounded more like a dream than reality. I was immune to the pox because I already had it. Barely survived, but that's another story. The same was true for the planet's chief of security, which is why he was the last to leave. Crazy lunatic was murdering every prisoner he could find. But since I had some pull with the judge, I convinced the security chief to take Julian with him on his transport and deliver him to a medical facility on Beta Three."

"How could you be sure he would do it?" I asked. "He wanted the prisoners dead."

"A bribe greased the wheels, and I followed in my glider to make sure he would keep his word. Then I personally checked Julian into the hospital under a false name. I stayed with him day and night until he started recovering and I knew he would make it. I guess our Willises-are-tougher-than-rawhide genetics gave us an advantage somehow. When he got back into his right mind, he asked me to look for you. He heard through various grapevines that you had escaped from Captain Tillman, but no one knew where you had gone. He also said he would rescue the wishing-well prophet when he got out of the hospital. Finding you was more important, so that was my job."

I pointed at myself. "I already found the prophet, and I can tell that story later, but does that mean my father is still in the hospital?"

Jillian shook her head. "I checked on that by radio. He's out, but I don't know if he was declared fully healed and discharged by a doctor or he just left on his own. And I've been worried about that. If a person's system isn't fully cleared of this pox, it can go dormant and come roaring back. And I also don't know if he was able to get a ship. He might be trying to commandeer one as we speak, or maybe he's on his way to Beta Four to try to find the prophet."

"And now we're in the Alpha system," I said, "and I can't go to the Beta system again, not with Crystal and Zoë in danger and on their way to Gamma." After heaving a heavy sigh, I nodded at Jillian. "Go on with your story."

"There's not much more to tell. I finally tracked you down in the Delta system and followed you." She pointed with her thumb toward the rear of the ship. "I wake-surfed your tail, hoping to stay undetected and learn your final destination. Then I would find Julian to tell him."

"Why undetected?" I asked.

Jillian shifted uneasily. "Well … I didn't want to have to tell you this long, tedious story, especially about what I did to your father in school."

"Why not?"

Her emerging smile seemed uncertain. "Because my career as a cool aunt would be over real quick."

"But my father forgave you." I rose from my seat and hugged her. "And I forgive you, too." I smiled and kissed her forehead. "Aunt Jillian."

"Thank you, Megan." She brushed a tear from her eye. "Okay, back to the story before it gets too sappy in here. Julian said after he rescued the prophet, he would try to get to Gamma Five and to look for him there once I received word about you. How far down on his to-do list he got, I don't know."

"But he'll eventually go to Gamma Five, so there's no reason for us to change our plans." I drummed my fingers on my thigh. "But I wonder why he's trying to go there."

"I'll let you work on that puzzler. He was barely able to talk when he gave me my marching orders." She looked toward the ceiling. "Emerson, I haven't greeted you yet. How's my old by-the-book buddy?"

His voice came from a speaker above. "I am functioning at one-hundred-percent efficiency. And how are you, Captain Willis, or should I say, Captain Jillian Willis to avoid confusion? Unless, of course, you now have a married name."

"I'm too busy and too ornery to ever get married, so it looks like I'll be a Willis till I croak. Anyway, what's protocol? When I trained here in the Nine, that was a few ranks ago. Now that I'm a captain, who's in charge, by the book?"

"You have seniority over Megan militarily, but she remains captain of this ship unless she voluntarily surrenders her position to you or you declare her incapacitated."

Jillian nodded firmly. "Then Megan's in charge. I'm in no mood to run this rusty bucket of bolts. It's actually a good idea to decommission. No offense intended, Emerson."

"No offense taken. This ship has, indeed, seen an abnormal amount of duty."

"So we'll just go along with Megan's plan to decommission and steal … ahem … procure the ship when we're ready."

"Wait." I walked slowly around the table as I thought out loud. "The Alliance would never accept me as captain of this ship. In fact, they might execute me on the spot, so we can't just sail into port with me at the helm. In fact, all records of me as captain should be erased from Emerson, because the first thing they'll do is a data dump from his memory banks. Officially, I'm dead, and Oliver has taken control of the Nine."

"True," Jillian said, nodding. "Keep going. Your brain's puttering along just fine."

I continued pacing. "They probably won't believe Oliver's story. He's an escaped slave. Just a kid." I halted and pointed at Jillian. "We need you to be the legit captain. We'll say we stopped once more at Beta

Three for some sort of supplies, and you came on board to hitch a ride to Alpha One. When you saw Oliver was in charge, you both decided it was best for you to take over."

"Okay. That works. But why was I on Beta Three?" Jillian asked. "According to your story, that is."

I waved a hand. "I don't know. You come up with something."

She grinned. "I'm pretty sure I can cook up a saucy tale."

"And then when we dock for decommissioning, I'll hide somewhere on the ship while you and Oliver officially report your arrival. Then Camille will be satisfied that he was telling the truth and that I'm dead. Then you can declare an emergency and take the Nine out again. No stealing. No worries that she'll be reported missing."

"I suppose I have to come up with an idea for the emergency." Jillian sighed. "I'd better crank up my tale-telling engine. It'll have to be a doozy."

As we traveled toward Alpha One, Emerson taught Oliver how to find and delete all references to me as captain of the Nebula Nine from the time I left the ship on Delta Ninety-eight, including audio and video of my presence. After we turned off all cameras and microphones in the ship, I searched for the best place to hide, taking only Perdantus with me. The fewer people who knew where I chose, the better. No torture, lie-detector test, or truth serum could extract my location from anyone.

During my hunt, I walked into the quarters where Dirk once slept to see if a panel there still opened to one of the maintenance channels. Crouching with Perdantus atop my shoulder, I pulled the panel open. On the floor of the channel lay the tiny camera and receiver screen he had once used to spy on Gavin Foster. They would come in handy.

After pocketing the items, I peered deeper into the ship's innards. I whispered to Perdantus, "This might work perfectly. Almost zero gravity and lack of air will keep any search effort quick and careless."

He hopped to the floor and took a step inside as he peered with me. "Will I go with you?"

I nodded. "In my suit. Not much air in the hull space. But don't worry. I don't stink anymore."

"Not as badly, you mean." Perdantus chirped a sigh. "I will do what I must."

After I moved my spacesuit to Dirk's room, I returned to the bridge with Perdantus. While no one else was looking, including Emerson now that we had blinded him, I set the spy camera on his console in the shadow of a data monitor.

Perdantus, perched on Emerson's console, looked on. "Well hidden, I think."

Two seconds later, Oliver walked in from the mess area, tapping on a computer pad. "Okay, that takes care of the media of us eating tacos. I think you're completely scrubbed post-Delta-Ninety-Eight. Jillian is setting up fake videos and audios of everything we scrubbed to take the place of the ones we erased. And we stowed her glider with the land rovers. We're all set."

I looked at the digital countdown on Emerson's monitor—00:07:54. "Good thing. Less than eight minutes till docking." I touched my ear. "You got your earbud turned on?"

"Yep. I'll be close enough to Jillian so you should be able to hear everything we say."

Jillian clapped her hands as she entered. "Positions everyone. I will be calling HQ in two minutes to coordinate the decommissioning." She sat in the Captain's chair and pointed at the first mate's station. "Oliver, put your butt there and get your game face on. It's time for action."

Grinning, Oliver plopped himself down. "Butt in position, Captain."

"Keep it there until I say to move it." Jillian waved a hand without looking at me. "Megan, go disappear. You're a ghost now. The moment you leave, I'm turning on Emerson's bridge cameras and microphones. He won't know you've been on the ship. We have to keep it that way."

"Okay, but I need to do something first. Less than a minute." I unfastened the necklace that carried my locket and draped it around Oliver's neck, whispering as I refastened it. "The dragon's eye is connected to my life. If it's glowing, you'll know I'm alive, and it should strengthen your healing power." When I finished, I set my thumb on the back of the locket for several seconds, then pressed his there, lifted it, and pressed it again. When the clasp popped open, I closed it, kissed his forehead, and drew back. "Just in case."

Before he could utter a word, I scooted off the bridge and into the living quarters, Perdantus flying next to me. As I padded noiselessly toward Dirk's room, I withdrew the spy camera's receiver. When I arrived, Perdantus landed on the bed, and I set the receiver next to him. While we watched the screen, I put the pressure suit and tank on. "Perdantus, do you want to get in the suit with me now? The hull space usually has enough air to breathe for a while, so you could wait. If you get uncomfortable, I could open my visor for a few seconds to put you inside."

He bowed his head. "I prefer to wait, thank you."

On the spy screen, the viewing window in front of Jillian flashed. A gray-haired woman wearing an Alliance emblem on her coal-black shirt appeared, her thin smile twitching in a nervous sort of way. Two children, a boy and a girl, maybe ten to twelve years old, stood a step or two behind her. Wearing Alliance-style uniforms, also black and perfectly pressed with a shirt logo displaying SS, they looked on with blank expressions.

My heart seemed to skip a beat. The SS Squad? Were they active now on Alpha One? Their blank stares provided no clues about their role, but their position behind the woman and her nervousness spoke volumes. These kids were enforcers of some kind.

The woman spoke with a stern tone, her voice coming through my earbud. "Your sudden appearance on the Nebula Nine is highly irregular, Captain Willis. My understanding from Admiral Fairbanks is that Oliver Tillman would be piloting the ship into the dock."

I put the helmet on and fastened it in place. So Camille somehow became an admiral. I didn't know she was in the Alliance military at all. Might she have used the SS Squad to put herself in that position?

"But," the woman continued, "then I read your missions report, and I must say that your explanation for your presence has a number of time gaps. After you dock, you will be expected to report to HQ to answer questions."

"Understood," Jillian said. "I will be glad to provide a full account of my whereabouts with a complete timeline of events."

Taking the screen with me, I opened the panel access door, crawled inside, waited for Perdantus to join me, and closed it behind me. I rose and jogged hunched over toward the airlock door while Perdantus fluttered along at my heels. This woman's orders couldn't be good. It meant that Jillian had to report to the land-based headquarters. That would make it a lot harder for her to get back to the Nine in a reasonable amount of time.

The woman's eyes shifted slightly, and she smiled. "It's good to see you again, Oliver. Do you remember me?"

Oliver cleared his throat. "Of course, Captain Fossil."

Her smile tightened. "Fossella."

"Right." He chuckled nervously. "I apologize."

"No need. You were only six when I last saw you." Her nervous twitch returned. "Considering your age and the fact that you are now an orphan, we have assigned foster parents for you on Alpha One. When the ship docks, you will be escorted to a transport cruiser and taken to your new home."

As I funneled air from the tank into my suit, I looked at Oliver's blank expression, unable to tell how he was reacting to Fossella's announcement. We hadn't anticipated the foster-care issue—another snag in our plans.

After the pressurization step, I passed with Perdantus through the airlock door and its usual procedures, then hurried on, scrunching under the lowering ceiling. As our distance from a gravity-enhanced floor increased, I grew lighter and lighter. All the while, I stared at the screen and continued listening.

"I'd rather go with Captain Willis," Oliver said. "She's Megan's aunt. Since Megan and I were such close friends, the captain and I hit it off right away. She feels like *my* aunt now."

Captain Fossella's eyes narrowed. "Odd for such a short time together, but I will see what the officer in charge has to say about that."

"Who is the officer in charge?" Jillian asked.

"Admiral Camille Fairbanks. She has just arrived in the Gamma system and is overseeing the Nebula Nine's return and decommissioning from there. I will ask her your question now, but, because of the distance, it will take a while to receive a response." Fossella began typing on a keyboard, and the girl behind her stepped closer and watched.

I crawled out of the access shaft into the hull space. So Camille was personally making sure the Nebula Nine docked for decommissioning. The mystery deepened.

Perdantus flew to my shoulder, laboring a bit due to the thin air, but he seemed to be tolerating it well enough.

While waiting for Fossella to complete her message, I walked to the central support column and sat on the platform that encircled it. As I had done the last time I was here with Dirk, I pulled safety line from my belt spool and attached the carabiner to a hook on the platform. I unfastened my visor, lifted it, and turned my head toward Perdantus. "Let me know if you need air."

He fluffed his feathers. "I will, but it's not bad so far."

I inhaled. Yes, it wasn't bad—thin but tolerable. It might be best to conserve as much air in the tank as possible. I turned off my suit's tank and focused on the spy screen now resting on my gloved palm. Fossella pushed her keyboard to the side. "Oliver, when the admiral replies, I will let you know. For now—"

"Wait, wait," Jillian said, waving a hand. "The order of events isn't adding up. We know Camille Fairbanks was in the Beta system two days ago. You read that in my report. How can she be giving you instructions about Oliver from the Gamma system when it takes three days to get from Beta to Gamma? She shouldn't be there yet. And even if she got there faster than we expected, how could her commands get to you so fast? It's impossible."

I clenched a fist. Good for her. My aunt was on her toes.

Camille walked into view and stood behind Fossella, a hand on the shoulder of each of the two children as her tall form allowed her to look over Fossella's head. "Well, Captain Willis," Camille said, a hint of derision in her tone, "you just had to force the issue, didn't you?"

I gasped. Camille Fairbanks was here? Then what happened to Crystal and Zoë and the Astral Dragon?

"It's clear," Camille continued, "that you're too much like your brother."

Jillian huffed. "Since he's the smartest man I know, I'll take that as a compliment."

"Don't. I was referring to his rebellious nature, his stubborn pride, and his refusal to stay quiet when necessary."

"Pardon my frankness, Admiral, but that proves you don't know him. He stayed quiet about my cheating for years. It's all in my report. It's my main reason for returning to Alpha One. I want to fess up and take my punishment."

"Obviously he stays quiet when he shouldn't, but when I find him, he will talk. He will want to keep his daughter alive." Camille walked out of view, calling behind her, "Proceed with the arrival maneuvers. I am on my way to their dock."

I stiffened. What did she mean about my father wanting to keep me alive? She thought I was dead, crushed in a collapsed tunnel. Maybe she was planning to tell my father that she had me in custody, knowing he couldn't prove otherwise since my body was buried. On the other hand, maybe she didn't believe a word of Jillian's tale because Jillian had no motivation to "fess up"? She had nothing to gain but a long stint in the brig. Maybe Camille suspected that the entire decommissioning story was a ruse, and somehow I was part of a larger scheme.

The Nine's viewing window flashed again. It now showed the enormous docking station, an orbiting parking garage shaped like a mammoth cylinder. A light at the top of the central tube probably meant that the station housed an administrative office there, likely where Fossella and Fairbanks were when I saw them on the screen.

As we closed in, a light moved down the central tube, probably a car in an elevator shaft that connected the office with the docking levels below, Camille its passenger. After a few seconds, it stopped at the third level down out of nine, at least according to my count, uncertain because the lights mounted around the station's perimeter were too dim to illuminate the details.

Our docking station, a square hole with metal framework all around, allowed us to glide in. Two figures in spacesuits holding docking hooks attached to cables waited, one on each side of the framework. Ahead, Camille sat in a four-person rover as it hovered on a ramp that jutted from the open elevator car, the glass top protecting her and her passengers from the airless environment.

Moments later, the ship's viewing window fell dark. Twin clanks sounded through my earbud, the docking hooks hitting the ship's metal frame on each side. Noise from the thruster engine died, and the Nine's front ramp began dropping open. The inner airlock panel had already been lowered from the ceiling and attached to the floor of the ramp, blocking the bridge's view of the outside.

Although I couldn't see it, I knew that Camille's rover was now gliding onto the outer part of the ramp while another airlock panel lowered behind her. Seconds later, the closer airlock panel began rising, revealing Camille and a uniformed male escort as they stepped out of the rover, its top now open.

They walked side-by-side up the ramp to the bridge, the man carrying a black toolbox. Jillian and Oliver rose, Jillian saluting with an arm over her chest. Camille halted and returned the salute while the man bypassed the pilot's chair and walked straight to Emerson's console. He ducked low where I could no longer see him, probably accessing the floor cabinets to plug a data cable into Emerson's storage units.

Camille lowered her arm. "At ease, Captain."

Jillian relaxed her stance. "To what do I owe the honor of your personal attention to this decommissioning?"

"It's quite simple." Camille folded her hands behind her. "I have employed a new force of troops called the SS Squad that I plan to use to bring all Alliance opposition to heel."

"The children I saw?" Jillian asked. "Two of them with Captain Fossella. I noticed their logo."

"Yes, those two are part of the force, but they're not ordinary children. They have special powers, but I won't go into detail now. My purpose is to make sure my plan has no further obstacles. At this time, only one man stands in my way." She paused, waiting for the obvious question.

Jillian complied. "Who is the man, Admiral?"

"Your brother, Julian Willis."

Of course, I expected that answer, but it made me gasp anyway. Now the lack of air became more noticeable. I would have to turn the tank on again soon.

"Julian? How could he stand in your way?"

Camille began pacing in front of Jillian, a finger to her chin. "I'm not sure what I should tell you."

Her theatrical pacing gave me a chance to get my question aired. Worried that a whisper wouldn't get picked up by my earbud in the thin air, I spoke at a normal tone. "Oliver, can you find a way to ask her about the Astral Dragon and her crew?"

The slightest of nods let me know that he heard my question.

Camille halted and looked at Jillian. "Let's just say that he has re-sources that make him considerably more than just one man, and I am going to my training camp to pick up a person who should be able to neutralize him."

"Excuse me," Oliver said. "Is it all right if I ask a question?"

Camille smirked. "You already did, but you may ask another."

"I was wondering about my friends, Crystal and Zoë. You said you were taking them to Gamma Five, but now you're here. What happened to them?"

"I sent them to Gamma Five on the Astral Dragon with one of my allies who is able to deal with gifted children."

"Oh?" Jillian said. "How does this ally battle against the gifts?"

Camille chuckled. "As if I would reveal that secret here."

"So they're safe," Oliver said. "Safe on Gamma Five."

"Whether or not they are safe depends on how well they're cooper-ating, and I intend to find out when I arrive."

I breathed a sigh of relief. At least they were probably alive.

Camille strode closer to Oliver, squinting at him. "Why are you wearing an earbud?"

"Um …" Oliver removed the bud from his ear. "To talk to Jillian while we were getting the Nine ready to dock. I forgot to take it out."

"And I lost mine," Jillian said. "It must've fallen out somewhere."

"Nonsense. You have speakers and microphones throughout the ship. You don't need earbuds." She snatched the bud from Oliver and stepped past the pilot chairs. "Scan the ship and find where this is trans-mitting. The other bud will have a signal like this one."

Her escort rose, blocking my view. "Yes, Admiral."

I yanked my earbud out. Leaving it turned on, I rose to my feet, dropped it on the platform, and kicked it over the edge. It fell slowly into the lower reaches of the hull space. I could have turned it off or even crushed it, but if they couldn't find it anywhere, they wouldn't be-lieve Oliver's excuse. Now maybe they would. At least it would be far away from me.

"Time to make ourselves disappear." I grabbed Perdantus and pushed him through the visor opening. He settled on my shoulder, somewhat smooshed by the suit, but he stayed quiet. I set the spy screen next to my chin, pinned between my cheek and the helmet, shut the visor, and turned on the air. Now for some gymnastics.

Hugging the central support with all four limbs, I climbed to the top until my helmet touched the roof, easy with gravity so low. From there, I looked at the chute we tried to use to eject the buzz biter from the ship several months ago, a metallic tube that extended from the engine room to the hull. At the point where it exited, about eight meters away, a metal rod protruded from the hull wall, a handhold for a mechanic.

I set my feet against the column and flexed my muscles to supercharge my legs. Bending my knees, I thrust myself toward the rod. In the low gravity, I sailed past two support beams, but my shoe clipped the second one. I fell short and rammed into the ejection chute, slapping against it with the side of my head. I grabbed the chute with both arms and hung on.

The spy screen's tinny speaker sent a man's voice rising to my ear.

"My scan indicates that the receiver is at the bottom of the hull space. There are no cameras in the area to verify. The schematics show that it is in a recess that isn't accessible to humans. It could have been dropped there, as Captain Willis indicated."

"Go look," Camille said. "Take the infrared scanner for heat signatures."

I gulped. For some reason, Camille was on a mission. She was sure someone else was in the Nine. I had to get out in a hurry. I shinnied up the angled chute to the hull, grabbed the mechanic's rod, and popped open a panel in the chute near the end, an access door to reach into in case something got stuck in the chute. I couldn't fit through the opening, but someone else could.

"Perdantus, can you hold your breath long enough to fly down the chute to the engine room? Once you're there, you can use your beak to pry open the access panel at that end, then you'll have more air. But it won't be easy. The second you open the panel, air will rush into the chute from the engine room. You'll have to push through the rush and close the panel from the other side."

"I will do my best." His feathers tickled my cheek as he spoke. "What should I do when I get there?"

"Press the ejection button. That will open the hull escape hatch on this end for about twenty seconds. Then I can pull the chute away from the hole and get out through the hatch while you sneak back to Oliver. The ejection trigger is the gray button on the console closest to the chute, but don't forget to close the access panel, the one you'll go through to get to the controls, before you push the button."

"I understand."

While holding to the chute with my legs, I opened the visor and set my face against the open access panel. "Go."

He hopped out of the visor and half skittered, half flew, down the inside of the chute. I closed the panel, relocked my visor, and watched the spot where I had emerged into the hull space.

Soon, Camille's henchman crawled out of the hatch I had used, carrying infrared goggles and a flashlight. All he had to do was put the goggles on and glance in my direction. My heat signature would stand out like a lightning bolt.

I swung around to the other side of the chute and set my body parallel to it. The chute hid all but my clinging arms and legs. I gritted my teeth and silently prayed, *Please, Astral Dragon, help Perdantus hurry.*

The man's voice came from the spy receiver again as he aimed the flashlight beam downward. "I located the earbud. It's lying at the bottom of the hull space, as expected. I'll start scanning for life forms."

A click reached my ears, the chute hatch opening, but the henchman didn't seem to notice as he put on his goggles. I grabbed the rod again and tried to turn the latch on the chute's flange to release it from the hull, but it wouldn't budge. Activating extra power in my legs wouldn't do any good. I had to turn the latch with my hand and do it in less than twenty seconds. My only hope was to use my dynamo powers on myself.

I closed my eyes and mentally focused on the dragon's eye. Warmth penetrated my skin where the locket rested on my chest. Power rippled through my body, along my limbs, and into my hands. I tried the latch again. It took all my strength, but it turned, freeing the ejection chute from the hull.

I looked down. The henchman was searching the area at his level. At any moment, he might glance toward me. I set the chute to the side. The little air remaining in the hull space began rushing out. I plugged the hole with my body and pushed myself through, then knelt on the exterior of the hull, reached in, and set the chute back in place. Unable to relatch it, I held the chute while waiting for its exit door to automatically close.

When it started sliding, I snapped my hand out of the way and exhaled heavily, whispering, "Well done, Perdantus," though he couldn't hear me.

I activated my magnetic shoes and rose to my feet. Now standing in an airless environment, I couldn't lift my visor to get the screen into a viewable position, so I listened for clues as to when to move and where to go.

After a few minutes, the henchman's voice returned. "No life forms detected in the hull space. That completes the infrared sweep of the entire ship."

"Then Oliver was telling the truth," Camille said. "Let's finish our work here and be on our way."

I walked toward the front of the ship, careful to keep my footfalls completely quiet. Of course, any noise I made wouldn't pass through the vacuum up here, but a careless clank in the wrong place might be heard inside of the ship.

When I reached the edge of the top level, I crouched low and watched the ramp in front of the ship. The rover glided out and entered the elevator car. When the car door closed, the light within rose two levels and stopped, maybe to allow the rover to enter a different ship, one that would take Oliver and Jillian down to Alpha One. And what of Perdantus? He probably hitched a ride with Oliver, maybe in his pocket to keep from being seen by Camille.

I heaved a sigh. I was on my own. I couldn't wait for Oliver and Jillian. It could take weeks or months for them to find their way back to the dock. I had to leave for Gamma Five right away, or at least as soon as I could.

Not knowing the decommissioning routine for a Nebula ship, I had to make some guesses. Or maybe I had to be bold while everyone was distracted by the admiral's presence.

I chose the bold option.

I turned off my shoe magnets, leaped to a steel girder in the dock's upper frame, and grabbed it. After turning the magnets on again, I attached my shoes to the girder and walked upside-down to the starboard side of the frame, then down the vertical girder until I reached another horizontal one that paralleled the ship. Once there, I found the hook attached to the ship at the end of a meter-long cable welded into the docking frame. I knelt, reached for the hook, and felt for the release mechanism. As I did, I noticed a sign on the wall next to the elevator, well-lit by a nearby shielded bulb—D4.

When I detached the hook, I rose to my feet and looked at the sign by the door to the adjacent dock—D3. In the near total darkness, a ship moored there took shape in my vision—another Nebula. Could it be Camille's?

I walked closer and read the label emblazoned on the bow—Nebula Seven. Yes, she had docked here. But where were her crew members? Lounging inside the ship? Or maybe in the station? If so, could I cripple the Seven without anyone noticing?

I grinned. Of course I could.

I walked to the Seven's stern and spotted its water port—a square flap with a pull handle embedded in the hull next to a similarly shaped waste port, both situated above a work platform about two meters from the girder, an easy leap in zero gravity.

Two hoses lay curled on the girder near where I stood, one for filling the fusion tank and the crew's drinking supply and the other for emptying the human-waste tank, both clearly labeled. I detached the adapter from the end of the water hose, attached it to the waste hose, and looked around for any sign of watching eyes. Since the station was inaccessible to anyone outside the Alliance, it seemed that no one worried about a ship's security beyond keeping foreign vessels from getting close. A lone saboteur could do a lot of damage.

With the end of the waste hose in hand, I toggled my magnets off, jumped to the platform at the adjacent dock, and held a vertical beam while I remagnetized my shoes.

Now upright on the platform, I opened the water access door and pressed the flush button at the side of the circular port within. Water spewed and flew into space, floating away from the dock in an undulating stream. When the flow ebbed to tiny globules of water, I attached the waste hose to the port and flipped the suction button on the opposite side.

As the ship drew the sludge into the water compartments, I imagined what might be going on inside the ship. If anyone was awake and paying attention, they could hear the suction engine, though it was inaudible out here in the vacuum. Several seconds later, I turned the suction off, detached the hose, and closed the door. That should keep the Nebula Seven at the dock for several hours, at least. Of course, Camille could always commandeer another ship, but even that would take a while.

After putting the adapter and hose back the way I found them, I scanned the Nebula Seven. What else could I do to sabotage it without taking a lot of time? As I thought about the systems, Camille's husband's boasts about the power of his enhanced photon torpedoes came to mind. They would be fired through the front weapons turrets. If I could somehow disable those, that would be a huge benefit.

I hoisted myself onto the casing that held the ship's retracted wing and walked on the hull to the front of the bow where the turrets protruded upward. I couldn't dismantle the turrets without the proper tools, but making them vulnerable to attack would be the next best thing. Disabling the protective shields would do exactly that.

Since the turrets stood upright, I was able to grasp the vertical exterior panel and pop it off, exposing the wires leading to the shield's generator. I pulled them free from the panel and rewired them to show positive feedback, making it impossible for the onboard computer to detect an outage.

After snapping the panel back in place, I disabled the other turret's shield in the same way and returned to the dock's framework. Once there, I retraced my steps to the upper girder, walked toward the port side of the Nebula Nine, and filled its reservoirs with water and isotopes, then detached the docking hook.

Now that the nine was floating freely, I hurried to the front of the ship, then, watching for any sign of a guard, crept up the ramp past the raised outer air lock panel. Seeing no one, I stopped between it and the closed inner panel and pushed the button to lower the outer one.

When it closed and air began filtering into the gap, I unfastened my helmet, took it off, and tucked it under my arm, then pushed the button to raise the inner panel. The moment it lifted high enough, I restarted my march toward the flashing light on Emerson's console. "Emerson, this is Captain Megan Willis."

Emerson's light flashed more brightly. "Voice and rank confirmed. Welcome back, Captain Willis."

"Good. You recognized me. I was worried that Admiral Fairbanks already wiped your memory."

"I detect that some of my memory was recently scrubbed, though, of course, I don't know what was deleted. According to my current memory, I have not seen you since you departed on the Astral Dragon. I hope that your journey was successful."

"It was in part, but the Astral Dragon has been hijacked along with my crew. I am declaring an emergency, and I am countermanding the Nebula Nine's decommissioning orders. We need to leave at once."

"Your authority to declare an emergency is recognized. You are in command, Captain."

I quickly shed my spacesuit. Leaving it on the floor, I hustled to my chair and strapped in. "Close the ramp, then full impulse power in reverse to leave the dock."

"Priority warning. We should first detach from the docking couplers."

"I already did that. I assume there are no sensors to give you that information."

"You are correct, and all cameras other than the ones on the bridge have been turned off. I cannot override that setting."

I slid my finger across my console screen, found the camera controls, and turned them all on. "You have eyes now, Emerson. Turn on the front viewing window and proceed with my commands."

"Proceeding."

The window turned on, giving me a view of the dock's elevator shaft. With a jolt, my body pressed against the straps, and the dock shot away, becoming a pinpoint of light against the planet.

I whispered, "Alpha One." Feelings for my birth home upwelled. Visions came to mind—prancing through amber fields of wheat with grain heads at eye level and splashing barefoot through cold streams. But since my mother and I joined my father's crusades when I was young, those memories were few and faded.

"Captain Willis, I am slowing our reverse momentum and rotating to a forward drive away from Alpha One. If you want me to plot a course, I will need to know the destination."

I shook away my reverie. "Gamma Five. The fastest way possible. Don't worry about g-forces. You know what I can endure. No one else is on board."

"But I am on board." Perdantus flew to my console and perched on it. "Your sudden departure from the docking station threw me against a wall, but I was not seriously injured."

I smiled and ran a finger across his chest. "Welcome aboard. I'm glad you're here."

"Oliver guessed that you would return, so I stayed behind to keep you company and assist you in any way that I can."

"You're the best, Perdantus. Really. I mean it."

He bowed his head. "As always, I am at your service."

"You'd better find the most secure place you can. We're going to shoot out of here."

"Give me ten seconds." He leaped up and flew from the bridge.

"You heard him, Emerson. He needs at least ten seconds."

"Acknowledged. Countdown in progress to ensure his safety." After the ten seconds elapsed, Emerson continued. "Now accelerating toward a safe wormhole entry point. We will arrive there in twelve seconds."

I retightened my straps. As the ship's speed spiked, my back pressed against the chair. The skin on my face pushed against my skull. Emerson was really pouring on the juice.

"Seven seconds to warp-speed jump … six … Captain, we are being hailed by Alliance Headquarters on Alpha One."

"Ignore it. Camille can't chase us for a while. And I have to trust Oliver and Jillian to take care of themselves. Go ahead and engage the warp engines at the programmed time."

"Warp engines engaging."

Once we were safely traveling through the wormhole, I unbuckled and whistled for Perdantus. He flew in and landed on my shoulder. "You called?"

"Yes. Tell me everything you heard, anything Camille said, or Oliver, or Jillian."

"Since I was with you most of the time, I don't have much—"

"If I may interrupt," Emerson said, "I can provide that information. My bridge cameras and microphones were turned on at the time."

"Great." I pointed at the viewing window. "Put it on screen from the time Admiral Fairbanks came in. Double speed. I'll tell you when to slow it down."

As the video played, I listened to the conversation, familiar because I had heard much of it through the earbud. Nothing unusual cropped up until Camille leaned close to Oliver as if whispering to him as they walked together toward the rover.

"Emerson. Pause it." The video halted. "Back it up to when Fairbanks leaned toward Oliver, slow it to half speed, and turn up the volume."

As the replay crawled along, Camille's voice came through at a slow pace. "You might be wondering why I demanded a search of the ship. I was convinced that Megan was on board, whether you knew about it or not. I know she survived my attack, exactly as I had hoped."

"Why are you telling me this?" Oliver asked, also in a whisper.

"Because I need her. I know she will stop at nothing to find her father, and I plan to follow her and locate him. I'm telling you because I know she'll eventually try to contact you. If you wish to stay alive, you will tell me when she makes contact. I will have eyes on you at all times, so don't think that you will be able to talk to her without my notice."

Then Camille and Oliver got into the rover with the henchman and Jillian, and they left the ship.

I smacked my palm against my forehead. "I can't believe I fell for it! She wants to follow me to find my father!"

"Yes," Perdantus said. "I heard."

"I played right into her hands. I thought that she thought I was dead. The thermal scan in the cave was a ruse. Maybe the torpedo got closer to me than she wanted, and she was really checking to make sure I was alive. Then she monitored Oliver to make sure he plucked me off Beta Four. That's why she thought I had to be on the Nine and why she scoured the ship searching for me."

"A fair assumption, Megan."

"Still, why would she spill the beans at that exact time?" I pointed at the window. "Emerson, run it back to just a few seconds before Camille leaned toward Oliver. One quarter speed."

The recording played again. The moment before she began whispering, she cast a split-second glance toward the ceiling. I leaped up and pointed. "There! She looked at the camera to make sure it was on. It was all staged."

"She wanted you to hear her secret conversation," Perdantus said. "But why?"

"To make me think she gave up on the idea that I was on the ship. To make me more comfortable with taking it to find my father. That also explains why she didn't wipe Emerson's memory and reset him to factory specs and why she didn't post a guard here."

"And what would she gain by your comfort?"

"My complacence. If I feel safe, I won't be as watchful." I hustled to a tool cabinet at the side of the bridge. "Emerson, scan every compartment of the ship for a tracker. It'll emit a signal of some kind." I opened the floor cabinet's door and pulled out a toolbox. "I'm getting a hand scanner for the places you can't scan."

"Scan commencing," Emerson said. "I will report any anomalies."

As I pictured the tracker Gavin planted on the Nine months earlier, another memory rose to the surface, and I spoke it out loud. "Some scanners don't constantly emit a signal. They can be intermittent or even dormant until they're needed. The tracker could be on a timer or have a locator to tell it when and where to start signaling."

"How does that apply to our situation?" Perdantus asked.

"Camille knows I'm going to the Gamma System. A tracker could stay dormant until we get there."

"I see. A sleeping tracker would make our search a more difficult one."

Sighing, I nodded. "Let's scan anyway and see what we can find. But even if we do find an active tracker, it could be a decoy to keep us from searching for another one." I clenched a fist so hard, it trembled. "I can't let her find my father!"

Perdantus fluttered to my shoulder and rubbed his cheek against mine, something he had never done before, probably to try to calm me down. "Megan, listen to me. The obstacles seem insurmountable, but we have time to search for your father and to ponder Camille's plan." He stepped back and looked me in the eye. "We need to be steady ourselves and consider our options with calm minds."

I exhaled. "Right. Of course you're right. Thanks. It's just that with Oliver and Jillian in danger, and my crew kidnapped, and my father out in space somewhere after barely surviving a disease …" I heaved another sigh. "You understand."

"Of course. Let's busy ourselves with the task at hand to take our minds off our troubles."

We began the long, tedious scan for trackers. Since Camille's henchman searched the entire ship when trying to find me, he could have placed trackers almost anywhere. The process did help me avoid focusing on my lost loved ones. Perdantus was right again.

Wearing a pressurized suit, I used the hand scanner to search the land rover garage along with the two rovers parked there and found nothing. But something was wrong. Oliver had said they moored the glider here, but it was nowhere in sight. Had someone removed it while I was working on the outside of the Nebula Nine? If so, where might it be now?

After combing the entire ship, I returned to the bridge, removed my helmet, and tossed the scanner back into the toolbox with a clank. "I got a big, fat zero."

Perdantus stood on my pilot's console. "I'm sorry to hear that, Megan."

"I found a signal," Emerson said.

I turned toward his monitor. "Really? Where?"

"At the bottom of the hull space. It is a conventional communications device."

I nodded. "My earbud. I'll have to get it. It might be useful." Since I already had my suit on, I returned to the hull space and used a hook and line to fish the earbud out of its crevice, not an easy task with so little gravity in the area.

When I returned to the bridge, now wearing only my Alliance uniform, I set the earbud on the console. "Even this could be a tracker, so I turned it off."

"Since it is now off," Emerson said, "may I suggest that you keep it in case you need it? Once you leave the ship, it will be your only means of communicating with me."

"Good point." I inserted it in my ear.

During the rest of the time in the wormhole, Emerson and I planned our approach to Gamma Five. We would emerge into the Gamma System less than three hours away from the planet, contact the Alliance outpost there, and request permission to land. A message from Alpha One couldn't have arrived there yet, and even if Camille sent one ahead of time in anticipation of our escape, she probably would have instructed the outpost to give us free passage since she wanted me to lead her to my father.

As part of our plan to prepare for landing, we decided we would orbit Gamma Five and search for the Astral Dragon from above. Although whoever took her to the planet was probably smart enough to turn off all signals emanating from the ship and shut Sonya down, she was programmed to set a timer to reboot herself if the ship were ever hijacked. By now, she was probably already sending a distress signal. We just had to locate it.

After the expected two days in the wormhole, we exited into the Gamma system and immediately hailed the Alliance outpost. To give me the needed authority, Emerson chose Jillian's voice print from the database of officers and altered my voice to match the print.

With Perdantus perched on the back of the first mate's chair, I spoke into my microphone. "Alliance outpost Gamma Five, this is the Nebula Nine. We are approaching your planet. Request permission to orbit and land. ETA is two hours, fifty-five minutes."

"Nebula Nine, this is Lieutenant Trevor Mixon. We detected your ship and are now tracking you. Our computer indicates that the closest voice match is Captain Jillian Willis. Please confirm."

I pressed my lips together. Although I had lied many times before, for some reason I felt like I needed to keep my lies to a minimum now. "This is Captain Willis."

"Ah, the still-reigning champion of the pilot-school points challenge. Your reputation precedes you."

My cheeks flushed hot. "Actually, my reputation isn't the best these days. You know, after the cargo ship incident."

"No worries. I read the report, and I'm still a fan. But I have a question. You're not registered as the commanding officer on the Nebula Nine. The last registered commander is Captain Tillman, and he's been logged as deceased. What's going on?"

I licked my drying lips. "I commandeered the Nebula Nine from the Alpha One docking port on an emergency mission. Admiral Fairbanks knows all about it."

He huffed a derisive laugh. "Admiral *Camille* Fairbanks, I assume."

"Correct. I am not at liberty to divulge the reason for the mission. You can contact her if you want, but I don't think a delay would be helpful to either of our careers."

"You got that right. She's not exactly …" He cleared his throat. "Duly noted, Captain Willis. You may proceed. Use one of the standard orbital paths and land wherever you wish, but realize that we will track your location. It's protocol."

"Understood, Lieutenant."

His tone turned boyish. "And if you could stop by the outpost before you leave, that would be great. I would love to meet you. Not to be too forward, but I see that you're close to my age and unmarried."

I smiled. It might be good in the long run to play along. "Well, Lieutenant, it's quite flattering that you want to meet me. And you're right that I'm not married. I'll see what I can do when I complete my mission."

"Oh, really? Wow, that's great. I saw your photo in the database, and you're quite—"

I switched the channel off.

"It seems," Perdantus said, "that you have a starstruck fan on Gamma Five."

"Jillian has a fan. Not me. But it helped to have him there. We're in the clear, at least for now. Camille hasn't poisoned the well yet."

When we reached Gamma Five and began a low orbit, we passed a huge spherical satellite with steady lights on its apparently metallic hull, some green and some red, but we weren't close enough to discern any details as we zipped by. Whatever it was would have to stay a mystery.

On my console's map, I watched hundreds of blinking pinpoints of light, each representing a signal coming from Gamma Five. Since Emerson was listening for anything transmitted on the three frequencies Sonya would use, I had time to read an article from Emerson's database about the planet itself, text and photos appearing on my console screen.

Gamma Five hosted three continents—Astatos, Placid, and Ragua—in the midst of an enormous freshwater ocean, and one of the three, Ragua, broke away from its bedrock and moved like a floating island. With so much movement, quakes were common, sometimes catastrophic. The initial break caused huge cracks that carved up the land and triggered tsunamis that flooded the coasts. Thousands of humans and other sentient creatures died, along with tens of thousands of animals. Although the climate there was always temperate and comfortable for humans, because the quake continued on a regular basis, most survivors of the big quake fled the continent and never returned.

I gazed at photos of the landscape and the creatures living there, each with a caption that described them. Approximately 1.3 million humans called Gamma Five home, a popular new abode for many Alpha One immigrants due to the similar atmosphere. Fewer than eight hundred lived on Ragua, the smallest of the three land masses, about ten percent of the planet's total ground area.

Animals that still lived on Ragua included highly adaptive species, like Montons, creatures that resembled bears but with mole-like claws that enabled them to burrow underground, thereby escaping unsuitable weather. Although many lived on Ragua at one time, most migrated to the other two continents when the quakes began, taking the opportunity when Ragua floated close enough to another continent.

Gamma Five also supported a number of ape species that humans had introduced as well as multiple cat varieties, some domesticated and some wild. Dogs also abounded, nearly all domesticated.

One of the most interesting facts is that the big quake occurred only several years ago. Scientists were still investigating the cause of the change, though some rumors said that the Alliance military conducted secret underground experiments that somehow dislodged Ragua from the underlying plates. They were also still conducting research on how the island could float from place to place without sinking. That, too, remained a mystery.

Emerson interrupted my reading. "I am detecting a distress call on an Astral Dragon frequency."

I spun my chair toward his console. "Where? Which continent?"

"Ragua. I am illuminating a locator point on your map."

I studied the map. The light appeared near the center of the continent, almost exactly on the equatorial line. "All right, let's get close enough for a visual inspection, say one kilometer. We don't want to be seen in case it's a trap."

"Acknowledged. We will deorbit in ten seconds, and I will shift control to you in case an emergency landing is necessary. As you are aware, I am not authorized—"

"To land the ship. I know. I'll take over." I looked at Perdantus. "Better go to your safe spot."

"I found a new one in the mess hall that allows me to see out a window. I will go there." He flew from the bridge.

When the Nine descended out of orbit, I grasped the yoke, extended the wings, and steered the ship into a deeper dive. With Perdantus safely tucked away, I could plunge into the atmosphere at a sharp angle and rely on the heat shields to protect us.

Once we had settled into a one-kilometer cruising altitude and closed in on the source of the distress signal, I searched below for any sign of the Astral Dragon. Tall trees covered most of the land, though many tilted at odd angles because of deep trenches that scarred the ground, probably due to the quakes.

The navigation map pinpointed the source of the signal, a grassy patch of land less than a kilometer away. We would be over it in seconds. As we approached, I dipped lower and stared at the area—nothing but green grass. How could that be? The signal was coming from that exact spot.

I scanned the surrounding area. With all of the deep furrows, could one of the channels lead under the pinpointed area? The Dragon's signal could easily penetrate the soil from below if she wasn't too deep. "Emerson, I'm going to do another flyby. Scan for a heat signature on that spot."

"Acknowledged."

I turned the Nine sharply and headed back at a downward angle until I reached an altitude of only fifty meters. Then I leveled out and decelerated as we flew over the area. "See anything, Emerson?"

"Infrared scan reveals anomalies."

"Put the image on my console." When it appeared, I narrowed my eyes as I studied it closely. The scan showed two orange circles side by side where the signal originated. What could they be?

I ran every possibility through my mind, anything circular in the Astral Dragon. Then it hit me. Those were the starting points for the wall climb in the holographic workout room. Sonya heated the floor coils to attract my attention, and since she heated only the coils, the Dragon was likely being watched. Otherwise, she would have lit up the entire ship. A guard would notice lights or engine noise but not the quiet-running coils. "That's her. That's the Astral Dragon. Underground."

"Acknowledged. I will search for a suitable place to land. That parcel of ground is too small."

"Look for a trench that points toward the Astral Dragon's location, a trench that disappears underground before it goes that far. I'm betting there's a tunnel that'll lead us straight to the ship."

"Search commencing."

I steered the Nine into another sharp turn and flew back once more. Three possible candidates for trench-tunnels came into view, but I couldn't find a decent place to land near any of them. If I could decide which trench was the right one, blasting a few trees away would make a serviceable landing spot, but that would attract too much attention.

"Trenches evaluated," Emerson said. "The trench that most accurately points toward the location of the Astral Dragon is the one I have labeled Candidate A on your map. The other two are labeled Candidate B and Candidate C, along with the angular degrees that they deviate from a direct line. The closest potential landing site to the point where Candidate A disappears into the ground is approximately five kilometers from that point."

"That's doable. We'll land there. Highlight it on my map, and I'll put us down."

"Acknowledged. You could take one of the rovers. That way, you would arrive at your destination more quickly, your landing options will be more plentiful, and your escape options will increase as well."

"Good thought. And when I find the Dragon, I'll look for my translator. No telling what kind of creatures I might have to understand."

When the landing site appeared on my map, I guided the ship to the spot, pointed the prow toward the Astral Dragon, and set us on a flat, grassy area, void of trenches. A line of trees, some vertical and some tilted, stood about ten meters away, tall enough to conceal a low-gliding rover.

I turned the engines off and called out, "Perdantus, it's safe now."

After unbuckling, I rose and looked at Emerson's console. "When we leave, go into self-defense mode. Shields up. Fire only if fired upon. Three-sixty monitoring for my distress signal."

"Acknowledged."

Perdantus flew in and landed on my shoulder. "I am ready, and I assume you will not need a space suit this time."

"Right." I grabbed a utility belt with an attached flashlight and laser blaster, then strode toward the ladder. "The atmosphere should be perfect for us."

"Excellent. I look forward to breathing fresh air instead of a malodorous Megan. No offense intended."

"None taken." As I descended the ladder, I smiled. It was so good to have such a smart, noble friend, one who felt free to say exactly what was on his mind. That's what real friends did. I had no idea what I would do without him.

We unmoored a rover and drove it toward the line of trees, Perdantus firmly perched on the back of my seat. Once in the forest, I dodged a few tilting trunks, dipped past a series of root balls, and descended into a ten-meter-wide trench. Some of the protruding roots swiped against the rover's sides, making a whipping sound, but they did no damage.

With sheer black walls of dirt on both sides, the trench deepened from one meter to three to five. Soon, the path transformed into a tube-like tunnel. Light from behind dimmed, forcing me to flick on the rover's twin headlights. Hoping to avoid detection, I aimed the beams at the ground and kept the engine at its lowest possible level.

Far ahead, a dark form took shape at the edge of the light—the Astral Dragon. It blocked the tunnel, its prow aimed at a ninety-degree angle to my path, meaning that it probably came here from a different direction. It couldn't have fit in the tunnel we traveled through.

I decelerated, landed a few meters away, and dimmed the lights as I watched for any sign of movement. If a guard were stationed outside, he would know he had a visitor, but maybe someone inside wouldn't have noticed our approach. Either way, I had to be ready for anything. But, so far, everything stayed motionless.

I turned the headlights off. With complete darkness and silence all around, I whispered to Perdantus, "Let's go."

Part
02

Gamma Five

11

Perdantus hopped onto my shoulder. I opened the hatch and stepped out into complete blackness. Grit crunched under my shoe, sounding like firecrackers in the stark silence. Cool, damp air penetrated my shirt, not enough to make me shiver, but it raised images of a drafty old house—eerie and haunted. I half expected to hear rattling chains and a low moan.

I unfastened the flashlight from my belt and flicked it on. The beam cut through the darkness and rested on the Astral Dragon's open front ramp. Mist floated through the light, swirling as I moved the air.

"Stay alert, Perdantus." I walked up the ramp, the light beam leading the way. Inside, the bridge seemed to be in order, no sign of a skirmish. My theory that Crystal and Zoë wanted to find the Starborn kids seemed more likely all the time. Otherwise, it was hard to imagine those two letting themselves get caught without putting up a fight.

When I walked onto the bridge, I looked at Sonya's monitor. A text message appeared and ran across the screen. *Do not speak a word. An intruder is on board. He is searching for information.*

I typed quietly on her keyboard. *Do you know what kind of information?*

A new message scrolled. *The intruders who commandeered the ship repeatedly asked where your father is, so I assume he's looking for any information that will provide clues to the answer.*

I typed, *Where is he now?*

In your father's office. He does not know that I am watching him. I am in stealth mode.

Understood. You can turn off the hologram coils now.

Already done.

Did you get any clue where Crystal and Zoë were taken?

Sonya's reply scrolled more slowly, giving me time to read the longer message. *To a training facility that lies deeper underground. Four guards conversed and gave me the impression that they could get there through a series of tunnels, but no one provided any details. Crystal and Zoë planned to overpower the guards once they found the camp, but everything changed when a woman arrived. She dismissed the guards and escorted Crystal and Zoë herself. The woman's confidence made me think that she held some kind of power over your sisters.*

I typed, *Thank you. I'll see if I can sneak up on the intruder.*

Sonya's next reply appeared in all capital letters. *MY PROGRAMMING INSTRUCTS ME TO PRINT OUT A FULL REPORT. IT IS IMPERATIVE THAT YOU READ IT.*

A low hum emanated from the printer below the monitor. I picked up the three pages and glanced at the front of the first. The text seemed to be a rehash of what Sonya had already told me. I could read the rest later. I folded the pages and slid them into my back pocket. Now to deal with the intruder.

I whispered, "Perdantus, stay on the bridge and warn me if someone sneaks up behind me."

Without a word, he flew off my shoulder and perched on the back of my chair.

Since my father's office lay beyond our sleeping quarters, I tiptoed there and peered through the open doorway. A flashlight beam knifed through the darkness, aimed at my father's desk. Hands rifled through a stack of papers, but I couldn't distinguish the figure holding the light.

I put my own flashlight away and flexed my biceps. Electricity arced across my fingers. One push with both legs sent me flying across my sleeping quarters. I slammed into the intruder and knocked him flat with a loud grunt. I propped myself on my knees and laid my hands on his upper arms, shooting electricity into his body. The jolt made him shake uncontrollably, unable to fight, though he let out a screech. But something seemed odd.

I shut off the electricity. His body settled to a tremble, and he quieted. I rocked back, grabbed my flashlight, and turned the beam on him. Shorter than one-and-a-half meters with smooth alabaster skin and small hands, he had to be twelve years old or younger.

His trembling arms shifted toward his face to block the light from his squinting blue eyes. "Who ... who are you?"

I lowered the beam to his chest where an SS logo emblazoned his long-sleeved black polo shirt. "Who wants to know?"

He blinked hard, still shuddering. "Oswald. Everyone calls me Oz."

"Well, Oz, I need to inform you that you're an intruder on my ship." I grasped his arm and hoisted him to his feet, making his height clear, about ten centimeters shorter than me. "And you are now my prisoner."

Teetering in place, he stared at me. "*Your* ship? Are you Megan Willis?"

"In the flesh." I forced him to walk to the bridge, my flashlight illuminating the way. As he stumbled along, my firm grip kept him from falling. The moment we arrived, I pushed him down to the navigator's chair. "Sonya, give me bridge lights."

When they flashed on, Perdantus flew from my chair, calling, "I will keep watch outside." He sailed down the ramp and out of sight.

I looked Oz in the eye and spoke with a stern voice. "What happened to my crew?"

He turned his head and broke eye contact. I pinched his chin, turned his head back toward me, and growled, "What … happened … to … my … crew?"

His tremors returned. "The two girls?"

I pinched harder. "Yes, the two girls."

"They went to the training camp. They're going to join the SS Squad."

"Then you're going to lead me there."

Oz scowled. "In your dreams. I was told to find some information here. They trust me enough to let me leave the camp. I don't want to mess up my assignment."

"You already messed it up. You let me sneak in and attack you. And what were you looking for in that office?"

"None of your business."

"None of my business? This is my ship!" I wrapped my fingers around his neck. "Do you want me to shock you again?"

His stare turned fiery. "You won't be able to."

"What makes you say …" Heat rose to my face. Something sizzled. I looked down. My shirt smoked, and tiny sparks began eating away the hemline.

I flexed my biceps and sent a charge into his throat. The jolt knocked him out of the navigator's chair. While he writhed and moaned on the floor, I batted the sparks until they died and the smoke cleared. "What are you? Some kind of firestarter?"

He sat up and wrapped his arms around his knees, panting. "How did … you do that?"

"Do what? You mean, shock you?"

"Well, that, too, but how did you keep me from burning you? Most people's clothes catch fire and they have to roll on the ground to put it out."

"So you *are* a firestarter. Were you born here on Gamma Five?"

He nodded, still breathing heavily.

"Maybe the shock weakened you." I stepped closer to him and set a fist on my hip. "Listen, Oz, we can keep doing this the hard way, or we can do it the easy way. If you fight me, I'll light you up again. If you cooperate, you can avoid more pain. Just lead me to my crew, and we'll get along fine."

His brow lifted. "So I don't need to tell you what I was doing in that office?"

"Well, yeah, you need to spill that story, too."

As his respiration slowed to normal, he looked up at me as if contemplating his options. Maybe he was thinking that taking me to the training camp would be a good way to get me captured and him released. And that danger did exist. I would have to be careful. But not going after Crystal and Zoë wasn't an option.

"No." He shook his head. "I'm not taking you there."

I blinked. "What? Why not?"

"You'll get captured, and I don't want that to happen."

I huffed. "Right. Like you're starting to care about me."

"That's not it at all. I mean, I know your reputation. Some say you're a pirate, and you deserve to be executed, but others think you're just a kid who's been influenced by pirating parents. Stories about what you did in the Delta system are going around, and once they find out you're a Starborn, they'll give you the choice to join the SS Squad."

"What's wrong with that?"

His pinch-nosed scowl returned. "I don't want a filthy pirate in our group."

"Listen, Mr. SS snob." I clutched his shirt around the squad logo, jerked him to his feet, and pulled him nearly eye to eye, making him stand on his tiptoes. "You're going to take me to the training camp, or your head's going to turn into a strobe light. Got it?"

He nodded rapidly.

I released his shirt and pushed him back. "On the way, you can tell me what you were doing in the office."

He shrugged. "You won't know if I'm lying or not."

"Good point. I'll wait till we're with Crystal. Then I'll make you talk. You can't lie to her."

"Whatever."

I looked at Sonya's console and spoke out loud instead of typing. "Sonya, can we take the same path out that you took to get in?"

She replied vocally. "Negative. As you could have read in the report if you had bothered to do so, the ship caused a collapse in the tunnel we traversed. That is why our captors left the ship here. There was no easy way out."

I opened a drawer under her console and found the translator earbud. "Did they leave a rover?"

"Negative. That is also in the report."

I pinched the bud and inserted it in my ear. "What about weapons?"

"Negative. They took all handheld and ship-based weapons, including the photon torpedoes. You could have learned that from the report as well."

"Okay. Don't pop a chip." I patted the laser blaster fastened to my belt, more to warn Oz than to inform Sonya. "At least I have this."

"And your cocky attitude," Sonya said. "I don't think you'll ever run out of ammunition for that weapon."

"Thanks. I'll take that as a compliment."

"It was not intended to be a—"

"Hush, Sonya. Turn off the lights when I leave." I nodded toward the ramp. "Lead the way, Oz." As he walked down the ramp, I followed close behind, relit the flashlight, and shone the beam in front of him.

Perdantus flew to my shoulder and chirped quietly, "I have nothing to report."

When we reached ground level, I aimed the flashlight at the Nebula Nine's rover—room for only a driver. We had to walk instead of taking it to the camp. Since there seemed to be no guards around and since the rover wouldn't respond to anyone but me, it would probably be safe.

Oz turned to the left and walked into another tunnel, smaller in all dimensions, forcing us to travel single file and prompting me to lower my head to keep from bumping into protrusions from the ceiling.

"How long does it take to get to the camp?" I asked.

"About twenty minutes. The SS leaders took your two rovers, so I'm sure they got there quicker."

I imagined Crystal and Zoë riding in the rovers, one in each, accompanied by a guard. "Two leaders?"

Oz nodded. "A woman named Raven and our training director, Morales. We all call him Moe."

As we continued walking, the tunnel's angle of descent slowly steepened. We turned into a side tunnel to the left, then into another to the right, a wider one this time with a higher ceiling. From each side, odd noises emanated from the dirt walls, like the sound of gnawing and chewing—pretty spooky in the cool darkness. "Any idea what's making that noise?"

"Excavations in other tunnels." Oz's voice sounded a bit labored, though we hadn't walked very far, and everything was either flat or downhill.

"I don't see any support beams," I said. "How do they keep the walls from collapsing?"

"The excavators know what they're doing."

"Do they use shovels? Pickaxes?"

"Claws and teeth."

The description raised a reminder of the Montons I read about. "Some kind of animal?"

"Of course. I said claws and teeth." His tone took on a sarcastic bite. "No wonder you captain a ship. You're brilliant."

"Yet, you're my prisoner. What does that say about *your* brilliance?"

"It says that I won't be your prisoner for long. You're walking right into our camp, and you don't have any idea what you're going to do when you get there. I'm brilliant enough to let you be that stupid."

"I guess we'll see about that." I stayed quiet for a while, mainly because he was right about one thing. I didn't have any idea what I was going to do. I had to decide when the time came. Maybe my sisters' strategy made sense, to learn what the SS Squad was all about from the inside.

After about fifteen more minutes, a glow shone ahead, growing brighter with every step. I shut the flashlight off, reattached it to my belt, and halted. "Is that light coming from the training camp?"

He nodded. "This tunnel ends at a ledge that overlooks the camp. It's completely fenced in, and you have to hike down a switchback trail to get to the gate."

"Guards at the gate, I assume."

"Of course."

"To keep intruders out, or to keep the trainees in?"

Oz shrugged. "Both, I guess. Some of the trainees don't want to be there."

"But you do. That's why they gave you your assignment."

"Right." He pointed at himself with a thumb. "I get special privileges because I do what I'm told. And now I'm supposed to be back for dinner and bed. That's why I decided not to resist leading you here. When you get chained to a bed in the dorm, Moe will probably give me merit points for capturing you."

I laughed under my breath. "As if you could." No longer needing a guide, I walked on. "See you at the training camp, Oz."

"Wait." He hustled to catch up and walked behind me, now puffing as if out of breath. "Do you have a plan?"

"Nope. I'm stupid, remember?"

"I didn't really mean that. You have to be smart to be a ship's captain. And you'd be stupid to tell me about your plan. So I guess I'll just watch and learn."

"That's the smartest thing I've heard you say yet." I picked up the pace and soon came to the end of the tunnel, a ledge to a precipice that plunged fifty meters or so to a circular expanse of fenced flat ground, most of it sodded, probably artificial grass in this subterranean environment. Still, bright lights embedded in the ceiling could be growth lamps, allowing real grass to survive.

To the left of the fence, ruts marred an open field of dirt, about a third of the size of the circular fenced area. Maybe construction equipment once sat there, but how it got out was a mystery, though it could have been dismantled and removed piece by piece.

Oz caught up and stood next to me, pointing at a path to the left. "That way. It's pretty steep. If you're not careful, it's easy to trip and fall."

I craned my neck to look at Perdantus. "This might be a good time for us to part company for a while. It'll be better if they don't know that I have a feathered ally."

He fluttered his wings. "What shall I do while I'm waiting for you to return?"

"Just hang around. Stay out of sight. Watch for chances to help." I rubbed his belly with a finger. "Think you'll be able to find something to eat?"

"I saw some crickets that looked tasty. I'll be fine."

"Good. I'll see you soon."

He flew from my shoulder and into the darkness behind me.

"I don't understand that bird's language," Oz said, "but I can tell he's super smart."

"That he is." I waved a hand toward the path. "Lead the way."

He walked down the narrow slope, and I followed. When the path switched back in the opposite direction, we continued, the cliff a few centimeters to one side and a sheer drop the same distance on the other. As before, Oz's respiration became labored. He didn't appear to be overweight or out of shape, just tired.

While watching the camp for any sign of movement, I glanced at the cliff face every few seconds. I needed a place to hide my blaster so I could retrieve it later. No sense in just letting them take it from me when I arrived.

Soon, a crevice in the wall came into view a few steps ahead. Since another turn in the path was coming up, and Oz would see me, I had to make my move without falling farther behind. Keeping my pace constant, I lifted my shirt, pulled the blaster from the holster, and set it in the crevice without a pause.

When Oz made the turn, he glanced up at me, but I kept my face expressionless. He marched on without a word. Soon, we arrived at the bottom of the cliff and walked to a gate, wide enough for two rovers to pass through side by side.

A guardhouse with an open door stood to the left of the gate where a uniformed man sat on a stool, blankly staring through a window at the grassy yard surrounded by the chain-link fence. When we arrived, I cleared my throat. "Hello."

He jerked, nearly falling off the stool. When he saw me, his mouth dropped open, then he squinted at Oz. "Did you bring a visitor, Oswald?"

"Nope." Oz gestured toward me. "Tell him."

I squared my shoulders. "I'm a Starborn, and I volunteer to be on the SS Squad."

12

"Volunteer?" The guard walked out of the guardhouse and looked me over. "What Starborn power do you have?"

I flexed to charge my hands. Electricity again arced from finger to finger. "I can shock people by touching them." I let the power die away and pointed a thumb over my shoulder at Oz. "Ask him. He felt it. I ran into him in my ship." I turned toward Oz and gave him a warning glare that he had better play along or he would be sorry.

"Yeah," Oz said. "I didn't announce myself when I boarded, so she let me have it. She really packs a punch."

"Your ship?" the guard said. "Why did you fly here?"

"I heard about the training camp so I landed close by. I figured it had to be big, easy to find. But if not for Oz, I would never have found it."

"Is that a weapons belt?" The guard lifted the hem of my shirt, revealing the belt.

"Yeah. Just a flashlight, though. I guessed weapons wouldn't be allowed."

"Most of you Starborn kids *are* weapons." The guard stepped back into his station and pressed a button. The gate rolled to the right on a set of wheels. "Oswald, take her to Raven. She'll decide what to do with her."

Oz set a hand on my back. "This way."

We walked together across the field toward a glass-and-metal building at the opposite side of the complex, shuffling across real grass, proof that the lights in the ceiling were enough to provide for growth. A sign above the building's door read, "Administration."

Oz whispered, "All right. I see what you're up to. You'll get in good with Raven and Moe and then try to escape with your crew. Smart. But you'll never make it. Guards are on duty all the time. Escape is impossible."

"Thanks for the warning."

"Anyway, the admin building has a couple of offices and sleeping quarters for the adults. The infirmary is there, too. We have a full-time nurse, and a doctor comes in to give us checkups once in a while." Oz pointed toward a barracks-like building to the right, a one-story wooden structure, maybe sixty meters across with multiple windows along the front and at the center. "That's the dorm and commons area. No one's in there right now. It's dinner time." He nodded toward a building to the left of the dorm and to the right of the admin building. "In the mess hall."

That one-story building, about half as wide as the dorm, displayed several windows across the front. From inside, quite a number of boys and girls watched us as we walked, some pointing.

Hoping to catch a glimpse of my sisters, I looked from window to window, but no familiar faces appeared.

When we arrived at the admin building, Oz opened the door, waved me inside to a waiting area in front of a counter, and followed. A thirtyish woman with shoulder-length jet-black hair that matched her black long-sleeved SS polo, rose from a seat behind the counter and smiled. "Well, who do have we here, Oz? The guard called me and said she volunteered, but he didn't know her name."

Oz gestured for me to answer, probably because he didn't know if I wanted to give her my real name. Since they could easily learn my identity, I decided to go for broke. I hoped to be gone before they could report me to Camille. "My name is Megan Willis."

The woman tapped her chin with a finger, touching her skin near a small mole. "Megan Willis. Why does that name sound familiar?"

I shrugged. "I guess it's pretty common."

She extended a hand over the counter. "I'm Raven, the training camp administrator."

I shook her hand but said nothing. Raven was the name of the woman who came to guide my sisters here. Did she have some kind of power over them? I couldn't detect any vibe from her at all.

Raven drew her hand back. "I called the training officer. He'll be out in a minute. He's sending a message to the admiral to get approval for you to join, but it'll take a while for her to reply. We heard she went to the Alpha system."

I kept a straight face. Again, I had to rely on escaping with my sisters in a hurry. But since the training officer hadn't heard my name yet, he couldn't relay it to Camille. Maybe she wouldn't order me to be put in irons right away. Still, if the officer told her about a volunteer showing up out of the blue, she would be suspicious, especially after what I did to her ship.

An office door opened at the far wall, and a man strolled out. Dressed in a uniform similar to Oz's, he walked toward the front with square shoulders atop a trim, toned body, maybe two meters tall. His bronzed skin made him look like the humans I had seen on Alpha Three, heavily tanned because of the sun-drenched lands there.

Smiling, he opened a gate at the end of the counter, walked into the waiting area, and grabbed my hand without waiting for me to extend it. "I'm glad to meet such a brave young woman. I'm Ashton Morales. All the trainees call me Moe."

I firmed my grip. "Megan Willis."

He drew back, his mouth dropping open. "*The* Megan Willis? The fabled pirate? Conqueror of the gray fox, Admiral Dwight Fairbanks?"

"Um …" I folded my hands behind my back. Hearing the admiral's given name for the first time felt odd somehow. "Yeah. I guess so."

Oz stared at me with wide eyes, but he stayed quiet.

Raven gave me an exaggerated nod. "Now I remember where I heard your name. We brought two of your crew members here because they were flying a pirate ship without a captain. When I learned that they're Starborn, I invited them to join us."

"Your abilities are already legendary," Moe said. "Almost mythical. Spreading throughout the galaxy like a bard's epic tale. And now you want to volunteer for us? Why?"

I shifted my weight from foot to foot, unsure of how to respond to this surprise welcome. "During my journeys I saw a lot of child slave trafficking, and I want to do whatever it takes to stop it. But how in blazes can one girl do that by herself? I figured if I could add my gifts to those of others like me, maybe we could make a difference as a team."

Moe pointed at me. "There it is. One of my favorite words. Team." He clapped his hands. "You got that right, Megan. We're a team. And our mission is to purge the galaxy of every evil plaguing every creature, no matter what the species. And child slave trafficking is definitely on that list. The SS Squad, because of our team's youthfulness, is uniquely qualified to—"

"Moe," Raven said with a scolding tone, "your motivational speech isn't needed. She volunteered."

"Oh." He cleared his throat. "Right."

Oz leaned close and whispered, "You sure pushed his buttons."

I concealed a smile. Maybe this wouldn't be as hard as I thought. But I had to watch out for Raven. She was likely involved with my crew's capture, which meant that she lied about not recognizing me. She might be my biggest obstacle.

"Back to business." Moe walked to the entry door and held it open. "Let's go meet the others."

We walked out into the yard just as two parallel lines of kids exited the mess hall. Dressed in black pants and long-sleeved black shirts under forest-green backpacks, they marched in sync toward the dorm, their arms and legs pumping in perfect rhythm.

I scanned the lines and found Crystal and Zoë marching side by side. Their heads pointed forward, but I caught Crystal glancing my way.

Moe joined Oz and me and gestured toward the dorm. "Megan, let's get you moved in. I'm sure we can arrange for you to bunk close to your crewmates."

As we walked toward the building, though not in a synced march, I imagined myself joining a parade like that. It sickened my stomach. Conforming to robotic obedience was far from my normal mode of operation. I couldn't tolerate being a performance monkey. Still, if it meant rescuing my sisters and figuring out how to stop Camille's plot, whatever it was, maybe I could be a monkey for a while.

When we arrived, we climbed three wooden steps to the building's door. I glanced down to the side of the stairs. Might there be a crawlspace under the building? The first floor's elevated position gave me reason to think so. A quick scan revealed the answer—a square panel at ground level, a latch securing it. Good to know.

We walked into a room with tables, chairs, and sofas placed here and there. Several boys and girls stared at me from their seats, some with books and laptops or computer pads in front of them. A closed door to each side appeared to lead to the rest of the building, but there were no windows to provide a peek. I scanned the starers for a familiar face but found none.

"This is the common area." Moe gestured to each side with a finger. "Girls' dorm to the left, and boys' dorm to the right." He looked at Oz. "You can go to the mess hall and see what you can find for dinner, then come to my office to report."

"Yes sir." Oz hustled out. Through the window, I followed his progress toward the mess hall, a slow pace and a hand on his chest. Maybe he was even weaker than I thought.

Moe set a hand on my back and led me to the left. "Let's find you a bunk." He knocked on the girls' dorm door. "It's Moe. When everyone is presentable, open the door."

As scuffling sounds and whispers emanated from the room, Moe smiled at me. "I don't go in there often. Raven does surprise inspections, so it's not like they're trying to hide anything."

I nodded but said nothing. A few seconds later, the door opened outward a crack, revealing a girl with closely cropped dark hair and bright green eyes, maybe a centimeter taller than me.

Moe nodded. "Good evening, Riddle. May I enter?"

"Of course." Her face expressionless, Riddle swung the door and spread an arm. "Come in."

"Follow me, Megan." Moe led the way along an aisle, two rows of bunkbeds on each side. After passing three sets of bunks, he stopped at a fourth. To the left, Crystal sat on a top bunk with Zoë on the bottom, both still dressed in their SS uniforms. They looked at me without a hint of recognition.

Moe gestured toward me. "I brought your friend, Megan. Don't you have anything to say to her?"

Crystal huffed. "*Used* to be our friend. We're not friends with pirate filth."

"Right," Zoë said. "Megan was leading us down a path of destruction. Now that we're here, we can battle the evil forces that possessed her to do so much harm to our cause. All rebels are trash."

Moe set a hand on his chest. "Hey, it's me. Not Raven. And besides, Megan's here voluntarily. She wants to join us."

Crystal's brow lifted. "Oh. Well, that's all right, then." She pointed at the bunks across from her. "No one's sleeping in either of those."

"Perfect." Moe waved toward the bunk. "There you go, Megan. I'll have Riddle bring you linens, clothing, and toiletries."

"Thank you, Moe." I climbed onto the bunk and faced Crystal and Zoë. When the door closed, I hopped to the floor and whispered to them with a hiss, "That pirate filth and path-of-destruction bilge you two vomited better be an act."

"Blazes, Megan," Crystal said. "Cool your blasters. Of course it was an act. We have to be convincing. They teach us to spew that kind of … of …"

"Verbiage?"

"That's a Willis word. I'll go with robotic rubbish. We quote their mantras when we have to."

Zoë rose and huddled close. "Acting like we're SS zombies helped us learn a lot, but we have to be careful about talking. Too many eyes and ears around. We're already being watched."

I looked toward the entry door. Riddle stood there with her arms crossed, her stare on me. She didn't appear to be buying my quick change from enemy to ally. I refocused on my sisters. "I can't wait that long. Once Camille gets word that I'm here, she'll storm right in and expose me. She won't believe my …" I drew quotation marks in the air. "Repentance from my evil ways."

"You think she'd kill you?" Zoë asked.

I shook my head. "Put me in the brig, maybe. I think she'll use me to lure my father into a trap, but I'm not sure. She's a crafty witch."

Zoë sat on the floor and gestured for Crystal and me to join her. "Let's get us all up to date."

For the next several minutes, we traded stories. While Crystal and Zoë told about their adventures, I pulled out Sonya's printed account and read her commentary, which added quite a bit of humor, such as, "When Crystal commanded a port turn, I knew she meant starboard, so I initiated a starboard turn, which turned out to be right, and by *right*, I mean correct."

At the bottom of the second page, Sonya included an odd statement that I read silently. *The passcode is 4NN31SMYH34RT.* I kept it to myself. Since the statement didn't seem to relate to anything in the report, I would have to ask Sonya what it meant. Obviously she didn't want to explain while Oz was there. No wonder she kept harassing me about reading the report.

Putting the passcode out of my mind for the moment, I told my harrowing tale. Crystal, because of her obsession with romance novels, seemed most interested in what Oliver said to me, but I shut her down.

"Hush, Crystal," I said, rolling my eyes. "I don't have time for that nonsense."

"Okay, then, spoilsport, back to business. The most important thing we learned is that the SS Squad isn't some kind of army they plan to use to take over the galaxy. It just means Special Service Squad. They're kids. Special kids, yeah, and some of them can kick serious butt, and some have creepy powers, but they're still just kids. No way can they ever be an army that'll take over anything more than a video arcade."

"Or a pizza joint," Zoë added. "They scarf anything by the shovelful. They're like food-frenzy furnaces."

I scrunched my brow. "Then why was Captain Tillman so worried about them? He said billions of lives were at stake."

Crystal lowered her voice further. "We have a clue. They take some of the kids aside and test them. Since I've been here, they've taken a group of four. Only three came back."

"So someone's missing?"

Crystal nodded. "I talked to one of them, a girl named India. She was weak and scared, so I didn't get much out of her, but she said they injected her with something and sent her into a tunnel and told her to look for something, but that's as much info as I could get before India started crying. Then Riddle barged in and told me to mind my own business. They're not allowed to talk about the test."

I clutched my shirt around my locket. "Since Captain Tillman wanted my dragon's eye to stop the SS Squad, the ruby and the test are probably related." I gestured with my hands as I explained. "Here's one theory. Every Starborn has a connection to their source of power. Maybe this test is a way to get them to use their connection to search for the source. We also know that Camille wants to catch my father. I learned that he's got the strongest connection to the source of power."

"So your father would give her a short cut?" Zoë asked.

"Could be. And maybe Captain Tillman thought the dragon's eye would lead him to the source before Camille could get to it. If she got a hold of it, it might give her enough control to kill billions of people if they don't bow to her wishes."

Crystal and Zoë stared at me wide-eyed. "Okay, Sister," Zoë said. "If you say so. But that sounds too twisted to be true. Is Camille actually using kids as guinea pigs and letting some of them die?"

I shrugged. "Maybe not all of them die. I saw two SS kids at the docking station at Alpha One. It could be that the weakest Starborn kids couldn't help her find the source so she's using them to twist a few arms to make her a bossy admiral. But I know some do die. Remember, I found dead kids in the Nebula One, and Camille's name was on the coffin tags."

"Right," Crystal said, nodding. "In the same room where they were stowing the glowsap, probably to sell it to the highest bidder. Murdering kids for profit."

Zoë clenched a fist. "That's serial-killer evil. We have to take her down."

"Exactly," I said, "but first, I have a question. You mentioned that Raven came to the Astral Dragon and brought you to this camp. Between the two of you, you could've strapped her to the infirmary bed and made her think she had the plague. But I guessed you went willingly because you wanted to see what was going on here." I cocked my head. "Or am I wrong?"

Crystal and Zoë glanced at each other, then looked at me. "Sort of right," Zoë said. "And sort of wrong."

Crystal nodded. "It's hard to explain. I asked her to look into my eyes, hoping she would spill some secrets, but when she looked, it didn't affect her at all. It was pretty embarrassing when she asked why I wanted her to look. My own brain felt kind of twisted, and I couldn't think of a single excuse."

Zoë raised a hand. "And I couldn't move even a hair on her head. My power's back now, but I want to test it later next time I'm close to her."

I pressed my lips together. "Weird. It sounds like she could drain your power somehow."

"Yeah," Crystal said. "Like she's an anti-Starborn."

Riddle walked up and tossed a backpack and a duffle bag onto my bunk. "Here's your stuff and something to eat. You'll have to take your bracelets off. They're not standard issue."

I began unfastening one of them. "Sure. Not a problem."

"Lights out in one hour." She turned and walked away.

I pushed the bracelets into the backpack. A wrapped sandwich and water bottle lay inside, but I didn't feel hungry at the moment. I lowered my voice again to a furtive whisper. "Do they dim the security lights outside when you go to bed?"

Zoë nodded. "It gets pretty dark out there, but they have a searchlight that sweeps the grounds all night long."

"Okay. I'll get a quick nap now, then at lights-out time, I'm going back to the Dragon."

"Why?" Crystal asked. "She's buried. No way out."

I leaned closer to them. "Couple of things I have to check on. I can't just leave the Nebula Nine out in the open, and I think Sonya's got some intel she couldn't spill while Oz was around."

"And how're you going to get over the fence and past the guards?" Zoë asked.

"The guards won't be a problem. Trust me."

Crystal heaved a sigh. "All right, Miss Mysterious, but let me tell you one thing. Don't trust Mr. Gung-Ho-Yay-Team."

"You mean Moe?"

"Right. He's a fence walker. He kisses up to Raven when he needs to, and then two seconds later, he's the kids' best buddy, or tries to be. You know, trust-me-because-I'm-your-coach kind of guy."

"Do you think he would rat me out if he saw me do something I'm not supposed to?"

"Yep. I wouldn't trust him."

I nodded. "Got it."

"Anything we can do while you're gone?" Zoë asked.

I paused for a moment. So far it seemed like Raven was the highest-ranked person here, and she probably wasn't lax about security. But maybe Moe had some intel we could find. "See if you can get the key to Moe's office. I want to snoop around in there."

Crystal and Zoë looked at each other for a moment before nodding. "You got it, Sister," Crystal said. "I can hypnotize him while Zoë lifts his keys."

"And do you guys know Oz?"

Crystal narrowed her eyes. "Yeah. Nerdy kid. Sometimes he acts okay, but he's got a short fuse. Won't talk to anyone except Chipmunk."

I lifted my brow. "Chipmunk?"

Zoë smiled. "Everyone likes Chipmunk. Some call him Chip. Younger kid. Really friendly. Probably the most athletic kid here."

"Okay. I'll remember Chipmunk. Maybe he'll be a good ally. But back to Oz. See if you can start up a conversation and find out why he was snooping in my father's office in the Astral Dragon."

Crystal pointed a thumb at herself. "Interrogation is my specialty. I'll get the answers out of his nerdy head."

"Perfect. Thanks." I pulled the uniform from the duffle bag and looked at shorts and a T-shirt at the bottom, probably loose clothes to sleep in. "Where's the washroom?"

Zoë pointed toward a door at the back of the dorm. "Two showers. Four toilets. I'm surprised they have running water here. Someone sunk some serious money into this place."

"Yeah. Selling glowsap is profitable." I pushed the uniform back into the duffle and carried it to the washroom. After using a toilet and changing into the uniform, including a pair of athletic shoes, I put my stuff into the bag and hurried to my bunk, trying to ignore all the stares from everyone in the dorm. Apparently the gossip network had made me famous … or infamous.

I climbed into my bunk and laid my head on the supplied pillow, thin but serviceable. With the duffle bag at my side, I fell asleep in seconds and dreamed about marching around in a monkey suit that I couldn't take off. In what felt like only a couple of minutes, someone tapped me on the shoulder.

I opened my eyes, but with the lights off, I couldn't see who the tapper was. "Who's there?"

"Crystal," she whispered. "It's two hours past lights out. I would've gotten you up earlier, but I zonked out, too."

"No problem. I needed the sleep." After taking the bracelets, flashlight, and weapons belt from the bag, I quietly rolled out of the bunk and set my feet on the floor, still wearing the supplied shoes.

A searchlight swept across the windows, illuminating Crystal's worried face and Zoë sitting on her bed before continuing its arc around the camp. "Six hours till wake up," Crystal said. "Hurry back."

I put the belt on, slid the flashlight into its holster, and fastened the bracelets on my wrists. "See you soon."

With a little light still filtering through the window, I tiptoed to the door leading to the common area, opened it, and walked out, careful to reclose it quietly. I padded to the exit door and tried the knob, but it wouldn't turn.

I stared at it blankly for a moment, then something clicked. The knob turned by itself, and the door opened outward a few centimeters. I spun. Zoë stood there nearly nose to nose with me, grinning. "I thought you might need a little help."

"Thanks. Good guess."

She extended a backpack. "You forgot to eat, and the pack might come in handy."

"True." I took it and put it on. "Thanks again."

After kissing her forehead, I walked out, closed the door behind me, and scooted down the steps. Crouching next to the stairs, I watched the searchlight beam pass along the chain-link fence line. The high point of the beam's illuminating circle touched the top of the fence while the low point brushed the ground. I would have to run to the fence, climb up one side and down the other, and hustle away, all during the time it took for the beam to make a circuit. And I had to do it all quietly enough to avoid attracting attention.

I visually followed the beam back to a tower where the searchlight sat atop a platform, swiveling slowly. A man stood under the platform in a circular crow's-nest perch, his elbows on the parapet surrounding the nest as he looked out over the yard from about eight feet off the ground. If he was paying attention, he would see me if I made a dash for the gate area, which meant that I had to climb the fence somewhere close to the dorm instead.

When the beam swung toward me, I opened the crawlspace panel, backed into the hole, and closed it. The beam brushed by, piercing my hiding place through gaps around the panel. The moment it passed, I crawled out, refastened the panel, and scampered around to the rear of the building.

The dorm's back wall stood about a meter from the fence, leaving a gap wide enough to walk through. Hiding behind the dorm, I pushed my fingers through the links and felt dirt on the other side. I snapped my flashlight from my belt, flicked it on, and shone it through the fence. A cliff face rose to a dirt ceiling that capped the compound, the same ceiling that held the lights that shone brightly during the camp's daytime hours. Escaping by climbing over the fence here would be impossible, but could the lights be disabled to give us a permanent night or at least a delayed morning? That might be helpful for an escape. Also, since my bracelets seemed to be fully charged, the lights were probably giving them the needed juice.

After putting the flashlight away, I climbed the fence, the dorm building at my back, shielding me from the searchlight. When my head rose higher than the roof, I watched the light as it rotated toward me. The moment arrived, I ducked under it, then quickly climbed the rest of the way.

Hanging on to the fence with one hand, I grabbed my flashlight with the other and shone the beam on the nearest ceiling light. The lamp variety was one I had replaced above the Nebula Nine's bridge a couple of times, but the wiring here seemed strange. An extra box had been attached to the side of the lamp.

I aimed the light directly at the box and squinted to read the label—Remote Detonation Receiver. I sucked in a breath. Someone rigged the ceiling to blow up. If each lamp had a similar bomb attached, the entire camp could get buried by the push of a single button.

With the searchlight beam closing in again, I put the flashlight away and hurried down the fence. Once I settled on the ground, I tried to slow my thudding heart. Of course, the bombs might simply be a way to bury evidence once they were finished with the camp and the kids were safely outside, but the plan might also be to bury the kids themselves and destroy even the living evidence.

Trying to put the thoughts out of my mind, I took a deep breath and exhaled slowly. For now, I had to concentrate on the mission at hand. My only chance to test an escape would be to time the searchlight's circuit, follow behind it at the fence line, and climb the fence close to the switchback path, all without being seen or heard.

While peeking out from behind the dorm, I retrieved my sandwich and began eating as I counted the seconds it took for the light to sweep around, ducking when it passed. By the time I finished the sandwich and bottle of water, I had counted 20 circuits, making me confident that it took 23 seconds for the searchlight to swing all the way around. That seemed doable.

When it passed by again, I ran on tiptoes out to the front of the dorm and followed behind the beam like a mouse trailing a clueless cat. After passing the gate, I stopped at the area in front of the trail, flexed my biceps to charge my legs, and leaped straight up.

As I neared the top of the fence, I slowed but still had enough momentum to clear the horizontal support pole. I grabbed it, swung over to the other side, and dropped. The moment I hit the ground, I bent my knees and rolled to keep from making a loud thud, but I dropped into one of the ruts where a loose metal rod protruded. It rammed into my gut, making me let out an *oomph* before falling to the side.

"What was that?" a man called.

I flattened myself in the rut, my cheek to the ground as I peeked at the tower. The searchlight halted, then swung back toward me. The beam crawled along the field on my side of the fence, getting closer and closer. Although I lay below ground level, I couldn't tell if the beam would pass over me or light me up like a super nova.

The beam halted directly over me. The man called again. "I saw something move."

Another man answered. "Should I go out there?"

A squawk responded, and a dark object appeared between me and the searchlight, its shape impossible to discern in the brightness.

"No. It's just a bird. I wonder how it got down here."

"Who knows? But I guess that's what I heard."

"Yep." The searchlight shifted away and returned to its cycle.

Perdantus landed in the rut next to my cheek. "You had better hurry. It doesn't take long for that light to come back around."

"I know. Thanks for the rescue." With Perdantus flying next to me, I ran to the switchback trail and scampered up the cliff face, staying as low as possible. Each time the beam came around, I stopped and curled into a ball, then after it passed by, I hurried on, listening for a call or an alarm, but no sounds rode up the cliff.

When I reached the top, Perdantus landed on my shoulder. I grabbed my flashlight again and turned it on. "I forgot to get my blaster," I whispered as I backed away from the cliff. "I left it in a recess on that trail."

"Risky to retrieve it," Perdantus said.

"Yeah. I probably won't need it." I retraced my steps toward the Astral Dragon, jogging as quietly as possible, again with Perdantus flying in orbits to keep from getting too far ahead.

Scratching sounds echoed through the tunnels, making it impossible to know where they originated. Oz had mentioned excavators, some kind of animal with claws and teeth. If they were trained to dig these tunnels, maybe they wouldn't pose a threat if I happened to run into one.

Soon, the Astral Dragon lay in view in the flashlight's glow, the front entry ramp still open. I walked in and set the beam on Sonya's console monitor, completely dark—normal, since I told her to turn the lights off. "Hey, I'm back. Anything to report?"

The console stayed dark. No sounds came from any speaker. Perdantus flew in behind me and perched on my console. "Strangely quiet."

"Yeah. Too quiet." I focused again on the monitor. "Sonya, can you hear me?"

Again, she didn't answer.

I opened the access panel under her console and shone the beam inside. No lights blinked. "Someone shut her down completely."

Kneeling, I reached in and flipped her override switch off and then on, but nothing happened. "There's no power at all. I'll check her battery backup."

I crawled in and found the recess where her battery was supposed to be, but it was gone. "Not good." I backed out and strode to my captain's chair. I sat and turned on the console, but it stayed dark.

"I'm checking the engines. I'll be right back." With the flashlight giving me sight, I hustled to the engine room and flipped on the manual ignition switch. Again, everything remained quiet.

I stooped, opened the engine access panel, and shone the beam on the main engine's fusion reactor. The platinum coil that usually protruded from the top had been taken—stolen. Without it, the engine wouldn't be able to cough, much less purr. Such a coil could be replaced, but it was too expensive to keep a spare one in inventory, especially since the coil was designed to work forever.

I straightened and looked around. How could I possibly get replacements for the coil and Sonya's battery? Without at least a battery, I wouldn't be able to figure out the reason for the passcode she gave me. Not only that, obviously someone had come on board since I was last here and sabotaged our power, someone who knew how to knock the Dragon out of commission. Might that person come again?

While trying to mentally trace an intruder's path to the ship, I imagined the damaged landscape on this floating continent. Because of the scant population, it probably had no spaceship parts stores anywhere close. Then, my mental sweep came across the Nebula Nine. It probably had a spare battery, and I could borrow its coil long enough for the Dragon to plow itself out of this hole.

I hustled to the bridge and flashed the beam on Perdantus, still perched on my console. "We need to check on the Nine."

He flew to my shoulder. "Let's hope the rover is where you left it."

I jogged down the ramp and turned into the tunnel we followed to get here. The flashlight beam shone on the rover, exactly where I left it. I accelerated, forcing Perdantus to hop off my shoulder and fly next to me.

When we arrived, I scanned the rover. The top cover had been taken off, and the interior panel that allowed access to the engine had been removed. "That's not promising." I climbed into the seat and spoke to the onboard computer. "Start engine."

Nothing happened.

I groaned. "Now I have to walk all the way to the surface."

Perdantus alit on the dashboard. "I could fly to the Nebula Nine and ask Emerson about the parts you need."

I lifted a finger. "Or I could try to call him with the earbud. I almost forgot about it. But since we're underground, I'm not sure it'll work." I reached into my ear and turned it on. "Emerson, can you hear me?"

Static filled the reply. "I am able to hear you, Captain Willis. The connection appears to be of low quality, but I am able to verify your voice."

"Good. Is everything all right out there?"

"For the time being. A potential intruder tried to board. I was able to keep the person out, but since he or she had what appeared to be a powerful gun, I attempted to raise the shields. They would not engage, and I was also unable to arm our defensive weapons. I suspect sabotage.

Therefore, I made the decision to leave in order to protect the ship from potential damage. I am flying the Nebula Nine at a low altitude in the general area. The ship should be safe for now."

"Wow, Emerson. I wonder how the shields and weapons went offline."

"According to the records, a higher ranking ship sent codes that disabled both systems. Whoever sent the codes knew how to bypass me."

I nodded. "Probably Camille Fairbanks told a local ship how to send the code. I don't think she's had time to get here herself yet. Anyway, the intruder could've destroyed the Nine, but since Camille's also trying to get information, she's not ready to do that yet. That intruder was there to look for intel."

"Your conclusion seems justified by the circumstances."

"Thanks. Listen, does the Nine have a spare battery that'll let me power Sonya on the Astral Dragon?"

"Affirmative. We have two compatible batteries in stock."

"Great. I also need a fusion engine ignition coil. I don't suppose you have one of those."

"Not in inventory, but since the Nebula Nine's engines need it only for ignition, the one we have can be taken as long as the engines are left running."

"Perfect. I can get to our prior landing site in about an hour. How long till you can land the Nine?" I slapped my forehead. "No. Don't say it. You're not authorized to land the ship."

More static filled Emerson's reply, making it barely distinguishable. "You are correct."

I adjusted the earbud. "But you can hover and extend the lower ladder where I can reach it, right?"

This time no reply came through, only static.

"Emerson? Can you hear me?"

Again, only static filled my ear.

"Emerson, I need to verify that you'll hover low and retrieve me with the rescue ladder."

When he didn't reply, I banged a fist against the rover. "Blazes!"

Perdantus looked at me, his head tilted. "I assume you did not get an answer. Would it be advisable for you to go out there anyway?"

I sighed. "It's an hour out and an hour back. If I knew I could get the parts, I would go, but I'm already risking a lot being here at all."

"I understand. It is often a poor choice to take on risk that cannot be estimated in the hope of gaining something that cannot be guaranteed."

"And it's a risk I don't really have to take right now. I can try again some other time."

"So you'll go back to the camp?" Perdantus asked.

I nodded. "Reluctantly."

With my flashlight aimed at the ground in front of us, we walked in the tunnel leading back to the camp. Along the way, I told Perdantus about Sonya's passcode, but he had no ideas to add that might solve the riddle.

When I again heard the scratching sounds, I stopped and listened. "Do you hear that?"

"I do. I will fly back and forth quickly to learn where the sound is loudest." He hopped up and flew a few dozen meters forward to the farthest limit of my light beam, then back about halfway. At that point, he flew in a tight circle. "Over here, Megan."

I hurried to the spot and listened. Yes, it was much louder here.

He landed on the ground and pointed a wing toward the side wall to the left. "I believe the sound is coming from that direction."

I walked to the wall and stood with my ear against it. The scratching grew louder and louder, like it was getting closer. Just as I took a step back, a wave of dirt crashed over me, knocking me flat. Something thumped on my chest. I wheezed a loud oomph. Then the pressure lifted, leaving me buried.

14

"Megan!" Perdantus called. "Are you all right?"

I spat a mouthful of dirt. "I think so."

As a series of grunts reached my ear, my translator provided the words. "So sorry. I did not expect anyone to be there."

I rose to a sitting position, pushing dirt out of the way, and pointed the flashlight beam toward the voice. A hairy four-legged creature, an exact duplicate of the Monton photo I had seen earlier, stood nearby, blinking its yellow eyes at me. Now that I noticed its tiny ears, it looked like a larger and darker version of the capybaras we had on Alpha One.

It spoke with clicks and low whistles. "Ah. A human. Then you probably will not be able to understand me."

"I understand you," I said, still spitting flecks of dirt. "I can't speak your language, though. I hope you understand Humaniversal."

"After all the orders your kind have barked at me, I certainly do. At first humans sounded like pigs squealing, the way they carried on. Now they are like clothed apes that …" He turned away. "Never mind. I am sorry. I should not spout my feelings like that. I hope I did not offend you. And I am sure I stepped on you. So sorry. It was not intentional."

"No worries." I set the flashlight on the floor to give us light, rose to my feet, and brushed dirt off my new SS uniform. "I'm not hurt or offended. But don't confuse me with the humans who are ordering you to dig these tunnels. I'm not one of them."

"Your uniform says otherwise." He aimed his nose at my shirt and snuffled. "That design is the mark of evil."

I touched the SS logo. "Do you mean this?"

"Yes. I will wager it was fashioned by the devil himself as a branding iron."

Perdantus flew from the ground to my shoulder. "I don't understand this creature's words, but I can tell that he is sincere. My negotiation skills have given me a lot of experience in evaluating honesty."

I laughed under my breath. "Yeah. Brutally honest."

The Monton squinted. "You are talking to a bird."

"Yes. He's my friend. Perdantus."

"I rarely see birds, much less talk to them. I do not trust them. Something about their beady little eyes."

At this point, I was glad Perdantus couldn't understand this Monton's jabber. He might have countered that Montons have beady little eyes themselves. I clutched my shirt. "Listen, I'm wearing this because I'm a spy in their ranks. I agree that it's a symbol of evil, and I'm hoping you'll help me figure out what they're doing."

The squint tightened. "A spy, you say?"

I nodded. "I've already been accepted by their training officer."

"But if you do not know what they are doing, why do you agree with me that they are evil?"

"Because I know their top boss, Camille Fairbanks. She is pure evil. And since she's behind what they're doing with the kids, it has to be evil."

"Camille Fairbanks. I know that name quite well. And speaking of names, mine is Massenbrook. What is yours?"

"Megan."

"Well, Megan, since you dared to call Camille Fairbanks evil, you have convinced me that you are, indeed, a spy." Massenbrook let out a chuckling sound that my earbud failed to translate. "I heard that humans refer to spies as moles. When I asked someone what a mole is, the answer made me laugh. It is an appropriate label. We underground diggers are well aware of the doings of those who dwell outside of our tunnels."

"Then will you help me?"

"As much as I can." His squint relaxed. "What are you trying to find out?"

"Why are you digging? Are you looking for something? Do you know what they're doing with the SS children? Since you know the bosses here are evil, why are you working for them?" I took a breath. "I guess that's all for now."

"Your last question is the easiest to answer." A low growl spiced his words. "The monstrous humans have taken control of my community on Astatos. They sent most of the adult males here to Ragua to work as slaves while the adult females take care of the little ones. If I refuse to work, the humans will kill my family."

Heat flashed in my cheeks. "That's terrible!"

"Yes. My mate and I have seventeen cubs. That would be seventeen murders of innocent Montons. Eighteen if they also kill my mate."

I reached forward to pet his head but pulled back, having no idea if that gesture would violate Monton personal space. "Let me help you. I'm here to destroy their work, to stop whatever they have planned."

"How can you be so sure if you do not even know what they're doing? And, pardon me for saying so, but you are so young. So small. I think your kind would call you a little girl. How could you defeat these monsters? And, not to be rude, but I do not think your bird friend will be much help."

I pressed a thumb against my chest. "I already defeated Camille's husband, I took over a Nebula series starship, and rescued slave kids in a distant system. I have battled tyrants all across the galaxy. You'll just have to trust me."

He snuffled again, louder this time. "No, I don't have to trust you. If the monsters learn that I worked against them, my family could die."

"They'll never know. It's just you and me."

He looked at Perdantus. "And the bird."

"Yes, and the bird, but he is completely loyal to me. I would trust him with my life. In fact, I already have multiple times."

Perdantus puffed out his chest but stayed quiet.

"Think about it," I continued, taking a step closer. "When Camille and her goons are finished using you, they'll probably kill you and your family anyway. They won't want anyone left alive who could tell what they did. No matter what you do, you'll all be dead. Your only hope is to try something different." I took a chance and set a hand on his head. "Massenbrook, I know you're willing to sacrifice for your little ones, but if all your sacrifices are futile, what good are they?" I stroked behind his ear. "Let me come beside you to help you defeat these monstrous slavers once and for all."

Massenbrook looked me over for a moment before replying. "You're quite a talker. I'll give you that. And convincing. You don't sound like a little girl at all."

I drew my hand back. "Then what do you say?"

"I suppose you're right. I don't see any end to the threats if I don't take the risk."

"Exactly."

"Very well. I will tell you what I know." He skittered on powerful, short legs to the hole he had broken open at the side of the tunnel. "My fellow Montons and I are searching for a power source that the humans want. For their part, the humans are testing gifted children they call Starborn who have some kind of mysterious connection to the source. I don't know what those tests do, but the humans are getting worried about the timing, as if something important will happen at Glandel's full phase."

"Glandel. I assume that's the name of your moon."

"Yes. One of two moons that will become full quite soon. The humans say if they can't find the source by then, they will have to remove the Starborn they have and begin collecting new ones."

I gasped, though more for effect than surprise. "Remove them? Does that mean kill them?"

"Knowing these monsters, I would assume so."

I nodded. "Okay. Go on."

"The humans built their camp here because the Starborn children say they feel the power source close by. Since the sensation never changes even as the continent drifts to other locations, the source must be at a fixed point in the ground somewhere."

"Why did they force you Montons into slave labor?"

He reared up to his hind legs and showed me his claws—long and pointed. "We are the best diggers in this star system. We can create a tunnel in hours that would take humans days to excavate. And we don't have to build any supports. We have a gland that secretes a liquid that seals the dirt in the ceilings and walls in place. We can either squirt it directly or let it ooze into our fur, and simply rubbing our fur against the dirt will instantly harden it. That is the more efficient method, because we don't have to stop digging to apply it."

I noticed a bulging sac near his belly—semitransparent and dark gray. Maybe that contained the sealant.

"Even with all of these abilities," he continued, "we have no way to sense the power source, but we believe we have a way to know if we're getting closer." Massenbrook lifted a pebble with his claws. "We think the power alters the soil—the color, the texture, the sheen. The differences are invisible to anyone but us Montons. So when we detect changed particles, we follow the changes, as if we were dogs chasing a scent, but all too often we will come to a boulder and have to dig around it, and then we lose the trail."

"That sounds frustrating."

"It is, especially since we realize that the power source might have once permeated the ground and later contracted into a single place, leaving remnants of its power scattered everywhere. That would make our efforts difficult, at best, because every lead could be nothing more than the source shedding its influence more heavily in one place, only to lessen its effects afterward. For example, just now I was following an especially promising trail when I ran into you." He scratched around in the dirt that had buried me. "This is strange. The particles here have been completely altered. They are shining brightly, as if …" He looked at me. "The power source is you."

"I can explain that." I lifted the chain and showed him my locket. "I carry a dragon's eye."

As I gave him a brief history of the gem and how it works, he listened carefully, grunting "Okay" and "I see" at times. Perdantus added a few facts that I translated to Humaniversal for Massenbrook, but I didn't reveal that the ghost of my great-grandfather lived in the gem.

When I finished, I dropped the locket back in place. "So, you see, I am *a* power source but not *the* power source. I get the impression that it existed on this planet long before I got here."

"What if they find out what you are?" Massenbrook asked. "Would they use you instead of the source they're looking for?"

I shrugged. "I don't know. I haven't figured out why they want the source."

Perdantus whispered, "His countenance has changed. What did he say?"

When I translated Massenbrook's question in Humaniversal, I added in Alpha One, "What does his countenance tell you, Perdantus?"

"That it's time for you to find an excuse to leave."

I gave Perdantus a long stare. I recognized his expression—I was in danger. And, as always, I trusted his judgment. I refocused on Massenbrook. "Um … listen. I have to get back to the camp. They're going to miss me soon, and I need to get some sleep before—"

He grabbed my wrist with his clawed hand. "No. Come with me. We can find the source of power together."

I flexed my biceps and sent a shock into him through the bracelet. He squealed and jerked his hand back. "What did you do to me?"

"Serves you right. You shouldn't grab me like that."

"I apologize. I was excited about finding the power source with your help. This has been a long and torturous task for me."

I massaged my wrist. The changes in this Monton's attitude were coming too quickly to believe.

"Whatever his words meant, Megan," Perdantus said, "they were a dodge, a false attempt to regain your confidence."

I replied again in Alpha One. "Yeah, I picked that up. This meeting is over. Let's hope I can run faster than he can." I took a deep breath and shouted in Alpha One, "Fly!"

The moment Perdantus leaped off my shoulder, I plucked the flashlight from the ground, spun in the camp's direction, and took off at top speed. When I reached the first turn, I careened around the corner and glanced back, sweeping the flashlight beam all around. Massenbrook was nowhere in sight.

I slowed to a jog and whistled for Perdantus. He landed on my shoulder and chirped, "Perhaps he is not a swift runner."

"That's my guess, but I'm going to keep—"

The tunnel wall to my left exploded, sending a blast of dirt across my body. I toppled to the side and landed with a painful thump. I cast the beam toward the new hole in the wall. Massenbrook charged at me, his claws swiping.

I rolled out of the way. He stumbled past me and spun back. Again rearing on his haunches, he pressed the sac on his belly. Black liquid spewed at me. Perdantus flew into the way and blocked the inky jet. The stuff splatted against him, and he fluttered to the ground, flailing his wings.

I charged my legs and slammed my feet into Massenbrook. He crashed against the wall and slumped to the floor. I snatched Perdantus up and ran, one hand gripping the flashlight and the other cradling my heroic friend.

Gasping for breath as I sprinted, I glanced at the gooey mess of feathers and Monton gunk. "Perdantus ... are you ... all right?"

"I can't move. This foul-smelling stuff is stiffening, and it's getting worse."

"I hope it doesn't restrict your breathing."

"It has not as yet, but as the hardening liquid tightens around my body, breathing could become more difficult."

"Then save your breath. I'll see what we can do at the camp."

When I reached the ledge, I snapped the flashlight to my belt and used the illumination from the searchlight to zip down the trail. At the bottom, I sprinted to the fence, charged my legs again, and leaped over the top.

With my free hand, I grabbed a vertical support pole and let it slide through my grip on the way down, slowing my plunge. Although the chain links rattled a bit, the sound wasn't super loud. Maybe no one would notice.

The moment my feet hit the ground, I dashed around the fence line in the same direction as before but on the opposite side of the yard, the searchlight beam only seconds behind me. When I arrived at the dorm, I leaped up the steps, opened the door, and pressed it closed behind me just as the beam passed.

I sighed with relief. Good thing Zoë had left the door unlocked. Smart, as always. But I wasn't so smart. In my rush, I had forgotten to grab the laser blaster from the cliff alcove again. Too late to get it now.

Trying my best to be quiet in spite of my quick breaths, I walked across the common room and tried to open the door, but something blocked it. I looked down. Light from the window cast a dim glow across Crystal as she lay curled on the floor, her head on a pillow.

I crouched close to her and whispered, "I'm back, and I need help."

"Oh. I was waiting for you." She sat up and rubbed her eyes. "What kind of help?"

I showed her Perdantus, now lying stiff and motionless in my hand. "No time to explain except Perdantus got doused with something that's tightening around him, cutting off his breathing."

"We have a healer. Like Oliver." She shot to her feet and opened the dorm door. "No use being quiet. They won't mind helping a bird. Just make up a good story."

She stomped in with me at her heels. "Galena, we have a sick bird. Can you heal him?"

After a few groans drifted around the dim room, a girl called, "I've never healed a bird before, but I'll try."

Crystal rushed to a bunk and waved a hand, hard to see in the dimness. "Megan, over here."

A light passed by, startling me for a moment. I looked at the dorm windows. A shade had been pulled down at each, muting the searchlight and giving the girls some privacy. I followed the call and found Crystal sitting on a bottom bunk with a little wisp of a girl. In the bare glow, her long hair looked like shimmering silver. "Megan," Crystal said, "this is Galena."

"Hi." I sat on Galena's other side and showed her my cupped hands, Perdantus nestled within. The other girls gathered around, including Riddle, her arms crossed, though her expression indicated concern.

Galena laid her small hand over Perdantus, not quite touching him. "Whatever that stuff is that's on him is crushing his bones. Some are already broken. And he can barely breathe." She lifted her hand and looked at me. "I can try to heal the injuries, but we have to get that stuff off him or it'll keep squeezing him. If we can't, he'll be dead soon."

I pinched an edge of the black stuff and gently pulled, but it had hardened like old glue to his feathers. "It's stuck. Does anyone have an ability that can get this stuff loose?"

"Oz," Riddle said, her arms still crossed. "He's a firestarter, and what he does to get a fire going might help, but I don't have a key to their dorm. I could knock and call for him, but he's a stickler for rules. He might not open the door."

From somewhere in the crowd of girls, Zoë called, "I can unlock it. We'll drag him here if we have to."

Zoë and Riddle hurried out of sight.

I set my ear close to Perdantus. The slightest wheeze rose from his motionless body. Whispers of "The poor bird" and "I wonder what that stuff is" and "How did he get down here?" pelted my senses, but I brushed them away. I couldn't deal with any questions right now.

"We're back." Zoë, with a hand around Oz's arm, guided him to the foot of the bed. "There's the bird."

Oz shook free. "All right. All right. I'll take a look." Wearing only gray shorts and a baggy black T-shirt, He knelt in front of us and touched the hardened gunk. "If I burn this off, it'll burn his feathers with it. Super dangerous."

Riddle spoke up from behind Zoë. "You told me once that your brain transforms stuff into something that can burn. Can you transform this stuff without setting it on fire? Maybe then it can be cleaned off."

Murmurs of agreement passed through the crowd.

"It's not as easy as it sounds," Oz said. "Stuff does transform, but it jumps straight to fire in less than a second. I've never done one without the other."

"Maybe …" I brushed a tear from my cheek. "Maybe we can douse his feathers the second they catch on fire."

"And," Galena added, "I can heal whatever gets singed. We just have to be quick with the dousing."

A girl near the edge of the crowd called, "I'll fetch water."

Oz gazed at me with narrowed eyes. "Have you told anyone how you found this bird?"

"Um … no. But does that matter? He needs our help."

He sighed. "I guess you're right. I'll try to help him. But we'll talk later." He cupped his own hands. "Let me have him."

I gently shifted Perdantus to him.

While everyone looked on, Oz stared at Perdantus. In the dimness, Oz's silhouette looked like a statue posed in prayer.

A surge of guilt flooded my brain. I hadn't prayed for Perdantus at all. How could I say I believed in a higher power when I tried to do everything myself without asking for help?

After swallowing to loosen my throat, I whispered, "Please, Astral Dragon … or God, or whatever you want to be called, help Perdantus. He got in the way of that stuff to protect me. He's such a hero, such a loving, sacrificial hero. If anyone deserves to live—"

"Get the water ready," Oz said. "I see smoke."

Zoë knelt next to him, a cup in her hands. Drops of water rose over the lip, drifted to Perdantus, and hovered a few centimeters above him.

Something sizzled. Tiny sparks drew threaded lines horizontally and vertically on Perdantus's chest, like a web of glittering silk. Thin streams of smoke rose from the lines, and his body twitched.

"He's suffering," Galena said. "It's too hot."

"The stuff is changing, but I can't keep it from burning."

Still sitting on the bed next to Galena, I leaned closer. "Calm yourself, Oz, and concentrate. Slow your breathing. Relax your mind."

"Easy for you to say. Your power comes from gadgets, not from your brain."

I kept my tone soft in spite of his barb. "You're right. Talk is easy. Forget about me and focus." I pulled the chain, drew the locket from behind my shirt, and clutched it in my hand. I needed to follow my own advice and focus on my power. I had to energize Oz.

I set my other hand on his back. "You can do this, Oz. I believe in you. We all do."

New murmurs of agreement rose, and words blended in.

"Yeah, Oz. I know you can do it."

"No one's better than you."

"You got this, Oz."

I peeked at my locket between my fingers. The glow from the dragon's eye seeped through the edges and painted a crimson aura on my skin.

The sparks on Perdantus faded, and the sealant glistened, as if liquefying. "Drip a little water," Oz said. "See if it'll wash off now."

Zoë let a few drops fall onto Perdantus. Crystal dabbed at his chest with a cloth. When she lifted it, long strings of goo rose as well. "It's coming off. Like melted pizza cheese. That is, if you use black cheese on pizza."

"I got most of it," Oz said. "But some of it's still hard. I'll keep it up."

I massaged his shoulder. "You're doing great, Oz. You'll get it all. I know you will."

After Zoë added a few more drops of water and Crystal mopped up the goo, Perdantus's feathers looked much cleaner, though some goo still clung to his lower feathers and legs. That probably wouldn't hurt him.

"My turn," Galena said as she slid her hand under Perdantus. "He's clean enough, but many of his bones are broken."

"Bird bones are hollow and brittle," Oz said. "Are you sure you can mend all of them? You've never healed more than a few scrapes and bruises."

Galena nodded. "I don't know why, but I've never felt so powerful before."

I glanced at my locket again. The dragon's eye pulsed like a scarlet beacon.

Cupping Perdantus in one hand, Galena laid her other hand over him and closed her eyes. "He's breathing but in great pain. The end of one broken bone is poking into a lung. Blood is leaking there. If I can't fix it, he will die quickly." She began humming a lilting tune, then added words.

Fair child of feathers
With bones so frail
Allow my fingers
To make you hale

My touch is healing
To mend the flawed
My touch is binding
A kiss from God

Galena inhaled deeply, then opened her eyes as she exhaled and looked at me. "The bleeding stopped, and the bones are mended. But I don't know if I did it quick enough. There's a pool of blood in his lungs."

I looked Perdantus over. His respirations gurgled. Blood seeped from his beak. His tightly closed eyes proved that every breath brought pain. Still, with the Monton sealant gone and his bones repaired, he had hope. "Thank you, Galena." I kissed her cheek, then Oz's. "Thank you both."

Oz touched his cheek. "Yeah. Sure. I mean, who wouldn't try to help a bird, right?"

I slid my locket to its place, rose to my feet, and held out my cupped hands while Galena gently moved Perdantus from hers to mine. As I petted his sticky feathers and walked toward my bunk, the girls dispersed, though Riddle, Crystal, Zoë, and Oz followed me.

"You have a lot of questions to answer," Oz said when we arrived at my bunk. "Where were you when you found your bird friend? How did that gunk get on him? And why are you wearing those bracelets again? I heard that Riddle told you to take them off."

Riddle gave Oz a gentle push toward the door. "She's my responsibility. I'll get the answers. You need to get back to the boys' side before an adult sees you here."

"All right, but I think she's trouble. We don't even know what her Starborn power is or even if she has a real one. For all we know, she could kill us."

"Don't be such a scaredy cat." Riddle gave him another push. "Go on, now."

While Oz shuffled out the door, Riddle watched him with her arms crossed until the door closed. She turned toward me, her brow raised. "Well?"

After glancing at Crystal and Zoë, I looked again at Riddle. "I was outside trying to figure out how to escape. That's where I found the bird."

Riddle eyes widened. "Okay, that's interesting. I expected a lie." Her head tilted. "Why do you want to escape?"

"You've seen what they do here." I waved a hand toward the other girls. "You're all guinea pigs in a dangerous experiment. When they take kids away to do their tests, some don't return. Don't you wonder what happens to them?"

"Moe told us what happens to them. The kids who do well in the tests are promoted to stations where they can help the Alliance stop the rebellion. That's what we all hope to do."

I huffed a laugh. "You have no idea, do you? They've pulled the wool over your eyes."

Riddle crossed her arms in front again. "Well, if you're so smart, Miss Bracelets, tell us what you think happens to them."

I pressed a thumb against my chest. "Oh, I *know* what happens. I was on the Nebula One, Admiral Fairbanks's ship. Not Camille Fairbanks. Her husband, Dwight. Anyway, they had glass coffins on board with dead kids in them, and the admiral said he confiscated their bodies from a laboratory that was conducting experiments on them. Supposedly he was taking them to their families for burial."

"And you think our camp was the laboratory?"

"Maybe you can tell me. Do you remember Penelope? Nine years old?"

Riddle nodded. "She was born on Gamma Five, but she was living in the Delta system before she came to the camp."

"Interesting. Admiral Fairbanks was in the Delta System when I found them. Maybe he really was taking her body home. And I saw a boy on the ship. Theodore. Eight years old."

Riddle loosened her arms and let them drop to her sides. "Also from Delta. He and Penelope were brother and sister. Penelope was almost ten, and Theodore was barely eight. They were close. I mean, tight. Like peas in a pod. They even let them test together."

"Well, I don't think they died together. According to the label on their coffins, Theodore died on day twenty-four and Penelope on day twenty-eight. Both of their death certificates were signed by Camille Fairbanks."

Riddle set a hand on her hip and thought for a moment before answering. "I'm pretty sure that's the number of days since they came to camp. Penelope got here before Theodore did. I don't remember if it was four days before, though."

"Do you remember what their powers were?"

Riddle nodded. "They could read people's minds in a way—some thoughts along with the emotions, you know, love, hate, embarrassment, pride. That's one reason they were so close. No one wanted to be around them, so …" Tears welled in her eyes. "So they stayed together." She bit her lip for a moment, then gazed at me as one of the tears tracked down her cheek. "I should've made friends with them, but I didn't. I wanted to fit in with the others, so I … I …"

"Went along with the crowd?"

She nodded, her voice cracking. "And now they're dead."

"Yeah. I know. And the certificates said something about failure code seven. Do you know what that is?"

Riddle shook her head. "All I know is they went to the tests and didn't come back. We thought they got promoted." She looked downward. "So … um … I guess the test killed them, huh?"

I set Perdantus on my bed and hugged Riddle from the side. "I'm so sorry."

She wrapped her arms around me and wept. "Megan, I'm supposed to be tested tomorrow. I mean, later today." She sucked in a halting breath. "I don't want to die."

I rubbed her back. "I won't let that happen."

She drew away and gazed at me with teary eyes. "What can you do?"

I looked her over. Since we were nearly the same height and her hair matched mine pretty well, maybe no one would notice a swap. "I could go in your place."

She blinked. "What? Are you kidding?"

"No. We look sort of alike. Maybe the tester won't notice. And I'll go in to blow the test to pieces. Ruin it somehow. Then no other kids will ever have to go again."

"Hold on, Sister," Crystal said as she took a hard step closer and shook a finger at me. "Are you out of your mind? Yeah, I know you conquered a crazed admiral and rescued slave kids and all that hero stuff, but you can't just barge in here like some kind of bulletproof supergirl and leap into a fire you don't know anything about. What's going on in that swelled head of yours?"

I set a fist on my hip and glared at her. "We have kids' lives at stake here, and you're telling me I should chicken out? What happened to my daring sister?"

"Oh, I'm still daring. I'm just saying you can't do this alone." She pointed at herself. "I'm going with you."

"Me, too," Zoë said as she stepped close. "The three of us together stand a chance against almost anything."

I smiled. "All right, I'm game for that, but how do we get you in? I doubt that you two will match the others like I match Riddle."

Crystal looked at the ceiling before refocusing on me. "They've got to have it all on a computer, right? You know, a list of today's guinea pigs. We could hack into the system and change the pigs' names to Megan, Zoë, and Crystal."

"If we had a good hacker." I turned toward Riddle. "Who comes in with the list of pigs … I mean, names?"

"Moe," Riddle said. "Usually right before we're called to morning exercises."

"How long till that happens?"

Riddle shrugged. "I haven't kept up with the time. Maybe about three hours. But if you need a hacker, I know the perfect person for the job."

"Three hours and seven minutes," a girl called from a nearby top bunk.

Riddle nodded toward the girl. "That's Echo, our hacker. She keeps a clock in her head that runs even when she's asleep. She's also a numbers genius, technology wizard, and all-around nerd."

I walked to the bunk and looked the young blonde over—petite, maybe ten years old, tiny nose, and big hazel eyes. "Why do they call you Echo?"

She smiled. "Why do they call you Megan?"

"Um … Megan's what my parents named me."

"Echo's what my parents named me."

"Okay. I think I get it. Sort of. Anyway, do you think you could hack into Moe's computer?"

Echo's brow furrowed. "Do I think I could hack into Moe's computer? That old clunker? I *know* I could hack it. It's running the Alliance standard operating system, but it's way behind on upgrades. More swinging doors than a barn. I had a chance to look it over when I reported to the infirmary a couple of weeks ago."

"Will you help us change the names of the test subjects?"

"Will I help you change the names of the test subjects? You bet. I'm on the list for today. I don't want to end up with a toe tag that says failure code seven."

"Super. But stop the echo effect. You're going to drive me insane."

"Can do." She put on a skeptical frown. "I hope."

"Just do your best. Back to the subject. Maybe while you're hacking you can also find out what the failure codes mean."

"If the codes are there, I can find them, but how are you going to get me in? There's a lock on the building door and another on Moe's office door."

"Leave that to my team."

"One problem," Zoë said. "When Moe comes in with the list, won't he think it's strange that the three newcomers are on it?"

Riddle shook her head. "He just tacks the list on the bulletin board in the common room and expects us to show up at the lab. Then he leaves really fast. He doesn't like being anywhere near me."

"Why?" I asked.

She tapped on the side of her head with a finger. "I'm a mind reader, like Penelope. I mean, I can't read thoughts like she could, but I'm better than she was at reading emotions. But only if you're close enough to me, like a step or two away. And that's why I decided to trust you. You've got love gushing out of you like no one else I've ever met."

Warmth flowed into my cheeks. Hearing those words felt good, but it also felt weird to have my emotions read by a Starborn.

Riddle set a palm on my cheek. "Please don't be embarrassed. I didn't mean to pry. And I won't tell anyone about any negative emotions I read from you."

My cheeks flushed even hotter. "Yeah … um … thanks."

"But there's something else you need to know. It's about Oz. He really liked being able to help the bird, but he's kind of nervous being around you. I think he admires your courage and spunk, but he doesn't trust you. He's jealous. He might try to get revenge."

I bent my brow. "Why? I didn't do anything to him."

"He's really touchy about certain things. You might've pressed one of his hot buttons without knowing it. Like if you did something that exposed his health problems."

"Health problems?" I thought back to the events from the moment I met him until the present time. When I tackled him, he went down like a rag doll. That probably embarrassed him, and I did see him huffing and puffing more than most kids would. "Can't Galena heal him?"

Riddle shook her head. "Galena's power isn't perfect. She can't help some people because they have barriers that prevent her from seeing inside to find out what's wrong."

"Riddle's right," Galena said as she walked closer. "It's like they're wearing a suit of armor. Oz has the thickest one I've ever seen, and it makes him mad that I can't see through it. I get the impression that something's wrong with his heart. That's why he doesn't go to workouts, and he gets special assignments that won't make him too tired."

I pressed my lips together. "I see. That explains a lot. I'll try to have a talk with him when I get a chance."

"Times a wasting," Crystal said. "That three hours will be gone before we know it."

I waved a hand. "Follow me. I've got a good read on the security out there. It's pretty lax, but we still need to be careful."

A weak voice rose to my ear. "Please take me with you."

I swiveled toward the voice. Perdantus stood on the bed, his legs wobbly. "You've got to be kidding me," I said in Alpha One. "You barely survived that Monton's goop attack. You're about as stable as a one-legged chair."

He extended his wings and flapped them as if to prove me wrong, then toppled on his side.

"Oh, Perdantus." I scooped him up and cradled him in my hands, holding him close to my lips as I whispered. "Thank you for saving me from that Monton. You're probably the most heroic bird in any world. But you're still recovering. Your bones need time to get stronger. I can't risk losing you."

He gazed at me with his serious avian eyes. "And I can't risk losing you. If I had not been with you when—"

"I know. I know. You saved my butt more times than I can count. But I'm not even leaving the camp this time. I'll be fine." I looked around. "Is there anything I can put him in while I'm gone that'll keep him safe?" I asked in Humaniversal.

"A shoe?" Riddle suggested. "Those shoes you were wearing when you got here looked strong."

"Good idea. They're magnetic and lined with metal." I looked at Perdantus. "Will that work for you?"

"You are saying that I will not be allowed to accompany you, and you will add insult to injury by subjecting me to your foot odor."

I nodded. "Yeah. Pretty much. And you're not in any condition to protest. Besides, you know I'm doing it for your own good."

He sighed. "Very well."

"Glad you're on board." I raised my voice. "Everyone on my team, get dressed." While they scurried around, I grabbed my magnetic shoe and gently placed Perdantus inside. After setting the shoe on my bed, I looked around at all the girls staring at me. Here I was, a stranger in their midst, practically taking over their dorm. Maybe some of them were excited about my mission to find out what was going on with the tests, and maybe others were more scared of the punishment they might receive. "Listen," I said, loudly enough for everyone in the room to hear, "I imagine you're wondering what's going to happen. You've heard stories about me that made me into either a shining superhero or a filthy pirate. And now I'm here invading your world like I'm some prima donna who thinks she knows your story better than you do. Well, let me set things straight."

I laid a palm on my chest. "Your story is also my story. I'm in this with you one-hundred percent. Not only am I a Starborn, I am the first Starborn."

A few gasps wafted through the room. I waited for them to quiet before I continued. "I am the reason the slavers kidnapped you from your families and imprisoned you down here. They want me to lead them to the source of a Starborn's power or maybe use me to get the power to come to them. Whatever these tests are, I'm sure they're somehow connected to trying to gain that power."

I extended a finger and swept it across the room, pointing at them as a group. "To them, you are expendable. You are guinea pigs. Lab rats. Nothing more. They don't care if you die." I lowered my hand. "My team … I call them my sisters … well, my sisters and I are going to the testing room in your place. We will learn what's really going on, how to put a stop to it, and then get you out of this pit and back to your homes."

Most of the girls smiled. A few clapped. Others seemed scared or nervous. I had to offer more.

I waved for everyone to come closer. When they gathered around, I lowered my voice. "My sisters and I have risked our lives a bunch of times to save other kids, and now we're ready to do it again. To succeed, we need your help. First, pray for us. Second, keep quiet about what we're doing. It's for your benefit, and if we get caught, we'll be the only ones who get in trouble. So don't think that ratting on us will make things any better for you. And third, be ready to leave at a moment's notice. I'm not sure what we'll have to do to escape, but we'll need you to start gathering your courage now. Keep your backpacks ready with your few belongings so we can bolt out of here." I took a breath. "Everyone got that?"

Nods spread across the room. A few seemed hesitant, but I couldn't think of anything else to say to make them feel any better about what we were doing.

"Ready," Crystal said. "All dressed and raring to go."

Now wearing her slacks and SS shirt, Echo finished tying a shoe and straightened. "And I'm all dressed and raring … I mean … yeah."

"Same here." Zoë pulled her empty backpack on. "I'm bringing my pack in case we need to steal … uh … collect things."

I nodded firmly. "Then let's go."

While the four of us walked toward the dorm's exit door, Riddle clapped her hands. "Everyone back to bed now. Reveille will be here before you know it."

By the time we arrived at the common room's exit to the outside, silence descended. I looked out the window and watched the searchlight beam. When it drew near, I waved for everyone to duck. We crouched lower than the windowsill and waited. The beam illuminated the room's interior for less than a second before moving along.

I whispered, "Now."

Zoë turned the knob and opened the door partway. I walked down the steps in front, signaling with a finger for the others to follow. When we gathered at the bottom of the stairs, I opened the door to the crawlspace. Once we had all squeezed inside, I closed the door.

"The next time the searchlight passes, we'll get out of here and run straight to the admin building, and we'll have to sprint because we'll be going in the opposite direction of the light, so it'll get back to us super quick. Zoë will lead the way because she has to move the lock with her mind and open the door for us."

As we waited, Echo slid her hand into mine. "I've never done anything like this before," she said with a trembling voice. "I hope I don't let you down."

"Don't worry. This is Plan A. If you can't find the information we need, we'll just shift to Plan B."

"What's Plan B?"

"Try Plan A again." The moment the beam swept past, I opened the door, crawled out, and waited for the others to join me before closing it again. "Go!"

Zoë took off. Crystal ran close behind her while I ran with Echo at my side. By the time Echo and I reached the admin building, Zoë was already holding the door open, waving a hand. The searchlight beam closed in. It would be over us in seconds.

As we climbed the steps, Echo halted and stared at the approaching beam. I grabbed her around the waist and hoisted her through the doorway. Crystal leaped inside, and Zoë lunged in next, closing the door behind her. "Everyone down!" I hissed. The second we crouched low between the front counter and the door, the beam zipped by, illuminating the office interior through the building's two windows, including us. If the guards were paying attention, they would've seen us .

We held our breath, expecting an alarm to blare, but none sounded. When all fell dark again, I whispered to Zoë, "We need the shades pulled."

She nodded and stared at the window on the left. The shade lowered on its own. When Zoë looked at the window on the right, its shade also drew low.

Echo whispered, "Are you worried the guards will notice that the shades are down when they weren't before?"

"Yeah," I said, "But it's better than them seeing us prowling around inside. More likely they're bored and won't notice anything that's not moving." I rose, flicked on my flashlight, and scanned the area beyond the counter. The desks and chairs seemed to be the only occupants, though Oz had indicated that some of the adults slept in this building. I leaned close to Echo's ear. "Who sleeps here?"

"Raven, Moe, and the infirmary nurse. The tower guards leave the camp to sleep. Two shifts. Moe's room is the closest to us, next to his office."

"Then we have to be super quiet." I turned to Crystal and Zoë. "I'll go with Echo to Moe's office. You two stand guard."

I opened the counter's swing gate, and the four of us entered the inner portion of the anteroom. Two doors stood closed on the far wall. The right-hand door, the one Moe came through when he first greeted me, had a sign with Ashton Morales printed on it. I led Echo to that door and waited while Zoë grasped the knob and stared at it, her brow deeply creased.

Something clicked. Zoë turned the knob and pushed the door open. I shone my flashlight inside. A desk sat two steps away with an office chair on the opposite side. The desk's surface held nothing, not even a computer.

Echo whispered, "He uses a tablet. Maybe it's in a drawer."

I walked around the desk and tried opening three drawers—all locked. "We'll need Zoë again."

At that moment, Zoë and Crystal bustled in and closed the door behind them. Crystal pointed toward the next room, her eyes wide as she whispered, "He's in there, sleeping on a cot. When I peeked in, he groaned a couple of times. I thought he might wake up, so we scooted in here."

I kept my voice calm. "All right. No worries."

"How's progress?" Zoë asked.

I pointed at one of the drawers. "I need your skills again."

She strode around the desk and pulled the drawer. It popped open with a noisy clank. We all sucked in a breath and held it. I exhaled slowly, whispering, "Who turned you into Miss Muscles?"

She smirked. "Probably you, Miss Dynamo."

I glanced at my locket. For some reason, redness pulsed from within. Maybe I *was* energizing my Starborn friends without even trying. Good thing. We needed to get this done super fast.

A computer tablet lay inside the drawer along with a notepad, a couple of pens, and what appeared to be an instruction manual. Echo picked up the tablet and set it on the desk, then pulled up the chair and sat.

As she tapped on the screen and various application windows flashed on and off, her eyes darted. "No problem getting past the password screen. I'm accessing the trainees database. It has fields for name, where we live, a description of our powers, a power quality rating, our most recent test evaluation, failure codes, and our next scheduled test."

"The last one is what we want to change," I said.

Echo nodded as she continued tapping. "I'm on it. I'll change yours and Zoë's and Crystal's to today, and I'll change the ones who were supposed to be today to … let's say … two weeks from now."

Looking over her shoulder, I scanned the entries. The failure code fields contained single numerals, mostly ones, twos, and threes. My eyes halted on a seven and shifted back to the name—Penelope Johnston.

I whispered, "Failure code seven."

"What?" Crystal asked.

"Penelope Johnston's failure code. I think everyone is failing the test at some point along the way, and Penelope's code is a seven, higher than most of the others."

"So maybe seven is a fatal failure?"

"That's my guess." I pointed at the name of someone who had a four. "Echo, do you know Chester Lentin?"

She stopped tapping and nodded. "Chester Lentin. Yep. He was a quiet boy. Kept to himself."

"Was? Didn't you see him after his test?"

She shook her head. "We never saw a bunch of them. We thought they got promoted."

I looked at the rightmost field, partially hidden off the screen. "Can you scroll horizontally?"

"Sure." Echo ran a finger across the scroll bar, revealing that field. "Hmmm. Looks like a place for comments."

I scanned the entries again. Several comments, including Chester's, said "Transferred."

I pointed. "I suppose transferred could mean promoted. Go back to Penelope's."

When Echo scrolled to her entry, I read her comments field out loud. "Drowned?"

"Some kids have said there's water deeper into the test," Echo said. "I never got that far."

"So failure code seven is probably connected to dying in the water somehow."

Zoë pointed at the tablet. "There's a nine."

"A nine?" I read the name. "Lyric Altera. The comment field is blank for her."

Echo's expression turned solemn. "Lyric Altera. She was a superstar—the strongest, smartest, and most powerful of all of us. They sent her to the test first, and when she didn't come back to the dorm, I heard Riddle ask Moe about it, and he said Lyric got reassigned. That's why we all assumed that the kids who don't come back get promotions. Since Lyric was the best, we guessed she passed the test and moved on."

"What was her power?" I asked.

"She could change her shape. Nothing crazy like from a human into a cat. She always stayed pretty close to the same size, but she could become another person, like you or me."

"Wow. That *is* powerful."

"Yeah. She became me once. It was like looking at a mirror. Scared the holy spitting spit out of me."

Something bumped next door, maybe Moe. I nodded toward the tablet. "Echo, are you finished?"

"Almost. Almost The system logs when the changes were made, so I have to fool it into thinking they were changed a couple of days ago when the last entries were made." Echo blinked. "Uh-oh."

"I don't like the sound of that," I said. "What's wrong?"

"What's wrong? The program won't save the changes without biometric proof."

"Biometric? You mean like a fingerprint?"

"A thumbprint, but yeah."

"Can you get around that somehow?"

"Maybe. It'll take some—"

The door slammed open, and the ceiling fluorescent light flashed on. Moe stood at the open doorway, dressed in gray boxer shorts and T-shirt, his fists tight and his face twisted in a furious mask. "What's going on in here?"

Crystal touched my shoulder. "I got this." She rushed to Moe and spoke in a serious tone. "Ashton Morales, it's good that you're here. I have to show you something really important."

His face reddened, seemingly ready to explode. "What could possibly be so important for you girls to be—"

She set a hand over his mouth and leaped at him. He instinctively caught her in his arms, and she wrapped her legs around his waist. "Look into my eyes," Crystal said as she drew her face close to his, "and you'll find the answer."

Moe blinked at her, and his facial muscles loosened. "The answer?"

"The answer to your question. Why are we here?"

"Oh … yes. Yes, of course. What is the answer?"

Crystal's cadence turned mysterious. "We came here because you needed help with deciding who should be next for testing."

He blinked again. "I did?"

"Yes. Don't you decide who gets tested?"

"No. Raven does that most of the time."

"So you sometimes decide who goes next?" Crystal asked.

"Yes. Sometimes."

"Well, don't you think the three newest trainees should go? They've never been tested before. And Megan has a lot of potential, right ?"

He spoke slowly, slurring some of the words. "Yeah. Raven thinks Megan might be the real deal."

"The real deal?" Crystal repeated. "What does that mean?"

"No one has ever passed the entire test, but Megan might be able to get through the final door."

"What's beyond the final door?"

"It's …" He blinked harder and shook his head. "It's not something I can …"

I whispered, "You're losing him, Crystal. We need his thumbprint."

Crystal set her hands on his cheeks. "Look into my eyes. Focus."

Moe stared at her. "I'm focusing."

"Good. Now that you've decided that Megan is going to the testing with the other two new trainees, you need to add your thumbprint. Isn't that right?"

"Yes, of course."

Crystal lowered herself to the floor, took his hand, and stepped toward the desk. "Then come this way."

Echo spun the tablet and pointed at the box for the print. Crystal extended Moe's thumb and pressed it on the screen. "There," Crystal said. "You did it. You authorized the change."

Moe nodded. "Yes, I did."

"And it was a good change. An excellent idea."

"Yes, it was."

I pointed toward his room. "Now give him a story to believe and put him back to bed."

Crystal nodded. "Us girls being here has all been a dream, Moe, but the change to who's getting tested isn't a dream. You really made that change." She led him out the door, and her voice faded as they walked toward the other room. "When you wake up in the morning, you'll be confident that your change was the right one …"

I glanced again at my locket. As before, it pulsed bright red. Crystal had become super powerful.

"The change went through." Echo showed the tablet to me. "Are we done?"

I scanned the data again. Now that Moe had provided a higher access level, maybe we could learn more. "Not quite. Since you got a thumbprint, did the system give you more options?"

Echo nodded. "One more option. A communications portal. We can use the tablet to contact anyone else on the channels this pad can use."

"Since they probably contact Camille Fairbanks, maybe it uses Alliance channels."

"It uses Alliance channels. Let's see who's listening." Echo pulled up a diagram that appeared to be a planetary map. "That's probably Gamma Five at the center," she said, pointing. "I see three blinking dots in orbit. According to the specs, two are Alliance ships, and one is unidentified."

"So this base is probably getting data from a planet outpost, like a relay." I squinted at the display. The two ships were on opposite sides of the planet, which made sense if one of them was Camille's, now that she had had time to get here. And the other was likely the Nebula Nine. Emerson would try to keep the planet between the two ships to stay away from her. The unidentified satellite might be that sphere we saw as we flew in. "Can you use the pad to call either of them?"

Echo nodded. "Can I use the pad … um … yeah. From the call log, it looks like Raven uses this pad to contact one particular ship pretty often. The code name is Mother Ship, and …" She ran a finger along the screen to scroll through data. "One of those ships is sending a signal on the frequency Raven uses."

"Hailing this camp, I'll bet. Camille's letting Raven know she's arrived."

"The other ship is running silent," Echo said. "No signals at all."

"If that's the Nebula Nine, I know a frequency it'll be monitoring, one that Camille might not pick up." I removed my communications earbud and showed it to her. "Can you get the pad to send on this bud's frequency?"

"Let me take a look." She took the bud and pinched it open, exposing its circuits. Narrowing her eyes, she moved her lips as she read something inside. "Okay. I've got the number. Let's see if this pad can use it."

After making sure the bud was still turned on, I put it back in place and watched Echo's wizardry as she tapped icons, slid windows from one place to another, and typed in all sorts of letters and numbers. After a couple of minutes, she opened a communications window and gave the pad an emphatic tap. "You're on. Just start talking."

"Super!" I cleared my throat. "Emerson, this is Captain Megan Willis. Can you hear me?"

"Megan?" The unexpected voice came through the pad's speaker.

I sucked in a breath. "Oliver?"

"Yeah. I'm on the Nine with Jillian, and we're playing cat and mouse with Camille. Her ship's the same class as ours, so we have the speed to stay away, but if she gets too close with those souped-up torpedoes, we're goners. Fortunately, Jillian has crazy-good skills. Even Emerson is impressed."

"Yeah. That's saying a lot." Pride in my aunt made my chest puff out a bit, but I didn't have time to dwell on that. "Listen, you probably have an amazing story about how you got off Alpha One and on board the Nine, but it'll have to wait. I'm calling you with my earbud frequency at the Starborn training camp, and I'm plotting a way to escape with everyone. But first I have to figure out what's going on here. Something about finding the Starborn power source. Anyway, I'm hoping to bust out with about twenty Starborn—"

"Twenty-four," Echo said, "including your crew."

"Twenty-four Starborn. Watch for us where Emerson dropped me off. I might not be able to contact you again. And I found the Astral Dragon, but she's out of commission. That's why I need the Nine. And if you keep Camille chasing you, that'll help me. The longer she stays away from the camp, the better."

"Got it," Oliver said. "We'll watch for you, but I can't guarantee we'll be close when you break out. Just keep hailing us with your earbud, and we'll eventually show up."

"Will do. And one more thing. Have Emerson look up what the locals say might happen when Glandel, one of the moons here, gets full. We might need to know."

"Glandel. Full moon. I'm on it."

"Great. I hope I'll see you in about one Gamma-Five day. If I remember the specs, that's twenty-two hours. Signing off." I nodded toward Echo. "Kill the stream."

She tapped the screen, and the communications window closed. "Signed off."

"Now do whatever you need to do to log out, and let's get back to the dorm."

Echo tapped on the screen again. "Logging out."

Crystal walked in and brushed the back of her hand across her forehead as if wiping sweat. "Whew! That was tough!"

I smiled. "Yeah, but also great, right?"

She flashed a huge grin. "It was pretty great, wasn't it? It took a while to get him to go back to sleep. I actually hummed a lullaby, and it worked."

"Good thinking. Now we need to scram."

After putting everything back the way we found it, including raising the blinds, we hustled to our dorm. While the others got into bed, I slid my shoe to the edge of my mattress and checked on Perdantus. He lay asleep inside, breathing steadily. I crawled into my bunk beside him, my head on the pillow but not close enough to the shoe to smell the odor.

I closed my eyes. With the mysterious test lurking, catching a couple of hours of sleep would help a lot.

After a few seconds, Riddle came to my bunk and whispered, "Is everything set?"

I looked at her, her outline visible in the dimness. "Should be. Is there a problem?"

"Maybe. I saw Oz." She nodded toward the window. "Talking to Moe for a minute or so."

"Think he's ratting on us?"

"I can't think of any other reason for him to be out."

"But he doesn't know we flipped the test assignments. He was gone before we planned it. What could he tell them besides Galena healing a bird?"

Riddle shrugged. "Must've been important, though. He thought it couldn't wait till morning. And when he came back, I peeked into the common room before he went into his dorm. He was storming mad."

"Maybe he didn't like what Moe said to him."

"I suppose so. I know he hates being ignored."

"Okay. I'll think on it." I pulled the bedsheet up to my chin. "See you in the morning, Riddle."

"See you, Megan."

When Riddle left, I closed my eyes. With so much going on and with danger around every corner, how could I possibly go to sleep?

But I did go to sleep, and I slept like a log until a knock sounded at the dorm door. "Wake up, girls," Moe called. "Everyone out in the yard for calisthenics."

The girls began rolling out of bed and changing to their SS uniforms. Since my sisters and I already had ours on, we had an extra couple of minutes. I sat up on my bunk with my legs dangling off the side and looked at Crystal. "The calisthenics. How long do they last?"

"About ten minutes." Crystal stretched her arms and yawned. "Just easy stuff to get our blood going before breakfast. You know, jumping jacks and running in place. Nothing to make anyone break a sweat, especially you." She nodded toward the toilets. "We'd better hit those before the line starts."

Careful to avoid disturbing the shoe, I slid off the bunk and ambled to the lavatory. After using a toilet, I walked out and noticed Riddle, already dressed, standing at the door to the common room, her head low.

I waved a hand toward my sisters. "Wait here. Give me a minute with Riddle. Oh, and check on Perdantus. I left him in the shoe on my bunk."

"Will do," Crystal said. "I'll find a hiding place for him."

"Good. Thank you." When I approached Riddle, she lifted her head and crossed her arms in front, her expression grim.

"Why the long face?" I asked.

She bit her lip. "When Moe showed up, I peeked out. He posted the test list, so I took a look."

"Oh? Any surprises?"

"Only one. You and Crystal and Zoë are on it, like we hoped, but so am I."

I sucked in a breath. "That's terrible. But it also doesn't make sense. I know Echo took you off the list. I saw her do it."

"Moe must've readded me." She held up four fingers. "They usually take four at a time. Either four girls or four boys. Exceptions for a brother and sister, like with Penelope and Theodore, but that's rare."

"Do you get tested one at a time? Do you go into a room by yourself? I don't have a clear picture of this."

"All four go together, but I've never gotten past the first trial. No one on my team has, no matter who goes with me. And I can't tell you what it'll be like, because they change it every time."

I grasped her wrist. "Don't worry. I'll be with you every step."

Her frown deepened. "That's what I'm really afraid of."

"Why?"

"Because you're bound to get your team past the first trial, and I'll have to go with you. It can only get worse from there."

"Okay. You've got a point. I don't know how to make you feel any better about it."

"If I die, just …" Riddle pulled me into a hug. "Please find my mother and tell her I love her."

"Riddle …" I rubbed her back and whispered, "I'm going to get you out of here so you can go and tell her yourself." I drew away, still holding her arms. "Got that?"

Now teary-eyed, she nodded. "Thank you."

I released her and turned around. Crystal and Zoë stood nearby, both with frantic expressions. "Perdantus is missing," Crystal said. "He wasn't in your shoe. We can't find him anywhere."

Although the news felt dark and sinister, I forced a smile. "He's probably just testing his wings." I whistled his usual call signal and waited, but he didn't show up or answer. As my smile melted, a lump swelled in my throat, forcing me to swallow. "That's not good."

"I'll get someone to look for him while we're gone," Riddle said. "I'm sure Chipmunk will be glad to. With a nickname like that, you know he loves animals. He even talks to birds."

Trying to squelch my worry, I gave Riddle a confident nod. "Thanks. I'm sure he's fine, but it'll make me feel better knowing someone's looking for him."

"Yeah. He's fine." Riddle opened the door to the common room. "Wait for the other girls before you go into the yard. Morales will want us to march like soldiers." She touched her tear-tracked cheek. "I have to go to the bathroom to wash my face. Be there in a minute."

"Sounds good." The moment my sisters and I stepped out into the common room, Oz did the same from the boys' dorm. He gave me a quick look, then hurried to the exit door, opened it, and hustled down the stairs, not bothering to wait for the others.

When the rest of the boys came out, they all gave me a long stare, some smiling, others stone-faced, a few frowning. With all the stories about me swirling in the air, I couldn't possibly know what truths or myths they believed. I just had to play it cool and not make any new enemies.

The boys lined up at the door and marched out with their arms and legs pumping in sync. When the door closed, Crystal, Zoë, and I walked to it and waited while the other girls lined up behind us.

"I'll go first," Crystal said, moving in front of me, "then Zoë, then you. Just march like we do. I know it looks stupid, but you can handle it."

I grinned. "You mean the looking stupid part? Yeah, pretty sure I can."

The door opened again, revealing Moe standing on the steps outside. "Well, just the trio I wanted to see." He looked beyond us. "Where's Riddle?"

I gestured with a thumb. "In the lavatory."

"All right. You three have a seat." He waved a hand. "Everyone else go to the yard. Do exercise routine number three, then go to breakfast."

Crystal, Zoë, and I backed away from the door while the other girls marched out. When the others had cleared the common room and the door closed, Riddle entered from the girls' dorm, her face now clean.

Moe looked out the window, and I followed his line of sight. The kids began doing jumping jacks, directed by Oz, though Oz appeared to be only giving directions, not actually exercising. "Okay," Moe said, "everyone's occupied. It's time to go."

Using a foot, he pushed a throw rug from its spot in front of a sofa, revealing a trapdoor with a handle. He grasped the handle and pulled the door open. Wooden stairs led down into darkness, a steep plunge. "Riddle, you've done this before. Lead the way."

As Riddle descended, I tried to imagine what lay below. I already knew about the crawl space, an area for water pipes and air ducts, but much more had to be down there. The testing facility, whatever that was, and with Montons available for tunneling, the chamber below, or even series of chambers, might be enormous. Time would tell.

I descended next. Although I wore my weapons belt, I had no flashlight, but a glow from farther down gave us enough light to see the stairs.

Behind me, I could hear creaking footsteps from Crystal and Zoë, then heavier tromps from Moe and a thump, the closing of the trapdoor. Of course, no one was left behind to put the rug back in place, but that probably didn't matter. Since all the kids knew about the trapdoor, the rug was likely there only in case a visitor came by, someone they wanted to stay ignorant about this cellar.

After about twenty stairs, Riddle stepped onto a concrete pad. A bare lightbulb hung in a ceiling fixture not far above my head. She pushed a metal door open and waved for me to follow. I walked into a brightly lit room with tiled floors and a slate-topped table to the left and another to the right. At one of the tables, four dome-shaped metal frames, about the size and shape of a pasta strainer, sat on the surface.

Directly ahead, a glass-enclosed chamber that looked like an elevator car protruded from a shaft in the floor. Raven stood in front of it, a white lab coat over her black shirt and pants. She stared at a computer screen mounted on the elevator car's exterior wall.

When she turned toward us, she smiled. "Well," she said with a cheery voice, "it's good to see our newcomers as well as Riddle. This is an excellent combination. Riddle will show you the ropes, and the three others will inject their new ideas into the situation theaters."

"Theaters?" I repeated. "Like scripted plays?"

"Far from scripted. Although we have sets and props that are fixed, you will compose your own lines on the fly, and the other characters will respond based on their artificial intelligence."

Crystal crossed her arms and huffed. "A simulation? Like a fancy escape room? What's the point of that?"

"It's far more than an escape-room scenario, which you will soon learn. The goals are real, and the consequences of failure are real. But you girls have powers that will keep you from harm."

"At every level?" I asked.

Raven blinked, her smile wilting. "Every level? What do you mean?"

"The other girls tell me there are multiple levels, some with water. I was just wondering if our powers will keep us out of harm's way the deeper we go into the theater."

Her smile returned, tight and thin. "It is best to assume that you could die at any point. That way, you will be as cautious as possible throughout the test."

"And what is the goal?"

"To find the source of your power." She picked up one of the metal strainers and placed it on my head. "Each of you will wear a thought monitor cap. As a team, your thoughts will combine to generate figments in the theater that you will all see and walk through in the first *level*, to use your term. It is a training scenario that will prepare you for the real-life obstacles you will face later. Using your powers against the obstacles will enable you to find the path to the source of the power."

Zoë tilted her head. "But how can our powers work on figments? I move physical objects, not make-believe ones. And Riddle reads minds, real ones, not computer-generated images."

"An excellent question, but you will see that your powers work on the figments just as well as they do on real people. Our computer is so-phisticated enough to respond to your actions appropriately."

I ran a finger along my cap's metal frame. "You don't even know what my power is. How can your computer respond to what I do?"

Raven patted my cheek in a condescending manner. "You, Megan, are an excellent challenge for our computer's artificial intelligence en-gine. It will learn your powers and construct the necessary obstacles to test you to your limits."

Prickles ran along my back. I wanted to swat this vixen's hand away, but, with the cap already in place, her move might have been a temper test for the computer to evaluate. I smiled and spoke in an even tone. "I'm looking forward to it."

"Your optimism will change soon enough." She walked behind the elevator and returned with four backpacks. As she handed one to each of us, she kept her focus on me. "Trail food, bottled water, a knife, and a flashlight."

When we put the packs on, Raven picked up another cap from the table and set it on Crystal's head. "Megan, it should be both entertaining and educational to see how you command your team in this exercise."

"What makes you think I will be in command?" I asked. "Riddle's the veteran."

Raven chuckled. "Don't kid yourself, Megan. We both know that one of your powers is leadership beyond what any other girl your age can normally achieve. You will not be able to resist taking charge. But I'm more interested in seeing what other powers manifest themselves."

I closed my mouth tightly. I was interested in that as well. How could being a dynamo work in a mental theater?

After Raven placed caps on Zoë and Riddle, taking a little extra time to fit a cap over Zoë's poofy hair, she opened a drawer built into the table and withdrew a capped hypodermic needle. "This is a sensory tracking serum. It's completely safe, and it will not alter your minds at all. It allows the computer to sense what you sense through all inputs and understand your mental reactions."

I shuddered. Her claim about mind-altering effects kicked my negotiation skills into gear. Why mention that idea when no one had even brought it up? It was a flashing neon sign that blared, *Mind-altering drug!* But was I overreacting? I needed time to think about it.

"I'll go first," Riddle said as she stripped off her outer shirt, exposing a sleeveless undershirt. "To show them it's safe."

"Thank you, Riddle." After rubbing Riddle's arm with an alcohol swab, Raven injected the pale blue liquid.

Riddle winced for a split second before relaxing. "Who's next?"

"I guess I'll go," Crystal said.

While she and Zoë took their turns, I watched the process. Was this a huge mistake? Of course, I would face enormous dangers to get the job done, but should I take stupid risks? Possibly forfeit my brain functions? Maybe I could argue my way out of it.

"Megan?" Raven said as she applied an adhesive bandage to Zoë's arm. "Your turn."

"Uh-uh." I shook my head hard, though I still wasn't sure. Now that my sisters had taken the injection, it felt strange that I would balk. But I needed more time to think and not cave to pressure. Let her make her case. "No way. I'm not letting you inject your mystery medicine into *my* brain."

"But it's essential for the test to work. And it's not mysterious at all. It just reads your sensory input and relays it to our computer. Your other team members took it without harm. Aren't you satisfied with that?"

I set my feet in a defiant stance, intentionally showing by my body language that they hadn't provided enough information to convince anyone with half a brain. "Satisfied? Just because someone else took your magic shot, I'm supposed to be satisfied?"

Moe stepped closer and spoke with a tone fit for a pep talk. "Listen, soldier. You're a ship's captain, one of the bravest I have ever met or even heard about. Your feats are legendary. As you know, a good leader takes risks, a principle that you've proven again and again. It's part of the universal code of honor. A leader sets the standard. She sets the course. She lights the way. And now it's time for you to do the same."

The more they talked, the more convinced I grew as rebuttals flew to mind. I blew through my flapping lips. "Rubbish. Pure Monton mucus. A leader does set the course but not when it's a slippery slope into a bottomless pit. I know for a fact that kids have died during these tests, and the only way I'll take part is if I go in with a clear mind, unpolluted by a drug that is promised to be harmless by the very monsters who sent those kids to their deaths."

"Skip the motivational speech," Raven said as she pushed Moe back. "This little wannabe captain understands only brute force." She looked me in the eye. "I assume you couldn't find your bird friend in your shoe this morning. Are you wondering what happened to him?"

I stifled a gasp, though I couldn't conceal a tight swallow. Was this the result of Oz's secretive talk with Moe? Maybe, but I couldn't let my rising fury get the best of me. I kept my voice steady and firm. "I'm not wondering anymore. You took him."

"I did take him," Raven said. "And it would be so easy to crush his fragile body with one squeeze of a tightening fist. And we could do it slowly to make his death as painful as possible. Does that make any difference to your clear mind?"

The image of a hand crushing Perdantus knifed into my thoughts so vividly, I could almost hear his bones cracking, but I refused to flinch. "My friend is also a soldier. He wouldn't want me to surrender my integrity, my very brain, in an important battle. Yeah, you can preach all you want about how safe your shot is, but the simple fact is this. I don't trust you. You've proven yourself untrustworthy, and I'm not going to trust my body or my brain to kid-killers or their promises. And if I surrender this time because of your threats, you'll keep making the threats the next time you want me to do something and the next time and the next time. It'll never end."

Without a word, Raven backed away and began a whispered conversation with Moe. Crystal jerked me close. "Blazes, girl! Why didn't you make that epic speech before Zoë and I took the shot? Now I feel like I have acid in my veins."

"Sorry. I needed time to think. I wasn't sure what I should do. But maybe it'll be okay. They don't have enough Starborn kids to risk losing them so easily."

She nodded. "Yeah. I guess that helps."

"Right," Moe said to Raven, now no longer whispering, "that might work. I just hate letting her get this win. It could start a pattern."

"Let me worry about that." Raven closed the drawer and walked to the elevator car. "It's time." She pulled a glass door open and gestured with a hand. "Enter, please. Your next stop will be the programmed theater. If you succeed, you will advance into the tunnel system that we believe leads to the power source. The source should draw you to it, but the paths are many, and some have obstacles that can kill you."

I led the way and stepped inside, making room as the other three joined me. Raven closed the door and pushed a button. The platform under us swished downward. Within seconds, darkness enclosed us.

"I don't get it," Crystal said. "A computer-generated theater makes no sense. How can it prepare us for real dangers?"

I shrugged. "Hard to say, but I know how real the holograms on the Astral Dragon feel. They penetrate your mind until you almost believe in them. And that belief might be necessary for us to use our powers as fully as possible. Maybe that experience will help us learn where to go."

"You might be right," Riddle said. "One time I heard Raven say something about us unlocking a door to the source. I never got far enough to see a lock, but maybe we'll find out this time."

The elevator car stopped. The door slid open on its own, revealing more darkness. I withdrew the knife and flashlight from the pack, slid the knife into my belt sheath and flicked the light on. The beam revealed an underground tunnel that split into multiple paths, a landscape similar to the one between the Astral Dragon and the training camp.

"No time like the present." I led our team out of the car. Hoping to memorize the area so we could get back, I scanned every centimeter around us. A swishing sound made me spin. The car lifted into a vertical tube and out of sight. I walked to the tube and looked up. Too narrow and steep to climb, we wouldn't be able to go that way without a rope. "Okay. That's not a good start."

"That always happens," Riddle said. "But the car will come back automatically if we fail the first obstacle. Last time I came here, I started in a jungle. You know, tropical trees, hanging vines, and a river full of crocodiles."

"How did you fail?"

"A big cat chased me and my team. I climbed a tree and tried to hide in the leaves, but the cat followed me. It slapped at me with its claws, and I fell. The next thing I knew, I was lying on one of those tables with Raven checking my vitals. Then she just sent me back to the dorm."

"Simulated death," Crystal said. "You lost the computer game, so you didn't advance to the real stuff."

"Well, the jungle was a lot scarier than this place. At least here we can see the stars. In the jungle, the trees were so thick, I couldn't see the sky at all."

I held up a hand. "Wait. The stars?"

"Right." Riddle pointed upward. "There's Uriel, the archangel." She shifted her finger. "And Darkantide, the alchemist and—"

I pulled her hand down. "There aren't any stars visible anywhere."

"Sure there are, Megan," Crystal said. "I don't recognize the names Riddle called them, but there are lots of stars all across the sky."

"And two moons," Zoë added, pointing toward one side. "They're giving us enough light to see the meadow and a few buildings maybe a couple of kilometers away."

I narrowed my eyes. "Meadow? Buildings? Are you serious?"

Crystal laid a palm on my forehead. "No fever. Maybe not taking that shot means you can't see the simulation."

I batted her arm away. "I can see fine, just not what you're seeing."

"What *do* you see?" Zoë asked.

"Reality. Underground tunnels. It's like I'm not in the simulation at all."

"Then how can you lead us if you can't see what we see?"

"She can't lead us," Riddle said. "What good is a leader who can't see the dangers we might run into?"

I spread my arms. "There aren't any dangers. No big cats. No trees to fall out of. Even when you were here last time, you only imagined climbing a tree. It wasn't really there."

"No. It was there. I can't climb an imaginary tree."

"You can *think* you're climbing a tree when you're really not. Your imagination can be a really good liar."

Riddle's tone sharpened. "Listen. I know what I saw. I know what I felt. There aren't any trees here because we're in a different place this time. You're trying to confuse me."

I set a hand on Riddle's shoulder. "Settle down. Calm yourself. Use your powers to read my feelings. You'll see that I'm not trying to confuse you."

After glaring at me for a moment, her tight facial muscles slowly relaxed. She took a deep breath, then exhaled and nodded. "Okay. You're right. I'll use my powers." As she stared into my eyes, I aimed the flashlight at my chest so the glow would give her a good view of my face. With my free hand, I pulled my locket into the open and clutched it. Maybe I could enhance her power so she could read my mind more clearly, but I couldn't take a peek at the gem without breaking eye contact. I had to hope it worked.

Soon, Riddle's eyes widened. Her body trembled. She let out a loud gasp and spun away, breathing heavily. "I … I've never … felt anything … like that before."

"What did you feel?" Crystal asked.

Riddle turned toward me again but backed away a step. "A holy presence, like I felt when I went to worship hour at home. A blazing light. Not hot. Just warm and soothing." She wrung her hands. "But it was too bright to look at. The radiance made me feel dark inside. Living in a shadow. I felt ashamed. So ashamed."

I released the locket and reached for her, but she backed away another step and held up a halting hand. "No. Stay away from me. You're something alien. Or you're not real. You're part of the simulation." She smiled at Crystal in a crazed sort of way, then at Zoë. "That's it. Don't you see? The real Megan got taken away, and we have this imposter who's trying to be our leader."

Crystal stepped closer and looked me in the eye. "Megan, is that really you in there?"

I turned my head, breaking eye contact. "Don't use your powers on me. This is no time for me to get hypnotized."

"But Riddle's power says you're not the real Megan. How else can I check to see if she's right or wrong?"

"You can't. I'm in dynamo mode. With your power boosted to the max, you could convince me of your own view of this simulation. I can't let that happen. I have to keep my view of reality. It's the only way I can be the leader."

"Maybe you shouldn't be the leader," Riddle said. "If you can't see what's going on, how can you help us pass the test?"

Zoë grasped my wrist. "I'm with Crystal on this one. Let her—"

I jerked my hand away. "I'm not letting her hypnotize me!" I glared at Crystal. "One of your powers is that you can tell if someone's lying. Well, listen to me. I am the real Megan. I am seeing the real world, not a simulation. Since I didn't take the shot, I'm not being fooled by a computer simulation. You should listen to me and do what I say."

"Well …" Crystal tapped her chin with a finger. "You definitely *think* you're telling the truth, but if you're a computer simulation, you're what one of my novels called an NPC, a non-player character. You really think you're Megan, so claiming to be Megan, in your mind, isn't a lie. I wouldn't be able to tell the difference."

I planted a fist on my hip. "So there's no way I can prove to you that I'm the real Megan. You've set up the boundaries that make it impossible. You let Riddle convince you that I'm not who I say I am, and you've known her for what? A few days? You put your sanity in the ejection chute and shot it into outer space."

Crystal copied my pose. "No need to slap me with a zinger. I'm just trying to figure everything out. Shouldn't I trust Riddle's power?"

I lowered my voice. "Think about it, Crystal. All she said was that I have some kind of blazing light in me. That doesn't mean I'm not Megan, just that I'm not her perception of Megan." I lifted my locket, pressed my thumb on the back, and popped it open. Inside, the gem glowed more brightly than I'd ever seen it. "My dragon's eye is blazing. Maybe she's sensing that."

Riddle shook her head. "It's your mind I'm reading, not a glittering rock. I know my power better than you do."

"That's true." I snapped the locket closed and put it back in place. "But you don't know me and how the dragon's eye affects me. That's my power. I supercharge the gifts of the Starborn, including yours. Everything's magnified way beyond normal, and you're not used to it."

"All right," Zoë said. "I'm changing my vote. I'm back on team Megan. This Megan, I mean. She's the real one."

Crystal nodded. "Yeah. I agree." She grasped my wrist. "I'm sorry, Sister. My brain lost a marble or two."

I returned the grasp. "No worries. It had to be super confusing."

We all looked at Riddle. She wrung her hands again, but her face had calmed. "I see your point. Just don't ask me to read your mind again. It's really scary in there."

I laughed. "I won't. We'll just—"

"Blazes!" Crystal said. "What happened?"

Zoë pivoted in place. "The meadow's gone. And the buildings. We're in a tunnel, like Megan said."

Raven's voice came through my cap. "Simulation completed, and the qualifications for the next phase have been met."

"What?" I touched the spot on the cap that emitted the voice. "Have you been listening to everything we've said?"

"Of course. We have to monitor everything to know how well you've done. I'm surprised you didn't realize that. After all, this is a test."

"I did realize it's a test. I guess I wasn't thinking about you listening in."

"That happens." Raven's tone turned sympathetic, but it sounded fake. "Test subjects often get distracted. But you all passed, and you can move on."

I growled to myself. Raven listening in meant that she now knew about the dragon's eye and my power to enhance the other Starborn. Not injecting me was her way of learning the truth, testing my leadership powers, whether or not I would be able to convince my three brain-addled friends that I was the only sane one. Yes, I was able. And that allowed our team to pass.

"How do we move on?" I asked.

"Choose one of the three tunnels. Let your Starborn powers guide you. From this point forward, I will not be able to give you any further guidance, and you can leave your monitoring helmets where you are. Because you care so much about your fragile friend, I trust that you will do whatever is necessary to find the power source, obtain it, and report back to me."

"Okay. Got it." I removed the helmet and tossed it to the ground. When the other girls did the same, I swept the flashlight beam across the three tunnel options.

Crystal scanned the tunnels. "Which way, Captain?"

"Since kids died down here, probably only one path is safe."

"And the others ..." Crystal slashed a finger across her throat. "Dead Starborn."

"Maybe. Or just a more dangerous path." I walked to the three-way divide and aimed the flashlight into the opening on the left. The tunnel narrowed as it progressed, then ended abruptly, though a dark spot in the floor at the end gave evidence of another passageway, maybe a hole. "A stairway?" I asked.

"Or a pit," Zoë said. "One of us could have a look and report back."

"Wait till I get a read on the other two." I shifted the light to the middle tunnel. This path widened before turning to the left—no apparent obstacles. I moved the beam to the final option. The ceiling seemed lower than in the others, and knee-high stalagmites pockmarked the floor. If we chose this one, we would have to duck pretty low while dodging the obstacles. I aimed the beam directly at the ceiling. Deeper in, huge bats hung everywhere. At least the dangling forms looked like bats.

I hummed, "Bats. Interesting."

Riddle grimaced. "You're not thinking about going that way, are you?"

"It's the obvious choice."

"Why?"

"Bats need a way to get outside to hunt for insects. That means this tunnel can't be a dead end. I didn't see bats in the other two."

"So," Crystal said, "tunnel number three is the closest to the outside. Sounds like a winner."

Riddle frowned. "But bats bite. And they carry diseases."

"Right," I said. "Exactly the reason why most kids don't choose that tunnel. We'll just have to be careful and not disturb the denizens."

Zoë rolled her eyes. "Another Willis word."

"It means inhabitants. Those who live here." With the flashlight beam leading the way, I walked into the tunnel on the right. "Let's go."

With nearly every step, I had to dodge stalagmites, forcing me to keep the light low, a good precaution anyway because it would be less likely to disturb the bats that dangled ahead.

I glanced back. Riddle kept up quite well, her body bent forward as she walked in my path to keep from ramming into anything. Crystal and Zoë did the same behind her, both shining their own flashlights.

I came upon the first row of the bat-like sacs hanging from the roof, but now they didn't look like bats as much as they did before. They seemed more like cocoons with a fibrous shell that emitted a slight glow. Slow movement within made the pliable sacs bulge here and there, proving that they housed something alive. As big as my head, if the sacs really held bats, they could easily do a lot of damage if they swarmed over us with snapping fangs and slashing claws. Letting them sleep had to be a high priority.

Ducking low, I passed under row after row of wiggling sacs. The other three girls copied my bent posture, all deathly quiet. The slightest crunch under our shoes sounded like a firecracker, making everyone flinch.

After a few minutes, we emerged into a circular chamber with a tunnel at the far end. I passed the flashlight beam all around. A curved wall of bare dirt surrounded us, no bat sacs anywhere. At the center of the chamber, a rod protruded from the ground, rising from a slot, like a control lever of some kind.

I padded to the shoulder high lever, wrapped my fingers around the upper end, and wiggled it. It moved easily. Maybe it really was a way to control something. I turned my flashlight off, fastened it to my belt, and grasped the lever with both hands, relying on the lights from the others.

"Megan!" Crystal whisper shouted. "What do you think you're doing?"

"What does it look like I'm doing? I want to see what this lever does."

"But trying something you don't know anything about might be how kids die in this place."

"And maybe not trying it makes kids die in this place."

"Wait," Zoë said as she aimed her beam at the exiting tunnel. "Let me have a look in there. If it seems safe, I vote to go on without trying the lever."

Crystal shone her light there as well. "I agree."

Riddle turned her flashlight on and joined her beam with Crystal's and Zoë's. "That's just common sense. Why take a risk?"

I heaved a sigh, both hands still on the lever. "All right. Take a look. But I'm staying here until you report, and I'm not committing to anything."

Visible in the other two beams, Zoë walked slowly to the tunnel exit and aimed her beam inside. As she took a step across the tunnel's threshold, she extended an arm and waved the light around.

"Do you sense the power source at all?" I asked. "That's what we're supposed to follow, some kind of sensation that—"

A loud clank interrupted. A gate with horizontal spikes shot out from the side of the tunnel and pierced Zoë's arm, pinning her to the opposite wall.

As Zoë tried to pull away, she grunted, "I'm stuck."

We all ran to her. A metal spike penetrated Zoë's sleeve and stretched it into a hole in the wall. Up and down the gate, horizontal rods in the gate's crisscross framework led into other holes.

I touched the rip in her shirt's fabric. "You're super lucky it got your sleeve and not your arm."

Zoë grimaced. "Oh, it got my arm, all right. I think it took a hunk of flesh into the wall with it. Hurts like dragon fire."

I whipped my knife out and sliced through the caught portion of the sleeve, freeing her. While Crystal held her light on the wound, I cut the lower part of the sleeve to have a look. Blood oozed from a gash on Zoë's forearm. "The wound's pretty bad, but there's a lot less blood than I expected."

Zoë breathed steadily, obviously laboring to stay calm. "That's because I'm using my mind to stop the flow. Maybe I can keep doing it till it clots and seals itself."

"Wow," Crystal said. "A mental tourniquet."

"Yeah. I've done it once before. I'll be all right soon."

Crystal shone her light on the gate. "I wonder if it was meant to skewer kids like a shish kabob or trap them inside once they passed it."

"Either way," I said as I strode toward the lever, sheathing the knife, "it's the wrong tunnel." I grasped the top portion again. "Get closer. Let's see what happens."

Once the other girls had gathered around, I pulled the lever along the slot opening, feeling resistance, maybe from a spring coil. As the lever moved, the entire room began a slow rotation. The tunnel exit hole shifted to a bare wall, then to another opening, then to a bare wall again, then to a third opening. With each appearance of an opening, a loud click sounded, as if counting the changes.

When I released the lever, the spring returned it to an upright position. The room slowed its spin, and the clicks slowed with it as the opening passed other exits. At one point, the opening revealed the closed gate, telling us that the room had completed a full cycle, and the gate retracted at the same speed as the rotation, disappearing into the wall, as if resetting the trap. Finally, the spin halted, and the opening revealed another tunnel, two openings to the right of the one with the gate, if I had counted correctly.

Crystal raised a hand. "I volunteer to check this one out." She looked at each of us in turn. "Okay. Since no one said 'No, Crystal, let me go instead,' I guess I'm elected." She tiptoed toward the tunnel, her flashlight beam shaking.

I grabbed my flashlight, flicked it on, and ran to catch up. As we walked side by side, I hooked my arm through hers. "Together is better," I whispered.

Her eyes straight ahead, she smiled. "Definitely."

We stopped at the new opening and aimed our flashlight beams inside. I studied the walls—no sign of holes for a gate. "Do you sense anything?" I asked.

Crystal narrowed her eyes. "Just a musty odor. I'm not feeling it, whatever *it* is."

"Same. No sensations." I pulled her toward the center of the room where Zoë and Riddle waited. "Let's try again."

When we arrived, I gave the lever a harder pull and let it snap back in place. The room spun faster, like a carousel made out of dirt and stone with a single tunnel opening instead of horses to ride. The clicks rattled almost too close together to distinguish, and the dizzying spin forced us to hold on to each other to keep from toppling.

Soon, the rotation slowed again, and the opening halted at a new tunnel. At least I thought it was a new tunnel. With the speed and dizziness, I wasn't able to keep track.

Again, Crystal and I walked arm-in-arm to the tunnel, this time not so much to calm her nervousness but more to keep each other from toppling over. We stopped at the opening and peered inside. "Feel anything this time?" I asked.

"Kind of. I'm not sure." Crystal gestured for the other two girls to join us. "This one's a maybe."

As they approached, I focused my own senses into the passageway. A slight strobe of red in my peripheral vision let me know that the dragon's eye had activated again. Deep within the darkness, far beyond the reach of our lights, something pulled on me—my feelings, my emotions—a deep longing I couldn't explain.

"I'm really sensing something now," Crystal said.

Riddle nodded. "Same here. It's strong."

"Right," Zoë said. "Almost like a hunger."

"Then this is the way we go." My flashlight blazing through the darkness, I marched ahead. Although no bat sacs hung from the ceiling at the beginning of the passage, a few appeared along the way, increasing in number, and these glowed more brightly than the others. Soon, the tunnel widened into an enormous underground chamber with an expanse of water that extended beyond my beam's reach, though the ceiling stayed at about the same level with sacs now hanging nearly everywhere, casting an eerie glow throughout the chamber, plenty of light.

"Well, here's the water," I said. "Maybe Penelope and Theodore drowned here."

As we turned our flashlights off and put them away, a call echoed. "Hello."

I turned toward the source of the voice. Oz stood at the edge of the water gripping a long pole, one foot on a raft made of logs.

I hissed in a whisper shout. "Quiet. Bats are everywhere."

"I don't think they'll bother us. And they might not be bats. Can't know for sure."

I strode to him, a tight fist ready to punch him in the nose, but I stopped two paces short and breathed deeply as I loosened my hand. "You ratted on my friend, and now he's in danger. Raven took him."

Oz blinked. "Your friend? What are you talking about?"

While I breathed again to cool my anger, the other girls joined me. "Perdantus. The bird. And don't pretend you don't know."

"I know about your friend, but I didn't rat on him. Someone else must've done it."

"I don't believe you."

"Why? I'm not the only person who thinks you're too stuck up for your own good. Even some of the girls think you're a cocky jerk. Ask Riddle. She'll tell you."

I turned toward Riddle. "Is that true?"

Riddle cringed. "Yeah. A couple. Not me, though. Or Echo. Or Galena."

"Well, you *are* cocky," Crystal said, "but in a good way. And Oz is telling the truth. He didn't rat on Perdantus."

"And does it really matter?" Zoë asked as she faced Oz. "Let's get down to business. First, why are you here?"

"To help you. I've been this far before. A little farther, actually, but I didn't have the strength for the physical stuff past that. Raven felt sorry for me and let me stay at the camp when I came back, but only if I promised to help anyone who made it this far." He shrugged. "So here I am."

I crossed my arms. "Raven has a heart? I doubt that. And how'd you get here so fast?"

"I left before you did, and I know how to choose the right tunnel. Raven didn't want me to tell you how because it's a test to make sure you're qualified."

"He's telling the truth," Crystal said. "I think we should do what he says."

I bent my brow and muttered, "For now."

Zoë pointed at the raft. "Are we going for a ride?"

Oz tapped the end of the pole on the ground. "That's why I have this."

"All five of us?" Riddle asked.

"Yep. I built it with my testing team. Us four boys probably weighed about the same as you four girls plus me. I'm no bigger than any of you."

"What happened to the other boys?" I asked.

Oz averted his eyes. "Um … they didn't make it."

"Did they die?"

"I don't want to talk about it." He nodded toward the raft. "Just get on when I push it out a little ways. It's shallow here." He waded out a few steps with the raft and vaulted on board. The raft bounced a bit, but the hefty logs kept it well above the surface. He stuck the pole into the water and held the raft in place. "Your turn."

I waded into the tepid water and, with help from Oz's hand, stepped up to the raft. Each time Oz pulled one of the girls aboard, he smiled. Chivalry appealed to him, a good sign, and I was glad to see it. I wanted to like him, but up until this point he hadn't give me a reason to. Of course, he didn't have much of a reason to like me either. Maybe I could look for a way to change that somehow, like stop being so cocky around him.

Using the pole, Oz pushed us farther into the body of water. "Raven told me they call this Treasure Lake. Whatever lives in those dangling bags fill the lake with … well … deposits, so the bottom is loaded with their organic sediment."

"Ewww!" Crystal lifted her foot and looked at the sole of her shoe. "You mean we were stepping in bat droppings?"

Oz laughed. "Ever since you came through that tunnel. But, like I said, I don't think they're bats. That stuff is a lot more flammable than bat poop. Our team found out the hard way."

Something dropped onto the raft. I crouched close to it—a thick droplet. "You're right. That's not guano."

As Oz poled on, he shrugged. "So I didn't use your fancy word. At least you admitted I was right."

I touched it with a fingertip. When I lifted my finger, a long thread of the sticky stuff lifted with it. As if awakened by my touch, the entire string and the rest of the droplet glowed.

"Wow!" Crystal said. "That's the shiniest poop I've ever seen."

"It's not poop." I lifted my finger toward my mouth.

Crystal grimaced. "That's gross, Megan! Don't eat it!"

"I'm not going to eat it." I touched the stuff with the tip of my tongue. The bitterness burned. I gathered saliva in my mouth, swished it around the burning spot, and spat into the lake. "It's glowsap."

Crystal blinked hard. "What? How can the ceiling drip glowsap?"

"Because the sacs have bramble bees in them. When you rubbed glowsap all over my body to help me heal from a bramble bee sting, I got a little of it in my mouth. I'll never forget the horrible taste. Burned like fire. This is the same stuff."

Zoë stared at the ceiling. "You told me these bees are deadly."

I huffed a laugh. "Oh, yeah. They're deadly. Much worse than bats."

Crystal pointed at herself. "Well, I know more about bramble bees than anyone here, and they never built sleeping bags over them like those they're wearing now."

I imagined a sleeping bee in one of the sacs. "Did you ever go where they sleep at night, or just to their spawning cave?"

"Um … just the spawning cave. I have no idea where they slept."

"We know they can knit a barrier to keep predators out of the spawning cave. Maybe they knit these coverings for safe sleeping."

Crystal stood on tiptoes and stared at a sac. "A hibernation stage. That makes sense. During the dead of winter, we wouldn't see active bees for a couple of months. That made it a lot easier to gather the glowsap they left behind, that is, until the new bees hatched. But I wonder how long they stay in hibernation. We don't know when they'll wake up."

I rose, wiped my finger on my pants, and looked at Oz as he continued poling in silence. "Glowsap is highly flammable. Whatever happened to your team, it was a glowsap fire, not a guano fire. Feel like telling us about it now?"

"All right, but it's not pretty." He nodded forward. "There's a place ahead where we set up camp on a narrow shoreline. It was colder then, and one of the guys wanted to start a fire. We couldn't find any wood, and we didn't want to burn our raft, so we—"

"Wait," Zoë said. "Where did you get the logs for the raft?"

"Long story, but when we got to the lake, we figured we couldn't go any farther, so we tried another tunnel that went outside to the surface. A cabin was close by with logs lying next to it. I guess they were going to split them for firewood, but it was obvious no one lived there anymore. You know, because of the quakes we get here on Ragua. Anyway, we dragged the logs all the way back to the lake and built the raft. That's why we wanted to make camp. We were exhausted."

Zoë nodded. "Got it. Go on."

"While I was searching for something to burn, one of the guys lit a match and accidentally dropped it. Then *phoom!* The floor around him went up in flames. I dove into the water just in time, but all the others got burned up."

"Blazes!" Crystal cringed at her own word. "Sorry. I mean, claw of the dragon! That's awful!"

"It was. Watching them burn made me puke. And I felt like a steamed clam myself, like the water might boil all around me, but the fire finally went out, and I waded to shore." He touched his head. "Luckily I was wearing a sensory cap, like a helmet."

I nodded. "We've seen them."

"Anyway, Raven saw the whole thing and sent some guards to come and make sure I was okay."

"So you went back to the camp?"

Oz shook his head. "Not right away. After checking on me, they told me to keep going. I had come this far. I should see how much farther I could make it."

"By yourself?"

"Yeah. It was scary. That's why I only went to the next big obstacle. I refused to try to beat it, and I just went back to camp on my own."

"Why did you refuse?" I asked.

"You'll see when we get there. I'm sure Raven will want us to go on now that I'm not alone, but it'll take a lot to convince me."

I let Oz's story tumble through my mind. The log raft proved that he must've gone to the surface at some point, but one detail bothered me—the matches. None were included in our backpacks. Why in theirs? They had a firestarter with them. No need for matches.

Crystal leaned close to me and whispered, "Oz is lying about something, but I can't tell what it is."

I kept my voice low as well. "You must've read my mind. I was thinking the same thing."

Riddle also leaned close. "I tried reading Oz's mind. He's putting up a mental wall to block me. Something's up with him."

"What are you whispering about?" Oz asked. "We need to be a team. No secrets."

I crossed my arms over my chest. "You spill your secrets, and we'll spill ours."

"Um …" He shoved the pole deeply into the water and pushed the raft more quickly forward. "My secrets are stuff I did in the past, so talking about them won't help anything."

Crystal gave me an affirming nod. He was being honest.

"All right, then," I said as I lowered my arms. "No secrets going forward. We were talking about the fact that you were lying about something. I think you started the fire that killed your teammates. It wasn't a match."

Oz flinched. He stayed quiet for a moment, biting his lip. Then he nodded. "You're right. I did start the fire. But it was an accident. I didn't know everything would blow up like that. I swear."

Crystal whispered, "True, again."

"Okay," I said, "accidents happen to all of us. I've had more than my share."

Oz lowered his voice. "Probably none that killed anybody."

"Actually …" I cringed as I breathed the awful words. "I've killed people accidentally and on purpose, including someone very dear to me."

Oz's eyes shot wide open. "You did?"

Heat surged along my skin as I waved a hand. "Like you said, talking about it won't help, and it's all in the past, so let's just move on. Tell us what we're going to face next."

"Yeah. Sure." His tone seemed friendlier. "Illusions are the next step. We'll go through a chamber that's filled with dangers that aren't real. That's why Raven, or whoever invented the tests, made a fake world in the first level, to see if we could overcome those illusions. The kids who pass that part of the test are supposedly ready for this one, but I get the impression that Raven didn't have anything to do with the second set of illusions. It's something she doesn't have control over."

"But how can illusions hurt you?"

Oz lifted a finger. "One of the things we'll see is real. We just won't know which one. So once the kids who made it this far figured out they're illusions, they let their guard down, and the real one killed them."

"How did you survive?"

"I tried to set everything on fire. Most of them didn't catch because they weren't real. But one did, a monster that looked like a cross between a dragon and a gorilla, like a muscular serpent with hair all over it. Anyway, when I set it on fire, it screamed like a zillion bats and dove underwater to douse the flames. Obviously, my fire power wasn't going to work while it was submerged, and I had no idea when it would come up for another shot at me, so I poled back the way I came as fast as I could."

"So you retreated."

He frowned. "What would *you* have done?"

I waved a hand. "Don't get me wrong. I'm not saying you should've stayed put and faced the beast. I'm just wondering if you could have gone forward to get away instead of backward."

"I don't know. Maybe. I guess I was worried that forward might be worse. I knew going back wasn't."

"Good point. But what you're saying is that the only way you could identify illusions was that they didn't catch fire."

"Right. They all looked so real."

"That means overcoming the illusions in the first level didn't really train you for this level."

"I guess so. Unless I was too scared to use what I learned. And, let me tell you, I was scared. You will be, too."

"I don't doubt that. What I'm wondering is how Raven knew to train you for illusions. Someone besides you had to report to her about them, someone else who survived that level. And it also probably means that whatever the monster is, it's guarding something, and Raven is using us to get whatever that is. The power source, I'm guessing."

Oz poled onward. "Makes sense, but I have no idea who reported the illusions to her."

I didn't need to glance at Crystal for confirmation. I knew he was telling the truth. "My guess is Lyric Altera. No one else had her failure code. Maybe she didn't fail or die."

Zoë, who had been quietly thinking for a while, spoke up. "Or she reported it and got sent back. Then she died during the second test."

I pointed at her. "That could be right. Maybe we'll figure it out when we get there."

"Assuming we *do* get there," Oz said. "More powerful kids than us have tried and failed."

"More powerful?" Crystal huffed. "Stand back, Ozzie. You ain't seen what our dynamo girl can do."

I kicked her ankle. "Hush, Crystal."

"Uh-oh," Oz said.

"What?" Crystal and I asked at the same time.

He pointed ahead. "I hope that one's an illusion."

Riddle gasped. Crystal clutched my arm. "Oh, man. Literally."

I looked in that direction. A giant man stood in the lake, the surface at his waist level and his head nearly touching the ceiling. With a huge axe propped on his shoulder, long dark hair and short beard, and muscles bulging through a flannel shirt, he looked like an impossibly big lumberjack.

I eyed the lumberjack closely. The glow from the bramble bee sacs passed through his body. He had to be an illusion.

"Do you see him?" Oz asked.

"Yep. Just push the raft right through him."

"You're sure he's an illusion?"

"Perfectly sure. Look how the glowsap light shines on the wall. He doesn't interrupt the glow."

Oz thrust his pole and pushed us faster than ever. "But that's so obvious. Why didn't I think of that?"

"Because you were scared. Fear can make people miss an obvious answer."

When we drew close, the man reared his axe and swung it at us. Oz dropped his pole on the raft and ducked. Crystal, Zoë, and Riddle bent low. I stood firm, though I flinched a little.

The blade passed right through my neck. My skin tingled, but I felt nothing else. The raft slowed to a stop within the man's reach. He roared with laughter and pointed at me, his finger nearly on my nose. "Most of you are cowardly rats, but I see you have a feisty wench in your crew. We'll see how long she keeps her courage."

I cocked my head. How could an illusion respond to our actions unless someone was monitoring us? A sentient being of some kind, or maybe an artificial intelligence computer, had to be speaking through this phantom lumberjack, and the words it chose didn't sound like anything Raven would say. Maybe I could get it to give me a clue by poking the brain behind the brawn.

I set a fist on my hip. "What's the axe for, bigshot? There aren't any trees down here. If you want to scare people, you'll have to up your game from stupid as a slug to at least dumb as a dunce, but I doubt your intellect can climb that high."

"Megan," Oz hissed. "Don't be so—"

"Hush," Crystal whispered. "This is one of her superpowers."

The giant let out a belly laugh. "I am going to enjoy bringing this lassie to her knees."

"Lassie? And wench? Where did you get that vocabulary? You sound like a novel set in Alpha One medieval times. I don't know of any other planet where they use those labels for girls."

"Aren't you the well-traveled logic queen? Let me give you a taste of my knowledge. From your attitude, word choices, and accent, I deduce that you are fourteen years old, an Alpha One native, and have been an active protester against the Alliance government, perhaps even dabbled in piracy. Am I right?"

I suppressed a look of shock at his accuracy and stayed in negotiation mode. "Let's say you nailed it perfectly. Since you know enough about piracy to guess what a pirate might act like, that means whoever you are, or whoever invented your computer brain, must also have some piracy experience. Otherwise, you wouldn't know it intimately enough to make that judgment. Simply put, it takes a pirate to know a pirate."

The man stroked his beard. "Maybe so. Maybe so. But you won't get any more information out of me. I will be leaving you. And you won't see any more illusions. With you aboard , they will be useless."

As he faded, I whispered to myself, "Useless?"

When the man disappeared completely, the area dimmed. "Let's go, Oz. Or I can do the poling for a while if you want."

"No. I'm fine." He picked up the pole and smiled. "That was pretty amazing. You're figuring all of this out, aren't you?"

"Slowly. That *useless* part tells me that the illusions are meant to get as much information out of us as I was getting out of him, almost like someone is checking our credentials."

Oz pushed the pole into the lakebed and scooted us forward. "Credentials?"

"Like an Alliance passport," Zoë said. "Unless you're a pirate like Megan, you have to show a passport when you arrive at nearly every planet in the galaxy. It gets scanned to prove who you are."

"Yeah, I knew all that. I'm just wondering why an underground testing place would need credentials."

Crystal whispered to me, "No, he didn't know all that. He's just saving face."

I kept my expression blank. I could've guessed that, but it didn't matter. His little fib was probably his way to avoid looking dumb in front of us, and that didn't bother me. In fact, I was beginning to see his quirks as an effort to be liked by others. And that was okay. Clumsy, but okay. "I'm getting the impression that whoever designed this obstacle course wants to filter out the weak-minded, the fearful, and those who aren't Starborn. The designer wants only the most capable Starborn to make it through the course."

Riddle shuddered. "Then the designer must be a sadistic madman. Those who don't make it die."

"Not all of them," Oz said. "I didn't. Maybe I'm one of the most capable."

Riddle huffed. "Well, goody, goody for you. Penelope and Theodore died. Your teammates died. And you're the one who sent them up in flames. I haven't sensed a sliver of remorse in you, just relief that you weren't the one turned to toast." She pointed at him and looked at me. "Megan, doesn't that bother you at least a little bit?"

"Which part?" I asked. "The sadistic madman or Oz's lack of remorse?"

"Both!" She shifted her pointing finger at me. "I sensed your emotions a minute ago. You're enjoying matching wits with whoever the madman is that set this place up. You'd better get your head on straight, or you'll end up getting us all killed."

Her rebuke stung. I did need to keep my head on straight and not let my emotions rule, and now was a good time to start. "You're right. Thank you for being brave enough to hit me between the eyes with it. Not many people will do that."

Riddle nodded, a hint of a smile bending her lips.

"But," I continued, smiling to acknowledge her smile, "it might not be a madman running things. It could be an AI program that's designed not to allow anyone in who isn't supposed to be here, and it protects itself from intruders. People should realize that if they're not supposed to be here, they should turn back, so the real sadistic ones are the adults who send kids here to do their dirty work."

"Yeah." She nodded again. "I see what you mean."

"But *we're* not supposed to be here, right?" Oz said. "The five of us, I mean."

A wave of confidence washed over me. For some reason, our journey felt like exactly what we were supposed to do. "Trust me, Oz," I said in a peaceful tone. "I think I was born for this."

As if calmed by my demeanor, Oz quieted and poled on.

After a few minutes, Oz set the pole on the raft. "A current takes over here that'll push us close to shore. That's where I met the real monster, right before the edge of the lake."

The glow from the bee sacs illuminated a gray wall that lay about fifty meters in front of us. At the center of the wall, an ornate wooden door blocked the way, like the door to an ancient castle. "Did you ever get a chance to try to open that door?"

"No. This was the end of the line for me."

Water splashed ahead of us. The front of the raft lifted, and a wave shoved it back. Crystal toppled off the starboard side, Zoë off the stern. Oz and Riddle flopped to their stomachs and held to the logs while I fell to my knees and searched for my sisters, watching for hands or feet protruding from the splashes as thoughts of Penelope and Theodore blasted into my mind.

Between us and the shore, the water roiled with foamy surges. A draconic head protruded from the surface, rising slowly.

I resumed my search. Zoë's head popped up first, then Crystal's a couple of meters away from her. Both gasped for breath. I grabbed the pole and reached it toward them. Zoë latched on to it first, then Crystal swam and clutched Zoë's foot. I pulled both of them aboard. The girls propped themselves on hands and knees, dripping as they tried to catch their breath.

Bracing myself against the rolling waves as the creature continued rising from the water, I staggered to the bow and, hoping to show no fear, stared directly at the beast's face. His scales glittered crimson, and his eyes pulsed with the same hue. As Oz had said, hair covered much of his body. His armor looked like a patchwork of fur and scales.

As he eased himself onto the shore in front of us, his long neck kept his head in place, his ruby eyes fixed on Oz. "I recognize the boy." His voice sounded like thunder in the distance as his Humaniversal words reverberated in the cave. "I am glad he has come for another visit. Our previous conversation was cut too short." His head shifted, and his eyes focused on me as Zoë and Crystal continued breathing heavily behind me. Riddle knelt while checking on them, and Oz propped himself on his haunches as he watched. "Your comrades appear to be unfit for battle, but you stand like a worthy opponent. What is your name?"

The dragon's toothy smile and piercing stare shot fear straight to my bones. After taking a deep breath to calm myself, I cleared my throat and spoke slowly. "I am Megan Willis, daughter of Julian and Anne Willis."

"And I am Tempest, for my breath is a raging storm when I am angered." He drew his head back a meter or so. "Why are you here?"

"I have come to find the source of power for the Starborn children."

"That is no surprise. The others who came before you had the same quest, though none were able to get past me. What makes you think you can?"

"I'm hoping that a simple appeal will work, Tempest. I don't understand why you would try to stop us. If we pass, it wouldn't hurt you, would it?"

"On the contrary. Opening that door would ignite a fire in this chamber so intense that the water would boil. Although you would be able to escape, I am too big to go through that door or the narrow tunnel you entered by. I would die in the steaming cauldron."

I glanced around. Bramble bee sacs hung everywhere. Apparently, they had deposited enough glowsap to create an inferno with the slightest spark, and that meant it wouldn't be safe for me to use electricity from my bracelets. "I see. That is definitely good motivation to keep us from passing, and it puts me at a disadvantage. Considering your huge size, razor-sharp teeth, and impenetrable scales, I don't think I can get past you by brute force, especially if you also have fiery breath. I would have to come up with another way."

"Your description of me is an obvious attempt to feed my ego, and once my head has swelled, you hope that I will make some sort of mental error. Is that your plan?"

"I am simply stating facts to answer your earlier question about whether or not I can get past you. Have I exaggerated your attributes? Do you have a weakness that I can't see?"

Tempest let out a deep-throated chuckle. "You are a clever one, trying to fool me into revealing a vulnerability. I will enjoy matching wits with you."

"But you're not matching wits, Tempest. You dodged my question just now."

"Intentionally and without deceit. I would be a fool to give away any secret that could compromise my safety."

"But your answer indicates that you *have* such a secret. Otherwise, there would be no need to mention it. You would've simply said 'I have no vulnerabilities.'"

"You have bested me on that point, Megan Willis, a tally on your scorecard, if you will, but knowing my only vulnerability would be of no benefit to you. I do have razor-sharp teeth, and I can breathe fire, but my scales are not impenetrable. They are tough and leathery, not hard and metallic. A sharp sword wielded by a muscular warrior could possibly make a shallow prick with enough effort, but I see no warrior of sufficient strength among you, nor a sword."

I narrowed an eye. "I see. You decided to tell me about your vulnerability to blunt the impact of my tally, knowing that I couldn't use it to my advantage. You are a clever opponent."

"And you should know better than to resort to flattery. It is insulting to think it would work against me."

"Fair point. No more flattery. Let me go back to my idea that I would have to find another way to get where I want to go." I tapped a finger on my chin. "Maybe I could offer to find a way to let you out. If you weren't here, I could pass."

"Nonsense. Only the man who set up this labyrinth, the man who made me a prisoner in this accursed pool, the man who forced me to guard this door, can do that."

"Who is that man?"

"He never told me his name, but he is a warrior like none other I have encountered, not necessarily in physical strength, but in ingenuity. In fact, you remind me of this warrior because of your own mental skills."

"A warrior? I hope he wasn't too cruel." I spread a hand toward the lake's surface. "You have plenty of water to drink, Tempest, but did this man leave you anything to eat?"

"Fish are able to enter this pool through an underground stream. An occasional turtle, as well. Even a wayward crab from time to time. And, of course, the infrequent human visitors are the most substantial meal. I have enough food to survive."

I resisted a shudder. He might have been lying about eating humans just to get a rise out of me. "Yeah, but raw meat? I like cooked fish but not raw." I snapped my fingers. "I forgot. You have fiery breath. You can cook your food."

Tempest released a humming laugh. "Very good, Megan. Very good. You want to see my fire breathing to prove whether or not I really have that power, but I will not dignify your doubts with a suicidal demonstration." He huffed twin plumes of smoke from his nostrils. "Unless you wish to be my target. We could die together."

I waved a hand. "No, no. I believe you can breathe fire. But all that aside, if I can find a way to get you out of here, would you let me pass?"

"Of course. As soon as an escape is available, I would leave immediately. I will no longer be here to block your way. But, as I mentioned, I know you cannot do …" He stared at me, his eyes flashing more brightly than before.

His stare drew a shudder. I couldn't prevent it this time. "Is something wrong?"

"You have a dragon's eye ruby."

I looked down at my shirt. My locket glowed so brightly the color shone through the material. "Does that make you angry for some reason?"

"Not at all. I can use the ruby to escape." Tempest extended a clawed hand. "Give it to me."

I glanced back for a millisecond. All three girls were now sitting up, though Crystal leaned her head on Zoë's shoulder. I could use her help hypnotizing this beast, but she seemed barely conscious. "Tell me how you plan to use it. Maybe I can help you."

"There is an ancient incantation. That is all I will say. Since you cannot possibly know the incantation, I have to do it myself."

215

I bit my lip. If it was the same incantation Thorne used to try to become immortal, Tempest would attempt to use the dragon's eye to absorb my father's life essence, but Barnabas was protecting against that. Yet, even if the incantation did work, how would that help Tempest escape? Maybe he could set the chamber on fire and survive the heat, but that still wouldn't get him out. He knew something I didn't know, and since he wouldn't tell me, it couldn't be good.

I clutched the locket through my shirt. "No. You can't have it."

"Then I will take it!" His head shot forward, teeth bared. We all flung ourselves down to the raft. I grabbed the steering pole again, hoping to use it as a weapon, but what good would it be against a dragon?

His head and neck whipped back and coiled, like an adder ready to strike again. "This is your last chance. Give me the ruby or die."

With the pole in hand, I shot to my feet and shouted, "Zoë! Get ready to toss some grenades at the dragon."

She squinted. "What grenades?"

"Stinger grenades." I whacked one of the bramble bee cocoons. It broke open. A bee flew out with an angry buzzsaw noise. I whacked another sac and another and another. More bees zipped out.

Waving her hands, Zoë mentally hurled the bees toward Tempest. As they swarmed around his face, he batted at them with claws and wings while I broke more cocoons.

Bees flew at me, but Zoë grabbed them with her mind and tossed them toward the dragon. In the midst of the buzzing din, I shouted, "Make a water shield around us. Then Tempest will be their only target."

"Will do." Zoë waved her hands faster than ever. Water shot up from the lake in a wide circle and covered the entire raft in a dome with me standing through the ceiling, getting soaked by the spray. I knocked down one more cocoon, sat on the raft, and drew the pole onto my lap as I watched the dragon through the dome.

With at least a dozen bees jabbing at his face, Tempest thrashed his neck to toss them from his head, but the bees followed every motion, relentlessly stinging him. If what he said about his scales was true, maybe the stingers were sharp enough to penetrate. I already knew they could pierce the tough hide of a Jaradian. Even if not, Tempest's eyes were vulnerable and maybe the inside of his mouth if he decided to open it and blast them with fire, but that would be a last resort, given the danger of igniting the glowsap.

Soon, Tempest's movements slowed, as did Zoë's. Breathing rapidly, she looked at me. "I can't keep this up much longer."

I clutched my pendant through my shirt. "The ruby's shining like crazy. You must be stronger than ever."

Zoë groaned. "I feel strong, but my arm wound is killing me."

"Right. I forgot. Try to hang on. He's been stung several times. Maybe he'll keel over soon."

She gasped for breaths between phrases. "Yeah. Sure. … But when … the dragon's dead … what then? … We still have … the bees to … deal with."

"We'll keep water over us while we run through the door."

"If it … opens," Zoë said.

Tempest's head smacked the shallow water. As the bees continued stabbing his neck, he stared directly at me, his snout submerged and his eyes pulsing with fury. He lifted his head and wheezed, "You will die with me."

"Uh-oh." I rose again into the watery dome, thrust the pole into the water, and shoved the raft farther out into the lake. "We need to get out of here!"

Tempest blew a stream of fire at us. Zoë threw more water into the dome, strengthening the wall and further soaking me. I ducked under the dragon's barrage. The flames sizzled against the wall of water, but some of the fiery stream hit the ceiling. The blaze raced along the rocky surface. The bramble bee cocoons exploded one by one as the firewall passed. More bees erupted from their shells and joined the others. A tremor shook the cave. Rocks broke loose and rained into the lake, raising splashes. Could it be a quake? If so, the tunnel could collapse.

Within seconds, fire coated every wall, and the water at the edges of the lake bubbled. Flames engulfed the escape door, though it still seemed solid enough to keep us in this death trap, a chamber that threatened us with at least four different ways to die.

Zoë toppled to the side, exhausted. The water dome collapsed and splashed in our laps. Tempest lay motionless at the edge of the water, bees swarming his lifeless head.

One of the bees flew toward us with a furious buzz. I shouted, "Watch out!" But before it could get to us, it exploded in flames.

I swiveled toward Oz. "Did you do that?"

"Yeah, but I don't think I could do it to the whole swarm. We'd better retreat and come up with a new plan."

"No retreat." As tremors continued to shake the ground and rip stones loose from the ceiling, I rammed the pole against the lakebed and shoved us forward. "We have to charge while most of the bees are still occupied with Tempest."

"But the door's on fire!"

"Even better." I pushed the raft on shore well away from the dead dragon and held the raft in place with the pole. "Everybody off! Hurry!"

With pebbles pelting our heads, everyone leaped to shore. I withdrew the knife and began sawing the rope that held the logs in place. "Zoë. Oz. Keep the bees away from us."

While they pushed bees or lit them on fire, I finished the cuts and pried a log free. "Everyone lift. And do it fast. We'll have only seconds before the bees launch another assault."

The five of us working together, we hoisted the log with me in front. I shouted, "Battering ram!" and we charged toward the flaming door. The end of the log bashed into it. The weakened frame shattered, and the hinges went flying. The door fell back and thudded in the next room, casting off most of the fire.

"Keep holding the log, and let's go." We ran through the gap with flames all around the doorframe. When we reached the other side and stood in a dark chamber, I nodded at Zoë. "Can you prop the door back in place?"

"Depends on how heavy it is." As she stared at the door, a bee flew in, but it instantly burst into flames.

I whispered, "Thanks, Oz."

The door rose a few centimeters, then dropped back to the ground. Zoë grunted, her face taut. The door lifted again, this time higher, slowly, ever so slowly. When it rose high enough, I called, "Let's prop it!"

Oz, Crystal, Riddle, and I set the end of the log against our side of the door and pushed until it stood upright and blocked the exit. The tremors died away, leaving the roof intact, though dozens of stones and pebbles littered the floor.

"Okay," I said with a loud exhale, "lower the log. Slowly now."

When we had set the log on the ground, a stray bee flew by. It, too, ignited and plunged to the ground in a sizzling flame. Light from gaps around the door illuminated Oz's grinning face. "You're welcome."

I patted him on the back. "Good job." I looked at each exhausted face, barely visible in the glow. "All of you."

"I didn't do anything but help carry a log," Riddle said.

Crystal massaged her scalp. "Same here. I think I hit my head on the raft when I fell off. Still pretty woozy."

I ran my fingers through her hair and came across a nasty lump. "Now's when we need Oliver or Galena." I gave her a hug from the side and turned toward the others. "Everyone stepped up when needed."

"Right," Oz said, looking at me. "I have to admit, you and Zoë were pretty amazing. That water shield Zoë put up was awesome, and the way you kept that dragon from killing us was double awesome. I'll never forget it. I promise."

The compliment felt good, but since he left Crystal and Riddle out, I wasn't sure what to say. "Well, we made it. That's what's important."

"But made it where?" Oz asked. "With the bee sacs gone, we need more light."

I looked in the direction we had been heading. Firelight from the door had dwindled, casting a flickering glow only a few meters into the new chamber. Darkness shrouded everything beyond. I unfastened the flashlight and flipped the switch, but it stayed dark. After shaking it and slapping it against my palm to no avail, I heaved a sigh. "That's not good."

"Probably got soaked," Crystal said. "I lost mine when I fell overboard."

"Same here," Zoë said.

A clicking sound emanated from Riddle's hand. "I have mine, but it's dead. Maybe they'll work after they dry out awhile."

"And was that a quake?" Crystal asked. "Another one of those might bury us."

"True." I picked up one of the fallen stones and tossed it away. "We'll have to worry about that later." I refastened the flashlight to my belt and turned toward the charred door. A two-meter-long broken strip of the door jamb lay on the floor, smoking but not on fire. I peeled off my saturated outer shirt, wrapped it around one end of the strip, and picked it up. "Oz, can you fire this up for me?"

"Sure." He stared at the strip as I held it upright. Sparks danced on the edges from the halfway point up to the top. Within seconds, a bright yellow flame burst forth, making the strip into a suitable torch.

"Thanks. Keep it lit, if you can."

"No problem. The wood looks pretty thick. It should last awhile."

Holding the torch high in front, I walked deeper into the new chamber, Oz next to me, Zoë and Crystal behind us, and Riddle trailing. Although Riddle's regret over not being able to help during the battle with the dragon concerned me, I couldn't do anything about it.

With rough dirt walls close to us on each side and a ceiling within reach of my torch, the new chamber proved to be a lower, narrower tunnel than the others. Since there were no supports within view, the Montons probably dug this one at some point.

The darkness and close confines prompted me to keep my voice low. "Oz, as far as you know, no one has made it this far, right?"

"Right, but I'm sure Raven wouldn't tell me if someone did. Maybe if I had kept count of all the kids who never came back, I could figure it out."

I halted and waited for the others to catch up. I turned and compressed Riddle's shoulder. "Do you know how many kids never came back from the tests?"

"Fourteen. Three boys on Oz's team. Penelope and Theodore. A second four-boy team. A four-girl team. And Lyric. She went by herself. After her, I guess they decided they'd better go in teams."

I gave her shoulder another gentle squeeze. "Thank you. That's helpful information."

In the glow of my torch, tears sparkled in her eyes. "Lyric was my friend. I hope we can find out what happened to her."

"We'll do our best." I pivoted and walked on. A few seconds later, another door appeared, blocking the tunnel. I stopped and waved the torch from side to side to get a fuller view. It appeared to be a thick, metal door, like a bank vault, complete with an alphanumeric keypad embedded in the center and a horizontal door handle on one side..

I pushed down on the handle. No click sounded. I pulled, then pushed, but the door wouldn't budge even a millimeter. "I guess we need an entry code."

"Then we're stuck," Oz said, "unless one of you knows a code somehow. I sure don't."

Each of the girls shrugged, Crystal adding, "Try something random, maybe, to see what happens."

I laughed under my breath. "No way. Whoever put this door here stationed a dragon to protect what's on the other side. The next obstacle is probably even more dangerous. A wild guess could kill us all."

Zoë sidled next to me and studied the keypad. "Is that a camera lens?" She pointed at a dark circle covered with glass.

I studied the object. A tiny red dot pulsed within. "If it is, that means we're being watched."

"And listened to, probably." She pointed again. "One of the keys has a question mark on it. Isn't that usually a Help key? Maybe it won't hurt to press it."

I looked at her. "Can you press it from a distance?"

"I don't see why not."

After setting the burning torch on the ground in front of the door I spread my arms, motioning for everyone to back away. "Let me know how far we can go."

We all took about thirty steps to the rear before Zoë said, "Stop." She squinted at the door, barely visible in the flickering light of the torch. The door beeped, and words emanated. "Enter the passcode." The familiar voice rattled my senses, the voice I had hoped to hear for so long.

"Papa?" I ran to the door and spread my arms in front of the camera. "Papa, it's me, Megan. Open the door."

I pressed the question mark key. The same voice said "Enter the passcode" in the same cadence.

"It's a recording," Crystal said as she joined me.

"But I know it's my father's voice."

Oz picked up the torch and made the flame brighten. "If your father recorded it, then he's the evil mastermind behind this entire obstacle course."

I balled a fist. "He's not evil!"

"How can he not be evil? Kids have died in this place."

I clenched my teeth, breathing hard as I kept my rage in check. "Like I told you before, he's protecting something that other people can't have. The evil ones are the monsters who send kids in here."

Oz backed up a step. "Okay, okay. No use arguing about it."

"Since it's a recording," Crystal said, "that means he's not here right now. Any idea what the passcode could be?"

"Yeah. Definitely. Sonya printed it out for me. " I reached into my back pocket and withdrew the sheets—wet through and through. When I carefully unfolded them, I looked at the top page—nothing but ink smears. I moaned. "The water ruined the print!" I flipped through the other pages. They, too, held nothing but smears. "There's no way I can read this mess."

"Did you read the passcode when Sonya printed it?" Crystal asked.

I nodded. "But it was a bunch of letters and numbers, not something I could remember without studying it."

Crystal tapped a finger on my forehead. "The passcode is in there somewhere. You just have to pull it out.

"But how? It was a long string, more than ten characters."

"Maybe I can help, you know, by hypnotizing you. I can talk you through the time when you were reading the page. You can read it out loud while one of us punches it in."

"Do you really think it'll work?"

Crystal shrugged. "Won't hurt. I don't see any other options. Besides, I haven't had a chance to use my skills on this crazy journey. This is my turn to be something more than a useless tagalong."

Riddle pressed her lips together, a tight expression I could easily read. She was stung by Crystal's tagalong comment. She hadn't used her skills either, and she desperately wanted to be an asset instead of an anchor.

I nodded. "Let's give it a try."

"All right," Crystal said, "but first charge me up. I haven't used my power to do something like this before. It's like I have to guide you through your own mind to unlock your memories."

"I'll see what I can do." I pulled the chain and drew my locket to the outside of my shirt. I clutched it and closed my eyes, concentrating on the power flowing through me. Now that I had gotten used to the sensation, it was becoming easier to transfer the power to other Starborn. And since I now knew that my father was behind this obstacle course, maybe the secret to finding him lay on the other side of this door, and igniting Crystal would be a snap.

"Blazes, girl! I can feel it. It's like a tsunami of power."

"I feel it, too," Zoë said. "But I already tried the door, and it's still not budging."

I opened my eyes. The fire from the torch blazed, and Crystal's eyes sparkled more brightly than I had ever seen them. Riddle crossed her arms, apparently more dejected than ever.

I touched her shoulder. "Can you work with Crystal? Maybe you can read my emotions while we do this and help her know how to guide me to my memories."

She nodded, though her expression stayed glum. "I'll try."

Crystal pointed at her eyes. "Okay, Megan, take a dive into my peepers. Let yourself go, and I'll take you on a journey into your past. I want you to speak every word you hear, not just your own."

"All right. Here goes." I looked directly into her eyes and allowed her power to penetrate mine. A sense of floating washed in, and the darkness paled to light gray.

"You're on the Astral Dragon." Crystal's voice echoed, as if coming from far away. "Imagine yourself there."

Within seconds, the darkness paled. I sat on the floor with Crystal and Zoë on the Astral Dragon bridge.

"So what did Oliver say?" Crystal asked as she leaned closer to me. "He missed you, right? I think he's got a huge crush on you."

I rolled my eyes. "Hush, Crystal. I don't have time for that non-sense."

"Okay, then, spoilsport, back to business." Crystal's voice altered to an echoing tone. "I think you read the pages by now, didn't you?"

I blinked at her. "What are you talking about?"

"The pages Sonya printed out."

I looked at my lap. "Yeah, I've been reading them while you and Zoë told your stories."

"Did you read the passcode?"

I nodded. "I have no idea what it's for, though."

"Read it again. Out loud this time."

"Why?"

"Just trust me." Her voice continued to echo. "It's important."

"All right, weird sister." I gazed at the page, but now the text looked smeared from top to bottom. I couldn't read anything. "That's bizarre. Everything's a smeared mess."

"Are you sure? Concentrate. Focus on what you saw just a couple of minutes ago."

"I don't need to concentrate. It's impossible to read."

Zoë spoke up. "She's getting angry, Crystal." Her voice also echoed, and it didn't sound like Zoë at all, though it seemed familiar, like it came from a stranger. "I think she might be disconnecting. Maybe talk about her father. Her longing to be with him is the strongest emotion she has."

Crystal leaned closer to me again. "Do you remember your father ever talking about a passcode, maybe a family secret between him and you and your mother? After all, to the Alliance, you were a trio of pirates. You must've had secret codes for communicating and keeping your loot … I mean … um … confiscated goods secure, right?"

I nodded. "We had a vault on Alpha Three. It had a secret passcode, but I never used it. Only my parents did."

"Didn't they tell it to you at some point? I mean, what if they died and you were left alone? They would've wanted you to get into the vault, right?"

A sensation of sadness swept in. I whispered, "My mother did die. And I don't know where my father is."

"She's grieving," Zoë said in her odd, echoing voice. "We need to fill that emptiness. See if you can take her back to a happier time, maybe a family get together when her father might have mentioned the passcode."

Crystal slid even closer and set a hand on my shoulder. "Megan, let's go back to when you were zooming around the galaxy with your parents in the Astral Dragon. All that danger and excitement, your dad and mom at the controls, and you navigating while keeping Sonya from snarking too much. Do you remember?"

As the images of those days came to mind, I smiled. "I remember."

"What about the first time your parents put stuff in the vault? That might be when one of them told you the passcode."

"I remember a day like that. We had just finished a raid on an armory in the Gamma system. It included a lot of gold ingots that we didn't want to haul around. They're heavy, and they make us a target for pirates." My mind took me back to that day. It seemed so real, I felt like I was there. I stood in a cave, my mother next to me. She held a torch, giving light to my father as he pressed letters and numbers on a keypad embedded in a metal door."

"Is that so?" Crystal said. "Is the door gray, and does one of the keys have a question mark on it?"

I leaned closer to the vault door. "Yes, to both."

"Then it's the same door. Ask your father what the passcode is."

"I don't know if he's set it yet. I could wait—"

"Megan," my father said as he pressed buttons, "I'm setting the passcode for this vault. I'm sure you already know that you can't tell anyone the code."

I grinned. "Not even Sonya? She'll get mad if you start keeping se-crets from her."

"Well, I might put it in a secret file in Sonya's encrypted database, and I'll tell you what it is, but you can't tell anyone else except in a life-or-death emergency. I'll program Sonya to provide you with the pass-code if there is such an emergency."

"Why would you tell her to do that? If you give me the code, I won't forget."

My mother caressed my cheek with her free hand. "Because when terrible things happen, it's harder to remember other things, even the most important ones. Grief and stress can crush our emotions to the point that our brains are compromised."

I smiled. "That's not going to happen, but whatever."

"Let's hope not," my father said. "Anyway, the passcode is based on a statement I often make about your mother." He smiled at her as he continued pressing keys. "It's 'Anne is my heart,' but there are no spaces and it's all caps, and the vowels, except for Y, are changed into look-alike numerals."

"You mean like, E is a three because they sort of look alike?"

"Exactly. I'll let you figure the rest of it out if it ever becomes nec-essary. I'm sure you're smart enough."

The scene faded, and the bridge of the Astral Dragon returned. The page in my lap clarified. I read the crucial sentence out loud. "The pass-code is 4NN31SMYH34RT."

The sound of beeps followed, then the snapping of fingers. "Come out of it, Megan. You got it done."

I blinked. The area darkened except for a flickering torch. Zoë stood at a vault with her finger on a key. "I punched it in, and nothing happened, but I haven't pressed Enter yet. Are you ready?"

I took a deep breath, then exhaled and nodded. "I'm ready."

Zoë pressed the key. My father's voice returned. "Passcode accept-ed. Welcome, Megan."

Zoë turned the handle. This time it clicked. She pulled the door open, letting a crimson glow pour out from the new chamber. "You did it!"

"We all did it." I spread my arms. "Bring it in, everyone."

As they gathered, we laid our arms over each other's shoulders, me between Crystal and Riddle. Oz dropped his torch and squeezed between Zoë and Riddle. "Listen, team," I said with a sincere tone. "Now everyone has used their Starborn gifts to get us here. Don't ever think that your gifts are less important than anyone else's. We were all needed."

"You got that right," Crystal said. "I couldn't've pried that memory out of you without Riddle. She was amazing."

Riddle offered a weak smile, the red glow from the doorway making her appear flushed. "Thanks. I'm glad I could help."

"All right, then. Now for some good news. My father said 'Welcome, Megan.' That means he knows that only I could've gotten this far. I think the dangers are over."

Crystal sucked in an exaggerated gasp. "No more near-death experiences? Won't that be boring?"

"Hush, Crystal." After winking at her, I lowered my arms and walked in front of the doorway. A gust of wind blew past, scattering my still-damp hair.

"That was a strange wind," Crystal said as she joined me. "Eerie. Sent chills up and down my spine."

"Doesn't that mean there's an exit to the outside somewhere?" Zoë asked.

"Maybe." I walked in, followed by the others. A radiant glow, reddish and sparkling, appeared farther in the tunnel, growing larger and closer.

Crystal whispered, "I hope I'm not the only one seeing that."

"You're not," I said. "Unless you're seeing something other than a red light."

"I'm here, Riddle." The new voice came from the glow, echoing throughout the chamber.

I halted and turned toward Riddle. "Do you recognize that voice?"

She padded close to me. "It's familiar … I think."

I turned forward again and called, "Who are you?"

When the glow halted about five meters away, a girl took shape within as if a red sun burned inside her, and her gentle smile added to her radiance. Wearing an SS Squad polo shirt, pants, and athletic shoes, she looked like a typical camp kid, except for the brilliant light within. "Riddle knows me. Ask her."

Riddle gasped. "Lyric!"

Lyric extended her arms. "Come to me."

"But …" Riddle shivered. "Are you a ghost?"

"Not at all. I am fully alive."

Riddle ran into Lyric's arms, and the two embraced, both crying. After a few seconds, Riddle stepped back. "Lyric, you're so scared. Why?"

Lyric's smile faded along with some of her glow. "I can't fool you, can I, Miss Mind Reader?"

"No, and I feel your fear so strongly. You must be terrified."

"I have fear, but I am not terrified. Your senses are just sharper now." She pointed at herself. "I have become the source of power for all the Starborn, and your own power is magnified when you're close to me."

"How did that happen?" I asked.

Lyric turned toward me. Her smile and glow brightened more than ever as she extended a hand. "You must be Megan Willis. I'm so glad to finally meet you."

I shook her hand. Her skin felt warm, sending a soothing sensation up my arm. "You already knew about me?"

"Maybe more than you know about yourself." She drew her hand away and laid a palm on her chest. "I'm sure you want me to explain everything, but first I have to give you an important message from someone very dear to you."

"Who?" I asked.

"You'll see." Lyric closed her eyes and spread her arms. Her size swelled, her limbs lengthening and her torso thickening. Her clothes morphed at the same time, changing from the SS uniform to spacesuit coveralls. As her hair shortened, her face turned darker and rougher. stubble sprouted on her cheeks and chin and grew into a man's five-day beard.

With each passing second, the man became more and more familiar. Soon the transformation was complete, and a perfect likeness of my father stood before me.

An urge to leap into his ... or her ... arms nearly burst through. My own arms seemed to rise on their own, begging to embrace this person, but I forced them down to my sides. Yet, I couldn't hold back a whispered, "Papa?"

He offered a sad sort of smile, an expression I knew so well. "Megan, I have ..."

I suppressed a gasp. That voice! A perfect rendition. Exactly like my father's.

He cleared his throat. "Megan, I have a million things to tell you, but I can't say them in person, so Lyric is speaking for me, as I requested if you were ever to make it this far. She can tell you the story of how we met and why she's here, but she can't fully express in her normal bodily form what I need to tell you with my voice, which is why she looks like me now.

"You see, since Lyric possesses the source of Starborn power, she contains every attribute of that power, giving her the ability to record my expressions, my tones, and my inner emotions, and now she will communicate them to you, not only through this manifestation of my body and voice, but also through an emotional channel straight to your heart."

Crystal sidled to me and held my hand. Zoë did the same on the other side. They knew that what was about to happen might absolutely bulldoze my emotions.

He folded his hands in front. "Megan, I heard about what you did in the Delta system, how you defeated Admiral Fairbanks, rescued the trafficked children, and arranged for them to go to a sanctuary planet." Tears sparkled in his eyes. "I am so proud of you, my dear daughter. I have known for a long time that you have the intelligence, courage, confidence, and most of all, the love within you to accomplish the impossible. You are the heroine I always knew you would be."

My father's sense of pride in me flooded my heart. Warmth coursed through my body. My chest swelled. My heart thumped. It felt like it might explode.

"And ..." He lowered his head. "I also heard what happened to your mother. My dear, sweet, wonderful Anne." When he refocused on me, tears streamed down both cheeks. "She was my joy, my love, my everything. We always knew one or both of us might die trying to stop the tyrants in the Alliance. I hoped if one of us had to go, it would be me, but it didn't work out that way. Still, I know she died with courage, honor, and selfless sacrifice. For that, I am proud of her, though my respect for her does nothing to reduce my heartache over her death."

Grief crashed into my mind—sadness beyond any I had ever felt. Of course, I grieved when Mama died. It broke my heart. But the feeling was nothing like this. A claw gouged my very soul and ripped part of it out. I bled within, and the hole wouldn't heal. The wound just kept bleeding, festering, and spreading. I could do nothing to stop it.

I cried. I trembled. My knees gave way. Crystal and Zoë held me up until I could steel my legs and stand alone.

My father, through Lyric, waited patiently, his own tears flowing. When I settled myself, he continued. "As you know by now, I had to hide the power source of the Starborn from Camille Fairbanks. She knows that I had possession of it, and even now I am leading her away from Gamma Five, hoping that the source will be safe in this underground chamber. Still, I knew she would likely press on with searching for the source here on Five in case my leaving was a ploy, which is why I set up a series of obstacles to prevent anyone from finding it."

"But how did you put this obstacle course together?" I asked. "It had to take months, and you were banished to Beta Four."

He nodded. "Let me give you a timeline. I have known about the power source on Gamma Five for years. In fact, you were only a one-year-old when we visited the planet. Your mother and I were searching for a base of operations, and our scanners detected an unusual power surge here. When we investigated, we asked some local animals to help us dig tunnels to find the source."

"Montons?"

"Yes. Deep in the ground under the surface of Ragua, we found an enormous cavern with a lake of red light, a pulsing body of scarlet gas. I touched the surface with a fingertip and felt no pain, so I filled a glass bottle with the gas, but as soon as I rose and began walking away, the gas spewed out of the bottle and back into the lake."

"Oh. That's interesting. The power wanted to stay together."

"Correct. I tried again and held a gloved hand over the top to keep it from erupting. As your mother and I began walking out, the uniting force became too powerful, and it knocked my hand from the top. The gas streamed toward the lake again, but your mother was in the way, holding you in her arms. The stuff splashed into you and filled you with red light. Then the lake surged toward us. Every molecule of the red gas plunged into your chest and lit you up like a scarlet beacon, drawn, I suppose, by the gas inside you.

"Then the ground began shaking. Apparently, the removal of the gas caused a fault somehow, and the entire continent of Ragua separated from the foundation and became a huge island. Although we survived, thousands of people on the surface died in the cataclysm—collapsed buildings, tsunamis, and floods."

I nodded. "Admiral Fairbanks … Dwight Fairbanks … hinted that you and Mama did something awful on Gamma Five. I guess that was it."

"Yes, that's likely what he meant. In any case, we called upon Barnabas, your great-grandfather, to help us figure out what to do. He knew of a procedure to remove the power source from your body and return it to the lake, but it was too late to restore the connection points for the continent. When the radiance left you, he told us that some still remained inside you, but it wouldn't cause any harm. That's how we knew that a person could carry the power source safely within.

"During the next several years, it became clear that children born on Gamma Five, specifically on Ragua, began developing unusual powers. Apparently, the quake caused the gas to seep into the ground and atmosphere. It entered some of the newborns, giving them their gifts and an internal draw toward the power source. That's when the human traffickers gained interest in the kids, and, of course, the corrupt power-hungry beasts in the Alliance also coveted them.

"The Fairbanks couple were among the beasts, but they wanted the source, not just the kids. When they began their mad quest to locate the source, that's when I vowed to protect it, and a few Alliance officers were on my side. In fact, Captain Tillman took you to keep you safe from Admiral Fairbanks, though I have since heard that he abused you badly."

Heat rushed through my body once more. Captain Tillman was on my father's side? Now that was stunning news.

"I was supposed to be executed, but my sister, Jillian, someone I never told you about, arranged for me to be sent to Beta Four instead, though she didn't know that your mother escaped her exile on that planet with Tillman's first mate, and your mother was unaware of my status. I searched for her on Beta Four for months. Finally, Jillian and I were able to commandeer transportation for me, and we escaped the planet."

"I found out about Jillian," I said. "I'll tell you more when I see you again."

He nodded. "I will look forward to that. Anyway, my first goal was to secure the power source, and this obstacle course is the result of my efforts with the Montons. I hoped to get Barnabas to help me, but I learned that he, too, was banished to Beta Four because he wouldn't tell the Fairbankses what he knew about the power source. I vowed to rescue him, but I needed to finish this project first because Camille Fairbanks had already established the Starborn camp.

"In fact, soon after I finished some of the obstacles, Lyric came from the camp, found the vault door, and knocked on it. I used a camera to check who was out there. She seemed innocent and frightened, so I let her in. Because she made it through the course, I decided to put a dragon in the lake, and I sent word to the camp that Lyric was dead, eaten by the dragon, and they shouldn't send any more children. Obviously, they ignored my message.

"Since I had Lyric, I thought it would be a golden opportunity to protect the power source by making it mobile, and she agreed to the plan. Since she is a Starborn, she was able to absorb the contents of the lake, and she became the embodied power source. Once I thought she was sufficiently protected, both by the obstacles and by her Starborn powers, I left to return to Beta Four to rescue Barnabas and to lead Camille away from Gamma Five. How I fared in my efforts, I can't tell you, because Lyric doesn't know."

A proud smile lit up his face. "I knew you would eventually come. That's why I designed this obstacle course, and later added the dragon, with you in mind. Every step of the way, I thought, 'What would Megan do?' and my design included a way to get through the course that you would figure out. And you did. Well done."

He heaved a sigh. "Now I ask you to decide what to do with Lyric. Whether you let her stay in this refuge or you think it better to take her somewhere else. I leave that up to you. I know you will make the best decision."

His pride in me chased away some of my grief, though a new sadness seeped in, and it felt like he was about to reveal the reason.

"Unfortunately," he continued, "since I couldn't guess how long it would take for you to come, I had to leave, setting bait for Camille to follow. My hope is to lead her to a place where I will have an advantage in battle. Since the Alliance will not carry out their duty to bring her to justice, I will take that mantle and put an end to her trail of tragedy and tears.

"But there is a risk greater than the danger to my own life. Camille will probably try to use you to lure me into a trap. That's why I am leading her away from Gamma Five and from you, and I have no way of predicting when we will get back together. All that to say, please don't wonder about my love for you. Don't think that my departure from Gamma Five means that I don't long to be with you. It is love that sends me away. It is my absence that protects you. As long as Camille thinks I hold the power source and that you can be an effective lure, she will not kill you." He chuckled. "And she has no idea that you are probably more of a danger to her than she is to you."

His laugh felt so good. How many times had he laughed in that exact way when tucking me in bed at night, teasing me about how dangerous I am? I laughed with him then, I laughed with him now, and I replied, even though I knew my real father couldn't hear me. "Papa, I know you love me. Never worry about that. And I know someday we'll be together again. I look forward to that day with all my heart."

"As do I, Megan. As do I." He extended his arms. "I am not really your father, but I can transmit his feelings of love into you."

My throat tightened, but I managed to squeak, "Okay." I pulled away from Crystal and Zoë, walked forward, and slid my arms around him.

He drew me close. As he stroked the back of my head the way he always did when he hugged me, he spoke with a hummed tune. "My daughter lives, in glory I stand, in awe of God's wonderful grace. My strength I pass, to her in love, to straighten the twisted disgrace."

His embrace and crooned words seemed to melt me through and through, though somehow I stayed erect. Never before had I felt such devotion, such tender compassion. Did my father really love me this much? He had said so many times, but now, through Lyric's gift, I truly felt it.

His body shrank in my grasp and pulled away. Within seconds, he transformed back into Lyric. Tears flowing, she gazed at me, her voice cracking. "Your father loves you so, so much. I felt his love then. I feel it now. You are so blessed."

I sniffed, trying to quell a new sob. "I know. Thank you for letting me feel it again."

"You're welcome. I have a wonderful father as well, but I was kidnapped and trafficked to a slaver who eventually sold me to Camille and Raven. Anyway, I hope to go back to my parents someday. They're wealthy and politically powerful. They'll help us make a difference."

As new strength swelled within me, I clenched a fist. "Until that day, I swear to you by all that is holy, I will protect you and the power source from Camille Fairbanks, and I will rescue every kid in the training camp, no matter what it takes. So help me, Astral Dragon."

Crystal joined me and touched my shoulder. "Cool speech, Captain, but what's your plan? Since Lyric shines like a spotlight, you have to leave her here, right? I mean, she'll kind of stand out."

I shook my head. "Raven sent us because she, and probably Camille, thinks the power source is still down here. She won't stop looking. And now that the dragon is dead, there aren't any unstoppable obstacles left. They'll come down here eventually. We can't leave her."

Lyric's glow faded. "I can control how brightly I shine. That's not a problem."

"Good," I said. "And since you can change what you look like, you can pose as any of us, even Oz."

"True, but I'd rather not be a guy if we can help it. I hear their dorm smells pretty bad sometimes."

"Let me think a minute." Her odor comment raised a reminder of Perdantus. How could I claim to Raven that I had gone as far as possible in the test unless I gave her some proof? Without the power source in hand, she wouldn't believe me, and she would keep Perdantus as a hostage.

I mentally traced our path back to the camp. We probably had to retie the log to the raft to make sure it could hold six of us instead of five, assuming the fire didn't burn the other logs, and we had to hope the bees were no longer flying around. Once they had gotten their fill of dragon meat maybe they wouldn't be so aggressive, and the fire might have killed them all. They also might have flown away, knowing how to escape after their hibernation period.

I mentally focused on the dragon corpse and whispered, "The dragon is dead."

"Yeah," Oz said. "You knew that. Did you bump your head or something?"

Crystal winked. "Megan's plotting. Get ready for a crazy idea."

"Not crazy," I said. "Just … well … aggressive." I looked at Lyric. "I would be absolutely shocked if my father left you without a weapon of some kind in case you needed it. What did he leave, and where is it?"

"He left a couple of things." She walked to a shadowy corner and returned with a serrated knife and an axe. "I've never fired a gun, so he gave me these."

"Perfect. But what about food? Did he leave a supply for you? Are you hungry? We have trail food we've been munching on. I have plenty left."

Lyric shook her head. "I am fueled by Starborn power. I never have to eat. And with no eating, no need for a toilet."

"Must be nice." I waved a hand. "Everyone follow me. If you're thirsty, we can get water in Treasure Lake. If you have to use the toilet, we'll figure that out, too. But be ready for something gross. It won't be pretty."

23

With my thumbs behind my backpack straps in front, I led the way out of the elevator car and into the laboratory, my shoes still damp, leaving footprints on the floor. Raven lay on the table with a pillow under her head, apparently asleep. When the others joined me, we gathered next to her, and I cleared my throat loudly.

"What?" Raven shot to a sitting position and blinked at us. "Oh. You're back. You were gone so long, I fell asleep."

"Yeah. We noticed. I'm guessing it's the middle of the night by now."

"You're right." She smiled. "Well, obviously you didn't die. What do you have to report?"

I hiked the backpack higher. "We'll share our report in the dorm in front of everyone. I want witnesses."

Raven slid off the table and stood on the floor. "Witnesses? Why?"

"You said you would return Perdantus to me if I succeeded. I want everyone to be there to force you to keep your word."

"Of course I'll keep my word. But our deal stated that you had to get to the end of the test tunnel. Did you find the power source?"

"That information will be in our report."

"Well, aren't you the mysterious one? And insufferably stubborn. But I'll grant your audience. It will be interesting to learn why you're being so dramatic." She curled a finger. "Come with me."

We followed her up to the common room's trapdoor. When we had all emerged, Raven closed the trapdoor and scooted the rug back in place and pushed a table over it. She knocked on the girls' door, then on the boys'. "Everyone come into the common room," she shouted. With a smirk, she shifted to a sarcastic tone. "Our famous heroine, Captain Megan Willis, wants everyone to hear a report about her team's harrowing journey into the testing tunnel. I'm sure you will be entertained by this know-it-all newcomer and soon realize that it was worth waking you out of your well-deserved night's sleep."

The doors opened, and the kids streamed out, some yawning, most of them scowling with bleary eyes. I stood next to the table, took my backpack off, and set it on top. When everyone had gathered around, Raven gestured with a hand. "Megan, they're all yours."

"This won't take long. First, Raven took Perdantus, my bird friend, and threatened to kill him if I didn't go through the testing tunnel to the end. Now that we have completed our mission, I am demanding that she return him to me in front of all of you, my witnesses."

Raven crossed her arms. "What is your proof that you went to the end? Where is the power source?"

I looked her in the eye. "There is no power source at the end of the tunnel. It's just an empty chamber."

"Nonsense. If it's empty, why is a dragon guarding the door? I heard about it from a few testers who turned back in fear."

Murmurs rose from around the room. One boy said, "Oz told me about the dragon, but I didn't believe him."

"Is it true?" Echo asked me. "Is there really a dragon down there?"

"There is." I spread a hand toward my team members. "We all saw it."

When my team nodded to affirm my claim, Raven chuckled. "Do you expect us to believe that the dragon let you through that door? What proof do you have?"

"This." I pushed a finger into the backpack's outer pocket, withdrew a tooth, and slapped it on the table. "This is one of his teeth. We killed him to get through the door."

Gasps sounded from nearly every mouth. Many kids chattered excitedly, though a few cast skeptical stares at the tooth.

Raven picked the tooth up and looked it over. "Very clever. It's sharp and freshly plucked." She set it back down on the table. "Where did you get it? From one of the big cats in the wilderness? I know there's a tunnel that leads to the surface. Is that why you took so long?"

I pointed at the tooth. "You think that's from a big cat?"

Raven shrugged. "I don't know, but I don't believe it's from the dragon. I think you're lying to get your friend back."

"Well, maybe this will convince you." From the same pocket, I pulled out an eyeball and rolled it across the table toward her. "This is one of the dragon's eyes."

As gasps again flew around the room, Raven blocked the eyeball with a hand, picked it up, and looked it over. "My understanding is that a dragon's eye has a red pupil. This one is a dull purple."

I growled, "Because it's dead. There's no blood pumping through it anymore."

She rolled it back to me. "You could've gotten this from the same cat. The species on this continent have eyeballs this size with similar coloring."

"I thought you might be stubborn about this, so …" I unzipped the backpack's main pocket, grabbed a protruding spine, and jerked the dragon's head out of the pack. I slammed the head down on the table, splattering blood everywhere. "Does this look like a cat to you?"

Screams erupted. Kids scattered to the walls, leaving me staring at Raven, blood streaming down my face and hers.

With a finger, she wiped blood from her eye and smeared it on the table. "You really are quite the drama queen, aren't you?"

"Not drama. Proof. Proof that we did what we were called to do and proof that you don't want to admit that you sent these kids on a dangerous mission that turned out to be an insane hunt for a myth. This isn't a test, like you've been calling it. It's a suicide mission to nowhere. Why you created this hoax is a mystery, but if you still believe in the power source …" I pointed toward the trapdoor. "Then feel free to go down there and have a look yourself. The dragon's gone, and the tunnel carousel is deactivated. Even a powerless person like you can find the way. Nothing is there."

Raven crossed her arms tightly. "If it's a hoax and nothing exists beyond the door, then tell me why a dragon guarded it."

"How should I know? I'm just a know-it-all newcomer who exposed your charade. You're the one who has to answer your own question, not me." I extended a hand. "Now give me my friend back, or will you prove you're a liar in front of all these witnesses you sent into danger for nothing?"

The corner of Raven's lip twitched. "I am no liar. You'll get your bird in a few minutes, and I'll ask Morales to inspect what lies behind that door. And I will send a member of your team with him to ensure that he is guided safely by a Starborn you care about. That way, if he determines that you actually found the power source and hid it somewhere, you will be incentivized to reveal its location in order to get your teammate back."

Zoë raised a hand. "I'll go with him."

"No. Too eager." Raven's eyes scanned my other team members and stopped on Crystal. "You. The blonde. What is your Starborn power?"

"Um …" She glanced at me before looking again at Raven. "I can tell if someone's lying."

"Oh? Do *you* ever lie?"

Crystal nodded. "When I need to lie, you know, to help someone."

"Then I can't trust you. Maybe you have other powers that will scuttle Morales's mission." Raven locked her gaze on Riddle. "Ah. The perfect candidate. I know your powers well, and I'm sure by now Megan has taken a liking to you since you are one of the weakest of our trainees. She'll stay out of trouble until you return with Morales."

Riddle bowed her head but said nothing.

Raven clapped her hands. "Everyone else to bed. Riddle, you come with me." While the kids streamed toward their respective dorms, Raven's stare riveted on mine. "You'll have your friend in a few minutes, and you will stay in the girls' dorm until further notice. Understood?"

I firmed my jaw. It wouldn't hurt to throw her a bone. "Understood. I do want Riddle to return safely."

"That attitude will get your far." Raven draped an arm over Riddle's shoulders and guided her out of the building.

Oz gave me a quick glance before entering his door with the other boys while Crystal and Zoë stood next to me, one at each side. When every door had closed, the three of us quietly slid the table and rug away from the trapdoor, opened it, and helped the real Riddle climb out.

Crystal put her empty backpack over Riddle's head, and we hustled her into the girls dorm. With the lights out inside, we had no trouble sneaking her to the empty bottom bunk under mine.

The four of us huddled there, whispering. "Never would have believed it," Crystal said to me. "How did you know she'd pick Riddle?"

"Because she's a coward. She didn't want anyone who could overcome Moe. The hard part for me was convincing myself that Lyric was the real Riddle in case one of the kids could read my mind and rat on us."

"Same here," Zoë said. "I just tried not to think about her at all."

Riddle nodded. "You probably did fine. Chipmunk might have read your minds, but he won't tell even if you did slip. He hates Raven."

I looked at the door, imagining Oz lying in his bed. What was he thinking about all this? Since he didn't have friends in the dorm he could talk to, he probably felt alone. "I'm worried about Oz saying something."

"Why?" Riddle asked. "I didn't pick up any negative vibes from him. Not that I tried, but I usually feel anger from people even when I'm not trying."

"Yeah, but he's a stone wall. Galena can't see inside to heal whatever's wrong with him, so he might be able to hide his emotions, too."

"Why would he betray us?" Crystal asked. "What's in it for him if he does?"

"Avoiding death."

Crystal scrunched her brow. "Death? What do you mean? Is he in danger?"

"We all are, and Oz is smart enough to figure it out. When Raven hears that the chamber really is empty, she and Camille will think the whole obstacle course was my father's ruse, that he took the power source with him. Then every Starborn will be worthless to them. You know what Camille will tell them to do to the Starborn when she finds out."

Crystal slashed a finger across her throat. "And the sooner, the better. She won't want any witnesses."

"Right, but it'll take at least a little time for the messages to go back and forth between them and Camille, even if she's already in this system, so we have a little time. We should get some rest and plan for an escape during the next sleep cycle."

"You'll take me, right?" Riddle asked.

"Definitely. We'll take everyone."

Crystal's eyes widened. "Everyone? How in blazes are we going to do that?"

"I'll figure something out. I already got over the fence twice without getting caught. I just have to expand the idea to include more people."

"What'll you do if Oz betrays us?" Riddle asked.

"Then obviously we won't take him, and he'll suffer the consequences. But he should know by now that they won't reward his loyalty, that he's nothing but a throwaway in their eyes." I shrugged. "But I'm just guessing what he believes or doesn't believe. Like I said, it's hard to get a read on him."

Riddle nodded. "Next time I see him, I'll work as hard as I can to get a read."

"Good idea. For now, let's go to sleep. We'll watch for Lyric to come back from the tunnels. She might have more intel that'll help us plan our escape."

After using the toilets, we all went to bed, though I couldn't sleep. Not yet. Not until Perdantus returned. Raven said it would be only a few minutes, but it had already felt like an hour. Soon, the dorm door opened and quickly closed. The flutter of wings drew closer. Perdantus landed on my pillow and nestled close.

He spoke with whispered chirps. "I heard that you risked your life to keep me safe."

I nodded. "Same as you've done for me plenty of times. How are you feeling?"

"Much better. I have nearly all of my strength back."

"Great."

"And I also have some information. Since Raven thinks I am merely a dumb bird, she spoke freely in my presence."

"Oh? What did you hear?"

"Nothing that won't wait until morning. We should sleep. I haven't been able to since we were separated."

I grinned. "Worried about me?"

"I am not ashamed to admit that I was. You are my dearest friend."

I stroked his chest feathers. "Thank you, Perdantus. You're precious to me as well."

When I closed my eyes, Perdantus fluttered to my chest and lay there. I fell asleep almost immediately and dreamed about escape plans. I climbed the fence again and again. Since I didn't have my bracelets on, every attempt proved to be too slow and noisy. A guard shot me every time, and I dropped to the ground, only to get up and try once more.

After a while, however, the dreams ended, and I slept without a care until someone prodded my shoulder and whispered, "Megan, wake up."

I opened my eyes. Raven stood next to the bed, a hand on my arm. After stifling a gasp, I whispered, "Why are you—"

"Shhh. It's me. Lyric." Her face shone reddish for a moment. "See?"

"Whew. Good. You scared me."

Perdantus rose and stood on my chest, listening.

"Sorry about that. Since Riddle's in the dorm, I can't be her anymore. I chose Raven so I could come in here without anyone asking me questions."

"Where's Moe?"

"While I was Riddle, I showed him the empty chamber past the dead dragon, then on the way back, he fell into a pit. I led him to it, of course, and I pretended to be oh, so sorry about it. Since he hurt his leg and can't climb out, he asked me to hurry back and get help. So I switched from Riddle to Raven and came to the dorm. He has a water canteen, and he wasn't bleeding, so I think he'll be okay for a while."

"Then Moe's out of the picture for now. That's perfect. We can use that."

"How?"

"Do you mind becoming him for a while?"

She grimaced. "Becoming male is … well … really weird. But I did it to become your father. I can do it again."

"Good. Did the kids here ever do climbing exercises, like going over a wall?"

Lyric nodded. "Moe had a portable wall that he put in the yard, but some of the boys roughhoused on it and broke the top board. He said he would fix it, but I guess he never did 'cause I didn't see it again. Maybe he fixed it since I left. I don't know."

"When you did climb, did he time you, like with a stopwatch?"

"Yeah. He had a competition. I never did very well, but at least I wasn't the worst. Kind of in the middle of the pack. Chip was always the fastest."

"Who was the worst?"

"Of the girls, Galena. Of the boys, Oz. Most of the time, he couldn't get over the wall at all."

"Yeah, we think he might have a heart condition." I looked at Perdantus. "Where did Raven keep you?"

He responded with quiet chirps. "In a cage in Morales's office."

Lyric's eyes widened. "You're talking to a bird?"

"Of course. Don't you have any intelligent birds on Gamma Five?"

She shook her head. "Just scavengers and birds of prey. Not many this bird's size."

"His name is Perdantus." I refocused on him. "While you were in the office, did you notice a stopwatch anywhere?"

"Yes. Morales opened a desk drawer that contained various items, including a stopwatch."

I nodded. "You said you have more intel. Now's a good time to tell me about it."

Perdantus spread his wings as if ready to explain with avian gestures. "Just before Raven released me, she used Morales's computer tablet to send a verbal message to Camille Fairbanks telling her that the dragon was dead and that she sent Morales to see what was behind the dragon's door. She told Camille that you claimed that nothing was there, and she asked Camille for instructions on what to do if that was proven to be true. Raven offered her thoughts on possible options—Plan A, kill all the Starborn except you so Camille could use you as bait to catch your father, and Plan B, kill everyone, including you, Morales, the guards, everyone. And destroy the training camp and bury it. She did not mention a Plan C, but she added that they had to hurry because of Glandel's phase. I'm sure you remember that the Monton mentioned the moon issue."

"I remember." I hummed in thought for a couple of seconds. "The Monton said Glandel's full phase is coming soon, and that'll cause trouble of some kind. Raven's probably worried about that and wants to get her plan done before it happens."

"Yes," Perdantus said. "That explanation matches her words quite well."

"And her words mean that I guessed right. If Raven finds out that nothing is in the chamber, she'll want to kill the Starborn, but we have to let our plan finish hatching. To keep the deception going, our fake Morales has to show up and give a report. Otherwise, Raven will send more guards into the tunnel and find the real one."

"So," Lyric said, "what do we do?"

"You'll be Moe, like I said before. Go ahead and report to Raven that the chamber was empty and there's no sign of a power source anywhere. Since she is obviously Camille's right-hand woman, and Moe is just a stooge, Raven will start Plan A or B rolling. We don't know if Camille's still in orbit around Gamma Five or if she took off after my father, so we don't know how long till Raven gets the go ahead to start killing kids. And that means we have to escape during the next sleep cycle." I looked at Lyric, still a bit uneasy about seeing her wearing Raven's face. "Here's my plan."

I stood outside in front of the perimeter fence, my fingers poking through a few of the gaps between the links. After our recent lunch, I felt heavier than usual, but maybe the food would give me more strength. With no bracelets on my wrists, I needed a boost.

While the other kids stood in a group and watched, Moe, that is, Lyric in disguise, held his computer tablet and the stopwatch Zoë and I had taken from his desk. He called, "Go!"

I leaped up, grabbed more links, and set my feet in two gaps below. The fence rattled, making me cringe. Like in my dreams, it was far too noisy for a stealth escape. I would have to figure out a way around that problem.

As I climbed, the memory of my practice runs in the Astral Dragon came to mind, and my training kicked in. I scaled the top in a hurry and shinnied down, planting my feet emphatically on the other side.

Moe pressed the stopwatch button. "Twelve point seven seconds. Not bad. Not bad." He scanned the group. "Anyone think you can beat that?"

A boy's hand shot up.

"Chipmunk," Moe said, pointing at him. "Let's see what you can do."

Chipmunk, a short, thin boy with pale skin and white spikey hair, sauntered up to the fence, grinning at me. "That was really quick, Megan. Good job."

"Thanks, but I hope you can do even better."

"I'll give it my best shot." He spat on his palms and rubbed them together. "Ready."

"Megan," Moe called, "come on back in through the gate. It would be better if we don't have too many kids outside the fence."

"Sure. Okay." As I walked toward the gate, I looked at the admin building. Raven strode toward Moe, her fists tight.

"What do you think you're doing?" she shouted as she drew near.

I walked through the gate, left open by the guards for the exercise. Now it was time for Lyric to put on her best acting performance.

Moe showed Raven the clipboard. "Climbing exercises. I never got around to fixing the practice wall. I thought it was about time we exercised that set of muscles."

"Fine. Exercise is great." She waved a hand at the fence. "But using the security fence? Isn't that inviting trouble?"

Pursing his lips, Moe shook his head. "I don't see why. It's a strong fence. They won't break it like they did the practice wall."

"That's not what I mean." She drew him close and whispered something I couldn't hear. Even when I walked closer and joined the other kids, their voices stayed too soft for me to listen in. I would have to ask Lyric about it later.

When Raven drew back, she lifted a finger. "All right. One climb each, but no more. I want everyone back in the common room for studying."

"Understood." Moe turned again toward the fence. "Chipmunk, get ready."

Chipmunk nodded. "Born ready."

"Go!"

He jumped and scurried up the links. When he curled over the top, he simply let go and dropped. The moment his feet slammed into the ground, he bent his knees and rolled.

Moe stopped the watch. "Eleven point six seconds!"

The other kids clapped and cheered, and I joined in. That was an amazing climb.

Chipmunk shot to his feet and pointed at me, grinning. "Too bad you can't try again."

"Yeah," I called back, "but I don't know if I could beat your time. You did great."

When Chipmunk returned, Morales sent the rest of the kids through the exercise one by one. Crystal and Zoë did quite well, as I expected—thirteen point nine for Crystal and thirteen point seven for Zoë. Two of the boys bested their times, but not Chipmunk's or mine.

Most of the kids, however, did much worse, some climbing the fence in twenty seconds or more. Riddle fared a little better with her time of 18.4 seconds. Oz barely made it at all with a time of more than thirty seconds. Somehow, I had to get them to climb faster. Tonight, they had to get over the fence before the searchlight could sweep past and catch them in the act.

After finishing, we walked back to the common room. I joined Chipmunk and patted him on the back. "Great climbing."

He kept his gaze forward, smiling. "Thanks. You, too."

"I noticed your technique. Really clever. Especially how you just let yourself drop. That sped things up."

"Yep. Falling is always quicker than climbing. You just have to know how to land. Most of the kids are probably scared to try it."

"Tell me, do you think you can teach that to the other boys? Maybe practice in your dorm by jumping off a top bunk?"

He looked at me, his eyes narrowing to suspicious slits. "Why?"

"You saw the dragon's head, right?"

He laughed. "Yeah. Coolest thing ever."

"Then you know I'm a good leader."

"Everyone knows it, but some are scared of you."

"That's fair. I'm a stranger." I pinched his sleeve and drew him closer. "Listen, something's about to happen that'll be a lot scarier than me. I have an important plan that'll mean the difference between life and death for all of us. We'll need everyone to be able to land safely, just like you did. Please trust me on this."

"Trust the dragon slayer? No problem. Get the boys to jump off the bed? Also no problem for most of them. They like to do stuff like that. But Oz won't want to. What'll I do about him?"

I released his shirt. "Yeah, Oz might be a problem, but don't worry about him. I'll deal with him myself."

"All right. You're the famous captain. I'll get it done."

"Thanks." I split off from him and walked the rest of the way to the common room with Crystal and Zoë. "Everyone climbed pretty well," I said as I opened the door.

Crystal kept her voice low as we entered. "Don't kid yourself. Most of the kids climbed way too slow, especially Oz. And with him, now you have to hope he'll betray us. Otherwise, he'll slow us down so much, we'll all get caught."

We left the door to the outside open and passed several kids who were already seated at various chairs or sofas, reading books or writing in notebooks. Others, including Riddle, were in the dorms gathering their study materials. My sisters and I chose a four-chair arrangement in the far corner and sat in three of them. When Riddle came out, she set my backpack on my lap and sat in the fourth chair. Perdantus flew in behind her and perched on my shoulder.

After I gave Riddle and Perdantus a summary of what we already talked about, I added, "I'm not going to plan on Oz being a traitor. I just have to find a way to fix the problem. But a bigger problem might be the noise. Did you hear the fence rattling?"

Crystal shook her head. "I wasn't paying attention."

"I noticed," Zoë said. "I can't imagine a way around that. It's not like we can wrap the links with blankets or something."

I sighed. "If I can't come up with a solution, we might have to drop the plan. Or maybe I can go first and see what happens. If I get caught, I'll be the only one, and nobody else will get in trouble."

Crystal huffed. "You're a lot more likely than anyone to get over the fence without a sound. Galena was pretty clumsy and nervous. And if Oz goes with us, we're sunk. He'll rattle that fence like it's a choir of castanets."

"True. I'll keep thinking about it."

Riddle gestured toward the backpack. "Your bracelets are in there. You could easily escape without a sound."

I unzipped the pack and put the bracelets on. "That's great for me, but I'm not leaving without saving every last one of these kids, that is, the ones who want to be saved."

Perdantus extended his wings. "I might have a solution."

I twisted my neck to look at him. "Let's hear it."

"No need to speak it. Just leave the fence noise problem to me." Perdantus flew off my shoulder and out the open door to the yard. Although a bit of the black goo still clung to a few of his feathers, he seemed able to ignore it.

"What did he say?" Riddle asked. "I still don't understand his chirps." After I gave her a quick recap, she wrinkled her nose. "So he didn't tell you his plan?"

"Nope. He's like that sometimes."

"But you trust him?"

I gazed out the door, no longer able to see Perdantus. "With my life."

"Same here," Zoë said, lifting a hand.

"In a heartbeat," Crystal added. "He's been my friend longer than anyone here. I know he won't let us down."

Riddle inhaled. "Okay. Since you're so sure, I'll trust him, too."

For the rest of the day, we read various books, though I had no course of study to follow. From time to time, I glanced at the rug covering the trapdoor, expecting that at any moment the real Morales might push his way out and expose our plan, but it never happened.

Our Morales, that is, Lyric, checked on us every hour or so. He barked at a few kids who seemed to be loafing or just pretending to read. His gruff voice combined with his rah-rah words sounded so real. Lyric almost had me convinced. But when he walked close and looked at us, a hint of red glimmered in his eyes, likely on purpose, reminding me who he really was.

After evening exercises and dinner, the four of us returned to the common room and continued reading in the corner. Raven came in from the yard with Moe and pointed at us. "There she is."

They walked to our corner. Raven set a fist on her hip, while Moe crossed his arms. "We have come to a decision," Raven said. "Since there is no power source to search for, we are shutting this operation down. The entire training camp. Everything."

"Okay." I rose from the chair. "Why are you telling us instead of everyone at the same time?"

"The others will learn about the plan soon." Raven pointed at me. "I'm telling you now because I need you to go with me on a special assignment. The rest of the trainees will be processed out and returned to their homes as soon as possible."

"What kind of assignment, and when?"

"First thing tomorrow you will accompany me on a transport cruiser that will rendezvous with Admiral Camille Fairbanks's ship. From that point on, you will be under her command. Don't bother asking what she plans to do with you, because I don't know."

I gave her a defiant stare. Of course, I would never go anywhere with Camille, but if I absolutely refused, Raven would say that I didn't have a choice, which would give me a good reason to try to escape tonight. That would cause her to keep a more careful watch over me. I didn't want that to happen. Maybe I could craft my response to avoid scrutiny. "I'm no fan of Camille Fairbanks."

A hint of a smile crossed Raven's face. "Nobody is, but she commands a lot of power. It's no wonder you're scared of her."

"Scared of her?" I snorted. "I just led a team that slayed a dragon. I'm not scared of that overrated, self-appointed ..." I drew quotation marks in the air. "Admiral."

Raven cocked her head. "Okay. I can believe that. Then I guess you won't mind going with her, seeing that your mother is dead and your father is missing."

"I can stomach being with her. Since you want everyone to go home, maybe I can get her to help me find my father. I've been looking for him for a long time."

Raven chuckled. "Believe it or not, she might be more than willing to help you with that. Just remember to stay on her good side. You'll be better off."

I wanted to grumble, "She doesn't have a good side," but I simply nodded and said, "I'll remember."

Raven pointed at Moe with a thumb. "Morales will stay with you until you're ready to go in the morning."

I lifted my brow in mock objection. "What? I don't need a guard. I said I want to go with you tomorrow. And what about your rules? You can't let a man come into the girls'—"

"Don't get so worked up. First, these are Camille's orders, not mine. Apparently, she thinks when you hear about her plans, you'll try to leave. Second, you and Morales will sleep in the common room until you and I leave in the morning. You can stay as far away from him as you want as long as you don't leave the room. You may, of course, go to the bathroom if necessary, but if you don't return quickly, he has permission to barge in and find you. For now, pack your personal belongings before Taps tonight, and be ready to go with me at Reveille. You are welcome to wear the clothing we gave you when you arrived."

When Raven left, Moe stayed behind and stood with his hands folded in front, an assignment Raven likely cooked up to keep me from scheming with my teammates. I scooted my chair closer to the others and sat again. "Okay, it's clear that Camille approved of Plan A. Processing the trainees is Raven's way of saying she's planning to kill you all. And you know she won't flinch about it. She's already sent several kids to their deaths, knowing the dragon was down there. So we need to tell everyone to be ready to escape, let's say, three hours after Taps."

Riddle wrung her hands. "What if the other kids don't believe us? I mean, some will, but probably some won't. Maybe most."

"And," Crystal said, "the ones who don't believe might turn coat and spill our plan."

Moe cleared his throat and spoke softly while barely moving his lips. "Leave that to me. At Taps, have everyone gather in the common room."

I nodded without saying anything. As Morales, Lyric could probably help a lot, though I couldn't yet figure out what she had in mind.

After dinner and evening exercises, both of which I missed because of my banishment to the common room, the other kids returned to the dorms. I put my few belongings into a backpack, including the bracelets, and I attached a new flashlight to my belt, then I said good riddance to the dorm room and returned to the common area.

Crystal brought my dinner on a tray, a super nice meal—steak, purple mashed potatoes that tasted better than any potato I had ever tried, and a strange vegetable that looked like asparagus with arms and legs, all of it tender and savory. Apparently, Raven decided to use up the best food they had left over—a last meal for condemned prisoners.

When the bugler played Taps, Moe doused the lights in the common room and called for everyone to gather around, the open doors to the dorms furnishing a glow from each side. The children sat quietly in chairs or on the floor. Each serious expression reflected the notion that something important was about to happen.

Standing near the middle of the room with every eye on him, Moe spoke in a hushed tone. "You know I have always encouraged you kids to be the best you can be. I have been tough sometimes, maybe too tough, and I'm sorry if I pushed you too hard. I hope you'll forgive me. And maybe now you will, because I am risking my life at this moment. If Raven knew what I am about to tell you, she would have me put to death."

A few stifled gasps filtered through the room. When everyone had quieted again, he continued. "We are all proud of Megan, Zoë, Crystal, Riddle, and Oz for slaying the dragon and ending the dangerous tests you have all endured, but I learned today that Admiral Camille Fairbanks is canceling this program because she thinks she no longer needs you."

When a couple of kids reacted with smiles, he held up a hand. "It's nothing to be happy about. What sounds like good news is actually terrible. In order to hide her ghoulish activities, she plans …" He lowered his voice further. "And you must react quietly to this. She plans to kill you all."

New gasps sounded. Some of the kids clapped hands over the mouths of others, though every pair of eyes widened with alarm.

Moe laid a hand on his chest. "But I'm not going to let that happen. We … our dragon-slaying team and I … have a plan to get you all out of here safely. Since Raven and the guards have weapons, I can't overcome them myself, so we'll have to rely on stealth and silence. You will have to call on your powers, the physical strength you've gained during your training, and, most of all, your absolute silence from now on. We can't let anyone else know about our plans."

I looked at Oz. He sat on a chair in a corner by himself and watched me with narrowed eyes. He knew that Lyric could look like anyone she pleased, though she couldn't exactly mimic their word choices or mannerisms without studying them for a long time. He likely figured out that she had transformed into a copy of Morales, but what would he do with that knowledge? Maybe I could get a hint before he exited to his dorm.

"Therefore," Moe continued as he walked to the boys' door and opened it, "we will meet here again in three hours. I know it will be difficult, but try to sleep. I will wake you up when it's time to go, and I will inform everyone about the rest of the plan." I sidled over to Oz and stood next to him while Moe continued. "Wear your uniforms to bed. That'll save some time. You won't be able to take anything with you besides what you wear or carry in your backpacks, so put your necessities in your packs before you go to bed. Also, when you leave your beds, make it look like someone's sleeping there. That way, if someone were to peek in, it would look like you're still there."

When everyone headed toward their dorms, I caught Oz's sleeve and whispered, "Everything all right?"

"Not really." He nodded toward Moe. "I know what you're doing with Lyric, and it makes me nervous. I'm guessing she's going to pretend to be him long enough for you to get everyone out, maybe order the guards to do something that makes them look the other way."

I nodded. "Something like that."

"What about Raven? He can't tell her what to do. She reports to Camille Fairbanks and no one else."

"We can neutralize Raven."

He bent his brow. "Neutralize? Do you mean kill her?"

"I don't think that will be necessary. We can take her by surprise and tie her up. Gag her. We'll make it work somehow."

"This plan sounds like an unfinished bridge. You'll come to the end and drop into a canyon 'cause you don't really know what you're doing."

I pointed at myself with a thumb. "I've escaped places a lot tougher than this underground cracker box, and I've learned that anytime you make a detailed plan and think you've considered every possibility, it never works. You just have to think fast on your feet and somehow dodge the problems that pop up. It's all about experience, flexibility, and teammates you can count on."

"Yeah, you're great with words, but words aren't good enough for me. I mean, I'll escape if everyone else does, and I'm not gonna rat on you, but leave me out of the planning."

I narrowed an eye. "Is it because of how we have to escape?"

"What do you mean?"

"We'll have to climb the fence. That's why Lyric had us practicing today."

Oz winced. "Okay. You got me. I know I can't climb that fence quick enough. But why don't you just have Lyric order the guards to do something besides watching the gate?"

"Because they would probably ask Raven for confirmation. The guards wouldn't want to get into trouble with her."

He sighed. "Yeah, you're probably right about that."

"That's why we have to get over the fence super quick. I'll come up with an alternative for you."

"What alternative could there be?"

"Like I told you, I'll think fast on my feet." I set a hand on his shoulder and looked him in the eye. "I give you my solemn word that I'll get you out of here."

He glanced at my hand, prompting me to draw it back. "What about the fence noise?" he asked. "The guards will hear us."

"Perdantus said he would take care of the noise."

He blinked hard. "The bird? Are you serious?"

"That bird has never failed me yet." I glanced at Moe. He stood patiently at the boys' dorm door. We needed to finish up. "Perdantus will get it done. Trust me."

"That's just it. I don't trust you. You've been here a couple of days, and you think you're in charge of our lives. I don't believe they'll kill us, but I do believe we might die trying to escape."

I nodded toward his dorm door. "You'd better get going. Just don't squeal. All right?"

"I won't squeal." He spun and stalked through the doorway.

When Moe closed the door, he exhaled heavily. "That didn't sound good at all."

"You're right, but I think he'll come around. He did against the dragon."

"True. He seems kind of wimpy on the surface, but he gets the job done."

Now alone in the common room, I sat with Moe on a sofa. Since the room was dark, he transformed back into Lyric. "So," I said. "let's talk about how to keep Raven and the guards occupied while we climb the fence."

Lyric whispered, "Poison."

I sucked in a breath. "Poison? You mean, you plan to kill them?"

She nodded. "Since we don't have guns, it's the only way I can think of. I found a bottle in the kitchen that should do it." She shrugged. "They deserve to die, right?"

I firmed my tone. "I don't care what they deserve. We're not going to kill anyone unless it's in self-defense."

"I thought of that, but we *are* defending ourselves. If we don't kill Raven, she'll kill us."

"Not necessarily. We're only guessing she's going through with Plan A, and maybe we can escape without killing anyone."

Lyric's brow furrowed. "How?"

"Like you said to the others, stealth and silence. I trust that Perdantus will do something about the fence noise, and you can distract Raven and the guards, maybe disable the searchlight. I want to get out of here without spilling a single drop of blood."

"All right. Good." Lyric touched her stomach. "I was feeling queasy about poisoning people."

"Yeah. No wonder." I set a hand on her shoulder. "Listen, our goal is to rescue, to save lives. Every decision we make needs to focus on that. We'll kill a murderer if we have to but only to save other lives. Since we might have to alter our plans on the fly, keep that in mind. We are all about saving lives, not taking them."

She gave me a firm nod. "Got it."

"I suppose you don't need to sleep."

"Nope. Powered to the max all the time."

"Well, I need to." I leaned my head back against the sofa cushion. "You still have the stopwatch, right?"

She withdrew it from a pocket and showed it to me. "Yep."

"Then wake me in three hours unless something comes up."

She transformed back into Moe and clicked the start button. "Sleep well."

I took my backpack off and set it at my side, then closed my eyes and tried to sleep, but my brain kept running through different fence-climbing scenarios. Considering the times the kids posted during the exercise, it seemed impossible for them to get over the fence and run to the switchback trail before the searchlight could catch them in the act. Somehow, Lyric would have to sabotage the light.

After nearly an hour, I finally dozed off. I dreamed about the escape again, and the dreams raised the noise problem. The fence rattle magnified and spread into a ground tremor and then a full-fledged quake. The ceiling collapsed and buried everyone alive, making the camp a death trap that would soon become a graveyard once the debris had crushed the life out of everyone underneath it. And then an earlier idea hit me. The explosive boxes I saw on the cavern ceiling could be an easy way for Raven to kill the Starborn. She would get her allies out and blow up the ceiling—all evidence buried forever.

Something touched my shoulder. I snapped my eyes open. Moe stood next to me, though the red gleam in his eyes told me he was really Lyric. "We still have fifteen minutes to go," he said, "but I have to use the toilet first."

I raised my brow. "Really? I thought you didn't need to do that anymore."

"When I was with Raven, she wanted us to sit down and chat while drinking coffee. She said she made my favorite kind, something caramel. Anyway, I thought if I refused, she might get suspicious. It was a big mug, and my digestive system still works, so now I have to go."

I nodded toward the boys' dorm. "Then go."

She glanced that way with a nervous pause. "Yeah, I could, but I'd rather go as a girl. I'll change back to Riddle for a minute and go in our dorm."

I smiled. "I can't blame you for that."

When she left, I rose from the sofa, put the backpack on, and yawned silently, stretching my arms. The moment I flopped my arms to my sides, something thudded close by. I snapped my flashlight from my belt, flicked it on, and aimed the beam toward the sound.

The rug over the trapdoor lifted, then slid out of the way as the door opened fully and slapped against the floor. Moe's head appeared. As he emerged, he groaned, obviously in pain. When he saw me, he extended a hand. "Megan. Great. Help me up."

I glanced at the dorm door. How could I signal Lyric to stay inside without alerting Moe? "Um … sure." I grasped his wrist and pulled.

Groaning again, he climbed the rest of the way out, then sat on the floor and looked at me. "Well, that was torture, but I followed my own advice and never gave up. It's like a chant I teach to all the kids. Never give up. Never give up."

I shifted the light so that it stayed out of his eyes. "What happened?"

"Riddle and I went …" He blinked at me. "Wait. You mean Riddle didn't get out? She didn't tell you to come and look for me?"

Ten different ways to answer ran through my mind, each dangerous for multiple reasons. I chose a semi-true one that might satisfy him, but if he checked with Raven, that could be a problem. "Riddle came back and told us you fell somewhere, but she wasn't sure how to find you. I asked what happened just now because I was wondering if you broke a bone or something."

He rolled up a pant leg, revealing a swollen ankle. "It might be broken. I'm not sure. Looks pretty bad. And I probably made it worse climbing out of that hole I fell into."

The girls' dorm door opened. Lyric looked out. When she saw Moe, she stifled a gasp and closed the door. Fortunately, Moe was looking at his ankle.

"It does look bad." I searched his belt for his canteen. "Did you have water?"

"I had enough. Drained my canteen and left it in the hole." He extended a hand again. "Can you help me get to the infirmary?"

My mind again reeled with possibilities. With Moe in the infirmary, Lyric couldn't be him, and that would ruin our chance for her to distract the guards. "Um … it's a long way to walk on that ankle. Why don't I help you lie down on the sofa and prop that ankle on a pillow? Then I'll see if I can get a wheelchair from the infirmary and another canteen."

"You'd do that for me? Thanks, Megan."

The dorm door opened again. Raven came out, though I assumed she was Lyric. I couldn't see any other possibility. "Morales?" she said as she hurried closer. "You're injured."

"Maybe a broken ankle. Hurts like crazy." He lifted his arms. "Can you help Megan get me to the sofa?"

"Of course." She and I each supported him under an arm as we lifted him to one foot, then we helped him hop to the sofa and lie down. With nearly every move, he grunted, obviously in a lot of pain.

After we set a couple of throw pillows under his ankle, Raven sidled close to me and whispered, "I'll go to the infirmary and see if I can get a sedative from the nurse. If Moe's sleeping, he won't talk to the real Raven." She leaned over and touched Moe on the shoulder. "I'm going to the infirmary to get you something for the pain."

He grimaced as he tried to smile. "Thanks. That'll be great. And water."

After giving me the stopwatch, she left and closed the door quietly. I glanced at the watch—nine minutes to go. The boys' dorm door opened, and Oz poked his head out. He likely knew that it was almost time to gather for our escape, but he probably didn't know that the person lying on the sofa was the real Morales.

I hurried to him and grabbed the doorknob, whispering in his ear as I tried to push it closed with him in the way. "It's not time yet."

"I know." He pushed back and slipped out. "I'm just trying to figure out what's going on. Why is Lyric on the sofa, and why was Raven in here?"

"Well …" I looked into his eyes. At times like this, I would often lie to keep people safe from harm, but Oz was my teammate. He risked his life to help us slay the dragon. How could I lie to him? "Um … that's not Lyric on the sofa."

His eyes widened. "The real Morales came back?"

I nodded. "He's hurt. We're getting pain meds for him."

His whisper sharpened. "Then we're sunk. Lyric can't be Morales anymore. She can't distract the guards."

"If the painkiller knocks Morales out, she can change into him and—"

"What? You can't be serious. He might wake up, and you'll have two Moes." Oz shook his head hard. "You can't do this. I won't let you."

"But they'll kill everyone in the morning. It's better to take our chances and try to escape."

"They won't kill us. No one is that cruel."

I growled as I spoke. "I watched Camille's husband's ship aim its photon torpedoes at a temple filled with children. If I hadn't stopped him, he would've blown that building to pieces with all the children inside, and I've heard that Camille is even crueler than he was. She doesn't want anyone to know how she's been sending kids on suicide missions to find the Starborn power source, and she'll eliminate all witnesses who aren't loyal to her."

"Maybe that's what we should focus on. If we were loyal to her—"

"Stop it!" My own whisper spiked in volume. "We can't be loyal to a kid killer. That's not happening."

Oz let out a deep sigh. Then he looked me in the eye for several seconds, his expression softening. "Listen, Megan, I don't want this to sound romantic or anything, but you're the most amazing girl I've ever met. I know you want to save the kids, and you'll risk your life and break your back to get it done. It's just that I don't think your plan is going to work. I think if we wait to see if they really are planning to kill us, then we can rise up and fight. With all of our combined Starborn powers, they can't possibly beat us."

"Yeah, well, good luck with battling guards with guns. They'll mow you down before you can set a shoelace on fire. Sure, you'll have helpers, but getting twenty different strange powers together as a unified front won't be easy. Besides, Raven knows what Starborns are capable of." I wanted to reveal our theory that Raven was an anti-Starborn, that she could sap our powers, but I had no proof. "She'll be ready. She probably already is ready."

Oz crossed his arms. "Oh, yeah? How?"

I lowered my voice another notch and eased closer to him. "Have you looked carefully at the lights on the ceiling?"

"No. Not really. Why?"

"I climbed the fence behind the dorm and studied one of them. It has a remote receiver attached with extra wires leading into the dirt."

Oz shrugged. "So?"

"A label said Remote Detonation Receiver. It's a remote-controlled bomb. Raven set this camp up so that it can be buried, and everyone left here would suffocate."

Oz's lower lip quivered for a split second. "I don't believe it. Yeah, you saw the detonator, but they might be there to cover the camp after everyone's gone. You're just paranoid."

"I thought of that option, and maybe you're right, but you asked how Raven could be ready." I gave him a shrug of my own. "And now I've told you."

The common room exit door opened. Raven—Lyric in disguise— walked in with another woman following her, likely the nurse. They huddled together near the sofa, whispering to Moe. After the nurse helped him drink from a cup, she gave him an injection, and he fell asleep within seconds. When the nurse left, Raven strode to me with a shoebox in her hand. She looked at Oz. "Why are you here?"

"Don't play boss lady, Lyric. I know who you are." He nodded toward the box. "What's in there?"

"Something for Megan." She set a finger to her lips. "And don't talk so loud. I know I can't change into Moe now, but I can still help out by being Raven. I passed by her room, and she's sound asleep."

I looked at the stopwatch. "Less than three minutes. We have to move forward."

"Have you heard from Perdantus?" she asked. "About the fence noise, I mean."

"Nope. But he'll get it done. I know he will."

Oz huffed. "Way too much confidence in that bird."

"That's not possible." I pointed toward the girls' dorm door. "Raven, please wake everyone up and gather them quietly. While you do that, I'm going to show Oz what trusting in your team is all about."

"Sure." Still holding the shoebox, she opened the girls' door and went inside.

I grabbed Oz's sleeve, pulled him to the exit door, and opened it. Outside, the searchlight revolved in its usual circuit, illuminating the fence. When it drew near, I closed the door, waited for it to pass, and opened it again. While the kids gathered in the room behind me, I listened carefully.

Something metallic rattled, then stopped. Seconds later, the rattle returned, louder this time. One of the guards called from the tower. "Did you hear that?"

"Yeah. I'll take a look."

The searchlight stopped and swung back to the section of fence where we practiced climbing. Something small clung to the links about halfway up, bobbing in time with the rattles.

"It's a bird," a guard said. "What's it doing?"

"Catching bugs. Looks like crickets."

"We have crickets down here?"

"Yeah, I've seen them before. For some reason they're attracted to the fence. Go figure."

"Bird's gonna feast for a while. Get fat on crickets." The searchlight shifted away and returned to its usual circuit.

"There," I said as I closed the door. "Perdantus solved the noise problem, just like he said he would."

"Gotta admit, that's one smart bird." Oz furrowed his brow. "But how did he get those crickets to stay on the fence?"

"I'm not asking, but we have to get going before he runs out of them."

Lyric, still looking like Raven, unzipped my backpack and put something inside as she whispered, "I found the box in Raven's room. Looks like mechanical parts. I'm putting them in your pack."

I nodded but said nothing. Apparently, she didn't want Oz to know, and I couldn't blame her for that. The parts were likely the engine ignition coil and Sonya's battery. We would definitely need them if we hoped to escape the planet aboard the Astral Dragon.

She rezipped the pack and handed me my bracelets. "I saw them in there. I guessed that you would want them."

"Good call." I snapped the bracelets in place.

"And I told all the kids who I really am. I hope that's all right."

"Works for me." I turned toward the gathered kids. "Now pay close attention. We all have to climb over the fence as quietly and quickly as possible in the spot where we practiced. When you make it to the other side, run to the switchback path that climbs the steep cliff, hustle to the top, and hide until we all get there." I showed them the stopwatch. "I'm going to time the searchlight's revolution so we'll know how fast we have to be. I'll start the watch when the light passes the point where we climb."

The moment the sweeping beam brushed past Perdantus, I pressed the button. We all watched through the window in silence. When the searchlight beam shot into the common room, everyone ducked, even though I hadn't told them to. A good sign. They didn't need me to tell them everything.

Again, the light passed by Perdantus. I clicked the watch button. "That circuit took …" I read the time. "Twelve seconds?"

"You seem surprised," Oz said.

As a lump formed in my throat, I swallowed. "Um … yeah. It's going faster tonight than it was when I checked last time."

Oz pointed out the window. "So we're supposed to run from here to the fence, climb over it, and hide, all in twelve seconds?"

"Well, no. You run behind the beam while it's heading toward the climbing point. Then when it passes that point, you have to get over the fence and hide before the light comes around again."

"So we'll have twelve seconds to make the climb and hide. And that's after running from here to there. Not even Chip can do that. Neither can you. And I know *I* could never make it."

After everyone ducked under the beam's next pass, Crystal pushed to the front and turned toward everyone. "We can do it. All of us." She set a hand on my shoulder. "Because we have Megan. She's a dynamo. That's her Starborn power. She can make us all stronger and faster. And our Starborn gifts will get souped up. I know. She's done all of that for me."

"And me," Zoë said as she stepped forward and joined Crystal. "I believe in Megan."

"But most of us have never seen it work," Oz said. "I mean, I saw Megan do some pretty amazing things, but you're asking us to risk our lives to trust someone to get us over a fence in less than twelve seconds, someone who's never even done it herself."

I pushed the stopwatch into Oz's palm. "Eight seconds."

"What?" He blinked at me. "What do you mean?"

"I'm going to make it over the fence and hide in eight seconds. Time me while everyone watches." I lifted my dragon's eye locket from behind my shirt. It was already glowing much more brightly than I expected. "Look for the little red light."

Oz huffed. "Easy for you to do with those muscle-enhancing brace-lets."

"You're right. Too easy." I unfastened the bracelets, stuffed them into my backpack, and put the pack on. "Get ready. Here it comes."

When the beam passed again, I opened the door and ran to the left, close to the perimeter, then turned toward the guardhouse, chasing the beam. Yes, it was definitely moving faster than last time. Although I kept up pretty well, Oz and the other slower kids probably couldn't. I would have to come up with a solution.

I looked down at my locket as it bounced with my gait. The dragon's eye's glow burst through the clasp, giving me the same power I hoped to give everyone else. I held it out to my side to make sure Oz and the others could see it as I ran on. When I passed the guard tower, I noticed a crawlspace under the supporting platform. Maybe we could use that somehow.

The moment the beam flashed by Perdantus, I hustled to the fence, set my hands and feet in the link gaps, and shot toward the top, my muscles stronger than they had ever felt before. The fence rattles seemed no louder than Perdantus's pecks, giving me more confidence we could do this.

With a final push from my legs, I sailed over the fence and dropped. When I hit the ground, I bent my knees, rolled, then leaped up and ran to the start of the switchback trail. I crouched in the shadows to catch my breath and listen for an alarm, but the only sound came from the fence—the rattles Perdantus made as he continued plucking crickets from the links.

After the searchlight passed, once, twice, three times, I hustled back to the fence, climbed over again, and ran in front of it as it chased me

271

around the perimeter on the other side. When I arrived at the dorm building, I found the door partially open, dashed inside, and closed it behind me, ducking low and breathing heavily just as the light flashed through the window.

When the room dimmed again, someone grabbed my wrist and hauled me to my feet. Crystal stood before me, grinning. "Seven point five seconds, girl. That was awesome. It took you a little longer coming back over the fence, but you were tired. No one else will have to climb twice." Pats on the back came from all around along with whispers of amazement.

Oz set the stopwatch in my hand. "You proved yourself. Can't say I'm not impressed. But that's you. Everyone but Chip was slower than you in the exercise."

"I was slower," Zoë said. "But I'm willing to go."

Crystal reached into my backpack and withdrew my bracelets. "Same here. I know she can supercharge me."

"Maybe so." Oz sighed as he shook his head. "But I would have to cut my time by more than half. I don't think it's possible. I can't even run between here and the fence without coughing up a horse."

I took the bracelets and began putting them on. "I might have a solution. We can all sneak to a crawlspace under the guard tower and dash to the fence from there. That'll cut the running distance way down."

"Okay," Oz said. "This is getting better. But I'm still way too slow—"

"No time to discuss it. Just listen, and you'll see that you might not have to run at all." I snapped the second bracelet in place. "Groups of five. I'll take the first group. Chip, you're with me. Choose two other fast kids to go with us. Then Zoë will lead the second group. Crystal the third. Riddle the fourth. Oz the fifth with whoever is left." I turned toward Raven. "Lyric, you're in my group. Instead of running with us, go straight to the yard in view of the tower and distract the guards while the other groups are coming. We'll be sending kids over the fence one by one at the same time."

"Distract the guards? How?"

"You're the boss. They'll do whatever you say. The goal is to come up with a reason to turn off the searchlight or point it at something besides the fence and keep it there or shut it off until we're all out. Get creative."

"Get creative." She nodded. "I can do that."

"Good. And if the searchlight stops, I want all the groups that are still in this building to hurry as fast as they can to the tower right away." I patted her shoulder. "I know you can do it."

I pulled her to a crouch with my hand on the doorknob. "We'll go the next time the searchlight passes. Chip, are you ready?"

He joined Raven and me in our crouch with another boy and a girl. "We're ready."

I showed everyone in my group the glowing locket. "We can do this." The moment the beam passed, I opened the door. "Now!"

I ran to the perimeter behind the searchlight, glancing back. Chipmunk and the other two kids followed at the same speed, while Raven ran straight into the yard, barely visible in the dimness.

When she drew near the guardhouse, she looked up into their perch, waved her arms, and whisper shouted. "Hey. Turn the searchlight on me."

At nearly the same moment, Chipmunk and I arrived at the base of the tower and gathered the other two kids underneath. While we caught our breath, we watched and listened as the steady clinks of Perdantus plucking crickets continued.

The light stopped its rotation and focused on Raven. She set a hand in front of her face to block the brightness. "Raven?" one of the guards called. "What are you doing out here?"

I patted Chipmunk on the back. "This is our chance. You three go. All together. I'll see you at the top of the cliff."

While they skulked toward the fence, Raven blinked at the light. "You know about the plan for today."

"Yeah," the guard said. "Did something change?"

Zoë's group joined us, and I sent them along toward the fence except for her. I whispered, "I need you to stay in case the light starts up again. Maybe you can stop it."

She nodded. "I'll see what I can do."

"No change," Raven said. "I just couldn't sleep and wanted to make sure everyone's on board. It's a big day. I don't want any glitches. Tell me the steps I gave you."

When Crystal's group arrived, I kept her with me while the others headed for the fence. Louder rattles sounded from that direction, but the guards didn't seem to notice.

"It's pretty simple," the guard said. "We've got it covered."

Raven scowled and sharpened her tone. "Tell me the steps."

I whispered to Crystal, "Take the battery and coil from my backpack in case I don't make it. We need to get these kids out no matter what happens to me. And don't argue. Just do it."

While Crystal pulled the items from my pack, Riddle arrived with her kids. She whispered, "Something's up with Oz. I don't think he's coming, but I couldn't read his emotions. He's still got that blocking thing going on."

The guard heaved a sigh. "All right. All right." He altered his cadence, as if reciting a list. "When you and Megan leave, we'll gather the trainees in the yard."

"Understood," I said to Riddle. "Oz can stay if he wants to, but if the rest of the kids don't come because he won't lead them, I'll go back and get them." I patted her arm. "Now you and Crystal and your kids go to the fence."

When they hustled out, leaving me with Zoë, we continued listening while waiting for the last few kids.

The guard continued his recitation. "Then we short out one of the ceiling lights and tell the kids we're leaving to look at the circuits while they stay and do their exercises."

I gritted my teeth and whispered to Zoë, "Oz needs to hear this." I looked toward the dorms, but I couldn't see the building. The nearby searchlight was too bright. "Where is he?"

"Then," the guard said, "we detonate the bombs. The ceiling collapses, the SS Squad gets buried, and the danger to the galaxy is over. Everyone wins. Except the mutant kids, of course." He chuckled. "But you have to put the rabid dog down to keep everyone else safe, am I right?"

I clenched a fist. My guess was true, but I never imagined how callous the guards would be about murdering children.

"Very good," Raven said. "And where will you be when you detonate the bombs?"

"Outside. At the surface. We'll take the remote. And don't worry. We tested it at that distance. It'll work."

The fence rattled more loudly than ever. One of the kids must've jerked it too hard.

"That's no bird," the guard said. "Move the light over there."

"Zoë," I hissed. "Try to keep the light where it is."

"I'm on it, but you'd better zap me with extra power. That thing looks heavy." She scooted a few steps out and looked up with an arm extended toward the perch while I held the locket in my palm. I opened the clasp and exposed the ruby. It pulsed like a heartbeat—radiant and scarlet.

"I can't get the light to move," a guard said. "It's stuck. The joystick won't budge."

"Then we'll move it manually. I'll take this side."

While the guards grunted through their effort, Zoë held both hands high, her palms aimed at the perch. Grimacing tightly, she bared her teeth. Finally, she fell to her back and breathed heavily.

"We got it loose." The light swung toward the fence and illuminated Perdantus as he pecked at the crickets harder than ever. None of the kids were anywhere in sight. "I guess it was that blasted bird after all."

"Yeah. He's a greedy one. I'm surprised he hasn't bloated into a blimp by now. But it looks like most of the crickets are gone. He'll leave soon."

While they talked, I closed the locket, shuffled out, and helped Zoë crawl back into our hideout. Now that the beam pointed away, I could see the dorm building. The remaining kids had gathered in front of the door, safe for now because the light no longer rotated, but Oz didn't appear to be with them. They had no leader, no one to tell them to hustle over here. Maybe they would start on their own. If not, I would have to go back.

"Need anything else, Raven?" a guard asked.

Barely visible just outside the beam's glow, Raven looked at the fence, probably deciding that she had given everyone enough time to leave. "No. It sounds like you're ready. Thank you for putting my mind at ease."

One of the guards whispered to the other, but, crouching so close, I could still hear him. "Since when does Raven thank one of us peons?"

"Female bosses are weird," the other guard replied. "Just restart the searchlight."

The light began rotating again. I looked once more at the dorm. The kids were now walking toward the guard tower, probably not yet noticing the revived light and thinking they could get here safely at their slower pace. I had to go after them.

A woman's voice pierced the silence. "Who are you?"

I looked for the source. The real Raven strode toward her copy, only seconds away. "Did you hear me? I said who are you?"

Lyric transformed into a tall gray-haired woman and turned toward Raven. "Don't you recognize me?"

Raven halted and stared. "Moth—" She cleared her throat. "Admiral Fairbanks! What are you doing … I mean … yes, of course I recognize you."

I stifled a gasp. Was Raven about to call her Mother? But I couldn't ponder that more than a second. I looked back at the straggling kids. They finally saw the light and started running, but it caught up and swept past them. Fortunately, the guards were watching the drama in the yard and didn't seem to notice the new escapees.

One of the guards whispered, "Did you let the admiral in?"

"No," the other guard said. "I didn't even see her until just now. Something strange is going on."

I kept my stare on the two women. With the searchlight no longer aimed at them, the guards didn't notice Lyric's latest transformation. Not only that, the real Raven probably assumed the guards let the admiral come through the gate, so she had no need to ask them.

Lyric, posing as Camille Fairbanks, chuckled. "I know you're surprised, Raven, but I thought I would get here early and personally supervise this transfer. Megan is far more dangerous than you realize."

When the kids arrived at the crawlspace, I gathered them together. They all trembled, probably spooked after getting lit up by the beam, certain they were about to get shot. Climbing while scared would be harder than ever. "Zoë," I whispered, "if you can at least slow the light's rotation, we can make this work. We need to give these kids plenty of time."

"I'll get it done." She sneaked out again in sight of the perch and extended a hand toward the searchlight, then nodded at me.

I whispered to the kids. "Go. One at a time, after each cycle."

Raven set a hand on a pistol attached to her belt. "I assure you, Admiral, I can handle the likes of Megan Willis. Even she can't survive a bullet to the head."

I looked back at the dorm building yet again. The door opened, and Oz stepped out with Moe behind him, a hand on Oz's shoulder for balance. Was Oz going to betray us after all? But maybe I could thwart his plan. In Moe's groggy state, by the time he walked this far, the other kids would have had time to escape, but Zoë and Lyric wouldn't. I had to make a move before Moe could blow up our entire mission, and the only move I could come up with might end my life in a hurry.

"You're right, Raven," I said as I emerged from my hiding place. "A bullet would kill me."

As I passed Zoë, who still stood in a shadow, I whispered, "Go help Crystal. And don't you dare say no. I got this. Make your move as soon as the guards give us the spotlight."

Zoë ducked low and hustled to our hiding place. Now I had to delay everyone long enough for Crystal and Zoë to fire up the Astral Dragon.

I walked into the open, my hands raised. "I did everything you asked me to do. Why are you threatening me?"

The searchlight stopped rotating and aimed at us, my back to it as I faced Raven and Camille. Raven moved her hand away from her gun. "It's just insurance. You're unpredictable, to say the least."

I lowered my hands. "I'll take that as a compliment."

"Take it however you wish. Since you're going with the admiral peacefully, I don't care what you think."

"I will go peacefully on one condition." I nodded toward the dorm building. "You won't detonate the bombs and bury a bunch of sleeping kids."

Raven gasped. "Detonate bombs? Bury—"

"Don't try to snow me, Raven. One thing you should've learned about me by now, I'm not stupid." I gestured upward. "I checked out your bombs in the ceiling. I know you'll want to get rid of the evidence, including anyone who can rat you out."

She gave me a derisive smile. "All right. I admit it. You are smart, and you are right about the bombs and our plan to bury the evidence, including the Starborn. But we're not going to kill you. You're too valuable."

"But I won't be valuable once you get what you want. You'll—"

"Don't listen to a word she says!" Holding a handgun, Moe staggered into the searchlight's glow pushing Oz in front of him. "Oswald told me the whole story. The kids are escaping, and Megan is the mastermind behind everything."

Camille laughed. "You're so drunk you're about to fall down."

"Drugged, not drunk, but we have to stop that calculating girl before—"

"Come now," Camille said. "Megan's smart, but no one's smart enough to get the Starborn children past a secure fence without our guards noticing it." She looked up at the tower. "Right, gentlemen?"

Standing next to the searchlight, one of the guards waved a hand. "Right, Admiral. We've been watching the fence all night. No one could've gotten past us."

"See?" Camille nodded toward the admin building. "Now go to your room and sleep it off."

"Don't believe me? Check for yourself." Moe pointed toward the dorm building. "They're gone. Every last one of them."

"Did you actually go into the dorm rooms?" Camille asked.

"Well … no. I just took Oz's word for it."

Raven crossed her arms. "Oz, what's going on? It looks like Morales is too addled to give us a sane answer."

I glanced toward the fence, barely visible outside the reach of the beam. Perdantus had left, which probably meant Zoë had made it out.

Maybe he flew to tell Zoë and Crystal that I was in trouble and trying to buy them some time.

Oz looked straight at me as he answered. "Moe heard a noise that woke him up. He grabbed me and started choking me to find out what was going on. His eyes were wide, like a crazy man's." Oz focused on Raven. "Anyway, I tried to tell him everything was fine, but he wouldn't believe me, and he squeezed my throat more. I told him an insane story about the kids trying to escape and Megan was behind it all. He finally let me go."

"Liar!" Moe shouted. "I hardly squeezed your throat at all. I was just holding you so you wouldn't run."

Oz glared at Moe. "You were drugged. You don't know how hard you were squeezing. I could barely breathe."

"This is easily settled," Camille said, eyeing Moe. "I'll walk back to the dorm with you while Raven watches Megan and Oz."

Raven narrowed an eye at Camille. "Why are you going with him?"

"I don't want to rely on a drugged witness." Camille shrugged. "Besides, in his condition he might take a tumble and knock himself out."

"As if I care about that." Raven heaved an exasperated sigh and crossed her arms. "All right. We'll wait here."

"Let's go." Camille grasped Moe and walked with him toward the dorm.

While they faded into the darkness, I sneaked a glance at Raven. She stared at the dorm, unblinking. Whether or not she was suspicious of our fake Camille, I couldn't tell. I then focused on Oz. With wide eyes and jittering body, he seemed terrified. He knew, of course, that the Starborn children were gone, but he probably hadn't guessed that Camille was really Lyric, and I had no way of telling him.

Yet, even though *I* knew, I still couldn't figure out what Lyric had in mind. Earlier, she had mentioned poisoning someone in order to save the Starborn. Might she decide to kill Moe to keep our secret? Was she that desperate?

After a couple of minutes, Camille and Moe returned side-by-side, Moe walking more easily now, though still favoring a leg. Moe gave Raven a nod. "I guess I was really wiped out. The kids are all in bed. I apologize."

"Apology accepted, but to make up for your stupidity …" Raven drew her gun and laid it on Moe's palm. "You know what you have to do."

He stared at the gun and sighed. "Yeah. I know."

"Then do it. Now."

He offered a resigned nod, aimed the gun at Oz, and shot him in the chest.

I gasped. "Oz!"

Oz dropped to his knees, his mouth agape as he stared at me, his eyes begging for help. He fell forward and hit the ground face-first.

I lunged at Moe, but Camille blocked my way and held me with both arms wrapped around mine, pinning them to my sides as she barked, "He'll shoot you next if you don't settle down. I still need you to help me." She whispered into my ear, "We all need you."

"Well, that's done." Raven took the pistol from Moe and holstered it. "Guards, lock the door to the dorms while I wake up the nurse. We're leaving in five minutes. Then we'll go outside and bury this camp. The kids will die peacefully in their sleep." She looked up at the guard perch. "Did you hear me?"

One of the guards gave her a weak salute. "Every word. We'll be ready to go."

Camille nudged Oz with a foot. "What about him?"

"Is he still alive?" Raven asked.

"He's breathing. That's all I can tell."

Raven waved a dismissive hand. "Just leave him. He'll be dead soon, one way or another."

Heat roared into my ears. This witch was worse than a demon, maybe even worse than the real Camille. I struggled against her hold, but she seemed unnaturally strong. "Raven," Camille said, "tell your guards to open the gate. I'm taking Megan to my ship."

"Of course." Raven waved at the guards' perch. "You heard her. Open the gate."

"Right away." The guard left the perch and hustled down to the controls.

As the gate drew to the side, Raven narrowed her eyes at Camille. "Where's your sidearm?"

Camille touched her belt. "I didn't bring it. I had an armed escort with me, and we were accosted by a tunnel beast. My escort shot the beast but was wounded in the fight. I sent him back to the ship, but I neglected to take his firearm."

"Here." Raven extended her pistol. "Take mine. You can't expect to get this hellcat to your ship safely unless you're armed."

"You're right." Camille stepped away from me, took the gun, and aimed it at my back. "Go through the gate. Now."

I strode toward the opening. I didn't want to look back at Oz, but I had to. When I dared to take the glance, he lay on his side, blinking as he looked at me. He seemed so lonely. And no wonder. He was being left to die, to be buried under a mountain of dirt. And although it seemed that he allowed Moe to choke the truth out of him, who could blame him for that? He was scared to die. And now he was going to die anyway. Alone. I felt like more of a traitor than he ever was.

Trying to put the thought out of my mind, I focused ahead and passed through the open gate, Camille a few steps behind me. As we walked toward the switchback trail, the gate rattled closed, and it felt like my last chance to save Oz closed with it.

When we were well on our way up the trail, I looked down at the camp. The searchlight still shone on Oz as he lay motionless in the yard. My stomach churned. At any second I might vomit, but I held the spasms in check. I had to keep my wits about me to save everyone else.

As we neared the top, Camille transformed back into Lyric. Crystal and Zoë met us and both hugged me at the same time. "Blazes, girl!" Crystal said as she drew back. "We watched the last part of that disaster down there." She pointed toward Lyric with a thumb. "We thought she was really Camille, and we were ready to pounce on her when you got here. Good thing she went lyrical in time."

"Yeah. Good thing." I pivoted toward Lyric. "How did you convince Moe the kids were still in the dorm?"

She blinked her eyes, sparkling red. "I have a bit of Crystal's power. A smidge of hypnosis did the trick. In his condition, it wasn't hard."

"Good thinking." I refocused on Crystal. "Where are all the kids?"

"In the Astral Dragon. We replaced the battery and Sonya told us how to install the ignition coil. She says all systems are go. We're ready to try to plow out of there."

As I imagined the process, the thought of burrowing out and leaving Oz to be buried alive shredded my heart. How could I possibly do that? Trembling with emotion, I pointed at Crystal. "Listen. You and Zoë get the Astral Dragon out of its rut, then fly around. I'll be there as soon as I can."

"As soon as you can?" Zoë asked. "What're you going to do?"

I turned toward the precipice. "I'm going back for Oz."

Crystal grabbed my wrist. "Are you out of your mind? From where we stood, it looked like he ratted you out."

I shook free. "Moe choked it out of him. But then he lied for me, and it cost him a bullet to the chest."

"I saw him get shot. He's probably dead by now."

I took a deep breath. "I know. But I have to be sure."

Crystal's eyes flashed. "For a traitor? A coward? You would've chosen to die before betraying us, and you know it."

A growl erupted in my voice. "He's a human being. A kid. And I'm not leaving him behind. Got it?"

Crystal held up her hands. "Whoa! Yeah, I got it."

I exhaled. "Sorry. It's just that—"

"No. Don't apologize. I went mama hen on you, trying to protect you, and you went mama bear on me. It's all good. Go be a hero. Seriously. I mean it. It's what you do."

I waved a hand. "Go. Get the Dragon in the air and see if you can contact Oliver. We might need the Nebula Nine to help us if Camille's ship comes by to pick up Raven. When Raven figures out the truth, she'll want to punch a hole right through me."

Zoë pointed at Crystal. "You go to the Dragon and get the kids out. I'll go with Megan."

"Good. No way she's going alone." Crystal kissed my forehead. "That's not goodbye, Sister. That's hurry up and get your butt to the ship in one piece. And if Oz is dead, don't drag his corpse back with you."

I nodded. "All right. No dead bodies." I set a hand on Zoë's back. "Let's go."

We jogged down the trail as fast as the turns would allow. When we reached bottom, we ran to the gate. The guards were no longer there. Just as I set a hand on the chain links to climb, the gate began rolling open. Zoë and I squeezed side by side between the fence and the cliff face, a space so tight, the gate's links brushed against our bodies as they passed.

When the gate fully opened, Raven walked out, followed by the infirmary nurse, Moe, and the two guards. Leaving the gate open, they walked up the switchback trail and soon drew out of sight. Fortunately, they left the cavern's ceiling lights on at a dim setting, enough for us to see our way around.

We squeezed out of our hiding place and hurried to Oz. He lay on his side, gasping and gurgling, his face ashen.

I knelt next to him and held his hand. "I'm back, Oz. I'm back."

"I …" Bloody bubbles oozed from his lips as he squeezed my fingers weakly. "I hoped you would come."

"Don't talk. Zoë and I are going to get you out of here."

Zoë knelt next to me and shook her head. "It looks bad. Real bad."

"His only hope is Galena. I know she hasn't been able to heal him before, but I'm not giving up. I can't give up."

"No argument from me."

"We have to hurry before they blow the ceiling."

"You got a plan?" Zoë asked.

I looked at the trail leading up the cliff. "Carrying him together around those switchbacks would be impossible. I'll have to carry him myself. Help me get him up."

We worked together to hoist Oz over my shoulders, Zoë using her powers to add to the lift. Once I had him balanced, I pulled my locket out and clutched it in my fist. Now it was time to use my power to energize myself. "Please, Astral Dragon, help me do this and do it fast." I opened my hand. The locket pulsed red once more, grimacing under the load. "Now the fun part."

"Fun? Is that what you're calling it?"

"Optimism helps." My legs flexing powerfully, I marched with long strides through the open gate and to the beginning of the trail. As I climbed, I bent forward to keep from toppling back, and Zoë stayed at my rear to protect me from a fall. Tension racked my nerves. At any second, one of the guards might push the dreaded detonation button. Since the cavern's ceiling and its detonators spanned over the trail, the collapse would bury us with the camp. We would all die.

Every step sent pain through my shoulders and back, though the weight seemed less than I expected. And my legs were handling the burden just fine. When we reached the sixth switchback out of twelve, I spoke with a cheery tone. "It's not so bad. Maybe we can do this after all."

Zoë grunted through her reply. "Good. I'm lifting you with my brain as much as I can. You two are heavy."

"That explains a lot. Keep it up. I'm getting a good feeling about—"

An explosion erupted behind us, then another. The lights blew out, casting us in darkness. As more explosions rocked the cavern, sounding like massive thunderclaps, dirt cascaded on us. I shouted, "Run!"

Summoning all of my remaining strength, I broke into a quick jog. With no light to guide my steps, I had to slow my pace as I guessed where each switchback had to be, feeling with my feet to negotiate the turn. Spitting grit as it drizzled down my face, I called, "Are you with me, Zoë?"

I felt a tug on the back of my shirt. "Don't talk. Just keep going."

When I reached the eleventh switchback, a cascade of dirt knocked me down to my hands and knees. As the debris piled on, the weight grew heavier and heavier. Although I still had an air pocket under me, Oz probably didn't. He would suffocate in mere moments, and then I would soon after. "Zoë?" I shouted. "Can you hear me?"

A muffled reply vibrated through the soil. I couldn't understand the words, but at least it meant she was still conscious. Maybe she could hear me better than I could hear her.

I yelled as loudly as I could. "The dirt is still loose, and it's not a sheer cliff anymore. Climb through the dirt directly toward where the ledge was." I took a deep breath and held it. Trying to follow my own instructions, I pushed with my legs, straightened my body, and with one hand holding Oz, I used the other hand to pull against the dirt and haul us upward while pushing with my feet from below.

As I climbed, I talked to Oz, and also to myself. "Hang on. We're going to make it. The Astral Dragon wouldn't take us this far only to let us get buried a few meters before the top. Probably only a couple of more minutes, and we'll be there." Since the soil stayed loose, I was able to breathe and speak—unexpected, but not unwelcome as I set my feet and powered with my legs through the crushing soil again and again. Warm wetness penetrated the shoulders of my shirt. Was it sweat? Or maybe Oz's blood? I couldn't feel him breathing anymore. It might be too late.

I gritted my teeth. No. He couldn't be dead. It wasn't too late. I had to save him. Letting out a guttural growl, I climbed with all my might. As I pushed and pushed, the growl erupted into a scream. Then something grabbed my wrist and pulled. I broke out of a wall of dirt and staggered into an open area, my feet on solid ground. The grasp on my wrist held firm as I oriented myself.

A flashlight flicked on. Zoë stood next to me. Dirt covered her hair and shoulders, one hand clutched my wrist, and the other held the flashlight. "Good thing you screamed. I wouldn't've been able to find you in that mess if you hadn't."

"Yeah. Good thing." I bent my neck to look at Oz's face. Dirty blood dripped from his lips, but I couldn't tell if he was breathing. "Is he alive?"

Zoë touched his neck. "Yeah. Barely breathing, though."

I looked at a tunnel leading away from where we stood. "So where are we? At the ledge that overlooked the camp?"

Zoë shifted the light across the newly formed wall of dirt, sloping from the tunnel's ceiling down to our feet. "I think so. The ceiling here held up. No bombs close enough, I guess. The ground above the camp must've dropped and settled.."

I nodded toward the tunnel. "Then that's the way to the Astral Dragon."

"Yeah. It's pretty far, though. You can't possibly have much strength left. Maybe we can carry him together now."

I shook my head. "Too much trouble to get him off—"

The sound of an engine interrupted me. Lights appeared well down the tunnel's path, drawing closer.

"Friend or enemy?" I asked as I shifted Oz's weight on my shoulders.

"No clue," Zoë said, "but it doesn't matter. We don't have anywhere to run."

The engine noise, along with the sound of air jets, produced a familiar blend—a land rover. Seconds later, the two-seater rover arrived and
settled to the ground in front of us. The top dome's glass, coated with
grit, prevented a view of the driver, but I recognized the vehicle. It came
from the Astral Dragon.

"What's going on?" I asked Zoë. "I heard that the SS goons took
the Dragon's two rovers."

She nodded. "They did. When they brought us here, Crystal and I
saw where they hid them."

With a click and a hum, the dome lifted, revealing Crystal. Her
mouth agape, she leaped out and ran to me, extending her hands. "Is he
alive?" she asked as she and Zoë lifted Oz from mey shoulders.

"Barely. Get him to Galena right away." I shrugged to flex my
numbed shoulders. "Zoë and I will walk."

They settled Oz into the passenger seat. "No," Crystal said as she
rushed around to the driver's side. "Both of you get on top." She hopped
into the driver's seat and pressed a dashboard button. The dome lowered again and clicked in place.

I climbed onto the front of the dome with my legs over the side so Crystal could see where she was going, and I brushed grit from the glass to give her a better view. Zoë joined me, her legs over the other side.

Crystal pivoted the rover and glided down the tunnel, sending up a spray of loose dirt that collided against the side walls and curled back over Zoë and me. But that didn't matter. We were already filthy. We just blinked away the dust and held on.

After the two usual turns in the tunnels and a speedy run down the final straightaway, we arrived at the Astral Dragon, its front lights on and its entry ramp down. When the rover settled and the engine shut off, Zoë and I hopped to the ground. The moment I touched down, my knees buckled, and my calf muscles cramped. Pain roaring, I dropped to my side and flexed my toes toward my body, but the muscles kept knotting in tight, torturous spasms.

Closing my eyes, I bit my lip to keep from moaning. As I sucked in breaths through my nose, Zoë called, "Galena, get out here. We need your help with two patients."

I finally let out a moan, along with two words. "Oz first."

Crystal's voice followed, infused with a commanding tone. "We need people to carry our patients into the ship. C'mon, kids. Let's get a move on. If not for Megan, you'd be dead and buried."

Someone grabbed my wrist. I opened my eyes. Chipmunk slid a hand under me and lifted. "I've got you, Megan. Put your arm around me."

As I obeyed, another boy whose name I didn't know lifted from the other side. I reached an arm around his shoulders as well. Two girls lifted my legs, and the foursome carried me toward the ramp.

I looked at the rover. Galena stood at the side and laid a hand on Oz's chest. Obviously, she was trying to heal him. But could she?

"Stop. Let me down." I pulled my legs away from the girls, but the boys held on, propping me up. "Help me get to Oz." With one of the boys on each side, I limped heavily toward the rover, not knowing which cramping leg to favor. Both felt like steel vises, ready to snap.

When I reached Oz, I leaned over the side of the rover to get a closer view. Dirt smeared nearly every centimeter of his ashen face as he sat awkwardly in the seat, his head tilted to the side. Galena looked at me, tears streaming. "Megan, it's awful. So much blood. I repaired a hole on his chest and on his back, but he's bleeding on the inside, and I can't find where it's coming from. I've never been able to see past his ribcage."

"Maybe—" Something clogged my windpipe. I coughed out a wad of black mucous. "Maybe I can help." I lifted my locket's chain, opened the clasp, and set the locket on my palm. The ruby glowed but only with the normal brightness—my father's life signal.

I rolled my fingers around the locket and prayed, loudly enough for Galena and the growing crowd around us to hear. "Astral Dragon, I know Oz tried to betray us, but please forgive him. He knows now that he shouldn't've done what he did. *I* forgave him, and you're a lot more merciful than I am, so please do him this favor. Use my Starborn power to energize Galena so she can see into Oz's body and fix whatever problems she finds."

I heaved a sigh and looked again at the ruby. At first, the glow stayed the same, then it brightened and began pulsing. Gasps rose from all around. Everyone closed in to watch, blocking the Dragon's front lights and casting shadows over us.

"Get back," I called, "Galena needs—"

"No. Let them watch. I don't need light." Galena set her palm on Oz's chest and closed her eyes. Her facial muscles twitched as if she were guiding something with her mind. Then she crooned in a soft, lyrical tone. "I can see past his ribs and the bullet's path from his chest to his back, a path of carnage, a path of destruction. One of his lungs is bleeding from a hole that the bullet ripped through. The blood is pooling, and some of it is going up toward his mouth when he tries to breathe."

"Can you fix the hole?" I asked.

"I'm trying. There's so much damage. The bullet's path is already healing, but the lung is harder to sew back together. Even if I can stitch it, he'll still be in danger. Any jostling could rip it back open. No matter what happens, he'll be in pain for quite a while."

Chipmunk chimed in. "Oz is tough. He can handle pain. He's almost always in pain, but he gets through it."

"That's right," I said. "If you can, check out his heart while you're probing."

Galena nodded. Her eyes closed more tightly, and her brow furrowed. For nearly a minute, everyone watched in silence until Crystal sidled up to me and whispered in my ear, "We've got trouble."

I kept my voice low as well. "What kind of trouble?"

"I sent Riddle to the surface to watch for anything else that looked suspicious. A ship landed near the entrance to the trench that turns into the tunnel we're in. I asked her to describe it. It's definitely a Nebula ship. The second it landed, Raven and three other people came out of a hiding place and ran to it, probably the two guards and the nurse."

I winced. "If it's Camille in the ship, they'll find out they've been tricked, but they won't know that all of you are alive, just that I'm alive and whoever was posing as Camille. But the first place they'll look is here at the Astral Dragon."

"Then we need to load up and scram."

I nodded. "Get everyone on board. I have to stay here to keep energizing Galena."

"You got it, Captain." Crystal waved her arms. "To the ship! Now! Don't ask questions. Just go! Zoë, you get them settled inside while I guard Megan and Galena."

The Starborn kids hustled to the ramp.

Chipmunk set a hand on Oz's head. "I'm staying. He's my friend."

"That's fine," I said. "We all need a friend at a time like this."

A tear trickled down Chipmunk's cheek. "Oz asked me to stay. I'm reading his mind. He hears everything that's going on. He wants me to tell you …" Chipmunk swallowed as more tears flowed. "You're the reason he's fighting to stay alive. You fought so hard to save all of us, especially him, and he doesn't want to let you down."

As my own tears welled, I slid my hand into Oz's and compressed it. "Keep fighting, Oz. You're my new hero, and I'm here for you. So is Chip. And Galena. We'll help you get through this."

His hand flexed lightly, not much, but it was real. He definitely heard me.

"Megan." Crystal jogged toward me from the Dragon. "Everyone's ready. Sonya says we're in for a rough ride when we try to plow out of here, but we have way too many to buckle in. A lot of them are sitting on the floor holding on to something."

"It'll have to do." I looked at Galena as she continued concentrating. I couldn't ask her to hurry. She knew the dangers, both to Oz if she stopped the healing and to all of us if she couldn't finish before Camille and Raven showed up. All I could do was wait.

Zoë called from the ramp. "Something's coming. Sonya says it's a rover that's running dark, but she detected the engine. I sent Perdantus to see who's in it."

"Okay," I said. "Turn off our lights, start the engines, and raise shields in stealth mode. Try to shift the Dragon so our weapons are aimed at that rover."

"What about the ramp?"

"Raise it. If the rover is from hostiles, then once you're in position, open the cargo door in the back. We'll come in that way. I'm sure Perdantus will use that door, too."

"Got it." Zoë ran up the ramp.

"Almost finished with the wound in the lung," Galena said, her eyes still tightly shut. "I got a look at his heart. There's some kind of hole in it. I've never seen anything like it."

"A birth defect," Chipmunk said, his hand still on Oz's head. "He told me about it. It makes him get tired. He said the surgery to fix it is too dangerous, so he just has to live with it."

The Astral Dragon's lights flicked off, leaving us in darkness. Zoë had my flashlight, but she was gone. Fortunately, Galena worked her magic with her eyes closed.

The Dragon's engines rumbled to life, raising a hum that sent a tremor through the ground and walls. Dirt from the ceiling pelted us. Since the Dragon got here without collapsing the ceiling, might something else be going on? Another quake?

As if responding to my thought, the showers increased but then decreased, then rose and fell in a pattern, letting me know each time the Dragon shifted and rested as it turned toward the approaching light. A dim glow appeared from inside the ship, illuminating the door to the cargo hold. The Astral Dragon was now in position to face the rover.

Nearly invisible in the darkness, Perdantus flew to my shoulder. "A four-person rover is approaching on wheels instead of an air cushion, but no one is inside. I assume it is being controlled remotely."

"Probably carrying a bomb," I said. "Camille can't get her ship into the tunnel, so she's trying to blow up the Dragon any way she can. Tell Crystal to fire a laser in front of the rover. Maybe blasting a rut in its path will slow it down, but be sure not to hit the rover itself. An explosion could collapse the entire tunnel. I'll be on board as soon as I can."

"I will tell her." Perdantus flew toward the ship.

"He's patched." Galena lifted her hand from Oz's chest. "Not perfectly, but we can move him. We'll talk about his heart defect later."

A light pulsed from the front of the Astral Dragon, and the laser's telltale zinging sound followed. An explosion erupted somewhere down the tunnel, too far away to see.

I climbed into the rover's driver seat next to Oz, noticing for the first time that my muscles no longer cramped, maybe a healing gift from Galena. "You two board the ship through the cargo door. I'll be right behind you with Oz. But be careful. Lots of dirt fell between here and there."

Chipmunk took Galena's hand. "Let's go." They hurried toward the door, sidestepping the debris along the way.

With no time to raise the dome, I pressed the rover's start button. The air jets blasted grit in our faces. "Sorry, Oz." I pushed the throttle, sending us gliding to the rear door and into the cargo hold. Chipmunk and Galena met us there and helped me get Oz out of his seat while Perdantus returned and perched on the front of the rover.

When we set Oz's feet on the floor, his legs firmed, supporting his body as he tried to speak. "Let me …" His breaths still gurgled. "Let me walk." He coughed. A stream of blood dripped from his mouth and fell to the floor.

"Walk?" I pushed the cargo door's close button. That would signal the bridge that I was on board and safe. "No way. We'll carry you to the infirmary and get you cleaned up."

"It's all right," Galena said. "He's not bleeding anymore, and he needs to cough up as much pooled blood from his lungs as he can. Walking should help."

Chipmunk pushed a shoulder under Oz's arm. "Galena, you take the other side. We'll help him get to the infirmary while Megan does her Captain Hero thing." He looked at Megan. "Where's the infirmary?"

Just as I was about to point, Perdantus spoke up. "I will lead them."

"Good." Chipmunk nodded at me. "Go."

I charged my legs, ran to the ladder leading up to the bridge, and climbed in leaps, skipping most of the rungs. When I made the final jump and landed on bridge level, I stumbled into several kids who were holding to the side of the ladder. After righting myself, I ran to the bridge, dodging several more kids along the way.

When I arrived and stood behind the captain's chair with Crystal, Zoë, and Riddle, I looked at the viewing window. Our infrared scanner indicated four warm boxes in the rover, one in each seat—four bombs, likely enough explosive power to obliterate the Astral Dragon. At its crawling rate, the rover would arrive in less than a minute.

"Shields up," I called.

"Crystal ordered the shields up as soon as you boarded," Sonya said. "Our concern is that the bombs will bury the ship, making it impossible to leave. As Crystal put it, the ship will be our community coffin."

"She's right." I reached for my control panel and turned the head-lights on to their minimum setting. The twin beams revealed the rover. With its dome retracted, the boxes on the seats lay in clear view. Tiny lights blinked on each box, possibly indicating some kind of communications between the bombs and a remote detonator. "Is there a signal we can jam?"

"Negative," Sonya said. "I attempted a signal overload on more than a hundred frequencies. My efforts were futile."

"Then those lights might be timers. How long till the rover gets here?"

"If it continues at its present rate, it will arrive in fifteen seconds."

I sat in the captain's chair and turned the engines on. "Then full speed ahead. Let's blast out of here. Bridge crew, strap in! Everyone else hold tight! Perdantus, wherever you are, find a safe place." As the ship vibrated, sending grit across the viewing window, I grasped the yoke and pushed the throttle. We lurched forward, but the tunnel's sides kept us wedged.

"Nine seconds," Sonya said as Crystal buckled into the seat next to me. Zoë hustled to the navigator's station and strapped in.

"Gotta shake us loose." I shoved the throttle to max and jerked the yoke back and forth. The ship twisted and turned. More dirt rained in front.

"Six seconds."

Finally, we burst out and plowed ahead, slowed by the ship's sides scraping against the tunnel walls. We flew above the rover and hit the top of the vehicle hard as we passed.

"Split screen with front and rear cameras!" I shouted, unable to set the camera myself as I steered.

"Got it," Zoë said.

The window divided, showing the front view on the left and the rear on the right. An explosion lit up the tunnel behind us. The ship bucked and shuddered. Kids screamed. Dirt crashed over the explosion's burst of light, but the ship's rear beams kept the scene illuminated as we continued flying at much slower than impulse speed, maybe ten meters per second.

The tunnel ceiling behind us continued falling, and the collapse shot forward, as if chasing our ship. If we couldn't accelerate, the crashing cascade would catch up and bury us. Then, my memory kicked in. Ahead, this tunnel would turn into a trench without a ceiling, exposed to the air. The layer of ground above us had to be thinning as we churned forward.

I gripped the yoke and I shouted, "Crystal, arm the photon torpedoes and shoot at the ceiling ahead, say fifty meters. Let's blast this tunnel open ourselves and fly out of here."

"Sonya says three seconds to be ready to fire." Crystal moaned as she glared at her console. "We might not have three seconds."

As I watched the rear view, the collapse accelerated. Crystal was right. Burial was imminent.

Twin lights burst from the ship's front turrets. The torpedoes blasted into the ceiling ahead, ripping a gaping hole. Dirt dropped into a pile in front of us, but the hole above it remained open—our escape route, only a few seconds away.

To the rear, the collapsing debris buffeted our tail section, tilting our bow upward. We plowed into the ceiling and burst through into open air, the torpedo blast having loosened the thin barrier.

The kids cheered, but when a gust of wind shoved us to the side, they quieted. Heavy rain pelted the front window. Lightning flashed, and a clap of thunder sent a shudder through the ship.

Without the wings extended, there was no way I could fly in this storm. I pulled the throttle back and landed next to the trench. The ship slid parallel to it, sending a wave of muddy water to both sides and over the front window.

When the ship stopped, rain poured on the window, clearing our view. The ship's headlights illuminated the landscape—angled trees with roots partially exposed through the broken ground. Barely visible at the tops of the headlight glow, clouds boiled in the night sky.

I searched the air for any blinking lights. "Camille's got to be around here somewhere. Zoë, scan for a ship."

Zoë tapped her console. "I'm on it."

"I'm extending the wings," Crystal called as she slid a finger along her screen. After a few seconds, she slapped her console. "Blazes! They're not responding."

Sonya's voice emanated from the ceiling speakers. "Scraping against the tunnel walls narrowed the openings that allow the wings to extend. The wings are, for lack of a better word, stuck."

28

I regripped my yoke. "I can't fly through this storm without wings."

"I see a ship." Zoë slid a satellite-view map of the area onto the front viewing screen. "We're the red dot in the middle. The yellow dot is a ship heading this way. Arrival in seven minutes and fifty-one seconds."

A second yellow dot appeared, much closer than the other. "What's that one?"

Zoë scrunched her brow as she studied her console. "Another ship only a hundred meters from us. It wasn't there a second ago. It's also coming this way. Much slower, though. It'll be here in about a minute."

"That one's got to be Camille. She was waiting to see if we would escape. When she saw us come out of the tunnel, she fired up her engines. She probably didn't blast us because we broke out of the tunnel at a place she didn't expect. Let's hope the other ship is Oliver."

"Transmission request received," Sonya said. "Security clearance granted."

A new voice burst through the speakers. "We see you, Megan. We're on our way."

"Oliver!" Shivers ran from head to toe, good shivers. "Hurry! Camille's coming. She'll be here in ..." I looked at Zoë.

"Thirty-five seconds."

"Thirty-five seconds," I repeated to Oliver.

"Got it. We're accelerating. We'll be there in about six minutes. Hunker down and hang on because you might have more trouble than you realize. Emerson researched the moon-phase thing. When Glandel goes full every three years or so, it triggers quakes on Ragua."

"Yeah. We already went through one. The quake threat is probably one of the reasons Camille and Raven decided to bug out of the camp."

"Saving their sorry butts, huh? Figures. Anyway, we're going silent till we get there."

"And we're going stealth." I shut the engines off and doused every light except a couple on the bridge that I set to a dim level. I spun my seat and, looking at my crew and passengers, I spoke loudly enough to overcome the storm noise. "Camille and Raven are coming, and they'll be able to see a lot of heat signatures on board, so we have to scatter outside. I want them to keep thinking you kids are buried at the camp. Crystal, take half of the kids into the trench and spread out. Zoë, take the other half and go the opposite way." I touched the button to open the front ramp. "Give them lots of targets, too many to choose from. And someone alert Oz, Chip, and Galena in the infirmary. Let them know what we're doing."

My two sisters jumped up and began herding the kids toward the ramp. "What are *you* going to do?" Crystal asked amid the bustle and frightened murmurs.

"I'm staying here to draw fire away from the kids and buy them some time." I swiveled my head. "Where's Lyric? I might need her."

Zoë scanned the bridge. "She was here a minute ago."

Lightning flashed outside, illuminating a human figure standing in the rain beyond the ramp. "Who's that?" Zoë asked, pointing.

I turned a headlight on low and studied the person, a man with his back to us, his arms apparently crossed in front. Although I couldn't see his face, I recognized the stance. "He looks like my father."

"Has to be Lyric," Crystal said, "but what in blazes is she up to? Camille knows by now that we have a shapeshifter."

"No idea, but Camille and Raven will focus on him, not the kids. Perfect time to make the dash." I turned the light off and waved an arm. "Go!"

While my sisters and the kids ran outside, I hustled to Zoë's station, calling, "Sonya, turn the front microphones to max sensitivity."

The howl of wind and patter of driven rain poured through the ceiling speakers.

"Microphones set to maximum," Sonya said.

Outside, two lights knifed through the rain and highlighted my father's form. The Nebula Seven descended about twenty meters in front of him, its lights blazing past him and into the Astral Dragon's windshield. He stayed put, though wind and rain buffeted his clothing and hair as the ship settled on the ground.

When the Seven cut its engines, Camille's voice sounded from external speakers on her ship. "Am I to believe that Julian Willis stands before me? Or are you Lyric, the clever Starborn taking his form?"

As the rain abated to a drizzle, my father's voice came through my ship's speaker. "I am, indeed, Julian Willis. I heard my daughter might be in danger, so I came back for her. I always want her to be at my side. We're a team."

I nodded. That was my cue. I had to be out there with him … or her … or whoever it was. I turned my earbud on and hustled down the ramp. "Sonya, can you hear me?"

As I ran into the drizzle, her voice came through the earbud. "I hear you, but didn't your parents ever teach you to come in out of the rain?"

"Very funny. Just keep me up to date on Oliver's progress. I want to know how long till he gets here in half-minute intervals."

"At the Nebula Nine's current speed, the ship will arrive in four minutes, seventeen seconds. Updates on the half minute."

I splashed through mud puddles, leaped over a protruding root, and halted at my father's side, taking his hand. When he looked at me, his eyes glowed red for a split second, letting me know who he really was. Although I already guessed that he had to be Lyric, the realization hit me hard. My shoulders sagged, as if disappointment added to the rain.

"Four minutes," Sonya said.

Camille's voice returned. "If you are really Julian Willis, one of you should be able to tell me the location of the power source. If you do not, I will destroy the Astral Dragon and everyone aboard." She paused for a moment. "I see three human heat signatures inside. I assume you don't want to lose those crew members, whoever they are."

My father called, "Allow me to come on board, and I will guide you to the source. But if you do any harm here, I will never tell you where it is."

I whispered, "No. I can't let you do that."

He whispered in return, "She won't take me up on it. I'm just stalling."

Wind howled through Camille's reply. "How can you convince me that you're the real Julian Willis and not Lyric the shapeshifter?"

He raised his voice to compete with the wind. "Ask me something I would know that she wouldn't."

"With Megan standing there?" Camille chuckled. "What could I ask that you couldn't answer with your daughter in whisper distance? But there is another way to learn the truth."

"Three minutes, thirty seconds," Sonya said.

A woman appeared in the Seven's headlights, walking toward us. Although the brightness kept me from seeing her clearly, I already knew her identity. Raven, the anti-Starborn, had come to test the potential imposter. In mere seconds, she would probably be close enough to drain Lyric's power.

I glanced at my shirt. The locket glowed brightly through my damp material. Maybe I could make Lyric a dynamo and keep her from getting drained, or maybe her being the power source would keep her strong enough to stay in this form.

Raven halted about five paces away and stared at my father. "It seems that you really are Julian Willis, but verifying your identity isn't my only reason for coming." She extended a small rectangular box with a red button. "Camille is too patient with you, so I am taking matters into my own hand. She doesn't know this, but I installed a bomb on your ship's bridge that will engulf the Astral Dragon in flames. I will detonate it if you don't tell me where the power source is. You have to the count of five to comply. One …"

I stiffened. The count of five? Not nearly enough time to run back and save the others, especially Oz. And Oliver was still too far away. I had to come up with another option.

"Three minutes," Sonya said.

"Two." Raven's countenance stayed perfectly stoic as tiny raindrops collected on her black hair and sparkled in the Seven's headlights. "Three."

I crossed my arms to take on a confident pose. "You're bluffing. If you really put a bomb on the bridge, you would've set it off instead of sending that rover."

"That was a drone rover timed to detonate the bombs when it reached your ship. I wasn't close enough to use the remote on the bridge bomb." Her expression hardened. "Four. I am not bluffing."

"I believe you." I flexed my biceps to charge my hands and legs and leaped at her. I rammed into her chest, grabbed her throat with my electrified hands, and knocked her flat on her back. The shock from my hands made her stiffen and shake, her arms spread eagle and trembling. The remote fell from her grasp into a nearby mud puddle.

I released her throat and lunged for the remote, but she caught my ankle and pulled me back. I face planted and tried to claw forward, but the ground was too slippery to get any traction.

Two hands grabbed the remote. I looked up. Camille clutched it from one side and my father held it from the other. As they struggled, Camille's finger pressed the remote's red button.

An explosion boomed behind me. I scrambled to my feet and looked back. Fire gushed through the ramp opening as if the ship really were a dragon. I touched my ear. "Sonya! Fire suppression measures! Now!" I grabbed my father's hand. "Let's go!"

We ran together to the ramp and looked inside the ship. Flames roared throughout the bridge, a dozen sprinklers on the ceiling spewing water everywhere. Heat radiated from the inferno, almost too hot to stand. Breathing rapidly, I looked at Papa. "I have to go in. Oz, Chip, and Galena are in there. So's Perdantus."

He transformed back into Lyric and regripped my hand. "You can't. You'll get cooked. If they're still inside, they're probably already dead."

I shook free from her grasp. "I don't care if I cook. I have to check."

The moment I took a step to run up the ramp, Perdantus landed on my shoulder. "Megan, we're all safe. We escaped through the cargo door. It's fortunate that none of the children stayed on the bridge. They would have been killed."

I breathed a deep sigh. "Thank the Astral Dragon." I looked at my ship as the bridge compartment continued burning, though the flames had abated, but the ship couldn't possibly fly now, proven by the fact that Sonya hadn't given me any further updates. The computer was likely charred.

Raven set a hand to her ear. "What? How many?" She glared at me, my ship's flames dancing in her angry eyes. "Our crew notified me that there are child-sized heat signatures in the area. Did you get all those little lab rats out of the compound?"

I balled my fists. New rage coursed through my body. My chest heaved. My throat clamped shut. Good thing. If I tried to speak, I would cry for sure, and I couldn't do that. Not in front of Raven, my new mortal enemy.

"I'll take that as a yes, but I don't see how it's possible." Raven turned toward Camille. "Mother, now that we know Megan's father isn't really here, I see no reason to linger. Let's spray the grounds with laser fire and kill every last one of them."

Camille nodded. "Agreed." The two women turned and strode toward the Nebula Seven.

A hand touched mine. I turned that way. Galena stood next to me, her silvery hair shimmering in the remaining firelight. "Are we going to die?"

Fury broke through my aching throat as I growled, "Not on my watch." I craned my neck to look at my shoulder. "Perdantus, go to Crystal and Zoë. Tell them to put together a team of Starborn with whatever powers we need to go to war with these witches. I'll let them decide who to recruit. And tell the other kids to scatter even more and keep moving. Don't be an easy target."

"I will." He flew from my shoulder and out of sight.

I looked at Lyric and Galena. "You two stay behind the team that Crystal and Zoë put together. Galena will be there for healing anyone who might get wounded in battle, and Lyric ..." I shook my head. "Sorry. I don't know what you should do. Ask Crystal."

I spun toward the Nebula Seven. The entry ramp started rising, taking the two monsters with it.

I sprinted toward their ship. If I could get to the ramp before it fully closed, maybe I could leap inside. When I neared the ramp, a meter-wide gap remained. I bent my knees to leap, but my foot slipped. I fell to the ground and slid on my chest.

When the slide ended, I propped myself with my elbows and watched as the Seven's engines roared. The ship rose, its air jets blasting muddy water across my face. Dirty and wet, I scrambled to my feet and ran back toward the smoldering Astral Dragon.

Crystal, with Perdantus on her shoulder, stood in front of the ramp with Zoë, Chipmunk, and Oz. When I arrived, Crystal spoke rapid-fire.

"I assembled an assassin team. Chip's here to tell us what Camille and Raven are thinking. Oz will try to set their hair or clothes on fire. Zoë will try to crush their hearts and make them drop dead." She pointed at me. "But you have to make them dynamos. They all said they couldn't possibly send their power that far without you."

"Okay. I'll do my best." I looked up. The clouds raced away, revealing a full moon near the horizon, likely Glandel, a reminder of more danger. At the opposite horizon, morning light brightened the sky. In that direction, the Nebula Seven hovered about fifty meters above where it had landed earlier, probably trying to decide where to shoot first. If they were smart, they would target me and my newly assembled team. I had to take my own advice and move around, but could Oz keep up?

A laser bullet blasted the ground less than a meter in front of me. The impact sent us all flying. We landed on our backs and slid to the Astral Dragon's ramp. I charged my legs and leaped to my feet while the others struggled to rise. Perdantus fluttered up to perch on Crystal's shoulder again. "Chip," I said. "We have to run. You help Oz. Crystal, you and Perdantus find Echo and take her to the Dragon. If it's cool enough inside, see if she can get Sonya up and running. A surprise photon torpedo from our ship might be exactly what we need."

"I saw her a minute ago. I'm on it." Crystal ran from our group, Perdantus flying at her side.

I hustled to the trench, slid down the embankment, and crouched under the root ball of a leaning tree. When the other members of the assassin team joined me, we ducked as low as we could, gasping for breath. I anticipated more laser fire, but it seemed that the Seven just hovered in place, maybe tracking our movements.

"Okay …" I took a deep breath to slow my heart. "We're not an easy target now." I set one hand on Chip's shoulder and clutched the pendant with the other. "Since the Nebula Seven isn't moving, now's the perfect time to try to read the crew's thoughts. Look at their ship and concentrate. What's Camille's strategy? Why did she stop firing?"

He peeked around the roots. After a few seconds, he spoke softly. "Two women are arguing. One is saying to hold their fire until another ship arrives. The other wants to slaughter everyone but the Willis brat right away. The first says they need to get the approaching ship to surrender by threatening the Starborn. If none are left, then they won't have leverage to force the surrender. The second says to kill the lab rats. The Nebula Seven can win a battle against the other ship."

"It's good to hear they're arguing," I said. "It also means the Nebula Nine's almost here, and they see it on their scanner. Actually, I thought it would've already been here by now, but Oliver might be circling to come in from behind and force the Seven to turn. By now, both ships have their shields up. The Seven has enhanced photo torpedoes, but Camille won't want to waste them on the kids. She'll save them for battle against the Nine."

Chip nodded. "I picked some of that up from one of the minds, and that one wants to take you alive to lure Julian Willis. She doesn't care so much about killing the kids, but she'll go along with it."

"Probably Camille," I said. "So Raven's the one pushing to kill the Starborn. We need Oz and Zoë to try to take her out before those two witches and their crew can do anything. Chip, let me know if any important thoughts come through."

Zoë grasped Oz's wrist. "Let's do it." They emerged from under the roots together and faced the Nebula Seven while Chip continued staring.

"I can see them through the windshield," Zoë said, still holding Oz's wrist to help him stand. "I'll go after Camille's heart while you try to roast Raven."

Oz nodded, grimacing, obviously in pain. "I'll do my best."

The two focused on the ship. Zoë lifted her free hand and aimed her palm skyward. After a couple of seconds, Chip tugged my sleeve. "Camille's in pain, and Raven's screaming."

"It's working," I called to Zoë and Oz. "Keep it up."

Oliver's voice came through my earbud. "We're coming in from the Seven's flank, and we just dropped below the cloudbank. I thought she would've turned about by now, but she hasn't."

"We're keeping them busy," I said. "But they'll probably move at any second. Light them up while you can. I disabled the shields at the front torpedo turrets."

A photon torpedo shot out of the Nebula Seven and zoomed straight at us. Oz shouted at Chip. "Cover them!" He pushed me down and dove onto my back, and Chip did the same to Zoë. My chest splashed in the mud. Zoë and I let out twin oomphs. An explosion sent a storm of dirt, shattered bark, and photon particles rocketing into us. Both boys groaned, taking the brunt of the explosion's stinging debris.

The back of his shirt aflame, Chip rolled off me and into the mud. Oz, his shirt also on fire, stayed put, partly on me and partly on Zoë. I pushed him off to his stomach and threw muddy water over his back, dousing the flames.

Sizzles rose all around. Oz grimaced and moaned, his cheek pressed against the mud. Chip lay on his back, his arms folded tightly in front as he trembled. Both suffered horrific injuries.

The ground shook. The trench shifted, and a new crack formed at the deepest part, only centimeters from us, and the dirt we sat on began sliding toward the crack.

"Out of this trench!" I grabbed Oz's hands and started dragging him up the slope. Zoë did the same with Chip. The moment we got them to the top, the bottom of the trench collapsed into the depths, leaving a meter-wide abyss, too deep to see the bottom.

"Perdantus!" I shouted as the ground continued trembling. "I need Galena! Now!"

29

Above, the Nebula Seven zoomed past with the Nine hot on its tail. A photon torpedo shot from the Nine. The Seven surged nearly straight up, avoiding the shining missile. The Nine gave chase again, and the two ships rocketed back and forth, and up and down, with dives, spins, and loops that made my head swim. Jillian had to be flying the Nine. No way could Oliver pilot the ship through those expert maneuvers. And the crazy chase also meant that Camille and Raven had an expert pilot among their crew. They were likely too injured to fly the Seven themselves.

Now that the quake had ebbed, I looked at Zoë. "Are you okay?"

Mud caking her hair and face, she nodded. "Just bruised, I think." She wiped mud from her cheek with a relatively clean part of her sleeve. "A lot better off than the boys." A groan from Chip prompted her to grasp his hand. She let out a gentle shushing sound. "Help's on the way. Hang in there."

His shaking settled as he let out a deep sigh. "I'll be all right. Just help Oz."

"We'll help both of you." She compressed his hand. "I promise."

Perdantus arrived and landed on my shoulder, breathless. "Galena is coming. I told her to follow me. She is only seconds behind."

"Good. Thank you, Perdantus." I glanced toward the Astral Dragon. Smoke still rose from the scorched bridge. "Were you and Crystal able to find Echo and take her to the Dragon?"

"Yes. Crystal and Echo are both there."

"Can you check on their progress and bring back a report?"

"Of course." He flew away once more.

Above, the Nebula ships' flying acrobatics continued with occasional discharges of lasers and photon torpedoes. As the noise spiked to a near ear-splitting level, Galena ran into view. "There you are." She knelt between Oz and Chip, set a hand on Chip's chest, and closed her eyes. "His back is burned. Some projectiles are embedded in his skin. They're shallow, though." She opened her eyes and looked at me. "We should turn him over and pull the projectiles out."

"I can turn myself." Chip rolled to his stomach, groaning with the effort. "Okay. That hurt more than I thought it would."

"Then lie still and let us do the work." Galena looked at me. "Do you have a way to cut his shirt off?"

I touched my belt. The knife was still in its sheath. "Yeah. I'll do it while you check Oz." I drew the knife, cut into the shirt's hem, and began slicing upward.

Galena set a hand on Oz's back and closed her eyes again. After a few seconds, she jerked back. "Oh, no, no, no!"

I finished the final cut and looked at her. "What?"

She held out her hand. "Give me the knife." When I passed it to her, she began cutting through Oz's shirt. "It's bad. I'll tell you more in a minute."

While she worked, I began spreading the back of Chip's shirt open. Short, protruding spears of wood forced me to ease the torn material over them to pull it free. The process exposed bloody gashes on burned skin, and the spears made his back look like a morbid pincushion. Blood oozed from each stab point. It looked horribly painful.

I pinched one of the spears and plucked it out. Fortunately, since it had been a shallow piercing, Chip barely reacted at all, just a twinge. "Zoë, help me. Galena was right. They're pretty shallow." Working quickly, she and I removed every wood shard we could find. Only a little extra blood flowed, but the burned splotches made his entire back look like he had been licked by dragon fire.

Above, the roars of aircraft had silenced, allowing me to speak softly. "Can you hear me, Chip? Do you still have much pain?"

He squirmed. "Quite a bit."

"I got the splinters out." I closed the shirt over him. "I hope it helped."

"It did. Thanks." He breathed a sigh of relief. "Just let me know how Oz is doing."

"Yeah. Sure." I looked at Galena. She had opened Oz's shirt. Although his skin didn't appear to be as bloody or badly burned as Chip's, a thick dirty wood shard about a centimeter in diameter protruded from his back where his ribs protected his organs. "That looks terrible."

"It *is* terrible." Galena gave the knife back to me and laid her hand on his skin next to the wound. "This horrible stick pierced between two ribs and embedded in his heart."

The mental image seemed to pierce my own heart. How could he possibly survive such a wound? "Can you get it out somehow?"

"Not without killing him. If I remove it, blood will gush. I wouldn't have time to seal the holes before he bleeds out."

I slid the knife back to its sheath. "Even if I use my dynamo power to energize your healing power?"

"I doubt it. We're talking seconds, not minutes. I couldn't possibly do it."

"But won't the stick kill him if it stays?"

She nodded and set a finger to her lips. I nodded in return. Better to keep the bad news to ourselves for now.

Oz's voice rose in fitful gasps. "Answer ... her question ... Galena."

A tear trickled down my cheek. "She ... she told me, Oz. The stick will kill you."

"That's … what I thought. I'll die … either way."

I patted his shoulder. "Shh, shh, shh. Don't try to talk."

"Why? Because talking … might kill me?"

I bit my lip hard. He was right. Talking probably wouldn't make a difference. As I replied through my narrowing throat, my voice pitched higher. "Oz, you can say whatever you want to say. I'll listen."

He took a deep gurgling breath. "Cut the stick … down to … the skin, and … turn me over. I don't want … to die with … my face in the mud."

When Galena nodded her approval, I forced myself to speak with a bit more pep. "Sure, Oz. Of course."

I withdrew the knife again. As I set the blade close to the base of the stick, Chip rose to his knees and scooted over, his shirt hanging loosely on his shoulders. "How can I help?"

"You're his best friend," I said. "Right?"

"I've been trying to be his friend, but he hardly ever lets me."

"Good enough. Talk him through it. The pain'll be awful."

Wincing at his own pain, he nodded. "I can do that." He bent closer, his mouth next to Oz's ear, and began whispering, but I couldn't hear the words.

With both palms, Galena spread the skin around the wound while I cut the stick as low as possible. As I sawed, Oz groaned and twitched, and Chip's whispers grew audible. "I know you're scared. I am, too. But remember what I told you yesterday about fear? Love casts it out. These girls love you, and I do, too. And God does even more. You'll get through this. It's dark now, but light is coming. I promise."

Oz's voice weakened. "How can you … promise that?"

"For people of faith, life never ends in darkness. So whether you live through this or die, you will end up in the light."

Chip's words spread warmth throughout my body. He sounded like a gentle preacher—kind and soothing, keeping me calm as I worked.

When I finished the cut, Galena lifted her hands. Blood seeped from the wound, and the cut end of the stick had retracted out of sight.

As I slid my hands under Oz to turn him, the roar of a ship's engines made me look up. The Nebula Nine flew into view and descended near the Astral Dragon. But where was the Nebula Seven? Had Jillian and Oliver shot it down?

I turned my attention back to Oz. Galena, Zoë, and I lifted from below his body and turned him over. When he settled on his back, he let out a loud grunt, his eyes tightly closed.

Chip took his hand. "Look up, Oz. See the sky, how beautiful it is."

Oz's eyes blinked open. "Lots better … than mud."

"You bet it is." Chip pointed upward. "And that's where you're going. Through the sky. You'll fly to heaven where you'll never have pain again."

Blood oozed from Oz's lips. "That sounds good … but tell God … to get it over with, okay? I'm … I'm ready."

"Sure, Oz. And we'll get you through this."

Tears dripped from my chin. Earlier, I had called Oz my new hero just to encourage him. Now I knew it was true. He was a shield for me. If not for Oz, that stick might've stabbed my heart instead of his. I probably owed him my life.

I set a trembling hand on his cheek. "Thank you, Oz. I know what you did for me. Thank you."

He gave me a weak smile. "Best …" He swallowed. "Best thing I … ever did. You saved me … I saved you. … Fair trade."

Perdantus returned and landed on my shoulder. "Crystal and Echo are having trouble getting Sonya online, and the weapons are not yet functional. But they are still working feverishly on the project."

"Do they think they have a handle on how to get them working?" I asked.

"Not as of yet, but you know Crystal's perseverance. As she told me, and I quote, 'I would rather sleep with porcupines than give up.' And I believe her."

"I believe her, too. If you don't mind, please scout around. If anything happens that I need to know about, give me another report."

"I will." Perdantus flew away again.

"Megan!"

I turned toward the call. Oliver stood nearby, looking at us. "Finally found you. Listen, the Nebula Seven's nowhere in sight, but she might come back. So Jillian dropped me off, and now she's flying around looking for the Seven while we get everyone together, then she can land and load us in quick while the shields are down. We have to get moving. Now."

"You're right." I looked at Zoë. "You and Galena get the kids rounded up near the Astral Dragon and wait for the Nine. Don't forget Crystal and Echo on the Dragon's bridge. I know Crystal will want to keep working, but it's probably a lost cause. And find Perdantus. He'll check on stragglers from the air."

"We're on it." Zoë and Galena ran to Oliver, but Galena pivoted and looked back, tears tracking down her cheeks. "Goodbye, Oz. I'm sorry I couldn't heal you." She turned toward Oliver and lowered her voice, though not enough to keep me from hearing her. "Oz is dying."

"Is there any hope?" Oliver asked.

Galena shook her head, then she and Zoë ran toward the Dragon.

I turned to Chip and whispered, "Catch up with Zoë. See if you can find a cloth in the Astral Dragon, get it wet, and send it back with Galena. Probably plenty of puddles from the fire sprinklers. I want to wash Oz's face."

"You bet." Chip rose. As he hobbled out of sight, the sound of a ship rode the air.

Oliver looked up. "I can't see if that's the Nine or the Seven, but it's coming this way." He laid a hand on my back. "We have to go. Now."

"Go?" Anger surged. I shook my head and spoke through clenched teeth. "Someone needs to stay with Oz."

As the engine sounds grew loud, he leaned close and whispered, "Megan, don't make me drag you to safety."

I erupted like a volcano as I shouted with all my might, "I can't let Oz die alone!" I heaved fast, shallow breaths and lowered my voice. "I *won't* let him die alone."

Oliver stared at me, his mouth hanging open. He obviously had no idea what to say.

I heaved a deep sigh. "I'm sorry I yelled. Save the kids and leave me behind. I have to stay."

Oliver looked toward the sky again. The Nebula Seven zoomed past, followed by the Nine in close pursuit. "I think Camille's trying to separate enough from Jillian so she can take a shot."

"Then go. Save the kids. I'll be all right. Camille wants me alive."

"I'm not leaving without you." He knelt at my side. "Jillian won't land till I call her with my earbud. She can keep the Seven at bay." He set a hand on Oz's chest. "What's his injury?"

"A stick, like a wooden rod, through his heart."

Oliver winced.

"Galena's a healer, and she says she can't possibly repair the hole in time if we pull the stick out, even if I use my dynamo power."

"Yeah. I can imagine. But at this point, it won't hurt to try." He nodded toward my locket. "Get that dragon's eye lit up, and I'll see what I can do."

I touched Oz's hand. "Are you up for this, Oz? It'll probably hurt worse than anything you've ever felt."

"Yeah. Let's try." He grimaced. "One way … or another, it'll all be … over soon, right?"

"For the better, I hope." I clutched my locket, closed my eyes, and concentrated with all my might.

Oz let out a gurgling wheeze. "Are you … a healer?"

"Yes," Oliver said. "What's your power?"

"I'm a … a firestarter."

I peeked at the locket. It seemed normal—no extra glow. I had to try harder, but was that possible? Exhaustion weighed me down, like every drop of energy had drained from my body. How could I energize Oliver when I had no energy left to give?

"You can start a fire with your mind?" Oliver asked.

"Yes," Oz said. "I change … the surface to something … that can …" He voice died away.

"To something flammable? Like a carbon compound?"

Oz wheezed. "Yes. Carbon. Sometimes pure. Sometimes a compound."

"Then focus on the stick inside you. Try to change it to carbon while I do the healing part."

"Won't be easy." Oz's eyes shut tightly. "So … much pain."

"I can't imagine how bad it is, but maybe let the pain guide your power to where it hurts the most. That'll be where the stick is."

Oliver looked at me as if begging for help. I opened the locket. The ruby glowed, but, again, only at its normal brightness, indicating that my father was still alive, but nothing more. Grief stabbed me like a dagger, then anger at myself poured in. I had failed too many times. Cynda died. Renalda died. Would Oz now die because of my failure? I shouted into the air, "God, help me! I can't do this alone! Help me make Oliver a supercharged healer. Make Oz an energized firestarter."

A hand appeared in my peripheral vision and ran a wet cloth across Oz's forehead. "You can do this, Megan. I know you can."

The voice sounded different. As I turned that way, I opened my mouth to speak, but the sight of my father sucked the breath out of me. He knelt at my side, washing Oz's face. I could barely squeak, "Papa?"

He shifted behind me and set his hands on my shoulders. "Megan, we can talk later, but right now you have a life to save. You have been endowed with the power to empower others. You are the first Starborn. I know you can do this."

His words felt like audible energy. Every muscle flexed, and the dragon's eye burst with scarlet radiance. Beams shot out in multiple directions like a lighthouse with lamps that searched for someone to guide.

One of the beams poured into my eyes, coloring everything in a crimson hue. Another struck Oliver. He gasped and blinked, as if taken by surprise. A third beam washed over Oz. He arched his back and groaned. A fourth shot toward the Astral Dragon, but I couldn't see its target.

Oliver's eyes widened. "This is amazing. I can actually see inside you. And you're doing it, Oz. You're doing it. The wood is dissolving, and I'm sealing the wounds. Keep it up."

As hope filtered in, I let a smile break through. Maybe we really could do this. Maybe somehow a miracle was happening before our eyes. As if agreeing with my thoughts, the beams brightened even more, nearly blinding me.

The roar of an engine shook the ground. In the direction of the fourth beam, a ship zoomed toward us again, this time firing a barrage of laser blasts with another ship tailing it. If the other Starborn had gathered as instructed, their group was likely Camille's target.

A photon torpedo streaked from the ground toward the Nebula Seven. It blasted into one of the front turrets and shattered it, smashing a hole in the hull. Smoke streamed from the impact point. The ship keeled and swerved to the side. The Nine decelerated and hovered over the area as the crippled Seven flew away.

I exhaled heavily. Somehow, a second miracle happened, but I couldn't dwell on it. I had to finish the first miracle. As the dragon's eye continued pulsing, I focused again on Oliver. No longer red in my vision, he kept a hand on Oz's chest and spoke softly. "How do you feel?"

Oz coughed and spat a wad of bloody phlegm. "Better." His voice no longer gurgled. "Still a lot of pain inside, though."

"Yeah. Everything's sealed, but it's ugly in there. Your heart took a beating." Oliver looked at me and smiled. "We did it. All of us. You, me, and Oz."

The glow from the dragon's eye faded to normal. I closed the clasp and put the locket back in place. "You're right. We did. And I couldn't have energized you without …" I turned toward my father and found Lyric kneeling next to me. I gasped. "Lyric? It was you the whole time?"

She nodded. "You needed power, so I came to give you some, and I thought looking like your father might boost you even more."

The joy inside drained a bit. For a few moments, in the dizzying turmoil, I thought my father was really there, but I should have known better. Lyric had already changed into him twice before. "Thanks. I couldn't've done it without you."

"Yeah," Oz said, still lying on his back as he looked at us. "Thanks to all of you."

Oliver compressed his shoulder. "The Nebula Nine is on the ground. I'll get a stretcher from the infirmary and we'll—"

"Already here." Crystal stood next to Chip, a folded stretcher propped upright at her side. "The other kids are ready to board the Nine. Let's get Oz and take off."

We worked together to lay Oz on the stretcher and carry him to the Nine, hampered by our mud-caked bodies. He handled the jostling well, smiling and chatting most of the time, though a few grimaces revealed his ongoing pain. Even with those difficult moments, he seemed happier than I had ever seen him, as if the miracle had planted a fresh life inside.

I knew all too well how a brush with death can help a person treasure every living moment, no matter how much a moment hurt. I needed to learn from Oz's example, to march onward with a positive perspective, even though my father wasn't really with me.

I gave myself a firm nod. Soon, with God's help, my father and I would be together again. I could wait.

When we arrived at the Nebula Nine, Oliver and Crystal carried Oz up the ramp on the stretcher, Chip and Lyric trailing them. Chip grimaced with every step. He needed more healing help from Oliver or Galena as well.

I stopped at the edge of the ramp and looked at the Astral Dragon, still smoking only about twenty meters away. Echo descended her ramp and joined me.

"Status report," I said in mock military sternness, adding a wink.

Echo saluted. "Status report is as follows: Sonya is functioning but only as a type-in terminal. All shields are toast, navigation is fried, targeting is roasted, and only one of the torpedo turrets escaped broiling, but fortunately, it was enough."

"Yeah, I saw the torpedo, but if the targeting system wasn't working, how could you have possibly hit a moving target? It's hard enough to do that *with* targeting."

"That part was Zoë. I got the weapons system up, but she guided the torpedo. With wind and gravity affecting the flight path, hitting the Seven was a miracle."

I nodded. "Exactly my thoughts."

As Echo and I walked up the Nine's ramp, Jillian, sitting in the captain's chair, fixed her stare on me. A hint of a smile cracked her stoic expression. "The things I do for my crazy niece. Do you realize the g-forces I suffered to keep those insane women from blasting you and the other kids?"

I walked behind her while she swiveled her chair and kept her eyes on me. "Nope," I said as I leaned against Emerson's console, working hard to keep a straight face. "I've been lazing around. You know, sabotaging a Nebula ship, slaying a dragon, escaping a prison camp with two dozen kids, getting buried in a cavern collapse, that kind of stuff."

Jillian flapped her lips. "Lazy critter, aren't you?" She rose from the chair and extended her arms. "C'mere, you."

I ran into her embrace. She kissed my forehead, and, standing on tiptoes, I returned the kiss to hers.

When I drew back, I noticed Echo's feet protruding from the floor cabinet under Emerson's console. "What are you doing down there?"

"What am I doing down here?" The cabinet muffled her voice. "I'm checking to see if this ship's computer has a chipset Sonya needs. It's often redundant in the more advanced computers, so maybe I can borrow one."

Jillian called, "Take anything redundant you need. Emerson won't mind, right, Emerson?"

His voice came through the ceiling speakers. "Although it seems that the decision has already been made, I am not opposed to the removal of a chipset for an ailing computer. My designer provided redundancy for this very reason."

"Emerson," I said, "it's good to be back on board the Nine with you."

"Thank you, Captain Megan Willis. It is good to see you again."

I looked around the bridge, but no one else stood in view. "Where is everyone?"

Jillian motioned with her head. "Infirmary. Galena's patching up Oz and Chip, applying something for their burns. Pretty crowded down there, I imagine, and they're all excited. Oz even got off the stretcher and climbed down the ladder. You should've heard the cheers. Anyway, I told him I'd send you to the infirmary when you showed up. They all want to thank you for what you did."

Warmth flooded my cheeks. "Yeah. That's nice and all, but I don't really want to—"

"Stop right there, Miss Humility." She wagged a finger at me. "This is for them. After all you did, they feel like they need to thank you. It's all they have to give."

I nodded and added a sigh. "You're right. I'll go."

Echo called from the cabinet. "I found the chipset. Once I remove it, I'm going back to the Astral Dragon and install it."

"Works for me, but be ready to bolt back to the Nine if you feel a tremor. Since the moon has set, though, quakes might not be a problem anymore." I walked off the bridge and slid down the ladder. Once on the lower level, I followed a path of mud toward the infirmary. When I drew near, I waded through at least fifteen wet and dirty kids, all smiling and patting my back as they shouted words of praise. I smiled and nodded through the gauntlet, wondering for the first time what we were going to do with all of them.

Inside the infirmary, cheers greeted me from several more kids crowded in the room, including Oz and Chip sitting shirtless on a bed with Galena behind them, working on their backs. Oliver, Crystal, and Zoë stood on the far side of the bed, all beaming. Perdantus gave me a head bow from Oliver's shoulder.

Chatter flew back and forth. I tried to listen to everyone, but it seemed impossible to catch all the words. I learned that when Echo managed to fire a torpedo from the Astral Dragon, and Zoë guided it, that a red beam of light had energized them, enabling them to do the seemingly impossible. They knew the light came from me and the dragon's eye.

When the chaos settled, everyone looked at me, obviously expecting me to say something. As more kids pushed in to listen, I looked around. I had accounted for the friends I had gained on Gamma Five except one. I had not seen Lyric since I boarded, and she wasn't anywhere in sight.

Trying to ignore her absence for the moment, I pivoted slowly to address everyone. "Thank you for the kind words, but you all get equal credit. Everyone did their part, even if it was just being brave enough to climb that fence. Without your contributions, we never would've made it."

New chatter buzzed across the room until Crystal clapped her hands. "Quiet!" When everyone obeyed, she grinned and gestured toward me. "Make it short, Captain. We're all filthy, and there are only two showers on the ship, so we need to find a lake or a river before Perdantus has a stroke because of the odor."

After smiling in return, I continued. "We'll take off in a few minutes and find a place to bathe. Once we're clean, we'll fly again, this time into orbit around Gamma Five. Then we'll talk to each of you about finding your homes, and we'll check with the local authorities to get you there. If you have any questions, ask Crystal."

Crystal blinked. "Wait. What?"

"Answer their questions. I have to find someone." I waded through kids as I walked out. When I was alone near the ladder, I called toward the ceiling. "Emerson, have you seen a girl named Lyric? If you don't know her yet, maybe you could tell me if someone is alone here on the ship."

"There is a girl in the maintenance room, sitting on the cot you used to occupy. I thought she was you until you boarded and I recognized your voice. This girl looks exactly like you."

"That's Lyric." I hustled to my old quarters where I found a copy of myself sitting on my cot, her head low. "Lyric? What are you doing?"

She gazed at me with tear-filled eyes. "Imagining what you've been through. Emerson told me you were chained in this very room, a condemned prisoner wearing a deadly shock collar."

"All true." I sat next to her. "But why are you doing this?"

Lyric slid her hand into mine. "To gain some of the courage that lifted you from prisoner to captain of a spaceship."

I compressed her hand. "Lyric, that's really nice of you to say, but I don't understand. Why do you want to be inspired? What do you plan to do once you find your home?"

A tear trickled down her cheek ... or my cheek. Looking at a weepy version of myself was confusing. "I contacted my parents with the Nebula Nine's radio, and Jillian gave them our coordinates. They'll be here in less than an hour, and they'll help us get all the kids back where they belong. Also, my father said he'll enjoy repairing the Astral Dragon. He loves tinkering on spaceships."

"Wow! That's great, Lyric, but that still doesn't explain why you're here, looking like me."

She rose, took my hands, and pulled me to my feet. As we faced each other, she transformed back to her usual self. "I know you want to leave as soon as possible so you can find your father. Leave everyone here with me and take off in the Nine without any delays." She touched her chest. "I'll be their new leader, their new Megan Willis. We'll form a Starborn-protection unit to keep traffickers from ever bothering us again. I have to do this. For us and for you."

"Thank you, Lyric." I pulled her close and hugged her tightly. When we separated, I took a deep breath. "Well, I guess we'll take everyone outside again and tell them the new plan. I suppose Crystal and Zoë will want to come with me. At least I hope they do. Perdantus, of course. And probably Oliver. Since you have a healer, you won't need him."

She set a hand on top of my head. "Stop thinking, and let's do this."

During the next several minutes, while Jillian kept her eye on the scanner to watch for the Nebula Seven and whatever vessel Lyric's parents might fly, we gathered everyone outside. As expected, Crystal and Zoë opted to go with me, saying they could find their families later, as did Oliver and Perdantus. Everyone else wanted to go home.

By the time we finished our plans, Jillian called from the Nine's bridge. "A large craft is coming. About five minutes away. Looks like a cargo ship."

Lyric grinned. "That's my dad."

I blew a relieved sigh. "Good. Then I can take off without worrying about you."

After we all exchanged hugs and said our goodbyes, I gathered my crew. Just as we made ready to board the Nine, Chip joined us. "I need to tell you guys something."

I nodded. "Okay. Sure."

He focused on me while the others listened. "The last time the Nebula Seven made a run at us, your dynamo rays were shining all over us, and I could read Raven's mind clearly. I thought it didn't matter since Zoë and Echo kicked her butt, but I'm not so sure now." He pushed his hands into his pockets and took a deep breath. "Camille's dead."

I drew my head back and looked at the surprised expressions on the faces of my crew. "Are you sure?"

He nodded. "Raven was thinking about it, and I got no thoughts from Camille."

"So I guess Zoë killed her. Stopped her heart."

"Right, but Raven blames you for killing both of her parents. She doesn't care about the other Starborn at all anymore." Chip pointed at me. "She just wants to kill you."

"Okay. Good to know. But why did you decide to tell me now?"

"Something Riddle said a couple of minutes ago. She read Raven's anger. Her need for revenge will never stop. It's an obsession. Riddle didn't know it was directed at you, but when she told me, I knew. That's why I decided to tell you."

"So I need to watch my back. Thanks for the warning."

Chip raised a finger. "And one more thing. Raven was also thinking about Epsilon Six. Does that mean anything to you?"

"Sure. It's a planet in the Epsilon system. I've been there with my parents a couple of times. The system, not that particular planet."

"Raven wants to go there, but I don't know why. She was also thinking about Epsilon Five, but that wasn't as important to her."

As I gazed at him, a stream of thoughts rushed through my mind. My father wanted to lure Camille and Raven away from me. Maybe he left a trail that led to Epsilon Six, and Camille and Raven thought about chasing him there but stayed in the Gamma system, hoping to take me with them as bait. Epsilon Five had to be relatively close to Six. Maybe that was her second guess regarding where to go.

I patted Chip's shoulder. "Thanks again."

"Please be careful." Chip hugged me. The gesture took me by surprise for a brief second before I hugged him in return and patted his back.

When he left, the sound of a distant engine reached my ears. I called into the Nine. "Jillian, is that the cargo ship?"

"Yep. Lyric's father radioed me. It's all good."

I scanned the sky and spotted the ship as it drew closer at a fast clip. It would arrive with Lyric's parents in seconds.

"Megan," Jillian shouted, "I got another blip on the scanner. Looks like a glider is tailing the cargo ship. Someone's playing one of my tricks."

"If it's a Nebula Seven glider," I said, "it could be armed."

Oliver grabbed my wrist. "Then let's—"

Zoë leaped in front of me. A laser bullet blasted into her chest. I screamed, "No!"

Oliver threw his arms around me and half-carried and half-dragged me up the ramp, shouting, "Raven's after you. If we get you out of here, she'll chase us and leave the others alone."

Knowing he was right, I stopped fighting and let him hustle me into the Nine. "What about Zoë?"

"Galena's with her. So's Lyric and her parents. She'll get good care." Oliver ushered me to the first mate's chair next to Jillian and pushed the ramp-close button just as Crystal ran in with Perdantus flying at her side.

"Shields are up," Jillian barked as the engines roared. "Strap in. We're taking off."

Crystal leaped to the navigator's seat, and Perdantus flew from the bridge. Oliver strapped me in, then wrapped his arms around me and held on. "Hit it, Jillian!"

Jillian pushed the throttle. The Nine shot forward at a steep climb. The front viewing window switched to a rear camera, showing a gray glider in pursuit. At ground level, the Starborn kids gathered around Zoë, shrinking quickly as we zoomed away.

I stifled a sob. "She took a direct hit." My words shattered as I continued. "I've never ... seen anyone ... survive that. And ..." A spasm throttled my voice to a squeak. "And I'm not there ... to energize Galena."

As we entered space, the g-forces eased. In the camera view, the glider lagged farther behind, just a glimmering winged disk, still in pursuit. Oliver released me and knelt at my side. "Lyric will figure something out. She doesn't have a dragon's eye, but she is the power source. We can hope for the best."

"Speaking of hope," Jillian said as she looked at her console, "I hope Raven keeps following. I'm going slow to let her stay fairly close, but … oh, wait. Another ship's closing in from orbit. Nebula class. Gotta be the Seven."

Oliver rose and looked at Jillian's screen. "It's heading for the glider, not us. They're picking Raven up."

She nodded. "So they can keep chasing us even if we make a hyperdrive jump, but I have no idea where we're going."

"Epsilon Six." I turned toward Crystal. She stared blankly at the viewing window as if lost in thought. "Crystal, chart a course for Epsilon Six."

She gasped, startled. "Oh. Okay. Epsilon Six. Sorry, I was thinking about Zoe." She began tapping her console screen. "I'm on it."

"Why Epsilon Six?" Jillian asked. "It's pretty far. Maybe three weeks in a wormhole."

Trying desperately to push Zoë out of my mind, I took a deep breath. "A hunch. My father might be going there to lure Camille and Raven away from me and the Starborn power source."

Jillian winked. "A hunch from you is better than hard facts from most people."

"Course charted," Crystal said. "Eight minutes to the wormhole jump point. Four minutes if you step on it."

"We're stepping on it." Jillian pushed the throttle. "Megan, let's go find your father."

Part
03

Epsilon Six

I paced on the bridge from Emerson's console to the viewing window and back again. So many questions and doubts hammered my brain. Did I make the right decision to commit to traveling in the wormhole to the Epsilon system? With no proof that my father went to Epsilon Six, I could be wasting the twenty days it was taking to get there. He might have planted evidence of an Epsilon journey for Camille and Raven to find when he actually decided to go elsewhere. Not only that, I had no way to contact Lyric to find out how Zoë was doing, if she survived the laser blast at all. She could be—

"Megan!"

Now close to the viewing window, I pivoted. Jillian frowned at me from the captain's chair as she used a hairband to tie her locks into a ponytail. "If you keep worrying yourself with all that pacing, your body's going to rebel and leave your brain on the floor. Then what would you do?"

"Probably keep worrying."

"At least you'd have good reason to. Being brainless is bad for your health." Jillian sighed. "Listen, we still have six hours till we get through the wormhole. There's no reason for you to be on the bridge.

All I'm doing is studying the maps to learn more about the planet, and I certainly don't need you here for that."

I strolled toward Emerson's console once more, this time at a leisurely gait to keep her from thinking I was still worrying. "What should I do instead? We weren't planning a long trip, so we didn't bring any books, and when we docked at Alpha One, the technician erased Emerson's library."

"Oliver and Crystal are playing chess. Last I heard, Crystal's catching up to him in total wins. Why don't you get in on the action?"

I looked toward the mess table room where they had set up the chess board. "They don't like playing me because I always win."

"Then play Perdantus."

"But *he* always wins. Once he learned the game, he never lost again. Playing him isn't fun anymore."

"Now you know how Oliver and Crystal feel." Jillian gestured toward the viewing window. "Then go ahead and keep pacing. When your brain is flopping around on the floor and your body's aimlessly roaming the ship, don't come complaining to me."

"I'll remember that." I sauntered to the first mate's chair and slid into it. "Have you checked lately for another ship in the wormhole?"

Jillian rolled her eyes. "Like I said the last seven times you asked me that, the Nebula Seven wouldn't shadow us. It's too dangerous. Besides, they wouldn't come without repairing the hole in the torpedo turret, so they'll be at least a day behind us. So, in short, find something else to obsess about." She nodded toward the galley. "Maybe use some of that pent-up energy to cook dinner. I don't want to eat rehydrated beans from a foil bag again. I get gas."

"Yeah. Perdantus has been complaining about your—"

"Wait a minute." Jillian set a finger on her console screen. "Epsilon Six has a Zeta Sphere in orbit. Or at least it used to."

"Zeta Sphere?" I bent my brow. "I've heard of that somewhere. What is it?"

"More like what *was* it. It was an experimental base the Alliance abandoned about fifteen years ago. My guess is you've heard of it because Julian would've talked about it back when you were younger." Using her hands, she formed a ball in the air. "As the name suggests, the base is spherical, and the prototype was built in the Zeta system. A ship could transport from a docking bay on the sphere to any system in the galaxy as long as they had a similar sphere at the destination. Instead of days or weeks, the trip took from less than an hour to a few hours, depending on the distance. The Alliance had working Zeta Spheres in low orbit around Alpha One, Beta Three, Gamma Five, and Delta Nine. I didn't know about the one at Epsilon Six until now."

"My father did talk about the concept. Super-fast transport was his dream, but he said it was too dangerous."

"Far too dangerous. Early tests were great. Unmanned travel from Alpha One to Beta Three worked without a hitch, so the Alliance built the Gamma and Delta spheres in a hurry while keeping the technology secret. When they finished, they sent unmanned ships to and from all four spheres unscathed. The first manned craft was supposed to go from Alpha One to Gamma Five, but it disappeared, never to be seen again. After more successful unmanned tests, they decided the lost passenger mission was an anomaly and tried again."

"Let me guess," I said. "It disappeared, too."

Jillian splayed her hand. "Poof. Like pumpkin pie on my dessert plate. Gone in a flash never to return."

"Why didn't the Alliance keep using the spheres for unmanned ships, like for cargo transports?"

"Because those started having problems, too. Part of the cargo would be missing or some of it arrived ruined, like the transport process was degrading over time. Huge mystery. But they kept the spheres in case they can someday come up with a theory for fixing the problem. Since they stay in orbit, they're not in the way."

"Are they dark gray and about the size of the Alpha One docking station?"

Jillian nodded. "Have you seen one?"

"I saw a sphere orbiting Gamma Five. It had red and green lights in a network on the surface."

"That's one of them. The lights are the transport bays. Green for departure. Red for arrival. Since they're on, they're still operational." Jillian drummed her fingers on her console. "I wonder what the Alliance is up to. I would've thought they would be shut down. Maybe the lights are on just to show their positions on a scanner, you know, to keep ships from crashing into them."

"Maybe we should visit the Epsilon sphere and see what's up. It's as good a place as any to look for my father."

Jillian pointed at me. "Good idea. It's better than anywhere else I could think of. Knowing Julian, he'd want to figure out how to use the sphere to quickly transport back to Gamma Five after luring Camille to Epsilon Six. He could be the one who revved up the Gamma sphere."

"He would try to transport even though people on board disappeared?"

Jillian sighed. "You know your father. His technical expertise is unmatched, and so is his confidence. Maybe he thinks he can solve the problem."

"That's a huge maybe, and we're just guessing. He might not be at the sphere at all."

"True. But we'll start there. Since it's a docking station, we can check to see if it has supplies. We're running low on some things."

I smirked. "No shortage of beans."

"Or gas." Jillian swiped a finger across her screen, sending a document to my console. "Study the sphere's blueprint. Memorize its layout. That'll give you something to do till we get there."

For the next few hours, I read the specs and pored over the structural diagrams. I also looked up the environment on Epsilon Six—pretty much a desert planet with a single outpost building occupied by a lone sentry. Since nothing of value existed on the planet, the Zeta Sphere stood as the only reason my father would come to Epsilon Six.

Although I didn't understand the most technical aspects of the transport system, this much seemed clear—the sending sphere would atomize a ship with all of its contents and send the package of atoms through some kind of directional space warp, and the atoms would arrive at the destination where the ship would be restored by a stabilizer in a bath of laser-like rays.

The atomization and restoration process worked locally with humans, that is, the two processes happened in the same room without any transport. The test subjects reported that they retained all of their functions and memories. They were perfectly healthy. Obviously, the transport step had to be the faulty one.

Since I stayed busy with my new project, Oliver and Crystal teamed up to make our wormhole-exit dinner, a mishmash of reconstituted potatoes, gravy made from beef jerky, and a salad consisting of asparagus, beets, and tofu that tasted vinegary, probably from an intentional addition of vinegar to hide the real flavor. Jillian was right. We needed to restock some supplies.

When the time came to exit the wormhole, everyone gathered on the bridge. Jillian and I took the command seats, Crystal worked the navigator's console, while Oliver sat at the physician's station with Perdantus on his shoulder.

Popping out of the hole raised the usual splash of colorful sparks, but I focused beyond them, hoping to catch an early glimpse of the Zeta Sphere. From our exit position about three megameters from Epsilon Six, a sphere of its size in low orbit would be just a pinpoint of light, and it might be on the other side of the planet.

Jillian slowed the Nine to the usual planet approach speed and rose from her seat. "Megan, take us into orbit and find that Zeta Sphere."

"Um … sure. What are you going to do?"

"Rest in my room." Without another word, she strode from the bridge into the sleeping quarters.

Crystal stared after her. "That was … unexpected."

"Yeah," Oliver said. "Kind of abrupt."

Emerson spoke up from the ceiling speakers. "Rest is an appropriate course of action. Captain Jillian Willis was at her station for approximately nineteen hours, studying log entries I made during our journeys in the Delta system and afterward. She is more impressed with her niece than ever before. Based on that and conversations I had with her while you were sleeping, I think she is concerned about usurping your role as the leader of this quest."

"I … um … don't know what to say."

"Nothing." Crystal pointed at the captain's seat. "Just put your butt in that chair and do you job."

"I can do that." I shifted over and sat again with my hands on the steering yoke. "Who'll be first mate?"

"Definitely Oliver. He's the third best pilot on board. I'll claim fourth best."

Oliver snorted. "Says the girl who learned to fly the Astral Dragon in about two minutes."

"True. But I'm the nimbus of navigating. I should continue to be effulgent at this station."

"Someone got bored and started reading the dictionary." Oliver moved to the first mate's chair and looked at the console. "Any sign of that sphere?"

I studied the scanner—blank so far except for a signal on the planet's surface, likely the outpost. "Not yet. If we see any blip at all, that'll probably be the sphere. No reason for anything else to be orbiting a desert planet."

"There." Oliver touched his screen. "Just showed up. Coming around the left side."

"Yep. I see it." I steered toward a point ahead of the blip's path, guessing on the best route and speed to intercept. Of course, Crystal could plot those parameters, but docking at a spherical station was something new. It might be a fun challenge.

As we drew closer, the shape of the object became obvious—definitely spherical. Landing bays all across the surface made it look like a slowly turning honeycomb, and the red or green lights shining above each bay proved that it was, indeed, a Zeta Sphere. We would be there in only a couple of minutes.

Goose bumps ran along my arms. Might my father be there? Were we finally going to see each other for the first time in well over a year? After thinking he was dead for so long, the idea of reuniting felt impossible, and since he might not be on the sphere, I had to put the thought out of my mind and focus on the task at hand—landing the Nine in one of those bays.

As the sphere made a complete rotation, I counted thirty green arrival bays and an equal number of red departure bays. Apparently, the Alliance had planned for substantial activity at this station, which made sense. The Epsilon system boasted three major trading planets, and creating a hub at a less-busy outpost would allow travelers to choose one of the destinations and avoid traffic at the other two.

Opting for one of the arrival bays near the sphere's equator, I guided the Nine into the opening at the slowest impulse speed, flying at an angle to keep up with the station's spin. As the ship drew near, the green light on the exterior turned off, and a bright white light flashed on within the bay, illuminating the docking chamber, apparently automated arrival actions.

I had piloted a ship into a bay like this only once before with my father watching over my shoulder. He warned me that most bays inside a space dock had artificial gravity, and the moment the ship entered, I would feel the pull from below. I needed to compensate with a quick burst of the lower jets to keep us from banging down on the bay's floor.

The moment the bow entered, the downward pull started. I switched on the lower boosters just in time, easing the Nine slowly to the floor. When we touched down, I activated the magnets on our landing feet. Once the ship attached, I shut the engines off. The bay door began sliding closed, and a sign on the wall flashed, "Pressurized suits required." A smaller sign next to it read, "Air concentration 20%," and the number rose steadily.

Since I had studied the specs, I knew about this airlock system, but I wasn't sure it would work automatically without anyone operating the sphere. The fact that it did, saved us from having to put on space suits and helmets.

I looked at Oliver. "It just dawned on me. Isn't it strange that an abandoned station has electrical power, filled air tanks, and functional sensors? After a few years, the batteries would've died, and the air would be spent."

Oliver nodded. "Someone's been servicing the station."

New goose bumps erupted on my arms. "Let's hope it's my father, but just in case it's not …" I strode to the supply room and picked up a belt, a handheld laser gun, and a flashlight. After strapping the belt on and attaching the gun and flashlight, I inserted a comm bud in my ear and hustled back to the bridge. The sign on the wall now indicated 100% air capacity, and the pressurized suits sign had turned off.

"We are receiving a query," Emerson said. "A sentry on the planet's outpost wants to know why we have docked at the sphere. I told him that the captain is asleep. He asked me to awaken her. He already knows that the Nebula Nine's captain is officially Jillian Willis."

I furrowed my brow. "Interesting. That's a recent update."

"Not so recent that the data could not have arrived by now through traditional channels. Also, sphere-to-sphere data transmissions are instantaneous."

"Instantaneous? Really? Then why hasn't a Zeta sphere been put in orbit around Alpha One? That's Alliance headquarters. They would want data access to the other systems."

"According to my records," Emerson said, "one of the early spheres was installed in orbit around Alpha One, but a saboteur recently destroyed it. A new one is being planned."

"Okay. I'll have to look into that someday, but here's another question. Why can data be sent instantaneously, but physical stuff takes an hour or more?"

"That is a conundrum that I cannot solve," Emerson said.

"Conundrum," Crystal repeated. "Sounds like a Willis word."

I grinned. "The word conundrum is a conundrum for you. It means a puzzle or a mystery."

"May I remind you," Emerson said, "that the sentry is still waiting for Jillian to respond?"

"Should I wake her up?" Crystal asked.

I shook my head. "Patch him through, Emerson. Audio only. Make my voice match Jillian's."

"Commencing." Light static came through the speakers, followed by Emerson's voice. "Captain Willis is now on the bridge and is ready to converse."

"Greetings, Captain Willis," the sentry said, apparently a young man. "I am Ensign Kit Miles, sentry at the Epsilon Six post. I apologize for awakening you, but an Alliance military ship docking at this station is highly unusual, and I was concerned that your ship might be in trouble."

I let out a long yawn, giving me time to hatch a plausible story. "Thank you for your concern, Ensign. We are having some trouble. We sustained a water leak that is draining both our drinking supply and our fusion reactor, and this sphere showed up on my scanner as the closest safe docking station. My maintenance expert is searching for the source of the leak, but it might take some time. I decided to get some rest while he works."

"If you're low on water, there is a tank at the station. I can send you a map of the facility to help you find it."

"No need. We had the specs in our computer already. Now that I have your permission, I will send a team to fetch the water."

He chuckled. "A captain doesn't need permission from an ensign, but I appreciate the gesture. Stay as long as you want, Captain, and rest well."

"Thank you. I will." I pressed the call-terminate button on my console. "Well, that couldn't have gone any better."

"You're quite the talker." Jillian walked in, rubbing an eye. "Short naps are better than nothing, I guess."

I studied her face. A tear track smudged one of her cheeks. Since she hadn't bothered to wash the smudge or maybe hadn't noticed it, it would probably be better to ignore the issue and move on. "I'm going to lower the ramp and take a look around. Want to come along?"

She smiled, though the expression seemed forced. "No. You go. Someone needs to stay with the ship."

"True, but if my father's here, you'll want to see him right away."

"Of course, but I can wait." She waved a hand. "Go ahead. Just give me lots of updates."

When everyone else had joined me, including Perdantus perched on Crystal's shoulder, we stood in front of the viewing window while Jillian lowered the ramp. Once its far end touched the floor, I took a deep breath and walked out on it, my legs rubbery. Oliver stayed at my side, whispering, "You got this, Megan. And I'm here for you, all the way."

"Thanks." I steeled myself and strode on with more confidence. When we walked onto the landing surface, I looked around. Various machinery lined the walls and ceiling—scanning lenses, metallic protrusions that were probably the battery of laser guns that emitted the regeneration rays, and sensor screens that provided atomic particle measurements. Other scanners gave security updates to the station operator, including a report of any unusual movement in the bay. In short, a local operator, if he existed, knew we were here.

Something swished. A door in the side wall slid open, revealing a dim corridor, lit only by the lights in the bay chamber. I gazed at the door, hoping my father would walk through it, but no one came. The automated system might have opened the door for us, assuming that we had had time to disembark. The next step was probably to go to some kind of processing office to log our arrival, especially since we showed up unannounced.

I touched my ear. "Jillian, we're going through the door in front of me. Stay in touch."

"Will do. I would tell you to be careful, but I know you'll do the opposite, so just don't die. All right?"

"I'll do my best." Waving for the others to follow, I walked into the corridor and stepped along its curved path to a stairway, one flight leading up to a landing and a switchback second flight, and another leading down to a similar switchback landing, both directions illuminated by dim wall fixtures.

I looked both ways but couldn't see past the second flights in either direction. I pointed upward. "Based on the specs, the command-center deck should be that way." I shifted my finger downward. "The computers and a lot of the machinery are that way. If my father is here, he could be either place."

"I vote for down," Crystal said. "If he were at the command center, he would've seen you and run here to greet you."

"Not enough time. It's a long way. He would have to take an elevator to a landing, then thirty flights from there to here. I guess I should've chosen a bay closer to the command center."

"Then up. We might meet him on the way." Crystal formed circles with her thumbs and fingers and set them around her eyes. "And if a robot finds us and starts zapping us with his laser vision, it would be better to be up there. We could run down to get back to the Nine. Faster that way."

I nodded. "Fair point. Kind of bizarre, but it's fair." I grasped the railing and started a quick march up the stairs. "Let's go. I can't stand waiting any longer."

Crystal and Oliver followed while Perdantus flew ahead. "I will be a scout and make sure Crystal's laser-eyed robot isn't waiting to zap us."

I smiled as we hurried on. A door stood closed at the top of each pair of switchback flights. Out of curiosity, I opened the first one and found a hallway that appeared to lead to other bays like ours, but I had no time to investigate. I closed the door and moved on.

The climb sapped a lot of energy. Although I could have used my bracelets to charge my legs, I opted to climb with my normal strength, not wanting to leave my friends behind. After about twenty flights, we all grew tired, forcing us to slow our pace. We plodded on to the top of the thirtieth set of stairs and exited into a corridor that led to an open freight elevator door and an empty car, big enough for several people.

Perdantus stood on the floor in front of the opening. "When I heard you on the stairs, I took the liberty of pressing the button to call the car. I have seen no sign of robots or any other laser-eyed villains."

"Thanks, Perdantus. Hop aboard." He flew to my shoulder and perched while I entered the car with Oliver and Crystal. I pushed the button for the command center level, and we rode up together in silence. As each second passed, the tension increased. According to the specs, the elevator would open directly into the command center. If my father was there, I would see him in a few seconds, but, if so, why didn't he come to greet me?

Finally, the moment arrived. The elevator stopped, and the door opened.

31

Within the command center, dozens of computer screens encircled a thirty-meter-wide central floor, illuminated only by the screens' projected images. A work surface protruded from the wall under the screens—a shelf laden with keyboards and other input/output devices, including printers, microphones, and speakers.

Someone, most likely a man, though the dimness made it difficult to be sure, sat motionless in a wheeled desk chair, his eyes aimed away from us.

I padded slowly toward him, Perdantus on my shoulder and the others following. When I drew close, I cleared my throat and whispered, "Hello." Still, he made no sound or movement. I walked around the chair and looked at him. Although a two-week beard covered his cheeks, and his hair had grown graying ringlets over his ears, the changes couldn't hide his identity. My father sat in that chair, his eyes closed.

Holding my breath, I set a hand on his chest. It moved with normal respirations. I exhaled in relief. I whispered to the others as they joined me. "He's alive. Just sleeping. No wonder he didn't come to meet us." I reached for his shoulder to wake him up. "I'll just—"

"Wait." Oliver leaned closer to him. "Something's wrong. Give me your flashlight."

I snapped it off my belt and handed it to him. "What is it?"

He flicked it on and shone the beam in my father's face, revealing tiny, raised bumps across his forehead and more bumps partially hidden by his beard, dark red and oozing yellowish pus. "Some kind of sickness."

I touched my ear. "Jillian, that pox you told me you and my father had. What do the sores look like?"

Her voice entered my ear. "Little lesions that ooze clear fluid. Kind of reddish. Why?"

"Clear fluid? Not yellow?"

"It turns yellow in the final stages before death." Her voice spiked. "Megan, tell me what's going on. Right now."

Pain stabbed my gut. As my throat narrowed, I forced my voice to stay steady. "I found my father in the command center. He's asleep, or out cold, I guess. I think his pox came back. You said something about that, right?"

Jillian's tone calmed. "Listen carefully, Megan. Don't touch the lesions or any part of his skin or even his clothes. And find something to cover your face. I don't think it's an airborne contagion, but he might sneeze a load of deadly droplets on you."

I looked at my hand. "I already touched his shirt with my hand."

"Are you close to water? Can you wash?"

I looked around at the walls, visible enough in the dimness—no toilet facilities. "Not at the moment."

"Then don't touch your face. Wash that hand as soon as possible." Jillian sighed. "Megan, I hate to say this, but the pox is in its final stages. Your father is dying. There's no hope for him now."

A sob threatened to erupt, but I forced it down. "I can't let that happen."

"I'm immune. I see on the diagram where the command center is. I'm on my way."

"What's up?" Oliver asked.

Crystal set a hand on my back. "Yeah, Megan. Don't keep us in the dark. We can't hear Jillian."

"My father has the pox. He's dying." A tear trickled to my cheek. I brushed it away, then looked at my hand, the same hand that had touched his shirt. But I didn't care. If I got the pox and died with my father, I would be okay with that. Still, I had to protect my friends. They needed to know the risk. "It's contagious. Jillian is coming to help because she's immune, but you should leave."

Crystal blew through her flapping lips. "Who's scared of a deadly pox? After what we've been through, this'll be a breeze. A strong breeze, I guess. Maybe a hurricane. But I'm staying."

"Same here. I'll try to heal him." Oliver reached a hand toward my father.

I grabbed his arm with my clean hand and pulled him back. "If you touch him, you could catch it."

"Megan, since when do we let danger stop us from saving lives?" He pulled his arm away. "Now charge me up. I've never healed a pox before."

"And I," Perdantus said as he extended his wings, "will find Jillian and lead her here." He flew into the elevator car. Using his beak, he pressed a button, and the door closed.

"Thank you, Oliver." No longer caring about my contaminated hand, I gave him a hug, then hugged Crystal. "Thank you both."

Crystal crossed her arms and walked toward one of the keyboards. "I guess while you two do your thing, I'll fiddle with the tech to figure out how it all works. Don't worry. I won't blow up the universe."

"Sounds iffy, but go ahead." I pulled the locket from behind my shirt and opened the clasp. The dragon's eye glowed but just barely. My father's life was hanging by a burnt thread. "Let's do it, Oliver."

He set a hand on my father's cheek and closed his eyes. "I'm sensing something kind of … well … creepy, I guess. Darkness. Cold. Like walking in a haunted house with an icy draft blowing."

"I guess that's the disease. It's not like a wound. Maybe you have to counter it with the opposite feeling."

"Light and warmth." He nodded. "I'll try."

My hand trembling, I plucked the dragon's eye from the locket and set it on my palm. The faint glow flickered. As a cold chill invaded my body, I closed my hand around the ruby, and whispered, "God, please help Oliver. And help me energize him like a dynamo. We have a lot of Starborn power from Gamma Five, but I know it all really comes from you." As new tears flowed, my throat tightened, and stifled sobs throttled my voice. "I need you … to heal my father. To me, that's … that's the most important thing … in the universe. But … but it's also important to others. There is so much more to do. To help enslaved kids. And stop the slavers. Together, Papa and I can do so much more …" I wept through my final words. "Than I can do alone."

As I cried, Crystal hugged me from behind. "You'll never be alone, Megan. Not if I can help it."

My whole body trembled. "I know. I know. But I need my Papa. My Mama's gone. I can't lose him, Crystal. I can't lose him."

She let out a shushing sound as she tightened her embrace. "I'm here for you, Sister. I've got you."

Oliver, now with a hand on each of my father's cheeks, grimaced. "He's so cold. And his heart is skipping beats."

I glanced again at the dragon's eye. It's light now pulsed erratically between its dim state and darkness. Why wasn't my power working? Why wasn't Oliver's? Did I need Lyric with me again?

I imagined Lyric appearing in my father's form next to me. When Oliver healed Oz, it was at that moment that the dynamo power erupted within. At other times, I was able to energize a Starborn without Lyric around, so what was the true catalyst that triggered my power? Might it be the emotions that flowed at the moment? Compassion? Selflessness? Love? Maybe all three? What could I do that would help fill him with light and warmth?

After setting the gem back in the locket and closing the clasp, I pulled free from Crystal and sat in my father's lap, curling my body to fit. As Oliver shifted to the side, I slid an arm around my father's shoulders and my cheek against his cheek.

Oliver moved his hands to my father's chest. "His heart settled a bit. Keep it up."

"You're the healer. I'm just the catalyst." I hummed an old tune Mama used to sing at bedtime after Papa finished reading a story with me on his lap in a rocking chair. As the lyrics returned to mind like a distant echo, I sang them with a tremoring voice. "Dear child of mine, enfolded in my love." I lifted his arm and laid it over me. "You need not fear the dragons up above. They spew their flames, they threaten with claws. But you and I will soon escape their jaws. Together today, together tomorrow, we'll catch and surpass even through sorrow. For love abounds inside warrior hearts, a love that lasts. It will never depart."

As I let the final note fade, I glanced at the locket. The gem's glow passed through, sending radiance across my shirt.

"It's working," Oliver said, one hand on my father's chest and the other on his cheek. "I feel warmth stretching from his heart to his brain, like it's trying to make a connection."

I kissed my father's forehead. "I love you, Papa. I will always love you. Please come back to me. I need you."

"Wow!" Oliver said. "That was like fuel for the fire. The cold is retreating."

Papa squirmed under my weight. He winced and let out a low moan. I got off his lap and stood next to the chair with his hand in mine. It felt warm in my grasp. "Papa, I'm still here. Keep coming. You're almost back with me."

He compressed my hand. The sensation sent a surge of warmth throughout my body. Was he healed? I leaned close to his face. Most of the lesions had faded to light pink, and some were completely gone. "Oliver?"

"Yeah. The two heat sources hooked up, and the stream of warmth is spreading. The darkness is almost gone."

The elevator door opened. Jillian walked into the room with Perdantus on her shoulder. She strode straight to the chair while Perdantus flew to Crystal. Jillian bent close to me, whispering, "How is he?"

Barely able to hold back a shout, I forced my voice to stay low. "He's coming around, Jillian. My Papa's going to make it."

"Wonderful. But I shouldn't be surprised at any miracle from this crew." She kissed my forehead. "You two keep it up while I look around. I noticed something going on in our arrival bay, and I want to check it out from here. I'll tell you later."

I nodded. "Work with Crystal. She's been scoping things out."

"Will do." Jillian straightened and walked to one of the control monitors where Crystal stood.

I refocused on my father. The lesions had all disappeared, and the pain lines in his face relaxed.

Oliver lifted his hands and gave me a nod. "It's done. I think his body's exhausted, though. No idea how long he'll sleep."

"You did it." I wrapped him in my arms. "Thank you, Oliver! Thank you so much!"

"You're welcome." He hugged me in return. "It was a team effort."

"It was." I pulled away and held his arms. "Now we have to watch for symptoms ourselves, but as long as you're around, I think we'll be fine." I released him and looked again at my father. He breathed easily, a contented smile on his face. I wanted so badly to wake him up, but I had waited this long for our reunion, I could wait a little while longer.

I hooked an arm around Oliver's and walked with him to Jillian and Crystal as they studied a computer screen. "Any startling revelations from the snarky brain trust?" I asked.

Jillian turned toward me and tousled my hair. "I love hearing that saucy spark in your voice, Mophead."

I grinned. "Mophead?"

"My new nickname for you. Get used to it." She pointed at a monitor that showed the Nebula Nine parked in its arrival bay. Letters and numbers ran vertically on the right side of the screen. "The computer is analyzing our ship, like it's checking it for anomalies after it supposedly went through the deatomization process."

I read a header at the top of the screen—Alliance Cruiser Nebula Nine. "So it recognizes the ship because it's an Alliance vessel."

"Correct. It probably has a database of every ship in the fleet."

"Check this out," Crystal said as she walked to a nearby workstation and tapped on the keyboard. The screen above it filled with squares, each with a view of a docking bay. "We can watch for Raven. I set the system to sound an alarm if anyone shows up."

Jillian pointed at a flashing string of words on the first monitor. "See that status? It says the Nebula Nine has been cleared for transport. I'm guessing an arrival bay can also be a departure bay. A flip of a switch can send the Nine to any of the other spheres in short order. That is, if it works according to spec. Since it's unmanned, it might be safe, but we can't afford to lose our only transport out of here."

"The Nine's not the only transport," Crystal said. "I see another in a departure bay. It's a big sucker."

Jillian joined her and squinted at the screen. "It's a cargo ship. Ancient model. Usually just two seats for the pilot and first mate. Beds for long treks, of course, but no other frills. I wonder if Julian flew that hunk of junk here. Or maybe it was being used to test the transport system."

"Megan?"

I spun toward the call. My father stood in front of the chair, a weary smile on his face as he blinked. "Are you real?"

Tears burst forth. "Yes, Papa."

I ran to him. He caught me up in his arms and hugged me close, turning slowly in place. He whispered, "I can't believe it" again and again.

After we kissed each other on the forehead, he set me down and brushed tears from his cheeks. "Let me have a look at you." His eyes sparkled, and his smile brightened. "It's you, my little munchkin. It's really you."

I spread my arms. "In the flesh."

He ran a hand along my neck where the shock collar used to be. His smile twisted into a frown. "A burn mark. Those cockroaches will pay for what they've done to you."

I grasped his hand and held it. "They paid, Papa. Captain Tillman and his crew are all dead. So's Admiral Fairbanks. But you knew that, didn't you? Lyric morphed into you and spoke with your voice, almost like an AI persona."

His smile returned. "So you found Lyric. Good. Is she safe? Is the power source secure?"

"Safe and secure."

"And how did I get healed of that blasted pox?"

I gestured with my head toward Oliver. "This is Captain Tillman's son. He's a healer. I escaped with him and Crystal …" I gestured toward her as well. "From a slaver on Delta Ninety-Eight."

Papa bit his lip. "Oh. I see. I apologize for the cockroach comment, Oliver."

Oliver waved a hand. "No worries. I understand."

Papa narrowed his eyes. "What's with the bird on your shoulder?"

"He's Perdantus," Crystal said. "A great hero who's gotten us out of more deadly fixes than I can count. He understands both Alpha One and Humaniversal. He would speak for himself, but if you don't know Silver Jay, then you wouldn't understand."

"I have a translator earbud." He focused on Perdantus. "Greetings, Perdantus. Thank you for watching over my daughter and her friends."

Perdantus bowed his head. "I am pleased to meet you, good sir, and it was my pleasure to accompany and serve them through their many adventures."

"I'm looking forward to hearing all about it."

Jillian cleared her throat. "Hello, Julian."

He looked at her and nodded. "Hello, Sis. I saw you there. I assumed we could catch up in the lounge."

She ran her shoe along the floor, obviously nervous. "Sure, but first." She took a deep breath. "I know I confessed to cheating back in pilot's school, but there's something I left undone."

"Okay," he said, nodding. "Go on."

She shifted her weight from one foot to the other. "I've been working on how to say this for weeks, but I guess it's best to just blurt it out." She took a deep breath. "As you know, I cheated during our final battle, but I also changed my score on the final written exam so I would rank the same as you in the standings. If not for the change, we wouldn't have been tied, and we wouldn't have had to battle to break the tie. In short, I cheated to get the chance to cheat again. I was wrong, and I'm sorry."

He smiled. "I already knew that."

Jillian's eyes widened. "You did?"

"Even before the tiebreaker. I saw your test grade before and after, so I hacked into the system to see who changed it. I was tempted to change it back, but I left it alone. I figured it wasn't really my business."

Her mouth dropped open. "You hacked into the pilot school's computer?"

"Good training, don't you think? It started me down the road of piracy and computer technology. And who could've guessed that my sneaky sister was the reason for all my success?" He reached toward her. "Come here, sneaky sister."

The two embraced, rubbing each other's backs. "I forgive you," my father said. "For everything. The slate is clean." He drew away and smiled. "Without you, I'd be a human icicle on Beta Four."

She thumped a finger on his chest. "Now that's the truth. You need me. That's why I'm sticking around for a while. To keep you out of trouble, especially the refrigerated kind."

They both laughed, and the upwelling joy filled my heart to near bursting, but my father still looked exhausted. We needed to find a place for him to rest. "Papa, you mentioned a lounge. Can we go there and sit awhile? I have so much to tell you, and I want to hear what you're doing with this transport station."

"One floor up." He walked gingerly to a workstation and picked up a computer pad. "I'd better keep monitoring the bays in case we have unexpected company."

He and I walked hand-in-hand to the elevator car, and the others joined us. When we arrived at the next level, we walked out to the lounge, another large circular room with five plush sofas, seven recliners, and multiple coffee tables. And, speaking of coffee, a bank of urns with spigots stood on a table against the wall, a stack of Styrofoam cups at the end of the table.

Jillian looked at the urns hopefully. "Are they filled?"

My father shook his head. "But all the ingredients are in a drawer, we have electricity, and I could use some myself. Go for it."

"Anyone else?" Jillian asked.

When no one else asked for some, Jillian left to prepare the coffee. My father sat on a sofa's center cushion, and I sat at his side. Oliver and Crystal each chose a flanking recliner, angled them toward us, and settled back with the footrests extended. Perdantus perched on the arm of the sofa, looking more alert than anyone in the room.

When Jillian returned with two steaming cups, she handed one to my father and sat on his opposite side. "Okay, mystery man," she said, "what's up with these Zeta Spheres? We already know the basics and why the project was abandoned but tell us your connection."

He took a sip from his cup and settled back into the cushion, his eyes half closed as he took my hand and intertwined his fingers with mine. "You know I can't resist a mystery, so I scoped out the Gamma Five sphere and discovered that it was still active. I mean, it wasn't transporting ships, but the Alliance was using it for messaging. You might not know that the technology allows for communications between one sphere and another, and the Alliance has kept the spheres active exactly for that purpose, allowing them to send messages instantaneously, though they kept that knowledge secret within the Alliance military. The private sector doesn't know about it.

"In any case, the messaging system can be accessed remotely, so they don't need a human operator on board, but an operator *is* needed to send a physical vessel from one sphere to another. Since that project was abandoned and everyone thinks the spheres are useless satellite junk, they're left with only a military sentry on the planet who monitors activity."

He took another drink of coffee. "After learning the status of the Gamma sphere, I came to this one in an abandoned cargo ship in the traditional way, a typical wormhole. When I arrived, a sentry named Kit called in and asked me to identify myself. I told him I was a cargo pilot stopping in to get some coffee, use the toilet, and sack out for a while because the bed on the cargo ship has springs popping out of the mattress, and I sent him a photo to prove it.

"Since Kit didn't want to bother verifying my story by flying to the sphere, he told me to relax and take all the time I needed. I took advantage of his lack of diligence to be able to stay as long as I want and have free reign here. Anyway, I left clues for Camille Fairbanks that would lead her to Epsilon Six, and since there's nowhere else to go except this station, I hoped she would land in an arrival bay. Then I would flip it to a departure bay and send her into oblivion, assuming, of course, that the process continues to eliminate passengers."

He breathed a deep sigh and tightened his grip on my hand. "After that, I planned to return to Gamma Five in the conventional manner and find you, Megan. I knew only you could get through the obstacle course I set up to protect Lyric, though I didn't guess that you would track me all the way here." He kissed the side of my head. "You are every bit the courageous, clever, innovative daughter that I always knew you were. You are truly amazing."

His words warmed every part of my body, especially my heart, like I had flown into a Paradise that I hoped would never end. "Thank you, but you and Mama taught me everything I know."

His expression sagged. Tears welled in his eyes. "Anne's death is a crushing blow. I loved her more than life itself. But if I allowed that tragedy to sink in, it would cripple me. I can't let grief stop me from finishing our journey. I need to press on. We can talk more about your mother later. For now, unload your story on me. I want to hear every detail."

"All right. Well, first of all, we think Camille Fairbanks is dead, so don't expect her to show up at an arrival bay. But her daughter, Raven, painted a target on my back, so she's sure to come here looking for me." I shook my head. "That's later in story. I'd better start at the beginning when Captain Tillman took me away from you and Mama."

From that point, I spilled my entire saga. When I got to the part about finding Oliver and Crystal, they added some details that I had forgotten, but they later fell asleep in their recliners as I continued the long tale. Fortunately, Perdantus filled in other tidbits, as did Jillian, though she stayed quiet most of the time. When I finished, I exhaled. "And now we're here."

My father stared at me, his mouth agape. "Absolutely incredible. Truly stunning. I … I don't know what else to say."

I shrugged. "Don't say anything, I guess. I did what I had to do."

"And now we have much more to do. After we take care of the Raven problem, we'll finish looking at the data you gathered from Thorne and the computer drive you picked up from the dead Starborn, then together we'll search the galaxy for any remaining slave colonies, and we'll bring to justice any vermin involved in the trafficking, either now or in the past."

I raised a finger. "But first, can we use the instantaneous data connection to the Gamma Five sphere? I want to check on Zoë."

Papa ran a hand through his hair. "Let me think about the best way to do that."

I lifted my brow. "What's the problem?"

"Well, first, just sending a query to the Gamma sphere won't do the job. We would have to find a way to relay it to Lyric's parents. They will be the ones who are looking after Zoë, and they're probably holed up somewhere to keep all the Starborn kids hidden from Raven and the Alliance. Second, we'll have to come up with an excuse to use the communications system at all. The outpost sentry here is alone and pretty much unaccountable, but the personnel monitoring Gamma won't be so lax. I can watch what's going on at the Gamma sphere without being noticed, but once I activate a data channel, that'll raise suspicions, and they'll send the Epsilon Six sentry here to see what's going on."

"Maybe we can pose as that sentry and send a coded message to Lyric's parents. Since they're wealthy, it wouldn't be unusual for them to have some kind of ties to the Alliance, right?"

He firmed his lips. "Not a bad idea. Keep working on a way to do that without raising a red flag."

I nodded. "I'll ask Emerson to research the businesses Lyric's family is involved in."

"Good start." He set his computer pad on his knee and began tapping on the screen. "While you do that, I'll take a peek at what's going on at the Gamma sphere."

"Sounds good." I touched my ear. "Emerson, have you been listening?"

His voice came through the bud. "Affirmative. If I am to conduct research on the family, I will need their last name."

"Lyric's last name was Altera in the training camp database. That should give you a good start."

"Affirmative, though I don't know if my memory banks will contain that data I need until I conduct a query. Since the major erasure I suffered, I have noticed large gaps. I could contact the computer at the sentry post to download an update if such contact would not jeopardize our fabricated reason for being here."

"Contact the sentry directly and request a full download of anything that you have clearance for. Just a routine update after a long journey."

"Acknowledged."

My father's computer pad beeped. "Well," he said as he ran a finger along the screen. "This is interesting. An Alliance cruiser docked at a departure bay at the Gamma Five Zeta Sphere. It requested transport to the Epsilon sphere, and the Gamma sentry granted it."

I blinked. "What? Are they crazy? Why would someone risk death, and why would the sentry allow it?"

"No idea. Someone's desperate, I guess. But it's on its way. A fifty-eight-minute journey with …" He glanced at his pad. "About six minutes to go."

I gasped. "Six minutes! Can you see the ship's name?"

He looked again at his screen. "The Nebula Seven."

"That's Raven's ship. If she knows about the spheres, wouldn't she also know about the failed tests?"

"Not sure. But since she's Camille's daughter, maybe she knows something I don't know." He stared at the pad's screen once more. "I could close all the arrival bays, but that would alert the sentry, and he would just undo what I did. He might also shut down all the life support systems to stop us from doing anything else to cripple the sphere. That's why I wanted his cooperation. I can't override what he does."

"Then let Raven risk it. If somehow she makes it here, we'll be ready for her."

"Ready for her? My plan was to send her out of a bay. If she has a way to avoid getting obliterated, zapping her ship to another sphere won't do any good. She could just come back, and the sentry could halt everything we're doing." He rose to his feet. "I have to hustle to the command center. I can't get a visual on the arrival bays on this pad."

I shot to my feet. "I'll go with you. If Jillian will stay, we can let Oliver and Crystal sleep. She can watch over them."

"I'll stay." Jillian settled back in her seat and closed her eyes, smiling. "Gladly. Though I'm not sure how much watching I'll do."

Perdantus flitted to the back of the sofa. "If Jillian falls asleep, I will take over guard duty."

"Perfect." Papa grasped my hand. "Let's go."

We rushed into the elevator, rode down to the next floor, and hustled into the command center. Papa scanned the monitors, pivoting slowly. "The pad didn't tell me which bay the ship will arrive in, so we'll just have to wait for an alarm and see which one is activated."

"I'll tell Emerson to be on the alert in case he needs to raise the Nebula Nine's shields."

"Good idea."

I touched my ear. "Emerson, were you listening?"

"Affirmative. I will raise my shields on your order, and I will also be ready to raise them without your order if the ship is in danger."

"Perfect. Did you get any intel about Lyric's parents?"

"Affirmative. The download of all data updates is not yet complete, but I do have information about Lyric Altera and her parents. Her father, Robert, owns a manufacturing company, and her mother, Piper, is a capital management investor who helped finance the building of the Zeta Sphere that orbits Gamma Five. She is also the civilian overseer of the project. Their financial savvy has put them on the list of the top three wealthiest families on Gamma Five."

"Do they do any commercial trading with other systems, like Epsilon?" I asked.

"Affirmative."

"Good. Can you send a message through the sphere's instantaneous channel?"

"Negative. I do not have access."

"All right." I scanned the monitors for any sign of a communications window. "I'll see if I can send one from here to Robert and Piper Altera. Thank you."

"You are welcome."

"Let us know if you see—"

An alarm buzzed at one of the workstations. Papa hurried to it and looked at its monitor. "Ship transport arriving at bay number eight from Gamma in five seconds. The data says it's the Nebula Seven."

I stared at the empty docking bay on the screen, hoping to see a ship without a crew. Maybe the crazy mother-daughter duo was gone for good. "I guess we'll just watch and learn."

"Exactly."

A ship appeared within the bay. Although it was the size and shape of the Nebula Seven, scorch marks covered it from bow to stern, including its identifying label. "I think it's the Seven," I said. "Looks like it's been in a firefight."

Papa nodded. "But those don't look like laser blast marks. More like traditional fire exposure. Whatever that ship went through during the transport, it had to be superheated."

After the bay door closed and the air supply finished filling the chamber, the ship's ramp fell open and slammed against the floor. A slender woman walked down the slope, her gray hair uneven, as if chopped by a dull knife.

"Could that be Camille?" Papa asked.

"Not sure. The body shape and hair color are right, and her face is similar, but not exactly the same. I don't think she would be out in public with her hair looking like that, not if she could help it. And like I said before, a mind reader told us that Camille is dead. Raven was still alive when we left, but she's younger and has coal-black hair."

When the woman reached floor level, she looked around. Papa used the keyboard controls to zoom in on her face. A small mole on her chin revealed the truth. I whispered, "She *is* Raven!"

Papa squinted at the screen. "She's an older woman now. At least sixty Alpha-One years old."

"What could've caused such a transformation?" I asked. "Something related to the superheating?"

"I don't know of any way extreme heat can cause rapid aging." He flipped a switch on the console. "I'm turning off communications to the sentry. He'll eventually notice and fly here to investigate, but maybe it'll buy us enough time to figure out what's going on."

Raven's voice came through a speaker on the computer. "Is anyone here?"

I spied a microphone on the counter. "Should we answer?"

Papa nodded. "I'll disguise my voice. Maybe we can get some intel." He picked up the microphone and spoke with a gruff rasp. "Identify yourself."

She set her hands on her hips. "I am Raven Fairbanks, daughter of Admiral Camille Fairbanks. My crew and I departed in the Nebula Seven from the Zeta Sphere in the Gamma system hoping to arrive at the sphere in the Epsilon system. Can you tell me if I made it?"

"You arrived at the Epsilon station. Is your crew still aboard?"

She shifted nervously. "They … um … didn't make it. I'm alone."

"I checked our database. You don't look like the photos we have of you."

She huffed. "That's because any photos you have of me were taken when I was much younger. About thirty years have passed since then. I can't be sure, though. I haven't been able to keep track of time."

I sucked in a quiet breath. Thirty years? How could that be possible?

Papa covered the microphone and whispered to me, "Let's play along and see what happens." He returned to his gruff voice and spoke into the mic again. "According to our travel schedule, the Nebula Seven was supposed to arrive at this station twenty-nine years ago. Where have you been all this time?"

Raven laughed under her breath. "That's a story I don't want to tell. Suffice it to say that I was somewhere I definitely didn't want to be. It took every skill I had and years of planning to return to this reality, and I don't choose to relive it."

"This reality?" Papa asked. "Are you saying you traveled to another reality?"

She spoke with a sarcastic tone. "Well, aren't you the logic king?"

Papa looked upward in thought for a moment before answering. "Why did you attempt the journey? At the date of your departure, passengers were not allowed to be aboard the transport ship. The system was being tested for safety, and in all early tests no passenger ever showed up at the arrival sphere."

"I attempted the journey because the local head of the project told me that mechanics had fixed a glitch, and they have had more than a hundred successful tests with passengers since then. No problems."

"The local head of the project," I whispered. "That has to be Piper Altera, Lyric's mother. She double crossed Raven. You gotta love that."

After stifling a laugh, Papa replied through the microphone. "Interesting. I see no record of successful tests that early on. It seems that someone was lying to you."

Raven crossed her arms. "I'll be sure to find the scoundrel, assuming she's still alive after all these years."

"I can send you back to Gamma Five so you can confront the person who lied to you. We have had thousands of safe passenger transports since that time. No incidents in the last twenty years."

I gasped. My father was planning to send Raven to her doom.

"All right. I guess I can endure a short ride." She walked toward the ramp. "Let's get it over with."

Papa turned the microphone off and reached for the keyboard. "As soon as she's gone, we can leave the station before the sentry can show up and—"

"No." I pulled his arm back. "I know she's a terrible person, but you can't murder her."

"Murder?" His jaw tensed for a second before loosening. "Megan, she sent innocent children to their deaths. And she was involved with trafficking even more children. If anyone deserves to die, she does."

"I realize that, but no judge? No jury? We're just going to be the executioners?"

His tone sharpened. "Do you remember the judge who sentenced you to be enslaved? The judge who ordered you to be branded with a hot iron? Who put that choking shock collar around your neck? Who sentenced your mother and me to death? Is that the kind of judge you want?"

I stared at him without a word, knowing that his anger was directed at Raven and her ilk, not at me.

He set a hand on my shoulder and spoke with a calmer voice. "We're at war, Megan, and the powers in high places are the enemy. We can't count on them to serve justice. No judge or jury they appoint will ever convict a member of the elite class like Raven Fairbanks, even if she appears to be a crazy old woman now. That's up to us."

"I realize that. Like Mama always told me, sometimes you have to fight fire with fire. But Raven's harmless now. The Nebula Seven's cooked. Her crew are all dead. We can just take her as a prisoner of war and interrogate her to find out where she's been, or thinks she's been. Something strange happened to her. She doesn't come across as crazy."

After gazing at me for a few seconds, Papa blew a deep sigh. "You're right, Megan, and I'm sorry. I let my anger get the best of me." He kissed my forehead. "Keep me in line. I've been fighting this war for far too long."

Hearing his confession felt so good. He was still my Papa, a man who wasn't afraid to admit being wrong. "You're right about this being a long war, and we're close to winning it. For now, we need a plan to take Raven prisoner. She probably has weapons, and she's not going to go quietly."

"I have an idea." Papa turned the microphone on. "Is your ship capable of flight? It looks like it's been through a battle, maybe a losing one."

Raven walked down the ramp again and looked toward the camera. "If you knew what this ship has been through, you would be amazed that it looks this good. But, no, it's not able to fly. I assumed you would transport it. It doesn't need to fly."

"The transport doesn't require flight, but it does require hull integrity. I'm going to send someone to inspect the ship to make sure it's capable of travel."

"All right. I've waited this long. I can wait a little while longer." She walked up the ramp again.

I narrowed an eye at my father. "Let me guess. Jillian."

"Right. I doubt that the two have ever met, and Jillian's a natural when it comes to deception … I mean … acting."

"I know exactly what you mean, but she never really fooled you, did she? Weren't you on to her the whole time? You just didn't report her, right?"

"I was on to her, but she's my twin. We can't fool each other about anything. She did fool the school administrators, though. She had them eating out of her hand. She can be charming to the max."

"Sounds like a good plan, and maybe while she's inspecting, she can get Raven to spill her story. I think everyone needs to learn what that alternate reality stuff is all about."

"That's exactly what I was hoping," he said. "It seems that great minds think alike."

"True, but stupid minds also think alike. We'll see if Jillian thinks our plan is great or stupid."

We hurried back to the lounge and found Jillian asleep, fully stretched out on the sofa, while Oliver and Crystal continued napping on their recliners. Perdantus had nestled on Crystal's chest, but his eyes were open as he watched us enter.

After waking everyone, we told them about Raven's arrival and her bizarre story. Jillian agreed to act as ship inspector while we would board the Nebula Nine and listen to her conversation with Raven, transmitted to Emerson via a commlink in Jillian's ear.

From my memory of the sphere's layout, I led Jillian to a maintenance room where we found three sets of coveralls with a Zeta Sphere logo on the breast pocket. Fortunately, one of them fit, and the cap, also emblazoned with the logo, fit a bit too loosely, though probably not enough to worry about.

I gathered with Papa, Oliver, Crystal, and Perdantus at the Nine's bridge and listened to the ceiling speakers. Soon, Jillian's chatter came through. "Okay, homebase, this is Super Secret Agent Jillian Willis reporting. I am approaching the ramp of the Nebula Seven. I can already see that the hydraulic lift arms are busted. I'll have to deduct some points from the ship's ready-to-transport score for that, though it can be closed and sealed manually. And now I'm walking up the ramp, and I'm going silent until I need to talk to Raven."

My father, sitting at the navigator's seat, rolled his eyes. "That's my sister. Always the drama queen."

"You must be Raven Fairbanks," Jillian said in an official tone. "I'm here to inspect your ship."

Raven's voice came through, but at a much lower volume. "Thank you for coming. The ship has lost some of its functions, but I'm sure the hull is intact. A little scorched, but no holes that I could see."

"Yes, ma'am. I'm sure you're right. But I'll check every nook and cranny, maybe places you're not able to go. We want to make sure you get to your destination safely. That's what traveling with the folks at Zeta Sphere is all about."

"Thank you. After what I've been through, I do want to be safe."

"All you've been through?" Jillian asked. "Want to tag along and tell me about it?"

"Not especially." Raven's tone seemed weary. "It's a long story."

"I can see that you're tired, but I'm sure you know your ship better than I do. And since you were alone, I was just thinking you might want to bend my ear."

"Well, since you put it that way," Raven said. "I'll come with you. But more because I know the ship. I might tell you part of the story. We'll see."

"Sounds good. Let's go to the central hull space first. That's the area most people never go, and it's the most common place to find a hole no one's noticed."

"Works for me."

Except for footsteps, silence ensued for nearly a minute before Jillian continued. "The head operator told me you said you were gone for thirty years. I guess you know that's the coolest mystery ever. What's the first thing you remember happening?"

"Well, the moment the rays from the Gamma sphere's departure bay struck the ship, I remember a tingling sensation. Then a bright light flashed. I blacked out, but not for long, I think. I woke up, and my crew, three men and a woman, were out cold. I had a headache that pounded like a hammer, and that's no exaggeration. My skull literally throbbed. After shaking my crew members awake, I checked the scanner, but it wouldn't work. Nothing on the ship functioned."

"Do you think the atomization step fried the circuits?" Jillian asked.

"That was my guess at first, but I had no way of proving it. Anyway, we manually lowered the ramp and went outside, but we weren't in the Zeta Sphere anymore. It was a tropical jungle with tall trees, hanging vines, and a river. Since we had no access to repair parts, we had to go into survival mode. Fortunately, the river provided plenty of water, and fish abounded. Also, tropical fruit was easy to find.

"We subsisted on those for weeks, while venturing out in short forays to learn the extent of the jungle. But it seemed endless. I finally decided to pack up and go on a longer trek. I had seen a mountain maybe a two-day journey away, and I guessed I could climb to the top. When I arrived, I saw a circular chasm in the distance, but I couldn't tell if anything was in it. Other than that, the jungle extended as far as the eye could see. I also spotted a raging fire heading toward the ship and my crew. I had no chance to get there in time to warn them."

"Wow!" Jillian said. "So that's how your ship got scorched."

"Wait a minute."

Raven's tone sounded suspicious. The silence that followed tightened the tension in the air.

"Is something wrong?" Jillian asked.

"You seem familiar, like someone I knew before I left Gamma Five."

I looked at Papa. "Uh-oh. This is going downhill."

He waved a calming hand. "Let's give Jillian time to recover."

"Well, ma'am," she said, "I've never seen you before in my life. Of course, it was thirty years ago when—"

"Yes, you *are* her. Thirty years older. And you're no maintenance worker. You're in disguise. Why are you spying on me, Megan Willis?"

"Megan Willis? Who is that?"

A growl invaded Raven's voice. "I've seen that fake look of surprise before. You have to be her."

"She's busted." Papa shot out of his seat and ran down the ramp. "Megan, on my six!"

"Oliver. Crystal. Perdantus. Stay here and keep listening!" I dashed after him while checking the laser blaster on my belt. I caught up with him on our bay's floor, and we ran together to the stairwell and sprinted up. I called, "Where is the Nebula Seven's arrival bay?"

"Eight flights higher," he said, puffing. "Then five bays down the hall."

"Got it. Stay as close as you can." I flexed my biceps, powered my leg muscles, and zoomed up the stairs.

He shouted, "I'm on your six."

"Counting on it." I rushed to the proper level, flung the door open, and sprinted through the hall while drawing my laser blaster. When I reached the fifth door, I pushed a button labeled "Open." The instant the door slid to the side, I ran to the Nebula Seven's ramp and sneaked up toward the bridge, my legs bent and my head low.

Jillian lay prostrate on the floor near the Seven's main computer console, Raven standing over her with a laser gun of her own aimed at Jillian's head. "Admit it!" Raven shouted. "You're Megan Willis. You have to be."

"I'm not Megan," Jillian said. "I'm her aunt. That's why I look like her."

I crept closer. I needed to get a good shot, a hit that would disable Raven without killing her.

Raven set a foot on Jillian's back. "Don't take me for a fool. An aunt of Megan's would be at least fifty by now. Maybe sixty."

Stooping behind the pilot's command console, I took aim at Raven's gun hand.

"Raven," the ship's computer said with a calm male voice, "an intruder has come aboard and—"

I fired my blaster. The laser bullet struck Raven's wrist and sent her gun flying. I leaped from my hiding place and rammed into her, slamming both of us into the computer console. We dropped to the floor with me on top of her. I rose and propped my knees at her sides. After holstering my gun, I wrapped my hands around her throat and charged them up. Electricity arced from my fingers and shot across her face. Her body stiffened. Her eyes widened and her lips firmed as she stared at me, defiant.

I kept my hands in place. She deserved to die, but I knew I couldn't kill her. Not only was she too valuable; it simply wasn't the right thing to do, like I had said to my father.

"Megan!" Papa shouted as he ran up the ramp. "Everything under control?"

"Yep." I rose and set a foot on Raven's chest. "Got her pinned."

As Papa walked toward me, my limbs grew weak, and dizziness flooded my brain. My knees buckled, and I crumbled on top of Raven, making her let out an oomph.

Papa rolled me off her. Barely conscious, I looked up at him. The room spun halfway around my head, then snapped back and spun again, over and over. "Are you all right?" he asked.

"No. I'm … I'm weak. Dizzy. Like my life is draining from my body. I think it's Raven. She's doing it to me."

Papa grabbed Raven's laser blaster from the floor and pressed the barrel against her forehead, growling, "Whatever you're doing, stop it!"

She scowled. "Release me, and I will."

"I could put a laser bullet through your brain. That would stop you."

"You need me for something. Otherwise, you would've shot me already."

"I need Megan more than I need you." He pushed the barrel harder. "You have three seconds. One …"

Raven sneered. "All right. I stopped."

The dizziness faded, and the weakness ebbed. "I'm feeling better. Not completely, but better."

Papa drew the gun back. "You can sit up, but stay where you are."

Keeping the gun aimed at Raven, Papa helped Jillian to her feet first, then me. While Jillian leaned back against the computer console,

Papa guided me to a seat at the navigator station before focusing on Raven. "You might have figured out by now that it hasn't been thirty years since you left."

Raven glared at him. "I figured out that a girl who looks exactly like Megan is here and that a man is here who looks like her father. But I know that I spent thirty years in a jungle and that I'm thirty years older than I used to be. I can't put the facts together to make any sense."

"Your ship arrived," Papa said, "exactly at the expected time, fifty-eight minutes after you left the Gamma Five sphere. I have to conclude that you were in an alternate reality where time passes much more quickly compared to here. So you aged thirty years while we didn't age at all."

Sitting with her forearms propped on her knees, she narrowed her eyes at him. "Either I believe your story that time warps and my atomized body spent years in what felt like my physical body while suffering deprivation and torture in a jungle, or I believe that you two aren't who you look like, and by pure coincidence you're both here at the Epsilon station when I arrived." She shook her head. "I can't believe either crazy idea. You'll have to convince me of yours."

"Actually, I don't have to convince you of anything, but maybe we can agree to trade information."

"Maybe," Raven said, her tone dripping with suspicion. "What do you want to know?"

Papa slid the gun behind his belt in front. "During the tests of the Zeta sphere stations, no passengers ever arrived at the destination. Only the ships made it. How did you manage to show up at Epsilon Six?"

"All I know is that I left the Nebula Seven to find a high vista where I could look for civilization. While I was gone, a fire ravaged the area around the Seven and killed my crew. They could have taken refuge in the ship, but based on where I found their charred bodies, it looked like they ventured too far from the ship to make it back in time.

"When I returned, I lived inside the Seven. Fortunately, a few of the comfort systems still operated, like the solar-powered heater. And Nike, the onboard computer, kept me company, also powered by solar. I went on journeys now and then to find someone, anyone, but I always came back disappointed. Then one night, I was sleeping in the ship. A tremor woke me up. Light flashed everywhere. When the commotion stopped, I was here. End of story."

"Papa," I said, my mind now clear. "Could it be that time passes in that world at a set rate compared to ours? I mean, approximately two minutes here for every year there?"

"Maybe." He gave me a nod. "Go on."

"Doesn't it take longer than fifty-eight minutes to travel between other spheres? For example, from Gamma to Delta?"

"Definitely. Gamma to Epsilon is the shortest distance and time. Gamma to Delta is close to two hours, and Beta to Delta is the longest, about three and a half hours."

"So a three-and-a-half-hour trip translates to a hundred and five years on the other world. Two hours is sixty years. Any passengers who tested on those routes probably died of old age. And maybe their corpses weren't on board because they made a last-ditch effort to get out of that jungle and never returned to their ships."

He nodded slowly. "Good theory. And Raven was young and smart enough to survive on the ship." He looked at Raven. "Is that theory a satisfying one for you?"

"Satisfying?" She huffed. "Learning how I was marooned is enlightening but far from satisfying. If you knew what I suffered, you wouldn't even ask that question."

"All right. Is there anything short of killing us that would satisfy you?"

"Probably not."

"Maybe I can come up with an alternative." He tapped on Nike's console screen and studied the output for nearly a minute. "I see your mechanic's notes. One of the rear thrusters needs a part that's not in your ship's inventory, and the main engine's ignition switch is fried."

Raven nodded. "He reported both problems to me. He said the atomization at the Gamma Five station caused the problems. Something about incomplete reconstitution, whatever that means."

Papa closed a window on the screen. "The parts were probably already going bad. When they atomized, I'm guessing some of the particles weren't exactly like the ship's specifications, and they couldn't come back together properly because the computers reconstruct ships based on what they're supposed to be like, not on what they actually were like."

"My mechanic said something similar, but knowing what caused the problem didn't help solve it. We had only bananas, coconuts, and tree vines to work with."

"Of course. I'm sure your mechanic did the best he could. This bay is loaded with parts compartments. I can find everything I need." He walked to Jillian and whispered a lengthy message into her ear. She nodded and strode down the ramp and out of sight.

Papa refocused on Raven. "Tell you what. If I repair the Nebula Seven well enough to make it capable of transportation, and I allow you to go to any planet you choose, would you go there and stay? You would be a woman in exile, but you would live the rest of your years in the location you choose. To verify your compliance, I would inject you with tracking cells that would stay in your body, and I would always know where you are. If you leave your location, I would track you down and give you the punishment you really deserve."

"Death, I assume."

"Death is the only proper penalty for a murderer of the innocent."

I nodded. There it was, my father's offer, a start to the negotiation, but it had a flaw. Leaving her options open invited a counteroffer that could be a surprise. He was pretty good at this skill, but he hadn't been taught by Perdantus, like I had.

"I accept your conditions," Raven said. "I want to return to Gamma Five."

Papa's mouth dropped open, but he quickly closed it. Neither of us wanted Raven back on Gamma Five where the Starborn children live. She could continue her evil mischief there while still keeping to the parameters of the deal he offered. Unfortunately, his brief shock had weakened his stance, and she knew it. If he backed out now or tried to add more conditions, he would appear to be dishonest.

Raven lifted her brow. "Since you're staring at me like a dazed scarecrow, I assume we have a deal."

Papa shook his head as if to throw off a trance. Looking at her again, he heaved a resigned sigh. "We do."

I forced myself to stay calm. Letting Raven loose on Gamma Five would be a disaster. Still, I could tell by the calm look on my father's face that he had a plan in mind. Maybe he had hatched a better negotiation strategy than I realized, but I couldn't ask for an explanation. I would just have to be patient.

Raven eyed him coolly. "Interesting. I thought you would balk at my choice, but I suppose you're too self-righteous to change your mind."

He stared back at her. "As if you could be a judge of righteousness. Since the injected cells will only tell me you're on Gamma Five, I'll have to find someone there who'll keep closer track of you to make sure you stay away from the Starborn children."

"That won't be necessary, but I understand." She pressed her hands against the floor. "Am I allowed to get up now?"

"Yes." Papa fiddled with some of the controls on the navigation console. "But you'll have to stay in the ship for the time being. I can't have you wandering around this station, threatening my family while I work on repairs. I have to hurry in case the sentry shows up."

"Understood." Raven rose and dusted herself off with stiff movements. "Not that I can do much threatening after getting jolted by your daughter. I think half my body is still malfunctioning."

"You're lucky she didn't kill you." He pointed toward the aft with a thumb. "I'll start with the rear thrusters. They looked salvageable. Then I'll come back inside and check the ignition system."

"Since you're motivated to keep me away from your daughter, I'm sure you'll do your best to get me out of here as quickly as possible."

"You got that right." Papa laid an arm over my shoulders and led me down the ramp, whispering, "I sent Jillian to the command center and told her how to shift this bay to departure mode. Go see if you can help her. I'm wearing an earbud. Set yours to our family's frequency and encrypt the transmissions. Let me know when you're ready to send the Nebula Seven to Gamma Five."

I whispered in return, "So you'll keep your side of the deal by sending her to the planet she asked for, and you'll do it without killing her. She might die of old age in that jungle place, but it's just a stopover on the way to Gamma Five. I love it." When we halted outside the ship, I looked at him. Obviously, his negotiation skills were better than I thought. "Did you have that idea all along?"

"As a failsafe option. That's why I whispered to Jillian before Raven made her choice, to be ready in case she chose Gamma Five. I really didn't think she would, though. Asking for Gamma Five was a lot bolder than I thought she'd be." He patted me on the shoulder and walked toward the ship's stern, apparently to start repairing the ship, or pretend to.

After switching my earbud to the proper frequency and reinserting it, I hustled to the hallway and rushed up the stairs to the command center. Jillian stood in front of one of the monitors, studying the control icons. "Let me guess. Raven chose Gamma Five."

"Yep."

"Thought she would."

"Have you figured out the controls yet?" I asked.

Jillian nodded. "It's pretty simple. Julian told me to pull the trigger the moment you and he are out of the bay. Now I'm watching for him to leave."

I looked at the screen. Papa had the rear thruster compartment open and appeared to be working on something inside. "It looks like he's really trying to repair it."

"Knowing your father, that's no surprise. Maybe he wants to give Raven a working ship in that jungle."

"He did say he would send her to Gamma Five when the Seven was able to transport, but I thought that meant ready to transport through the sphere system. It's ready for that now."

"He's being kinder to her than she deserves. He's like that, even to scoundrels he despises. And, fortunately for me, to scoundrels he loves."

One of the monitors beeped. I looked at the screen. It showed a Nebula-class ship docking in one of the arrival bays. "Uh-oh. We have company."

I looked at a screen that showed my father carrying a box of parts toward the Seven's ramp. "Papa, a Nebula ship docked in one of the arrival bays. No idea why, but it'll be someone who'll be on Raven's side, not ours."

He increased his pace as he touched his ear. "You're right. Explains why she was so compliant." He hurried up the ramp and out of sight. "Maybe she had already arranged for backup, probably from the Alliance base on Epsilon Five. She was just biding her time until they arrived. I'll see what I can find out."

"And it also explains why the sentry hasn't shown up," I said. "He knew the Nebula ship would investigate."

"Maybe so. Going silent for now. Updates soon."

I shifted to the monitor that showed the Nebula Nine still docked, as expected. "We need to get the Nine to fly to that bay and be ready to open fire. Their shields will be down."

"Good call," Jillian said. "I should run the attack. Open the Nine's bay door as soon as the ramp's up. The automated system will probably close the new arrival's door. I'll need you to open it when I get there." She dashed into the elevator and pressed the button. "The moment you're sure they're here to help Raven, let me know." The door closed before I could reply.

I switched my earbud to its normal frequency. "Oliver. Crystal. Jillian's on her way back to the Nine. You two and Perdantus get ready to bug out and prepare for battle. No questions. Just signal your compliance. Jillian's got the scoop."

"On it," Oliver said. "Battle protocol."

I looked again at the Nebula Seven and switched my earbud back to our family's frequency. "Papa, I know you probably can't answer, but if you would leave the ship and get to safety, the Nine could attack the Seven, and we wouldn't have to worry about the new arrival. Or I could just open the bay door and suck out Raven's air. Since the ramp control's broken, she won't be able to close it." An image of Raven gasping for breath reminded me of Papa's promise. He wouldn't go back on his deal with her. "But I'm sure you'll do what's right. Maybe just give me a coded message so I'll know what to do."

After a few seconds of silence, he replied. "Megan, I have everything I need to repair the Nebula Seven except for one part, an FX stabilizer unit, model number four five seven seven four. Are there any in the station's inventory?"

I blinked. I had memorized every nut and bolt in a Nebula ship, but I had never heard of an FX stabilizer. Could it be something in the station itself? "I'll look. Give me a minute." I typed on the keyboard and searched for the label and model number. The computer responded with a diagram that resembled one of the gun-like objects protruding from the wall of the bay. The text described it as the atomizer/deatomizer gun, one of the most important pieces in the transport mechanism. The inventory report said there were five in stock. "Yes, the station has some."

"Have the inventory droid bring one to me. It's too heavy to carry. Besides, I want you to stay safe where you are, like you're in a kangaroo's pouch."

I drew my head back. A kangaroo's pouch? That was a code word our family used when we were raiding Alliance strongholds. It meant for me to pretend to stay in hiding when in reality I was supposed to follow him, but I had no idea where he intended to go.

After searching the screen, I found the option to take one of the units out of inventory, selected it, and figured out how to assign a droid to the task. The system reported that it would take three minutes for the droid to arrive in the bay with the part. I looked at the arriving ship. The bay door had closed automatically, and air began filling the chamber.

I pressed the button to halt the flow, trapping the new arrivals in their ship, at least until they could put pressurized suits on. That bought us a little more time.

On the screen that showed the Nebula Nine, Jillian ran into the ship, and the ramp began closing behind her. I pressed the button that opened the bay door. They would be able to leave in a few seconds.

A new voice crackled through a speaker. "This is the sentry at the Epsilon Six outpost. I see that someone is tampering with the controls in the Zeta Sphere command center. If you don't stop, I will remove the air from that compartment."

I dared not answer. Anything I said would prove that an unauthorized person stood in the command center. I just had to stop pushing buttons for a while. If the sentry removed the air, I probably had time to rush out to the Nebula Seven's bay.

An alarm buzzed. A message flashed on the Nebula Seven's screen—Departure atomization in twenty seconds.

I gasped. How could that be? I hadn't initiated the process. Could my father have activated it from a control console in the bay? Was he actually *trying* to go to that jungle? That would be insane for most people, but he must've had a plan. Could he have come up with a way to escape the alternate world? Maybe that's why he wanted the stabilizer. But the droid wouldn't get there in time. That's why he wanted me to follow him, to provide the part he needed and protect me from the new arrivals at the same time.

A hissing sound permeated the room. "I warned you," the sentry said. "You will be without air in thirty seconds."

That sealed it. I had to carry out my father's plan and do it now. I glanced at the Nebula Nine's bay—vacant. The ship had bugged out. At least my crew would be safe. Now I had to delay the new arrivals for as long as possible. Maybe removing their air would work. I pressed the button to open the door at their bay, then ran into the elevator.

As I rode down in the car, I imagined the disintegration of the Nebula Seven. Rays from the atomizer guns covered the ship and shattered it into millions of tiny particles that would zoom toward the Gamma Five station but probably pause in a mysterious jungle.

I whispered, "Papa, I hope you know what you're doing." Soon, I would have to figure out how to atomize myself and the stabilizer, but since my father was able to work the controls from within the bay, I probably could as well.

When I arrived at the stairway, I hurried to the proper hall, dashed to the door leading to the bay, and flung it open. The Nebula Seven was gone, and the bay door had closed. The droid, a one-meter-tall robot, stood at the center of the floor with the huge stabilizer ray gun sitting on a tray attached to the top of its mechanical head.

I searched the mostly empty bay for controls. I had to hurry. Every minute here equaled six months in the jungle world. After a few seconds, I spotted a panel of blinking lights on a wall. I charged my legs, leaped to the panel, and read the labels under various buttons and dials, including a timer that delayed transport for however many minutes the operator set, probably the one my father used to give him enough time to board the Seven.

I set the activation dial for five seconds, ran to the center of the room, and crouched next to the droid, my eyes tightly closed. A whisking sound swished all around me, like wind whipping autumn leaves into a frenzy. Tingles covered my skin and penetrated deep inside, as if winged insects were eating into my body all the way to my organs, though with no pain.

Soon, the tingles faded. I opened my eyes, straightened from my crouch, and looked around. Tall trees stood in all directions, so close, I could have touched two nearby trunks. Their huge elephant-ear-shaped leaves created a dense canopy over my head, providing plenty of shade from what appeared to be bright sunlight shining through the gaps. Warm, damp air penetrated my shirt, and running water flowed somewhere nearby.

The robot stood next to me, the tray on its head sloped at an angle, one side forced upward by a tree. Apparently sensing the precarious position, it rolled forward a meter or so to level the tray. I pressed a button on the robot that shut it off.

Now, where was Papa? Assuming it would be safe to leave the stabilizer, I tromped through fernlike undergrowth, following the running-water sound while breaking fronds so I could find my way back to the robot. A bird called with an odd hoot, and another answered with a laughing cackle. High above, a bird with colorful wings flew from the top of one tree to another several meters closer, maybe to get a better look at me. As Raven had said, this jungle seemed to be teeming with life, but might some of that life be dangerous and hungry? I would have to stay alert. Fortunately, I still had the laser blaster in my belt holster.

Within a few minutes, I came upon a slow-running river that cascaded over a ledge and dropped about three meters to a pool before running deeper into the jungle. Since the other side of the river lay only five meters away, I could jump there without worrying about carnivorous water creatures.

I flexed my biceps, charged my legs, and leaped across. After landing and running a couple of steps to get my balance, I walked away from the river, hoping to move beyond its noise so I could listen for any sign of my father.

Soon, all was quiet. I cupped my hands around my mouth and shouted, "Can anyone hear me?" The dense jungle growth seemed to catch and swallow my voice. My call probably didn't get very far.

A thump reached my ears, then another and another, like metal on wood. I followed the noise to a clearing where low stumps dotted the dark ground. A small cabin stood at the center of the clearing. Made of stacked logs from the chopped-down trees, with no hint of moss or mold, it appeared to have been recently constructed.

The thumping continued from the other side of the cabin. I walked around the edge and found my father using a hatchet to split a log supported by a pair of sawhorses. Several already-split logs lay on the ground close to his feet. Raven stood nearby, hanging clothes on a line stretched between two trees.

During a pause between thumps, I called, "Papa!"

His hatchet raised for another blow, he turned toward me. "Megan!"

I ran to him. He tossed his hatchet to the side and spread his arms. I leaped into his embrace and wrapped my arms around him. "I made it!"

"I knew you would." He spun me twice, kiss my forehead, and set me down. "Did you bring the stabilizer?"

I set a hand on my hip, half hiding a grin. "What do you think?"

He winked. "It's in your back pocket, right?"

"I wanted to put it there, but the shrink ray was on the fritz." I gestured with a thumb over my shoulder. "I left it near the river. A station robot is carrying it. Pretty sure it's safe."

"Most likely."

I glanced at Raven. She was now looking at us, but I couldn't read her blank expression. I leaned close to Papa and lowered my voice. "What's up with her?"

He glanced that way as well. "Long story, but we have an understanding. You might call it a mutual-survival pact with shared responsibilities. She knows she can't escape without me, and I'm keeping my word to send her to Gamma Five. Now that you're here with the stabilizer, I think I can get us all there."

I lowered my voice further. "Any idea if she's still itching to kill me?"

"Again, long story. When we arrived, she was a holy terror, raging like a maniac. After suffering here for thirty years, you can imagine what it felt like to come back."

"I can't imagine. Must be like escaping hell and getting thrown in again."

"So you can understand why it took me weeks to calm her down. If you had been here then, I probably couldn't have kept her from strangling you, but she's come a long way. She's not exactly a forgiving person, so she still holds a grudge for the role you played in killing her parents. But after all the conversations we've had over the past year, I think she understands why you did what you did."

"A year? Wow. I'm sorry it took so long for me to get here."

He chuckled. "About two minutes in our world. That's fast. I thought it would take longer. In fact, I was cutting wood to build a deck when you got here, but now we won't need it."

Raven walked closer and stood with her hands behind her back. "Hello, Megan. Welcome to our humble abode. I'll be playing the role of domesticated hostess, complete with cooking and cleaning duties. Julian can tell you that I haven't poisoned him … yet." Her persistent blank expression made her quip sound dark and authentic.

"Um … thanks." Hoping to avoid more awkwardness, I glanced around. "Where's the Nebula Seven?"

Papa gestured with a thumb. "Close by at a launchpad I made. The Seven flies now, though it's not able to leave the atmosphere for more than a few minutes."

"Holes in the hull after all?" I asked.

"No. The pressure regulator's broken."

"Ouch. That's not good. Out in space, it wouldn't take long for your head to explode."

"Exactly. And I don't have what I need to fix it."

"Or a helper," I added. "Takes two people to change out the regulator, and I'm guessing Raven isn't a willing apprentice."

"No, but she's come in handy for scouting, hunting, and learning why we came here."

I lifted my brow. "You have a theory?"

"A strong theory. Maybe a fact." He gestured toward Raven. "We worked together to figure it all out."

"Okay," I said, stretching the word as I glanced at her, "let's hear it."

"It's better if I show you." He set a hand on my back. "Let's all board the Seven, and we'll take a little ride."

He guided me along a narrow path, Raven following. Soon, we came to a larger clearing, completely bare of plants or even stumps. The Nebula Seven sat on its landing feet near the center. The scorch marks had faded, its ramp lay open, and a warped noise flowed from the bridge, low tones that sounded like an ancient foghorn.

As we approached, I looked at my father. "What in blazes is that racket?"

"Nike, the ship's computer, is sending a message. I have a theory that we can communicate with people in our real world, but the transmission has to be slowed to the pace that our world would understand. If I were to record a simple greeting, like 'This is Julian Willis calling for help,' that would take a few seconds here, but it would last a fraction of a millisecond there, too short for someone to notice and impossible to understand. So Nike is slowing the message to compensate for the difference. Even though it's a relatively short message, about a minute, he had to stretch it into a six-month-long message. He was able to create it quickly, but to actually send the message takes six months. If I'm not mistaken, he's almost finished, which might seem to be an odd coincidence, but I asked him to complete it before you showed up. You arrived a little earlier than I expected."

"You always taught me to be prompt." We walked up the ramp. "Who are you sending the message to, and what does it say?"

Papa lowered his voice to a whisper. "It's to Lyric's parents. I told them we would be arriving at the Gamma Five sphere soon, and I need them to come with a ship to pick us up. I also warned them to send the Starborn away from the planet as far as possible, maybe into a wormhole heading for Alpha One, though we need Lyric to stay. I'll explain why later."

"Sounds good." I slid into in the first mate's chair. "Let's get this ashcan off the ground."

Papa sat in the captain's seat, while Raven walked toward the navigator's station, frowning at me as she passed. Maybe she had become accustomed to being the first mate on their flights, but she didn't say a word about it. No matter. She had to know the new pecking order would turn out this way.

When the ramp began rising, squeaking a shrill complaint, I strapped in. "I'm guessing you had to improvise to fix the ramp."

He switched on the Seven's main engine. "Enough bailing wire and duct tape will fix just about anything."

"Yep. I sometimes add spit to lubricate stuff. You should try it on those ramp gears. That'll keep 'em quiet."

"Noted." As he studied the readings on his console, he grinned. "Next time I go to the ramp-repair store, I'll grab a bottle of sassy-girl spit."

"Cool. Expensive stuff, though." I checked the buckle on the strap, loose but good enough. "Will this be a long flight?"

Papa strapped in. "Nope. An hour, at most."

Raven huffed. "If we don't run into the same problem we faced last time. Considering how quickly the changes are happening, I won't be surprised if we do."

"You're right about that." He looked at the ceiling. "Nike, I don't hear the message. I assume you finished the transmission."

"I did, Captain," Nike said, still using a formal tone. "As you might expect because of the time-passage difference, I will not receive a confirmation soon, if at all."

"Understood." Papa grasped the steering yoke with one hand and activated the lower thrusters with the other, then pushed the throttle. "We're going to the cauldron. Shields up, Nike."

"Shields are now up, Captain."

We rose above the trees and glided over the jungle, an endless ocean of dense greenery, intermixed with shades of brown wood and silvery hues that coated vines dangling from outstretched limbs. The river I had jumped over sliced through the tapestry in a meandering path, looking like a sparkling serpent weaving through the underbrush, maybe hunting one of the tropical birds that laughed at me earlier.

As we flew on, in my mind, I repeated the strange word—*cauldron*. Of course, I knew what a cauldron was, but I had no idea what might be boiling within. I also wondered about Nike's label for my father. The only way Nike would allow him to be a Captain was if Raven authorized the promotion. Apparently, Papa didn't exaggerate. Their cooperation had risen to a high level during the past year. Since I had seen him only minutes ago, I had a hard time grasping the fact that the two of them had been working together for an entire year, and a lot can happen in a year. Yet, Raven still seemed aloof and sullen, not a hundred percent on our side, certainly not on *my* side.

After a hundred-or-so kilometers, the forest ended in a circular depression that plunged hundreds of meters straight down—the cauldron. Far below, boiling blackness covered the expanse, the color of crude oil or tar, apparently heated by thermal energy underneath. The liquid, however, didn't appear to be viscous—as thin as water, or even thinner. Spanning at least ten kilometers in every direction, this cauldron lived up to its label, maybe the biggest cauldron in any galaxy.

Papa flew to the edge and began a slow orbit around the center of the massive crater. "What's the black stuff?" I asked.

"Like I said, I have a strong theory, and now that you're here, maybe I can prove it." He sent the ship into a slow descent.

As we dropped, a sense of dizziness seeped into my brain, nausea roiled in my stomach, and my arms grew weak. I groaned. "I'm not feeling so good."

"That's what I thought." He altered the flaps. "I'll get us out of here." The ship continued descending. "Or not."

Raven's face tightened, and her voice spiked with pain. "It's happening again. I feel the pull."

Papa flipped on the lower thrusters and punched their throttle to max. We rocketed upward. G-forces pushed my body down. Pressure squeezed my lungs, forcing a rasping moan from my gut. Blackness leaked into my vision. If this kept up, I would pass out at any second.

Papa switched to the rear thrusters. The ship's drastic upward surge eased, but the shift jerked our bodies like a cracking whip. We zoomed forward horizontally, leaving the cauldron behind. With every second that passed, the sickness and weakness eased. "Feeling better?" he asked, his brow bent as he looked at me.

I nodded. "Getting there."

He looked at Raven. "And you?"

Her face pale, she exhaled. "It's over. Like last time, I didn't feel sick, just an overwhelming pull, and it's exhausting to fight against it."

"What pull?" I asked.

She waved toward my father. "Ask him."

I looked at Papa. "Let the explaining begin."

He turned the autopilot on and settled back in his seat. "First, let's talk about the effect our flight near the cauldron had on you. What was it like?"

"Well, sort of like what Raven did to me when she forced you to make a deal with her." I glanced at Raven. She glared at me, not menacingly, more like my comment merely annoyed her. "No offense intended."

"None taken." She smiled in a smug manner. "After thirty years in this God-forsaken world, I've progressed far beyond verbal sparring over trivial matters. In any case, your assessment is correct. The two feelings are equal, as your father will explain."

I turned toward him again. "I'm all ears."

"I thought of a corny joke," he said, "but I'll keep it to myself." He focused straight ahead. "As you know, Raven's power is to counter a Starborn's gift. For example, you are able to fill yourself with power and transmit it to other Starborn. She is able to drain power from you. In fact, she can cause all of your energy to drain, and you get weaker and weaker. If she continued, I think you would eventually die. The blackness you saw in the cauldron is the source of her gift. You might call it anti-energy, the opposite of the energy that Lyric carries as the power source."

"So you told her about Lyric?"

"Yes. She's not able to harm Lyric or remove her power, so I decided it's safe, at least for now. Since I needed her cooperation, I had to tell her everything I know."

"Okay," I said. "I assume there's more."

"There is. I think the anti-energy is seeping through some kind of crack that joins this world to Gamma Five. Normally, energy and anti-energy are in balance, but somehow a pool of each type formed in separate places—energy within Gamma Five and anti-energy in a cauldron here. The imbalance creates a vacuum of sorts that tries to draw them together, and that might be the cause of the seepage."

"Any idea how much of the anti-energy leaked from here into Gamma Five?"

"Enough for Raven to gain her power from it, but she refused to tell me how it happened. In any case, like Starborn are drawn to their power source, Raven is drawn to hers, which is why she and the entire ship were pulled toward the cauldron."

I resisted the urge to look at Raven. "Since Lyric is now the power source for the Starborn, I guess the anti-energy is drawn to her to restore the balance., Right? Shouldn't she leave with the other Starborn? Wouldn't that make the leaking stop?"

He lowered his voice to a whisper. "Maybe, but I hope she stays in the Gamma system like I asked. I'll explain why later."

I whispered as well. "If she does stay, could the anti-energy find her and maybe hurt her? Raven didn't hurt Lyric before. Could it be because Raven has to try to hurt a Starborn on purpose?"

"We don't know." He raised his voice to a normal level. "Considering how Raven can overcome your power, we think the anti-energy might kill the Starborn. That's why I sent the warning."

Raven raised a finger. "I sensed the growing influence of the anti-energy while I was on Gamma Five, but I had no idea what was causing it. I was getting more powerful, and I could conquer the gifts of any Starborn, including yours."

Warmth rushed into my ears. "It's true that you weakened me, but I didn't know what was happening. I was taken by surprise. I think I would do better if I had some warning."

"Exactly as you predicted," Raven said to my father. "She's a fighter. Hates to lose." She waved a hand. "Not to belittle you, Megan. The fact that you killed that dragon and sneaked all the Starborn out of the training camp right under my nose proved that you're a superb warrior. I couldn't be more impressed."

"Okay. Thanks ... I guess."

Papa focused on me. "Since we predicted your response, Raven and I discussed the possibility of a test to see if you can withstand an onslaught of her anti-energy after being warned. The contest is risky. If she overpowers you, she could kill you, but I will be standing close to her with a gun to blow her brains out if she tries." He looked at Raven. "No offense intended."

"Again, none taken. And I have no incentive to kill her because I want to leave this place. You're my ticket out of here."

The ship decelerated and angled downward. "We will land in twelve seconds," Nike said.

After the Seven settled to the ground and we deboarded, my father drew a laser pistol from his belt and set a hand on my shoulder. "Are you ready?"

"I'm not sure, but I'll do my best." I set my feet firmly and looked at Raven. She faced me, hands on hips. Although gray hair and wrinkles made her look considerably older than the Raven I knew, her cocky countenance was unmistakable.

Papa nodded. "You may proceed in a moment. If Megan withstands you for a full minute, I'll declare her the winner because that would be enough time for her to physically escape or find a weapon to neutralize you."

"Fair enough." Raven narrowed her eyes at me. "Defend yourself, Megan."

I inhaled deeply. My strength started draining immediately. My arm muscles loosened, and new nausea bubbled. Considering that she seemed to use her eyes to focus her power, it was probably best not to engage her head on.

Averting my gaze, I clutched my shirt around my locket. As the weakness worsened, I steeled my legs to keep my knees from buckling. I dug deep to recall the feelings that empowered me to energize Oliver when he healed Oz. Of course, when I thought my father had shown up, the energy soared. The emotional charge made my dynamo power skyrocket, but how could I resurrect that feeling? Trying to generate the emotions by sheer willpower would be artificial, wouldn't it? The emotional surge had to be real, organic, heartfelt.

Raven extended an open hand toward me and furrowed her brow. Her entire body transformed into her youthful self—dark hair, smooth skin, and rippled muscles. The black anti-energy flowed from her palm and streamed toward me. Had my imagination conjured this visual, or had my power made the anti-energy visible so I could do battle with it? Either way, the black stream looked real. I needed to raise a defense.

I reached both hands in front to shield my face from the flow. Light burst from the locket and expanded into a sphere around my hands that stretched down my arms and began enveloping my body in crimson. The black stream collided with the light and split into two paths that wrapped around me, rejoined at my back, and tied in a coil that tightened under my arms like a constricting snake.

My red suit of armor tightened with the coil, compressing my body and squeezing my lungs. I sucked in a breath and held it. Concentrating on the power surging within my body and mind, I forced the red energy to expand, to stretch the attacking serpent.

Raven extended her other hand. A second black stream poured forth and joined the first, strengthening the tightening coil around my body. A growl erupted from her throat. Her wrinkles deepened. Veins at the sides of her head thickened and pulsed. Her face tightened into a hideous mask, as if evil itself had erupted from her pores and painted her skin with vile corruption.

At that moment, I understood. Raven was cooperating with my father for one reason, to escape this world and return to Gamma Five so she could continue capturing the Starborn. Still evil to the core, she wanted to use her anti-energy to kill and to conquer, to continue her mother's quest for domination. And only I, the catalyst of the direct opposite of her power, stood in her way. She wouldn't kill me now, but she would try to kill me later. I had to show her that I would be a more powerful opponent than she bargained for. Every Starborn life depended on it.

I released the breath and sucked in another. Oliver came to mind— his kindness, his loyalty, his determination to do whatever it took to defeat the traffickers. Then Crystal and Zoë followed. Their love and devotion for me were as great as from any biological sisters. And, of course, Perdantus had changed my life for the better. In many ways, he was like a wise older brother. His loyalty was unmatched.

More faces appeared in my mind—Echo, Chip, Oz, Riddle, Galena, and other Starborn I didn't know as well. If Raven had her way, they would all be slaves to her whims.

And finally, Lyric took shape before me, not as a mental image but as a semitransparent girl standing at my side. Filled with red light, she looked like a scarlet phantom. Her eyes pulsed with the same redness— pure Starborn energy.

The red light flowed into me. I exhaled in a roar. My suit of armor burst forth, shredding the constrictor into frayed strips of blackness that fell to the ground and shriveled. The energy surged forward like a tsunami and blasted into Raven. She fell to her back and skidded several meters before stopping, motionless, her body reverting to its older appearance.

The energy lights faded. I inhaled a fresh breath into my aching lungs and blew it out again, shifting my respiration to quick, shallow gasps. Sweat trickled down my cheeks and back. Finally, I dropped to my knees and cried.

Papa leaped and knelt in front of me. "Are you all right?"

I nodded, unable to speak, knowing that I couldn't possibly look "all right" with tears flowing and spasmodic sobs wracking my body.

He compressed my shoulder and looked me in the eye. "You did it, Megan. You're more powerful than she is. I knew you could do it."

I nodded again and tried to spit out some words. "Maybe … you'd better … check on her."

"Right."

He rose and jogged to her. As he helped her to her feet, I climbed to mine. My legs wobbled under my weight, but they soon strengthened. I was recovering from the ordeal quickly.

Papa led Raven toward me. She limped, favoring one leg, then the other. When she looked at me, she offered a weak smile. "Congratulations,

Megan. I shouldn't be surprised about your victory. You always seem to overcome every obstacle you face, provided you are allowed a moment to plan and prepare. Once again, I am impressed."

I inhaled deeply and let the breath out slowly. I knew I was obligated to thank her for her gracious words, but I also knew they were designed to make her look good, not me. I now had no doubt that she continued to be my enemy who didn't deserve my thanks, but I could give her a similar speech. "I appreciate your evaluation of me, and I offer you a similar compliment. I have never faced an opponent as powerful as you, not even the dragon in the tunnel. I, too, am impressed."

Papa patted us both on the back. "Well, this mutual admiration is refreshing. I hope it continues because we have more obstacles to face." He draped an arm over me, pulled me away from our battle arena, and added a whisper, "Nice touch. I know you wanted to spit in her face instead."

"True, but sassy-girl spit is too valuable to waste on her."

Soon after the battle, we guided the robot and the stabilizer across the river on a makeshift bridge and stowed them in a woodshed Papa had built. Only minutes later, a drenching thunderstorm soaked the area. Papa and I took refuge in the ship while Raven stayed in the cabin—a one room structure he had built for her because, after living on the ship for thirty years, she didn't want to sleep there.

Once the storm abated, Papa and I gathered wood from the shed and built a campfire in the cabin's clearing. We each sat on a stump, the crackling fire between us. Although we were both exhausted, we knew we needed this time together without Raven close enough to listen.

As Papa poked the embers with a long stick, he explained the planet's cycles. A day lasted one-point-six times as long as those on Alpha One, providing extra sunlight that heated the humid atmosphere enough to trigger a thunderstorm nearly every day. Although they had been there roughly an Alpha-One year, it seemed impossible to know how long an actual year was here—no seasons, no alteration in the angle of their lone sun, and no change in weather. Raven verified that the climate stayed pretty much the same during her thirty years here except for a few droughts that always ended with a vicious thunderstorm. After a drought, lightning sometimes sparked a fire, which is what likely caused the inferno that killed her crew early on.

While he talked, I drank in every word. He loved teaching, and I loved learning, especially from him. Not that he was always right. He was always learning as well. But he never lied to me. No matter what the topic might be, he always spoke what he thought was the truth, even if he knew the truth might hurt.

I knew when a hurtful truth was about to come. His lengthy discussion of the planet's characteristics was his way of leading into a more difficult topic, allowing us both a chance to breathe before facing another challenge.

Papa let out a long sigh. "You know, your victory in the battle against Raven gives me a lot to think about."

I picked up a stick of my own and poked the fire. "I guessed that. Otherwise, you wouldn't have let me fight with her. You had a good reason."

"True. I needed to watch the powers you both exhibited and learn from them."

"Like how she emitted black ribbons of energy that I blocked with a red shield?"

He squinted. "Black ribbons? Red shield? What are you talking about?"

I showed him my palm. "The black streams that came from her hands. They twisted around me and squeezed my body like a python strangling a pig. But when I radiated the red light, it pushed the streams away. And while we were fighting, she changed to her youthful self for a while. That was bizarre."

His mouth dropped open. After staring at me for a moment, he rubbed his eyes, as if trying to clear his vision. "I didn't see anything like that. I mean, I did see you struggle like you were being squeezed, but I didn't see any colors or streams or a change in appearance." He shook a finger. "Actually, that's more evidence for my theories. I'm surer than ever about them."

"Your theories?" I let out a huff. "Okay, you've been delaying too long. Spill them. I mean, you haven't even told me what you plan to do with the stabilizer or how we can get out of this place."

"That's because I wanted to think about the battle for a while." He lifted his stick and gazed at the flame consuming the end. "You defeating Raven told me that your Starborn energy is more powerful than her anti-energy. And that's critical, because my theory on how to escape might cause her to gain power."

"How?"

He drew the stick close to his face and blew the flame out. "I'm sure you remember I mentioned that the anti-energy is leaking into Gamma Five through a rift between the worlds. If we could fly through that rift, we could escape, but we would have to pass through the pool of anti-energy to get there. My concern is that Raven would absorb the anti-energy like Lyric absorbed the Starborn energy. I wanted to make sure she could be defeated if she became powerful and returned to her evil ways."

I laughed under my breath. "You say *if* like it might not happen. She's still evil through and through. Our battle proved that to me. I'm guessing she's been pretending to get along with you."

"No doubt. Our relationship is strained, at best. And you're right. I saw the evil in her eyes while you were battling. She's been trying to hide it, but you exposed her."

I nodded. "So you're saying if Raven becomes too powerful for me to defeat, Lyric should be able to do it."

"Exactly."

"Okay. I guess we'll just have to wait to see if that happens, but what about the rift we would travel through? Is it big enough? I mean, if anti-energy is leaking through it into Gamma Five instead of gushing, the rift must be small. Could the Nebula Seven fit through it?"

"It's not a matter of fitting through it." He closed a fist tightly. "We'll have to *squeeze* through it. You see, according to Nike's simulations, our physical state is unstable. Our atoms are held together loosely, allowing us to compress or expand more easily. And, like I said, you seeing the red and black light only confirms my theory. You have a greater perception of the energy fields because of your gifts, and you see them more clearly now because of the diffusion of our atoms. In short, the energy is revealed through the diffusion gaps. That's evidence that we're far more flexible than normal. We'll be able to fly through the rift without harm. At least that's what the simulations indicate."

"So what happens when we come out on the other side? How do we get out of our loose state?"

He pointed at the shed. "That's where the stabilizer comes in. When I asked you to bring it, I had a different theory about how I would use it. That's all changed now. I thought if I could atomize the ship while here on this planet, it might trigger a resuming of our transport from sphere to sphere. But Nike ran thousands of simulations based on what we know about the spheres and the atomization process, and my idea simply wouldn't work.

"But to answer your question, we could use the stabilizer to increase our diffusion right before we pass through the rift and then reduce it afterwards. There is a danger, though. I believe this jungle world has properties that allow us to survive in a diffuse state, but in our world, our atoms might scatter. That means after we pass through, we would have to use the destabilizer instantly on the entire ship, or else we could disintegrate."

I shuddered. "That sounds incredibly dangerous."

"Risky, yes. Incredibly dangerous? Maybe not. We'll have the stabilizer ready to bathe the ship immediately, including itself. The simulation of that process showed a ninety-three percent chance of success if we time the restoration precisely."

"But where would we come out on Gamma Five? Not at an arrival bay at the Zeta Sphere, right?"

"Right. I don't have an answer for that. But since we will be fully restored, we'll be in a ship that can fly anywhere we need to go as long as we aren't in space more than a few minutes."

"Okay. That'll be great if we're not in an underground chamber like where you found the Starborn energy. And thinking about the arrival bay reminds me of another question. How did Raven get out of here after thirty years and show up at the Epsilon Six sphere?"

"When I studied more about the transport process, I learned that at a pre-arranged time, the destination sphere begins a pulling process that draws the diffused atoms to it. When that happens, the particles finish their journey and are stabilized at the destination sphere. That pulling process reseparates the atoms from their loosely fitted state. Since the ship is programmed as the container of the atomized package, if someone happened to leave the ship at the wrong time, the ship would depart without him. Fortunately for Raven, she was on board when the pulling began."

"How did the programmers calculate how much time to wait before the sphere starts pulling? Is it based on distance?"

He nodded. "They experimented successfully with short distances and extrapolated to estimate the time needed for the longer journeys. I believe, if the travelers weren't halted here in this world, the transport times would be instantaneous, like it is with data transmissions. The researchers' notes indicated that they were puzzled about the differences between data and physical transport, and now we know what causes it. I think the anti-energy on this planet draws atomized transport ships to it. Eventually, when it all leaks into Gamma Five, it won't happen anymore."

"Unless more is put here. I mean, it had to get here somehow. If there's still an influx, it'll never all leak out."

"Good point."

"Any idea how it got here in the first place?"

"Some idea. Fortunately, Nike's databases are loaded with ancient lore about the power sources. Apparently, anti-energy collects wherever great evil is happening, especially if it's occurring without restraint, and it might even cause the weird time discrepancy between the two worlds."

I tapped my stick on the ground. "Then why here? You haven't noticed any great evil going on, have you?"

Papa shook his head. "I've flown around quite a bit, and I haven't seen anything unusual, but I stayed fairly close to our base. This planet seems pretty big, so I could've easily missed something. I can guess, however, that the Starborn training camp might have been the evil that drew the anti-energy from this planet to Gamma Five. Since it's been destroyed, the seepage probably either slowed down or stopped."

I poked the fire with my stick again. With so much information flooding in, it seemed impossible to keep it all together. Also, more questions rose in my mind, like how this jungle world came to be and how it captured diffused transports, but Papa probably didn't know, and I was too tired to think about it any further. "So when do we start?"

"First thing in the morning, after a good night's rest. We'll put the stabilizer in the ship and take off."

The thought of going to bed incited a wide yawn. "What are the sleeping arrangements?"

He nodded toward the ship. "I've been sleeping in the captain's quarters on the Seven. You can have that or the first mate's bunk. Before I finished the cabin a few months ago, I camped in a makeshift tent while Raven slept in the ship. Since then, she's had the cabin to herself."

I smiled. "You didn't want to be in the ship with her, I guess."

"Nope. I would be vulnerable to an attack. I trust her about as much as I would a viper."

"I can't blame you for that." I yawned again, my vision turning blurry. I had to get some rest. "I'll take the bunk. You're probably used to the captain's bed."

"If only. I moved the bed to the cabin for Raven and borrowed a mattress from the infirmary. It's comfy enough, but the captain's bed was better."

I half closed an eye. "Why have you been so good to her? She's a kid killer."

"I'm not sure. Maybe when it's time for her to decide if she's for me or against me, she won't be quick to stab me in the back." He shrugged. "But either way, it's in my nature to win people over by helping them, no matter what they've done in the past. It's kind of ingrained in me."

I looked into his sad eyes. Maybe he was thinking about what Jillian did to him in pilots' school and the fact that he never exposed her, or maybe Mama came to mind, though I had no memory of her ever doing anything bad to him. The reason for his sadness didn't matter. I was here, and I could try to help.

I rose and extended a hand. "Let's put two mattresses in the captain's room, if that's all right with you."

"Sounds perfect." He took my hand and rode my pull to his feet. "Let's just hope I don't snore. Nike told me I've been sawing logs lately."

"If you do, you'll be camping outside again. But I'm so tired, I'll probably sleep like one of the logs you've been sawing. I won't hear you."

As we walked hand in hand toward the ship, I wondered about being able to sleep. The dangers of the coming day might spoil my hopes. Squeezing through the rift sounded super dangerous and probably painful. And what about Zoë? Did she survive the laser blast? How were Jillian, Oliver, Crystal, and Perdantus faring? Would Lyric be able to defeat a fully energy-infused anti-Starborn like Raven?

I heaved a quiet sigh. In the morning, we might learn the answers to every question, even if they broke our hearts.

35

We flew in the Nebula Seven at a low altitude toward the anti-energy cauldron. This time, I operated the steering yoke while Papa crouched next to the stabilizer between me and the viewing window. The device's gun pointed toward a side wall, and Papa had programmed it to swivel so that it could affect the entire ship and everything in it.

Behind me, Raven sat quietly in the navigator's seat. Although I couldn't see her without turning my head, I could almost feel her stare drilling into me, making a prickly sensation erupt on the back of my neck. After all of my father's preparation and calculations, she remained the unknown factor. Would she absorb the anti-energy? If so, how would she use it?

Of course, we could've left her behind, but Papa insisted that he had to keep his word and deliver her safely to Gamma Five. Half of me said it was okay to lie to a murderer who sent innocent kids to their deaths. But the other half agreed with him. If we left her to die in that jungle, even though she deserved it, we wouldn't be much better than she was. And those two wolves continued fighting inside me as I flew on.

To distract myself from the mental battle, I shifted the viewing window to show the jungle beneath us. Tree after tree zipped by, along with colorful birds either perched in the branches or gliding over the foliage with their wings spread. A monkey swung on a vine, and another stared at the ship, its eyes wide.

Then something odd darted from one tree to another, flying too quickly to figure out what it was. I switched to the camera's memory, ran it back to that moment, and magnified the view. The flying creature was a bramble bee. There could be no doubt about it. And where one lived, many more likely dwelled. But how did they get here? They were native to Delta Ninety-eight, a much colder planet. Could they have transported somehow in one of the Zeta Sphere's ill-fated tests? Or maybe it came from one of the planets Thorne had sent eggs or DNA to.

With no time to trouble myself about that question, I switched the window to a front view and flew on. We would arrive at the cauldron in less than a minute, and flying into the anti-energy pool would require all of my attention. "Fifty-three seconds," I said.

"Are you sure you want to fly this flimsy frigate?" Papa asked.

"Better than goosing that gizmo you're fiddling with. I have no idea how it works, but I do know how to fly."

"Agreed. Just follow Nike's radar guidance. Once you're in the energy pool, you'll be flying blind."

"Yep. I've flown through storm clouds at night with Emerson feeding me radar echoes. Shouldn't be much different."

Raven finally spoke up. "Just remember that the anti-energy will pull us toward it, so you'll be going faster than you expect, and it will make you feel sick again, so you should fly as quickly as safety allows."

I glanced toward her. "Good reminders. Thanks."

"You're welcome." She closed her eyes tightly, apparently straining. "I'll keep giving you updates on the effects. The pull is already increasing."

"Got it." I refocused on the viewing window. The cauldron lay in sight. The blackness in its depths bubbled at the surface, more active than yesterday. I angled the ship into a dive toward the coordinates

Nike had provided. Over the last few weeks before I arrived, my father had conducted flyovers high above with Raven aboard, and she reported where the strongest pulls occurred. That enabled Nike to calculate the most likely position of the rift below.

As Raven had warned, the ship accelerated toward the blackness. I compensated by altering our angle of approach, and with each increase in speed, I altered it more. The changes seemed to be gradual and consistent, but I couldn't count on that continuing. The pull could spike at any moment.

Weakness invaded my muscles, and my body trembled. I took a deep breath and forced myself to speak without a tremor. "Entering the anti-energy in five seconds … four … three … two … one … now." The ship plunged in. Darkness covered the viewing window. "Nike, you're the navigator now."

"You are on course," Nike said in his typical stoic tone. "No obstacles appear to be in the path."

Since I couldn't see anything visually, I shifted my gaze to the radar on my console. As Nike had said, no echoes appeared except for a solid wall at the target area. So far, the rift hadn't become evident, but since it was likely to be no more than a crack, it might not show up at all.

Dizziness made my brain swim. Still trying to ignore the effects, I looked at Raven. "Forty-seven seconds to the rift."

She grimaced. "Maybe not. … It's pulling harder."

I focused on my controls, battling against double vision. "You're right. Unexpected acceleration. Nike estimates thirty-one seconds now." A horizontal flaw in the wall appeared, nearly as long as the ship was wide but only a minuscule fraction as high as the ship's height. "Turn on the stabilizer."

"Prepare for a strange sensation," Papa said as he flipped a switch on the device. Laser-like radiance streamed from the barrel and sprayed the ship. As the stabilizer rotated, the radiance spread throughout the bridge and penetrated the hull, shooting through the metal like lightning through a conductor. The light rose from the floor into the device itself, shifting its own diffusion, but the radiance had no visible effect on it as the spray of light continued.

When the radiance approached me, I lowered my head to shield my eyes, though they would be affected anyway. Like the time I got atomized at the Zeta Sphere, a stinging tingle shot across my skin and penetrated to the core of my body.

When the stabilizer finished its circuit, Papa turned it off. "We're as diffused as we can be without flying apart in this world, but, like I explained before, we're too diffused to survive in our world. I set the device to restore us, and I'll turn it on the moment we're through the rift."

"Four seconds," I called as I looked at the crack in the wall, growing larger in my perspective, but not large enough. "Two seconds ... one ... zero!"

We slammed into the rift. The collision shook the entire ship, but instead of breaking up, the hull compressed around us as if it were made of rubber. The ceiling and floor pressed against me, but instead of crushing my bones, it elongated my body. The squeezing hurt but not as much as I expected.

After a few seconds, the compression eased, and the surrounding hull shifted back where it was before. My father still crouched next to the stabilizer, his arms around it, probably to keep it from moving.

"The Nebula Seven has arrived," Nike said. "I will conduct a scan to determine our exact location. I assumed it was safe to land the ship in order to prevent collision with any other objects."

Papa flipped a switch. "Restoring now. This might hurt quite a bit." As before, laser light shot out of the gun and began soaking the ship and itself in its wash as it rotated.

While I waited for it to hit me, I looked at my hands. My fingers trembled, aching like they were about to explode. My head pounded as if my brain was trying to escape my skull. Were my atoms ready to scatter?

As the pain spiked, I groaned. "I think I'm going to pop!"

My father rushed to me, scooped me out of my chair, and ran with me to a section of a wall the flow was about to strike. He sat me against the wall and ran to Raven. The radiance bathed me in its glow, quickly easing my pain. In my blurred vision, I could barely see him pick Raven's limp body up from the floor, carry her to a spot near me, and stand with his back to the wall while holding her upright, his arms under her shoulders. He grimaced, probably suffering the same torture I had felt.

When the radiance rotated past me, the remainder of my pain vanished, though weakness in my limbs continued. The beam then swept over them. Papa clenched his eyes closed and slid slowly down to the floor with Raven in his lap. He gasped and writhed while she groaned. For some reason, the restoration seemed to inflict more pain on them than it did on me. Maybe because they had been in their diffused state much longer than I had.

When the radiant beam finished its circuit, it shut off. I climbed to my feet, staggered to Papa, and knelt at his side. His eyes stayed closed, his arms hung limp, and Raven leaned back on his chest, but both breathed easily. They were alive.

"Papa?" I prodded his shoulder. "Can you hear me?"

He blinked hard before turning his head toward me. "I guess it worked."

"I think so, but what about Raven? Did she absorb the anti-energy?"

"I don't know. Did you see any blackness streaming toward her?"

I shook my head. "But I don't know if that means anything. I wasn't paying much attention to her."

Papa looked toward the ceiling. "Nike, status report."

"I landed the Nebula Seven in the midst of a dark cloud. I have been attempting to determine our location, but the cloud seems to be blocking my scans."

"Wait," I said. "*Nike* landed the ship? I thought Nebula series computers aren't allowed to land a ship. Only pilots can do that."

Papa smiled, though pain streaked his face. "I changed his programming. He can break Alliance rules now. The dumb ones, anyway. And I made myself the highest ranking officer with you second in command."

"Oh, okay. Thanks.""

Raven groaned and laid a hand over her eyes. "What happened?"

"Looks like we made it through the rift," I said. "We landed in a dark cloud, and Nike's scanners can't penetrate it."

"Maybe I can do something about that." She extended a hand. "Help me up."

I grasped her wrist and hoisted her to her feet. After wobbling for a moment, she blinked several times. "We're surrounded by the anti-energy. The ship's hull is keeping it from penetrating, but that might not last."

"Nike," Papa called, "hull integrity report."

"The hull integrity ranges from forty-three percent to sixty-seven percent, depending on the location. All values are dropping quickly. Catastrophic failure is likely in less than two minutes."

Raven pointed toward the bow. "Nike, open the ramp."

"Belay that command!" Papa shouted. "We can't let the anti-energy in here. And we're not sure yet we're on a planet with breathable air."

"Nonsense," Raven said. "We have to be on Gamma Five. There is no other possibility. And if you keep stalling, we won't have a ship that can fly us to a safe place."

Papa breathed a resigned sigh. "Nike, shields up. That might repel it."

"I have issued the signal," Nike said, "but the shields are not responding."

Raven walked toward the ramp. "The anti-energy is absorbing the shield's power. I'm going out."

"No." With my help, Papa climbed to his feet. "Nike, disable the ramp controls."

"Ramp controls disabled."

Raven chuckled. "You forgot that I installed a manual ramp latch during my thirty-year exile." She stopped at the ramp and pulled a lever to the side. The ramp dropped open and thudded on the ground, revealing a wall of blackness.

The blackness cascaded over the ramp and surged toward Raven. She lifted her head and spread her arms as if welcoming a family member. The blackness whirled around her body and enveloped her in a cyclonic spin that veiled her from view.

I slid my hand into Papa's. "I don't think we can stop whatever's going on."

"Not likely." He looked at Nike's console. "Are your scanners working yet?"

"Affirmative. I have confirmed that we are on Gamma Five, somewhere on Ragua. I will have a more precise location soon."

"Good. Then we can breathe more easily. Literally."

After nearly a minute, the flow of blackness ebbed, and daylight shone in through the ramp opening. Like a dark serpent, a final stream poured into Raven's eyes and disappeared. Her hair now black once more and her skin smooth, she lowered her arms and walked slowly toward us, her eyes like orbs of onyx. An aura of darkness moved with her, a surrounding shield of evil.

Papa whipped a laser blaster from a holster and pointed it at her. "Keep your distance."

Raven halted a few steps away. "I am not experienced enough with my newfound power to know if your little gun can hurt me, so I will restrain myself for now."

"What are you planning to do?"

"That's something I don't wish to tell you, but I will say this. Since you delivered me to Gamma Five as you promised, I will not try to harm you or your daughter at this time, but if you try to interfere with my future plans, I will show no mercy."

I huffed. "Mercy like my father showed you? If not for him, you would've died of old age on that jungle planet by now."

"And if not for you, dear Megan, my mother and father would still be alive, and the training camp would still be intact. So don't talk to me about mercy when I could punish you for your crimes against my family. And don't assume you can defeat me in battle just because you did before. Since I absorbed the anti-energy, only Lyric could ever hope to oppose me." She jabbed a finger toward me. "And you're not Lyric."

"No, I'm not, but—"

"Enough of your mouth!" She thrust her hands out. Her dark aura surged and slammed into us, driving us back. We crashed into the wall and crumpled to the floor. "Don't try to follow." She strode down the ramp and out of sight.

Papa and I struggled to our feet. Once we had balanced ourselves, I walked toward the ramp. "I want to see if I recognize where we are."

"Don't be long," Papa called. "We need to get to Gamma Five's Zeta Sphere. If Lyric's parents got our message, they'll be going there."

I halted at the end of the ramp and turned toward him. "Maybe you should try to contact them again. Give them an update."

He smiled as he saluted. "Aye, aye, Captain Willis."

My own smile broke out. "At ease, Captain Willis." My legs still somewhat weak, I walked outside. The landscape here matched what I saw during my previous visit—long ruts and angled trees. If my father's theory was correct and the training camp drew anti-energy through the rift, the site was probably nearby, and, if so, the Astral Dragon likely was as well.

I touched my earbud and turned it on. "Sonya, are you listening?"

Sonya's voice crackled through static. "Well, it's about time you returned. I have been fending off scavengers, human and non-human varieties."

"Sorry about that. We just arrived from … well … Epsilon Six, I guess. Hey, listen, can you see a Nebula series ship on your scanner? That'll be where I am."

"Yes. Until an hour ago, my scanner wasn't working, but Echo is here making more repairs."

"Echo's there? That's great!"

"Yes. Lyric's parents supplied her with everything she needed to repair the ship. She already had the knowledge necessary to finish repairing me, and now I am guiding her in repairing everything else."

"Perfect. Which way do I go to find you?"

"Your ship is two point seven kilometers to my southwest."

I sketched a mental map. The Nebula Seven had landed directly over where the training camp once stood. But the blackness wasn't here before. Maybe Raven's presence drew it from under the ground the moment we arrived. "I'll be there as soon as I can. In the meantime, watch out for Raven. She'll be looking for transportation. If she shows up, can you make it look like the ship still can't take her where she wants to go?"

"That will require no trickery. I am able to fly but not for long distances. There are too many holes in the hull. But I will add status reports that will make my condition seem worse than it really is."

"Good. See you soon." I hustled back up the ramp as fast as my sore legs would carry me. Inside, Papa sat at the captain's seat, speaking into the air. "Yes, Lyric. Megan just came in. Why don't you repeat what you told me? She's listening."

Lyric's voice came through the ceiling speakers. "Hello, Megan. Welcome back to Gamma Five."

Warmth flowed through every limb, as if she were there infusing me with energy. "Thank you. It's good to hear your voice."

"Yours, too."

"Before you repeat what you told my father, tell me how Zoë's doing."

"She's in good hands. Galena's been taking care of her. She should be completely well in a few days."

"And Perdantus?"

"He's been worried sick about you, but I already told him you're safe, so he's relieved. And he's completely healed as well. Everyone's fine."

"That's fantastic." I exhaled, my own relief flooding in. "Okay, so what else is up?"

"I am at Gamma Five's Zeta Sphere. My mother used her authority to take control of it and all the other spheres in the network. We've been in contact with your aunt in the Nebula Nine. They are ready to transport here from the Epsilon station."

"Wait. Did my father tell you about the jungle world? They'll get trapped there."

"Not anymore. My mother knew all about that weird place, which is why she demanded that the system be shut down until she could investigate it further. She said they were able to put a device in that world that gives her reports about the time shift. The shift is pretty much gone now. All transports should go directly to their arrival bays without any delays."

"And Jillian's going to test it? That's super risky."

"Not risky at all. My father already tested it. He's always been the daredevil sort. He went to Epsilon and back already. It's instantaneous now. At least going there was. Just a few seconds coming back."

"Any theory why it slowed down on the return?" I asked.

"Yes. Your father mentioned anti-energy collecting in that jungle world. We're guessing it's still collecting but not much has reaccumulated so far."

I nodded. "And that means eventually it'll get the way it was before. Long stops in the jungle world. We have to find the cause if we hope to keep using the spheres."

"You were there," Lyric said. "Any ideas?"

"Only that the anti-energy probably gathers where great evil is flourishing." I looked at my father in the captain's seat. "What do you think?"

"Good theory." He stroked his chin. "Maybe Emerson's decrypted that data drive by now. Something might be there that'll give us a clue."

"Good idea." I looked at the ceiling. "Hey, Lyric, let's get the Nebula Nine to your station. I need to talk to Emerson."

"Will do. They'll be at the arrival bay in a few seconds. When can you get here?"

"Probably in about—"

"Megan!" The voice came through my earbud. "It's Echo. I'll try to get through this without repeating myself."

"Hold a sec." I slid an icon on my screen that copied my earbud's output to our ceiling speakers. "Okay. Go.

"Raven barged in and took control of the Astral Dragon using some kind of strange power I never saw her use before. Like black magic. She tried to kill me, but I got away. Fortunately, I had an earbud. That's how I'm calling you. I'm hiding in one of the trenches."

My heart raced, but I kept my voice under control. "Stay hidden. We'll come pick you up."

Echo gasped. "The Dragon's launching. The Dragon's launching."

Papa strapped in and called toward Nike's console. "Shields up!"

The ramp began rising as Nike replied. "Shields will be activated as soon as the ramp closes."

A photon torpedo blasted into the ground in front of the ship. Dirt blew through the ramp's remaining gap and scattered on the floor.

"Evasive action!" I shouted as I leaped to my chair and strapped in. "Nike, get us off the ground. Arm the torpedoes."

The engines surged, and the ship shot straight up. G-forces pinned me to the seat. I couldn't even lift my arms to operate my console. Fortunately, Nike knew the protocol.

"Shields are up," he said in his unflappable tone as the ship shifted from a vertical rise to a forward surge, pushing me back in my chair. "The attacking ship is on the viewing window and is now fleeing at a low speed with its shields activated. We are giving chase, and our enhanced torpedoes are locked on the target. Awaiting your command."

I looked at my father. Now that we were both able to move our arms, we could take over for Nike. "What do you think?" I asked. "The Dragon's low speed is probably because the ship's crippled, but I'm wondering if she's baiting us for some reason."

"Could be. It's like she's begging for us to take a shot."

"But is your promise to her fulfilled? Is she fair game now?"

He nodded. "She's fair game. And she attacked us, unprovoked."

"Then no more questions. I'll take the shot myself." I flipped the cap off the photon torpedo switch. "Sorry, Sonya. Echo and I can repair you again." I pressed the trigger.

Twin balls of shimmering light shot from our front turrets and rocketed toward the Astral Dragon, but they curved away and missed the ship. As they continued flying, their paths arced and reversed course, heading straight for us.

I shouted, "Evade!"

36

We dropped nearly straight down, then shot forward again. My head snapped back, but the straps kept me in my seat. Huge explosions rocked the ship, making everything inside rattle.

"Our torpedoes struck the ground," Nike said. "They are no longer a danger."

"Is the Astral Dragon still on your scanner?" I asked.

"Affirmative. She is flying into the upper atmosphere."

I looked at my father. "It doesn't make sense to chase Raven. If she has that much power, she could turn any weapons against us."

He nodded. "Let's give her some space while we come up with a plan."

"In the meantime, let's find Echo." Since the channel to her earbud was still turned on through the system console, I spoke into the ship's microphone. "Echo, are you listening?"

"Yep, yep," Echo said. "You're signal's coming through like a digital bulldozer."

"Good. Come out of the trench and do something so I can find you."

"I'm already out. I'm waving my arms like a crazy person."

"Great. Stand by." I spoke toward the ceiling. "Nike, do you see Echo?"

His voice came through the speakers above. "Affirmative. Beginning landing sequence."

While the ship swerved toward Echo, Papa switched the outgoing frequency and spoke into the air. "Lyric, this is Julian Willis again. Prepare for an assault from Raven. We think she's heading your way in the Astral Dragon."

"Thank you," Lyric said, her voice now piping in through Papa's console. "The Dragon is already on our scanners. And the Nebula Nine is here. We'll have plenty of firepower to oppose her."

"Just be warned. She was able to turn our photon torpedoes toward us. We barely dodged them."

"Good to know. Fortunately, we have an amazing set of brains here, and the crew of the Nebula Nine just walked in. So we have Jillian, Oliver, Crystal, and Zoë. We'll figure out what to do."

"Super," I said. "Tell Crystal and Zoë their sister will be there in a few minutes. I'm picking up Echo."

"See you soon. Signing off."

My father nodded toward my console. "Take control, Captain. You'll be able to land faster than Nike would."

"Aye, aye, sir." I grasped the steering yoke and pushed the ship into a dive. When we landed at the edge of a trench, I lowered the ramp.

The moment it touched the ground, Echo tromped in, wearing military camo and boots. Dirt covered both cheeks, and blood trickled from a cut on the side of her head. "Raven used her mind to throw stuff at me. She has Zoë's powers. And a lot more. A lot more."

"Glad you could get away." I pointed at the navigator's station. "Strap in. We're going after Raven."

She hustled to the chair and buckled the belt. "Ready."

"Remember," Papa said, "the pressure regulator is broken. We can probably make it to the sphere without too much of a problem, but nothing more. And we have to elevate slowly to give the regulator time to adjust."

"Got it. Slow and easy." I engaged the lower thrusters and pushed the throttle. The Seven took off and ascended at an easy angle. "Nike, give me the fastest course to the Zeta Sphere based on our regulator's ability to adjust to the pressure."

"The course is now on your console."

I steered into the vector and pushed the throttle further, now rising slowly in a wide circle. "Based on your estimation of the Astral Dragon's speed, how long before she gets to the sphere?"

"The sphere is close," Nike said, "so the Astral Dragon will arrive in less than a minute, assuming its occupants can adapt to the lack of breathable air. I detected a number of breaches in the hull."

"I'm sure she found a pressurized suit, so we'll assume she survived." As we finally rose into the upper atmosphere, I imagined Raven arriving at the sphere. With her newfound power, there was no telling how much damage she could cause during our delay.

After what felt like an hour, a message appeared on my screen—Cleared for docking at arrival bay 3.

"Lyric's ready for us," I announced. "Two minutes, seven seconds to arrival."

"Let's hope that's really Lyric," Papa said. "Raven's already there. She could've learned where we're supposed to dock. We don't have to follow the order."

Echo ran a finger along the navigator screen. "I can change our approach path to a departure bay on the opposite side. On the opposite side."

Papa gave her a nod. "Let's do it. Let's do it."

Echo grinned. "Aye, aye, sir sir."

"Will any of the departure bay doors be open?" I asked.

She tapped on her screen. "Working on it. Working on it."

I squinted at her. "You're hacking the sphere's computer?"

"Of course. Of course."

"Well, get it done quick. Our air pressure is dropping. We don't want our skulls to crack."

"Almost done. Almost done."

A growing headache proved my fears. I had to ignore the increasing pain and get this ship landed as soon as possible.

As we closed in on the sphere, now in sight in the viewing window, I veered out of the original course and into the new one Echo provided.

Lyric's voice punched through the ceiling speakers. "Captain Willis, either Julian or Megan, what are you doing? You're off course."

A red flag shot up in my mind. Why would Lyric ask that? It wasn't like her to question my decisions, much less my father's. Could Raven be threatening her or even mimicking her? "No worries, Lyric. I got this. We'll be docking soon."

A whisper entered my ear through the bud. "Megan, it's me, Oliver. Listen. Something's up with Lyric. We can't trust her."

I turned my console's microphone off and gestured for my father to do the same. When he complied, I again transferred my earbud's output to the ceiling speakers. "I was wondering the same thing, Oliver. Lyric is not being Lyric."

"Yeah, we excused ourselves when Crystal detected that she was lying. We made an excuse that Emerson reported a major malfunction that we had to attend to."

"Are you back at the Nebula Nine right now?"

"Yes."

"Have you seen Raven?"

"No, but we know the Astral Dragon is in an arrival bay. I don't think Lyric or her parents would've allowed her to dock unless they thought the pilot was someone else."

"Or the bay door opened on its own." I imagined the process. If Raven could redirect enhanced photon torpedoes, she could probably open a door. "I'm thinking she has Zoë's abilities. She absorbed the power source for the anti-energy. I guess you could say she's sort of like the anti-Lyric. Probably can imitate her."

"Could she have other Starborn powers?" Oliver asked.

"Most likely. The real Lyric did. Finding her might be your top priority."

"Already on it. Jillian's heading out with a laser blaster to find the real Lyric. Crystal's going with her to detect lies, and Perdantus is joining them to suggest psychological tactics."

"Sounds like a great team."

Papa winked at me. "I think it's time to flush the fox."

His question sent my mind back a few years. He was referring to a trick he and my mother used to play whenever they needed to approach an Alliance outpost. The idea was to distract whoever was monitoring the arrival. "Yes. But don't lie. If she also has Crystal's power, she'll detect it."

"Good point. But how could she be mimicking all these powers if she's using anti-energy? Shouldn't she be limited to canceling Starborn powers?"

"Maybe she's draining the powers and then absorbing them somehow."

Papa stroked his chin. "That might be, but I can't see how she could keep it up. The conflicting energies would be at war in her body. If she's posing as Lyric, and I think we should assume she is, my guess is that she won't be able to use the other powers at the same time. The conflict could overtax her body."

"Do you think it's safe to lie to her?" I asked.

"I'm not sure, but it's worth thinking about. In any case, I should be able to do this without lying." He nodded toward me. "You're feeling the pressure drop, right? Do you have a headache?"

I laid a hand on my forehead. "Yeah, and it's getting worse. Aren't you feeling it?"

"I am. But I just needed to know if you were." He turned his microphone on. "Lyric, this is Julian Willis. Megan has fallen ill. Do you have a healer available?"

"Yes, Galena is in the control room with me. When you dock, Megan can come straight to us."

"Can you both come to Megan? Galena for healing and you to charge Megan up so she can energize Galena? Megan is feeling pretty awful."

Silence ensued. I held my breath. Was Raven buying Papa's charade?

"Yes, I will come with Galena. Go to the assigned docking port. I am on my way, and I will come into the bay as soon as the airlock procedure is finished."

"Perfect. See you soon." He turned his microphone off. "That'll keep Raven from monitoring our progress from the control room." He looked at Echo. "How's the hacking going?"

Echo made a final tap on her screen. "I have control of a bay door on the opposite side of the sphere to the bay Lyric assigned us. Level four. Bay six."

"Can you mimic an arrival in the assigned bay?" Papa asked. "You know, open the door, close it again, send air into the bay? That should make Raven think we're really going to that bay. There's no window at the door to check."

Echo studied her screen. "That's level three, bay two. It should be easy now that a digital bot I created is in the system." She winced. "And it's a good thing, too. I'm getting a rip-roaring headache. Rip-roaring."

"We'll need time to run from the other side of the sphere," Papa said. "Can you make our real airlock process fast and the one in the assigned bay slow?"

She began tapping on her screen again. "I'm on it. I'm on it."

Papa swiveled toward me. "You know what to do."

"Yep. Raven's distracted, so dock the Seven as fast as possible." My skull feeling like it might crack at any moment, I pushed the throttle. We zoomed around the sphere to the docking bay Echo had chosen for us, the only one on that side with an open door.

The moment I flew in with a rush and set the ship down, Echo closed the door from her console and started the airlock process. "Thirty seconds," she said. "I'm opening the bay door where we were supposed to go."

Papa looked at me. "Raven will see an indicator in the hallway telling her that the bay's opening. She'll think we're docking now."

As air flowed, I took in deep breaths. My headache slowly eased, a great relief.

Oliver's voice entered my ear and came through the ceiling speakers. "Megan, while you're waiting, Emerson wants to tell you something."

"Go ahead, Emerson."

"Captain Willis, I was able to decrypt the data drive you left with me. The contents were quite confusing. The girl, Penelope, was being tested at the Starborn training camp to determine her skills. Once approved, she was supposed to be transferred to a bramble bee mine for fifteen minutes, but she drowned during the test. Could the fifteen minutes be a mistake?"

"Fifteen minutes? That makes no sense. Maybe it's code for …" An image of an analog clock came to mind. The minute hand moved from the twelve toward the three, slowly, ever so slowly. I gasped. "An hour lasts thirty years. Fifteen minutes is seven-point-five years. They were going to send her to the jungle planet." The truth spilled from my lips in a flood. "I saw a bramble bee there. They must have mines. That's how Admiral Fairbanks got so much glowsap so fast. Whoever is running the mines at the jungle world is shipping the glowsap out. It still takes years to mine it there, but that's only minutes here."

Papa's murmured, "The most efficient mine possible. They torture kids at the usual rate, but they get the benefits immediately."

I pointed at him. "Right. And that's why all the names but one in Thorne's lockbox are reported missing. They're working the mines on the jungle planet. The one not missing is probably collecting the glowsap. His name is Omen, and we think he lives on Delta Ninety-one."

Papa gave me a nod. "Omen's probably paying the overseers a lot of money to do his dirty work for him, but since he must have imported tons of glowsap by now, he can afford it."

"Thorne was probably the grand schemer," I added, "and Omen took over the operation when Thorne died. But it must mean that Raven didn't know what was going on. Otherwise, she would've known a transport would take her to the jungle world."

"But Camille had to know. Was she keeping it from her daughter?"

"Airlock complete," Echo said. "I'll bring a computer tablet to monitor the system."

I pushed the button to open the ramp. "Thank you, Emerson. If you have more to report, we can talk about it later."

Papa, Echo, and I jogged down the ramp, Echo looking at the computer pad in her hand. "Airlock process started in our other arrival bay. I slowed it to half speed. That's the best I can do. We have one minute before Raven thinks she can enter the arrival chamber."

"What's that bay number again?" Papa asked as we headed toward our bay's exit.

"Level three. Bay two."

Papa accelerated. "On my six. I know the shortcuts." He threw open a door, ran to a stairway, and hustled down the steps. When we reached the bottom, he opened another door and looked down a curving corridor. "How much time left?" he whispered to Echo.

She looked at her pad. "Twenty-one seconds."

"Quiet now." He padded down the corridor, passing door after door, then he halted and pressed his back against the wall that stood closer to the center of the sphere. Echo and I did the same.

He leaned forward and peeked farther down the hall, then looked at me, a puzzled expression on his face. "She's not waiting at the door."

"Could she have already gone in?" I asked. "Assumed that enough air was in the bay?"

"Then she would've come right back out when she found it empty. And to return to the control room, she would've had to come up the stairs we just used. She's either in there or never came at all."

Echo looked at her pad. "Airlock process is complete. It's safe to check."

Papa walked to a door, opened it, and peeked inside. "It's dark."

"It is?" Echo tapped on her pad. "I'm showing that the lights are on."

I sidled to my father and peered into the darkness. "Smells like a trap."

Raven's voice came from somewhere in the bay. "Megan, I know you're out there. Come in, and we'll have a chat."

"Oh, sure. Walk into the spider's web, she said to the fly." I huffed. "Not a chance."

"I'm not asking, Megan. I am demanding that you enter. And you, alone." The blackness collapsed toward the center of the room, replaced by light. Raven stood on the vast floor with her foot on a writhing girl's back. Two other females lay on their backs nearby—Crystal and Jillian. Cuts and bruises marred Raven's face, and blood smeared her cheeks. "I'm sure you recognize your friends. Lyric proved to be a worthy opponent."

I balled my fists. How could Lyric have lost? My battle test against Raven proved that my positive energy was more powerful than Raven's negative, so Lyric should have won. And what did Raven do to Jillian and Crystal? Were they even alive? "I'll come in on one condition."

Papa grabbed my arm. "No. Raven wants to kill you. I'll go."

I pulled free. "Sorry, Papa. I'm more powerful than you are. And that's what she demanded. I have to be the one. I can't let my friends die."

Oliver's voice entered my ear. "Sounds like you need a healer."

I whispered, "Definitely, Oliver. Level three. Bay two."

"On my way."

"I'll lead them here," Echo said as she hurried down the hall, tapping on her pad.

"Since you paused," Raven said, "I assume you want me to ask what your one condition is. Rather dramatic, but I will acquiesce. What is—"

"No need to ask," I shouted. My cheeks felt on fire as I continued. "My condition is simple enough. Let my father come with me so we can take our friends to safety, and I will return alone."

"Very well." Raven shifted her foot to the floor. "You're fortunate that I can drain and mimic Crystal's ability to detect a lie. I know you will keep your word."

"I will." I grasped my father's wrist. "Can you go in without attacking her?"

Gritting his teeth, he nodded. "For now."

"Good. Let's go."

We jogged into the room and knelt between Jillian and Crystal. Both breathed without a problem, but their eyes were closed. Papa grasped Jillian's arm. "Hey, Sis. I'm getting you out of here." He hoisted her up and draped her over his shoulders.

I patted Crystal's cheek. She blinked, then grimaced. "She hit us with some kind of black lightning. Cleaned my clock. Both analog and digital."

"Come on." I held both of her wrists, helped her to her feet, and supported her as she staggered toward the door, Papa at my side carrying Jillian. When we arrived in the corridor, Oliver ran toward us. He helped Papa lay Jillian on the floor and set his hands on her head, probably to start any necessary healing process.

I guided Crystal to a sitting position and turned toward the door again. "Now to get Lyric. I'll do this by myself."

With both fists clenched, I strode to Lyric, not bothering to glance at Raven. As I crouched close to Lyric and slid my hands under her back, she whispered, "I couldn't beat her."

"I guessed that." Flexing the proper muscles, I shot power into my legs. I lifted Lyric into my arms, straightened, and walked toward the door, working with all my might to show no signs of weakness.

When I laid her on the floor next to Jillian, I flexed to rise, but she grabbed my arm and pulled me close. "She defeated me, but not because I didn't have enough power."

"Then why?"

"I lacked enough passion. My homecoming eased my pain." She set a palm on my head. "I lost because the fire in my mind was not hot enough." She moved her palm to my chest. "The burning anger in my heart had settled just enough to make me weaker." Lyric's eyes glowed red. "But you still have the heart, the passion to stop the monsters who enslave children, the evil that led to your mother's murder. The heat of that passion boils within you more powerfully than it ever did in me. You have to do what I could not."

"But how? You're the power source. Not me. I'm just an energizer. I could have all the passion in the world, but without the power, she'll mop the floor with me."

"You're right. You need the power. But do you really want it?"

"Um … yeah. I guess so. It's the only way to take Raven down."

"Very well, but be warned, the power is sometimes difficult to control."

I nodded. "I understand. What do I have to do?"

"Megan," Raven called. "Are you coming?"

I shouted, "Cool your jets. I'm making sure my friends are okay. I'll be there in a minute."

"Open your mouth," Lyric said.

"Open my—"

"Just do it. And keep it open."

"Okay." I held my mouth open. Bright red light streamed from Lyric's mouth into mine. Heat flowed with it, though not hot enough to burn. Every part of my skin warmed from my scalp to the soles of my feet. My muscles flexed. My vision grew clearer than ever before. Thoughts rushed into my mind, thoughts that couldn't be my own, maybe from those around me. Was I reading their thoughts? Could I also be a healer? Move objects with my mind?

When the flow of red stopped, Lyric closed her mouth. I did the same. She exhaled a long breath. "You have no idea what a relief it is to transfer the power source to you."

"Actually, I can imagine. I already feel like I'm about to pop." I rose to my feet. My father now stood with Jillian standing next to him, leaning against his shoulder while Oliver worked on Crystal, a hand on her head. I wanted a pep talk from Papa, but I had no time for that. "I have to go."

"Wait," Oliver said. "You didn't get to hear all that Emerson learned from the data drive. Raven was actually the mastermind behind the child slave market. She recruited Thorne to be the first slave master, and it was her idea to spread the bramble bee mines throughout the galaxy. For her, it was all about making money from glowsap. When Camille found out about the operation, the two joined forces, hoping to use Starborn children to find the positive power source so they could destroy it or harness it for their use. Raven also set up the bramble bee mines in the jungle world, and she knew how to go there and leave whenever she wanted, but we're guessing that too much anti-energy had collected in that world, and the pull the stuff had on her kept her on the planet."

"Wow! That's a lot to take in." I looked at my father. "Does that mean you could've left the jungle planet without her if she had told you how?"

He bent his brow. "Probably, but that's not important. Let's shift gears. Don't go in yet. Just stall her from here, and I'll run up to the control room and zap her back to the jungle. She can't leave without a ship."

"No. I gave my word to go back in there. Just like you gave your word to send her safely to Gamma Five. I have to do it."

He sighed. "All right. Go in. But I'm going to the control room to get the atomizer ready. If things get out of hand and I can isolate her, I'm pulling the trigger."

I nodded. "Sure. That's fine. I might need the help."

Echo walked closer to my father, her stare on the computer tablet. "You don't have to go to the control room. We can program the atomizer from here."

"Megan," Raven called again. "I'm losing my patience, little hero girl."

Heat surged within, hotter than I had ever felt in my life. I growled as I stomped toward the door. "You're about to lose something else."

As I marched toward her, she chuckled, "Oh, did I hurt your feelings?"

I halted just out of her reach, my heart thudding so hard, it sounded like a kettle drum. "I know you're the one who started the slave trafficking, and I know what you did on the jungle planet."

"Oh, you do?" She lifted her head in a snobbish manner. "For your information, we call that planet Delta Zero in honor of the system where I established the first bramble bee mine with Thorne." Her eyes glowed with blackness. "But my purpose here has nothing to do with that. I want only revenge. Because of you, my parents are dead. Now you will die as well."

Every word she spoke kindled the fire within me. She was proud of the chains, the fears, the murders. If not for her, Cynda would still be alive. If not for her, Renalda would still be alive. And countless other children suffered in toil and misery because of her greed. She was the one who needed to die.

Raven squinted at me. "Something's different about you. Why are your eyes glowing red?"

"I am seeing the blood that will soon spill from your veins." I glanced at my locket. My dragon's eye flashed like a brilliant red star. Energy stormed through my body. Knowledge flowed into my brain. I suddenly knew how to use every ability the power source bestowed. No use hesitating. I decided to go for broke. "Prepare to go to hell."

I reached toward her. A red stream shot out of my palm, plunged into her chest, and wrapped around her heart. Rolling my fingers into a fist tightened the streams. She gasped and clutched her chest. "How … how are … you doing this?"

"Shut up, witch." I flexed my biceps and sent a surge of electricity through the streams in sparkling arcs. They crackled and sizzled into her. The jolt sent her flying back, jerking her body from my grasp. She slid on the floor and lay on her back, breathing fast and shallow. I strode toward her, my hand extended to grab her heart again and finish her off.

The red stream flowed once more, but she lifted a hand of her own and sent a river of blackness that blocked my attack. The two streams splashed against each other, and the repelling force kept me from advancing toward her.

With her hand still extended to block me, she struggled to her feet, then leaped out of the way of my onslaught. She waved both hands at an atomizer. Its barrel rotated toward me. Just as I spun to swing it back, she used her finger to flip its switch.

Something flung me across the room. As I slid, I looked back. The atomizer shot my father. He instantly disintegrated.

I screamed, "No!" Now sitting, I reached toward the bay doors with both hands and wrenched them open. Air shot out of the room, sweeping Raven into the suction. As I skidded on my backside toward the opening, my feet in front of me, the vacuum sucked her into its void.

Careening out of control, I grabbed each door with my red streams and pulled them toward each other. They moved closer together, but they couldn't possibly shut before I got there. My feet slapped against the barrier, one on each door with a gap between them, wide enough for me to slide through. The suction pulled and pulled. My leg muscles knotted. They would give way at any second.

I flexed my biceps and sent new power into my calf and thigh muscles. I bent my knees and thrust myself back, giving the doors time to close with a barely audible click. Gasping for breath in the nearly airless chamber, I flipped over to all fours and crawled slowly toward the hallway. Every joint throbbed, but my heart hurt more than anything else. Papa was gone, maybe dead, and I had no idea what to do next.

New air hissed into the room. Within a few seconds, the door to the hallway flew open. Oliver and Crystal ran into the chamber. They boosted me from each side, dragged me to safety, and shut the door behind them.

They laid me on the floor. Heaving deep breaths, I tried to speak. "What happened … to my father?"

Echo knelt close, looking at her computer pad. "According to the station's computer, it was programmed to send him to Epsilon Six. I have no idea if he'll get there safely without a ship. Even if he does and he gets restored, he'll still be in danger until the arrival bay fills with air."

Oliver knelt at my other side. "Or there's enough anti-energy in the jungle world to hold him there."

I nodded. "Delta Zero. That's what Raven called it." I pulled my locket out from behind my shirt and opened the clasp. The dragon's eye ruby glowed. I exhaled, the ache in my heart easing. "Papa's alive. Somehow I have to find him."

"Let's see if I can locate him." Echo studied her screen. "Since the transports are supposed to be nearly instantaneous after Delta Zero lost its supply of anti-energy, he should've gotten there by now, but none of the bays are showing an arrival. None."

"Then he's on Delta Zero." I closed the locket and let it lie on my chest. "He has to be. And maybe since he's not on a ship, he's stuck there."

"Could be. Could be." Echo tapped on her pad and showed me the screen. "I've been tracking Raven. She's not moving. I'm sure she's dead."

The screen showed a body floating, barely visible in the darkness. Only the stars behind her allowed a view at all. A dense black stream flowed from her mouth and dispersed in the vacuum—her anti-energy flowing into nothingness.

Staying reclined, I glanced around. "Where are Lyric and Jillian and Perdantus?"

Oliver gestured with a thumb. "In the infirmary. Jillian helped Lyric get there while Perdantus scouted for trouble. They're all fine. And Zoë's been there ever since she came with Lyric's parents, but I don't know where the parents are. Jillian's looking for them." He touched his ear and listened for a moment. "Wait a second. Jillian says she found

Lyric's parents and Galena unconscious in the control room. She's taking them to the infirmary, so I'd better scoot. They'll need a healer." He kissed my forehead, leaped to his feet, and ran down the corridor. Now only Crystal and Echo remained with me.

Crystal plopped down with her back against a wall. "Blazes, girl! That was way too close!"

"Yeah. It was. For me, that is." I sucked in a deep breath and let it out slowly. "But my father got zapped. I have to find him."

"Of course you do, and based on what I heard, you'd better hurry to Delta Zeta or whatever it's called. It's probably already been a few years there."

"I don't think so. When Raven sucked the anti-energy out, Delta Zero's time started matching ours. It'll be a while before it's mismatched again."

"Good. So maybe we can get some food and find a bed. We can figure out how to get to Delta Zeta tomorrow."

"Delta Zero."

"Whatever."

I pushed myself up to a sitting position. "I need to see Zoë."

"Yeah. You should." Crystal rose, grasped my wrist, and pulled me to my feet. "I watched your battle with Raven. I guess since you have all the Starborn powers, I won't be able to lie to you ever again."

I half closed an eye. "Do you ever lie to me?"

She averted her gaze. "No. Of course not."

I deepened the furrows in my brow. "You're lying."

"Yep. You've got the power, all right." She hooked her arm through mine. "Let's go before you use my hypno-zonking power on me."

After saying goodbye to Lyric, her parents, Galena, and Echo, my crew and I sat in the Nebula Nine, me in the captain's chair, Jillian in the first mate's, Crystal in the navigator's, Zoë at the weapons' station, Oliver at the doctor's, and Perdantus on my shoulder. Jillian insisted that I take command of the ship, saying that I had earned it. I didn't bother to argue. Since no one wanted to find my father more than I did, I was glad to do it. And after spending three days at the Gamma Five sphere waiting for my crew members to fully heal, I was itching to leave.

During those days, I often paced the floor, thinking about Papa. Several times I was tempted to call on Barnabas for advice or maybe a prophecy about whether or not Papa was on Delta Zero, but I resisted. Through all of the dangers I had faced since I met my great-grandfather, I never once thought about seeking his help, and I survived. Now that I *was* thinking about calling him, I faced no danger, only uncertainty. If he came out of the ruby now, he wouldn't be able to help me when I really needed him. I just had to push aside my doubts and press forward.

I toggled my microphone on. "Echo, we're ready."

Her voice came through the ceiling speakers. "Good. Lyric's mom and I figured out how to send you directly to Delta Zero. Apparently, there's a Zeta Sphere orbiting it. I hacked a secret data section that has all the specs. We're guessing that this Omen character must've financed its construction. Anyway, that's where you're going."

"Any clue who's operating that sphere?" I asked.

"Nope," Echo said. "So you'd better scram out of there as soon as you can and fly to the planet's surface."

"Will do. Since my father doesn't know we're coming, it might take a while to find him. We'll want to get started right away. I'll bet he's already searching for the bramble bee mines and any enslaved children."

"Stay in touch," Echo said. "I gave Emerson instructions on how to contact us through the time shift. It won't be much of a shift to start with, but it'll get worse."

"Perfect." I swiveled toward his console. "Emerson, are you ready for that?"

"Affirmative, and may I say, Captain Megan Willis, after reading Captain Jillian Willis's log of events, I am most impressed with your heroism. It is an honor to continue in service to you."

"You got that right," Crystal said. "Let's not get separated again. I missed getting scared out of my wits nearly every second. I'm going to be on your six, seven, eight, and nine."

Perdantus chirped, "I agree. I was miserable when I couldn't help you any further in your adventures. I vow to stay at your side every possible moment."

"Same here," Zoë said. "Oliver gave my lungs a clean bill of health.."

Oliver grinned. "True, but only because you said you'd use your brain to tie my shoelaces to each other if I didn't."

"Guilty as charged," Zoë said as Oliver's hair flew straight up, as if sucked by a vacuum. "But he didn't lie. I'm good to go."

"True again." Oliver pushed his hair back into place. "But back to Megan. I agree with everyone. She's Captain Hero, and I'm proud to be in her crew."

Jillian reached over and laid a hand on my shoulder. "You are a hero, Megan, and you are well loved." She grinned. "But don't let our accolades go to your head."

"Accolades?" Crystal rolled her eyes. "Those Willis words are going to drive me nuts."

We all laughed for a moment, until Perdantus spoke again, looking me in the eye. "Megan, now that you possess the power source and have access to all the powers of the Starborn, may I suggest that you embark on this journey without consideration of those powers? As they were given to you in a moment, they could also be taken away in a moment. In fact, on Delta Zero they might not work at all. Do not let the powers inflate your confidence beyond its rightful boundary, and summon the courage to go as if you had no powers at all, save your love for your father and for the enslaved children."

My friend's words penetrated deeply. As thoughts of my father and the children came to mind, the warmth of love spread throughout my body. I nodded firmly. "You're right, Perdantus. Of course, I would go even if I could only crawl, but your reminders are wise and well placed. Thank you."

He bowed his head. "You are welcome."

Jillian strapped in. "Are you ready, Mophead?"

I strapped in as well. "More than ready."

"Echo," Jillian called, "press that disintegration button and send us to Delta Zero." She set her hands on her yoke and smiled at me. "Let's go find your father … again."

Cast of Characters
(In order of appearance)

Megan Willis—freedom fighter, daughter of Anne and Julian Willis

Crystal—Megan's crewmate who has mentalist powers

Zoë—Megan's crewmate who has mind-over-matter powers

Sonya—*Astral Dragon*'s computer system

Perdantus—silver jay, a master negotiator and Megan's friend

Camille Fairbanks—New admiral in the Alliance

Barnabas—Prophet from the Beta Four "Wishing Well"

Oliver Tillman—Friend of Megan and former slave

Emerson—*Nebula Nine*'s computer system

Jillian Willis—Megan's aunt, her father's twin sister

Captain Fossella—Alpha One docking station officer

Lieutenant Trevor Mixon—Gamma Five outpost officer

Oswald (Oz)—Training camp boy with firestarting power

Camp Guard—One of multiple camp guards

Raven—Camp director, daughter of Camille Fairbanks

Ashton Morales (Moe)—Camp training officer

Riddle—Camp girl with emotion-reading power

Massenbrook—A Monton (burrowing animal on Gamma Five)

Galena—Camp girl with healing power

Echo—Camp girl with technical wizardry

Tempest—Dragon in the testing maze

Lyric—Camp girl with body morphing power

Chipmunk (Chip)—Camp boy with mind-reading power

Ensign Kit Miles—Epsilon Six sentry

Julian Willis—Megan's father, a freedom fighter, Anne's husband

Nike—*Nebula Seven*'s computer system

About the Author

Bryan Davis is the author of fantasy/science-fiction novels for youth and adults, including the bestselling Dragons in Our Midst series. Other series include The Oculus Gate, Reapers, Dragons of Starlight, Tales of Starlight, Time Echoes, and Wanted: Superheroes, several of which have been bestsellers.

Bryan was born in 1958 and grew up in the eastern US. From the time he taught himself how to read before school age, through his seminary years and beyond, he has demonstrated a passion for the written word, reading and writing in many disciplines and genres, including theology, fiction, devotionals, poetry, and humor.

Bryan is a graduate of the University of Florida (BS in Industrial Engineering). In high school, he was valedictorian of his class and won various academic awards. He was also a member of the National Honor Society and voted Most Likely to Succeed. He continues to expand his writing education by teaching at relevant writing conferences and conventions.

Bryan was a computer professional for over twenty years before becoming a fulltime author in 2003. He and his wife, Susie, homeschooled their four girls and three boys, and they now work together as an author/editor team.

BRYAN DAVIS

ASTRAL ALLIANCE

— BOOK THREE —

AT THE SPEED OF MIND